Author's Note

Thanks for your interest in *The Briscoe Situation*. Please be advised that this action-packed novel is a work of fiction. Therefore, it cannot be everyone's cup of tea. The story begins in the autumn of 1964. Julius Briscoe's older brother, a Chicago lawyer, has been named an equity partner in his firm and needs Julius' financial aid in closing the deal. So the Briscoes of Philadelphia journey to Chicago with a briefcase full of money to witness Lenny Briscoe's promotion.

The Briscoe Situation contains language and situations that some people might find offensive and upsetting. If things such as human behavior, foul language, ethnic intolerance, sarcasm, unspeakable crimes, profound insights, evil terrorists, A-list gangsters, and class warfare concern you, please read no further.

Although some of the locations and characters in this book are based on actual people and places, they serve only to set the scenes so that you, dear reader, might get some sense of what it was like to live in those times. They aren't meant to titillate, shock, confound, infuriate, incite revolution, or trigger the premature concluders of this world. *The Briscoe Situation* is not a true story, although many real places and events serve as a background for these fictional characters. And if they remind you of your ex or your cousin Roberta, well, that's just coincidental, or someone's projecting.

The Briscoe Situation takes place in a time when people turned the other cheek and had a healthy respect for their neighbors and coworkers.

If you are experiencing difficulty understanding some of the references to life in those days, feel free to reach out to the baby boomers in your address book. They'll be glad to help. If you don't have any seniors in your circle of trust, you might want to visit a nearby Seniors' Center for a consultation. We old folks have little else to do, so we'll be glad to help you young'uns out.

Compared to these modern times, post-war America was practically the Dark Ages. Color TV was just getting traction; telephones couldn't fit in your pocket, people got their news from one of three television networks or their local newspapers or radio stations. There was no internet. No automatic conformity, no Facebook, Instagram, TikTok, or any of that. It was a different world than the one we now find ourselves in.

The main character, Julius Briscoe, is a culturally Jewish, agnostic eighteen-year-old boy living in or near Philadelphia. As our story begins, we find Julius settling old debts and about to take his very first ride in a big old jet airliner. Enjoy.

Richard Ettinger

June 2025

richardettingerauthor.com

The Briscoe Situation

ISBN: 979-8-9862163-9-3

Chapter 1
Greetings from Atlas City!

"The emptiness is endless, cold as the clay
You can always come back,
But you can't come back all the way."

Mississippi
~ Bob Dylan

I thought I had it all figured out. The next sixty or seventy years with Gracie Gold by my side, sitting atop of the world. We would raise our extraordinary children, become pillars of our community, and run successful businesses. Live our lives without a care or a worry.

I hadn't yet finished with compulsory education, but I was already a multimillionaire, the owner of several thriving businesses, a made man in the Jewish mafia, and a fearsome psychic assassin. As they used to say, the world was my oyster.

Then a trio of mindless backwoods fucks changed all that. How, you ask? They killed Gracie. That's how. I killed them right back. It was the least I could do.

"But they were just teenaged boys goofing around."

"They meant no harm."

"There goes the State Championship."

"Boys will be boys and all that," apologized the goodly folk of Atlas City.

I might have gone a bit overboard with the dispositions. Last October, the tiny village of Atlas City, New Jersey, lost many of its notorious citizens, courtesy of yours truly, Julius Truman Briscoe, with an assist from the *Psychic Brotherhood of Greater Philadelphia* and O'HANLON MOVING AND STORAGE.

The job was finally done. Jeremiah 'Dead Eye' Dickinson was dead and gone, entombed in five hundred pounds of concrete on a plinth guarding the north entrance to the Atlas City Parkway bridge. It was time to move on.

Marva Mitchell's Pinelands Hideaway was a fifty-unit roadside motel on Route 30 just south of Hammonton. The Golds and I had been staying there for three weeks. I was using the name Richard Philbrick. The Golds were registered as the Silberbergs: Myron, Jacob, and Hiram. It had been our base of operations during our campaign against the many wretched souls of Atlas City. The Golds left for home last week. Their surveillance skills were no longer required. The rest of the dirty work was up to me.

I spent the next two days, using about a million of those tiny shampoo bottles and all the hot water the motel had, and I still couldn't get all of that concrete gunk out of my hair. I had no choice but to shave it off and start over. I hopped into the pickup and drove to a nearby K-Mart Shopping Plaza where one of the satellite businesses was a franchised barber shop.

My stylist did a good job. I was now as bald as Mr. Clean or Otto Preminger. I couldn't help but wonder what

Gracie would think of my new look. The thought made me sad. Or, well, as sad as I get. I wasn't very emotional before I turned psychic. I'm far less so now.

The next morning, I drove to downtown Camden. I parked the truck in a lot across from the bus station, left the keys under the sun visor, and walked over to the Trailways depot. I bought a ticket for the next bus to Philly. There were 45 minutes to kill, so I went into a nearby Army-Navy store and bought a Waverley blue knit cap, new boots, and a pair of mirrored sunglasses. Back in the bus station, I picked up copies of the CAMDEN COURIER POST and the PHILADELPHIA DAILY NEWS.

I was among the first to board and took an aisle seat on the starboard side, three rows from the front of the bus. I leafed through the newspapers as I screened the incoming status buttons. Weary, anxious, eager, thoughtful, and aggressively stupid Normals on their way to Philadelphia and all points west.

"You're in my seat, dipshit," growled the bully with a Brando attitude. He slapped the back of my head and knocked my watch cap askew, revealing my trend-setting new look. A move guaranteed to intimidate most Normals. In case you haven't been paying attention, I am not a Normal.

My antagonist wore a black leather duster, scuffed work boots, and a gold earring. He had a gold-capped tooth and an unfiltered cigarette dangling from his lips. Before I could hit him with a mild dose of FEAR & LOATHING®, he shouted, "Hey, you mother fucking pick-pocketer, that's my watch. Give it over. Right now. Punk."

Considering my position on Normals in general, you'd think that Normals with bad manners giving me shit on public transportation would have short life expectancies. You'd be right.

I stood up. The guy was huge. Jeremiah Dickinson, huge. Maybe not as tall, but filled out. Heavily muscled with a chip on his shoulder the size of the transistor radio in my shirt pocket. He probably was armed. He was menacing. Usually, he'd be dead already. But there were too many witnesses witnessing this confrontation for anything noteworthy to happen to that goon. So, instead, I put the bully into time-limited ZOMBIE MODE® and told him to sit quietly in the back of the bus. He'd revert to his normal Neanderthal self in about half an hour.

I got off the bus at the Reading Terminal Market, grateful to leave New Jersey behind me, and went inside to get a bite to eat. Norman the Neanderthal followed me in. I let him off easy before. I'd hoped he'd learned his lesson. It seemed that he hadn't. Who should we blame? The student? Or the teacher?

I made my way into one of our competitors, SHANGHAI SAL'S, and took a table in the back near the restrooms and pay phones. Thanks to my ingenious disguise, Shanghai Sal herself didn't recognize me. I studied the menu. It was one of those laminated deals that had color photographs of each dish. The photos were contrasty and over-saturated. I fucking hate those.

"I want that Rolex. Let me have it. Now you dumb-ass mother fucker."

Norman the Neanderthal stood opposite me, a snub-nosed revolver in his right hand and a shiny stiletto in his left.

Blame muscle memory. It's instantaneous. An unconditional response.

"Julius, there is a threat," says the inner voice in charge of self-survival.

"There's a gun pointed right at you. Eliminate the threat."

There was no opportunity for an internal debate. No time to reason things out. Happens faster than you'd think possible. Zap. Tall, dumb asshole from Jersey fell down dead. He landed on an adjacent table. His death fart was loud and stinky, souring everyone's afternoon. I got out of there as quickly as I could. I didn't want to talk to the police. Didn't want to show them ID. All I had on me was Richard Philbrick's, and I didn't want that name in any investigator's report ever.

I went into ETHEL'S BAGELS and bought an assorted baker's dozen, cream cheese, and a rum babka. At the florist, I purchased flowers for Mom, Aunt Connie, Nettie, Dahlia, and for Ellie and Grace Gold's graves.

I flagged down a cab on Market Street and told the driver to take me to the **O,** Eighteenth, and Spruce. Years ago, Nettie Gold taught me the value of the cat nap. "Rest is a weapon, Julius. Take the time to recharge your batteries whenever you can." I rode in the back of the cab with my eyes shut, my feet flat on the floor straddling the transmission hump, hands resting on my knees. Five minutes of this was better than a two-hour nap.

"Youse alright back there, bub?" Growled the cabby. "I don't need no hippie puke like youse to go overdosing in my cab."

I was in no mood. "Do yourself a favor, pal, and shut the fuck up."

He slammed on the brakes, shut the meter off, and told me to get the fuck out of his fucking cab right fucking now, this very minute, or he was going to beat the living crap out of me. As if he could.

Post-Gracie, there was no way I was going to take shit from Normals ever again. I told him to SHUT THE FUCK UP®, turn the meter back on, and drive me to Spruce and Eighteenth. Don't leave home without it.

We arrived at the O without any more controversy. I paid the meter and told the ignoramus he had to pick up a fare in King of Prussia. Best hurry. Off he sped. If you think about it, that motormouth got off easy. But why bother thinking about it at all?

The eternally smokin' hot Margot St.James rushed from behind the counter and gave me a hug-of-all-hugs. The very same hug-of-all-hugs that launched the chain of events that led to the death of my cousin Victor.

"Julius, I am so so sorry about Gracie. She was the sweetest, the warmest, the nicest person I've ever known. How are you holding up, sweetie? Doing okay?"

I told her I was hanging in there, that time heals all wounds, and that I was going to need lots of time.

"Where's Uncle T?"

"He's downstairs. Sweetie, if you need someone to talk to, I'm always here for you."

"Thanks. I gotta go. Great seeing you again, Margot."

Uncle Teddy's office door was wide open. He was lounging back in his chair, stocking feet on his desk; he had the telephone wedged to his left ear. Uncle T was wearing mismatched argyle socks. He looked up at me and grinned. "Listen, Fred, I'm gonna have to call you back." He didn't wait for a response and dropped the handset onto the base.

I got off the first shot, "Nice socks. I used to have a pair just like them."

Argyle socks—black and white, just like Dad's—are the Briscoe signature fashion statement. He stood up, and we gangsta-hugged.

"Nice haircut."

"Get with the times, Uncle T. All us cool kids are sporting the skinhead look these days."

"Julius, where the fuck have you been? What have you been up to?"

"You don't want to know, Uncle T. You really don't. It sure is good to see you. How's Mom and Aunt Connie?"

"We're all good, Julius. We've been worried sick about you. You coulda called!"

"Couldn't risk it. What's been going on here?"

"Well, let's see. Dr. Fields reached out a couple of times. He had another big job lined up. It had Willie Novichok written all over it."

"What did you tell him?"

"I had no idea where you were. If you were alive or dead. So I told him, you're gonna love this one, Jules, that you took your Longstride money and bought a vineyard in the Napa Valley and were no longer looking for wet work." I laughed. Who wouldn't?

"So Fields counters that the job happens to be somewhere in California, exactly where he didn't say. But that it was another big payday. This was right after we buried Grace. I told Fields that William Novichok had recently suffered a life-changing event and wasn't taking any assignments, and that Fields should find another assassin."

"Did Miles clue you in on my vineyard excuse? Or did you come up with it all on your own?"

"I cannot tell a lie, Julius; yes, he did. You and the Golds all went missing right after the funeral. When Miles showed up last week without you, I had questions. He told me you had decided not to do any more jobs for Morgan Fields. Is that true?"

"It was. But that was before Gracie was murdered. I'll tell you this much, Uncle T, I've gotten real good at killing and crippling people—namely, those who were responsible, in one way or another, for Grace Gold's death. Now I'm thinking that maybe I want to get paid for killing Normals. It's so easy."

"If someone wants someone dead, someone is going to make it happen. Right? That someone might as well be me. But I'm still on the fence. I told Miles I was done with Fields. Not necessarily done with contract work. Have you figured out how Fields finds his clients?"

"Not yet, no. But I'll dig deeper if you'd like."

"Please do, Uncle T. I've got to get going, many apologies to make and lectures to endure. Dig?"

"Hey Julius, almost forgot, I've got some good news to share. Leonard called to tell your mother he had been named an equity partner in his fancy-ass Chicago law firm. He needs to sell his share of BIG CORNERS to pay for his buy-in. Fucking lawyers, right?

Due to policies that remain unwritten, my brother and I inherited William Briscoe's shares of BIG CORNERS INC. My mother had to sign a pre-nup relinquishing any claim on the business. According to Izzy Blafken, the *undzer shtick's* chief accountant, the impetus for this blatant act of misogyny was Sam Briscoe's second wife. Olga Briscoe embezzled a quarter of a million bucks from the business and ran off to Toledo with Larry Robards, a traveling accordion salesman from St. Louis.

Chico needed me to buy his half of our inheritance for the low, low introductory price of five hundred thousand dollars. Which, at that time, I happened to have on hand in my safety deposit box.

So my absentee older brother Leonard was recently named an equity partner in the law firm about to be known as FLEMING, KIRKLAND, PORTER AND BRISCOE (FKP&B.) That's a big deal. Right? You betcha. There was going to be a ceremony at the annual pre-Thanksgiving dinner. We're all invited.

Whoopee kai a! I was finally going to ride in a big ol' jet airliner.

◊◊

Chapter 2
chicago bound

"You know you've got to go through hell
Before you get to heaven."

Jet Airliner
~ Paul Pena

We four Briscoes were among the last to board Flight #505 on the Tuesday before Thanksgiving. We were in first class, row 3, seats A, B, C, and D.

Mother and Aunt Connie took seats A & B to continue their evaluation of their favorite radio soap operas without any further interruptions. Uncle T insisted on taking the window seat, which was fine with me. He slid the Zero Halliburton case with my half a million under the seat ahead of him. He fastened his seatbelt without being instructed, pulled the window shade down, reclined his seat, and said, "Wake me when we get to the bridge."

I sensed a smidge of claustrophobia on every Status Button on board. There were more than one hundred loud, contagious, malodorous, insufferable Normals crammed into this one-hundred-fifty-foot-long tube. I had more than one hundred Status Buttons to keep track of. Any one of them a potential threat. Flight #505 had four. ~~Potential~~ Genuine threats, that is.

Century after century, every society known to man has benefited from and been plagued by various subcultures. Their methods and styles would vary over the millennia, but their role in society would not. Take armed robbery, for instance. Highwaymen, plunderers, pirates, marauders, bandits, and brigands were all predecessors of the skyjacker, the worst of the lot.

According to the wire services, skyjackers were currently trending at number three with a bullet on their top ten most hated lists. Four such daring villains were just minutes away from commandeering United Airlines flight #505–Philadelphia to Chicago non-stop. Men, women, and children headed home for the holiday—one hundred fifty-three passengers and crew.

Once our plane was off the ground and cruising at altitude, the passengers' Status Buttons gradually morphed into similar patterns and colors like they do with movie audiences. There are enough powerful constants in the air travel experience to turn most passengers' Status Buttons similarly placid. There were more model citizens on board that afternoon than there were rebellious Marxist hijackers. But then again, it only takes a few.

I poked Uncle T in the ribs. He opened his eyes and scowled. "Already?"

"No," I whispered. "There's going to be trouble—four assholes in the cheap seats. I can't tell if they're armed. But I can tell that they intend to act out. I should probably kill them before they get up and start making demands. But what if I'm wrong about their intentions? What if they're just fearful flyers like me? What do you think, Uncle T?"

"Can't you just paralyze them like you did to those *Submariners*?"

"Not until they are standing in the aisle. I'd explain why, but it takes too long."

"Well, then, you don't seem to have much of a choice. We're going to have to wait and see. Let's hope you're wrong. Julius, it's okay to be jumpy your first time in an airplane."

As if on cue, four skyjackers sprang from their seats and took positions in the first-class and coach cabins. The two we could see were nattily dressed in olive drab fatigues. Black and white striped undershirts. Faces painted white. They both were sporting Ruger semi-automatics. They wore those M1951 Field Caps that complemented the leader's Fidel Castro-style beard and the female's true believer vibe.

The leader stormed the cockpit. His partner, whom I've come to think of as 'Teri the Terrorist,' stood guard while mimicking the standard instructions given by stewardesses everywhere. She was about to demonstrate the use of the oxygen masks when a breathy voice came on the public address system: male, early twenties, New England accent.

"Good afternoon, my dear, dear fellow travelers. I am about to announce a minor revision of our flight plan. While I'm giving you this exciting news, my associates will pay each of you a visit. You are to give them your cash and your valuables. If you resist, you will be shot. My associates are armed with twenty-two-caliber pistols. A shot to your head with a twenty-two will kill you without the risk of putting a hole in the aircraft. So be cool."

"And oh, by the way, I sure hope you packed your swimwear. Our next stop is the fabulous Havana, Cuba, where the temperature just now is eighty-eight degrees. On behalf of the staff and management of *TRIA, Tabula Rasa Interworldwide Airlines,* we thank you so very much for your patronage. We realize that there are many airlines for you to choose from. Thanks for choosing *TRIA*. Now, start handing over that cash and those jewels. You won't believe what a decent hotel room goes for in Havana these days. Have a nice fucking day!"

I asked Uncle T to remove his loafers and conceal the Zero Halliburton case behind them.
I slipped my watch off and dropped it into my boot. When Teri the Terrorist reached row three, I was ready for her. I hit her with a TRUTH® bomb. Not only did she not scrutinize us, Teri the Terrorist wrote her name, phone number, home address, and the names of her favorite rock and roll stars on the palm of her left hand and showed it to me.

The visionary in charge of this squad of Marxist assholes called himself *Aristotle Lindberg.* Teri the Terrorist didn't know the man's real name but described him as a 'dickless shithead.'

Sure, I could kill them or paralyze them or cause them to feel enormous shame and writhe in a swamp of self-loathing. But too many were on board to witness and remain silent about such strangeness. Yes, I could cause *Aristotle Lindberg* to change his mind and reroute us to the closest airport where he and his followers would turn themselves into the nearest FBI or gate agent. The only fly in that ointment was that I would have to instruct *Aristotle Lindberg* verbally. In that crowded environment, it was not possible without being overheard. I'd never tried anything like that and worried about unanticipated variables. My main focus was on keeping my family and my money safe from those armed thugs. So I reclined my seat, closed my eyes, and kept tabs on the skyjackers and everyone else on board.

Like most big cities, Chicago, that toddling town, holds a Thanksgiving Day Parade that can't be beat. This year's theme is *'The 50 States.'* Each one of these United States was invited to send and did send representatives to march down State Street, that great street, bright and early come Thursday morning. Pennsylvania dispatched the award-winning Mummers Club, the South Street Strutters String Band. All fifty of them were seated in coach. Although they perform boisterously in garish attire, Mummers are regular Normal folks just like you and yours. They have families, mortgages, Pontiacs, fishing boats, and real jobs. About half of the South Street Strutters String Band were active-duty law enforcement. All of whom were armed. Their Status Buttons were lit up. Alerted. Shades of aggression and caution. I sat up and whispered to Uncle T, "There's a bunch of cops back there. Twenty or thirty of them. They are pissed, and they are itching for a fight. You strapping?"

"I am. My Beretta and that little pea shooter I took off of Connie."

"Be ready. But don't shoot anybody." I shut my eyes again. It's easier to observe Status Button interactions that way.

Most people don't carry too much cash, so when they're facing a gun, they'll give it up. Same with most jewelry, but not all. Things with sentimental value, a family heirloom for instance, are worth risking a bullet for.

I don't know who it was, but one of the aft cabin skyjackers tried to take someone's something of great personal value and died in the attempt. In fewer than ten seconds, the rhythm section of the South Street Strutters String Band had subdued the *Tabula Rasas* working the aft cabin.

A silenced .22 fired into the sternum of a delusional idealist skyjacker isn't much louder than the steady thrum of the four jet engines propelling us on our merry way. The sound didn't attract the attention of the two terrorizing the first-class travelers. Aft cabin terrorist #2 surrendered without much of a fuss. The mummer/cops huddled up, presumably to discuss what to do about the two terrorists in the front of the plane. I paralyzed *Aristotle Lindberg* and *Teri the Terrorist* and walked towards the aft cabin.

The leader of this band of policemen/percussionists was Delaware County's very own Sheriff, Max Hermann. When I went through the curtain between the cabins, Sheriff Hermann's reflexes told him to 'shoot first, ask questions after.' I anticipated this response and dosed him with PECKINPAH®, which causes people to move very slowly.

"Don't shoot. I'm here to help."

I unfroze the first-class terrorists as soon as Sheriff Hermann and his posse had surrounded them. Considering the situation, Flight #505 was given green lights all the way to Chicago—a squadron of fighter jets our escort. With the air corridors cleared, Flight #505 touched down on runway

9A West at Chicago O'Hare, twenty minutes ahead of schedule. Everyone safe and sound except one Ashton Livermore III, the fool who tried to take Sheriff Hermann's hand-me-down Bulova. The major downside? I wouldn't have an opportunity to question the three remaining skyjackers privately.

Before we were allowed to deplane, guys wearing those nerdy FBI windbreakers swarmed into the cabin, trying to look all rugged and daring. Leading the charge was good old Jasper Sexton, the recently promoted Deputy Co-Special Agent in Charge of the Chicago Field Office. They ushered us into an empty hangar large enough to hold a pair of Boeing 707s with room to spare. A dozen folding tables were set up under the skylight in the center of the hangar. The feds had fashioned an assembly line of sorts for the debriefing of the witnesses and inspection of our carry-on items and our checked luggage. They lined us up in reverse order of our seat numbers. The folks in the way back of the plane would be processed first. They hadn't witnessed much from their vantage. Their statements were vague and brief.

"Special Agent Sexton, why am I not surprised to see you here?"

"Don't be such a wise-ass, Briscoe; this here is serious shit." Just my luck, they put us in Sexton's line. He asked me a bunch of questions about the situation on Flight #505. I gave the same answers, practically word-for-word, as had my fellow passengers and the crew. I sensed he was about to get chummy and ask about Gracie and Emma. Not today. Not tomorrow. Not ever.

I disabused Sexton of the notion.

"Briscoe, Special Agent Coleman here is going to pat you down now. It's procedure."

"Fuck your bullshit procedure, agent. You need a warrant, and no judge in my town will give you one." That's my older and only brother, Leonard, to the rescue. He had bluffed, blustered, and bribed his way into the hangar. He was worried about me and his half a million in cash. It wouldn't be convenient to have the FBI rummaging through our belongings. They didn't.

Lenny put an end to this pissing contest by whipping out his updated business card that read:

Fleming, Kirkland, Porter & Briscoe
Attorneys at Law
Leonard C. Briscoe, Partner

There was an address on Wacker Drive, telephone and fax numbers elegantly printed on premium stock. It affected Special Agent Sexton like kryptonite affects Superman. He didn't go all weak at the knees or anything. He apologized to Lenny up and down and instructed a contingent of junior agents to help with our luggage. We had a lot of luggage. Uncle Teddy and Aunt Connie were flying off to Paris on Monday. Mother was meeting Ida May Lipshultz in Miami for some sun and house hunting. They were planning to move to the Sunshine State following my graduation, when I would take over running the family business. There was a lot of baggage to deal with.

Chapter 3
the second city

"It's a wild time!
I see people all around me changing faces!
It's a wild time!
I'm doing things that haven't got a name yet"

Wild Tyme
~Paul Kantner

Flight #505 may have landed ahead of schedule, but by the time we had been given a succession of thorough once-overs by a never-ending horde of well-meaning do-gooders, it was closing in on dinner time. We skipped several stops on Leonard's carefully planned itinerary and went directly to dinner at a restaurant in The Loop called THE BLACKHAWK.

Back in the good old golden days of radio, THE BLACKHAWK hosted a nationally broadcast show. It featured big band music performed by the Coon-Sanders Original Nighthawks Orchestra.

If you ever were going to amount to anything anytime soon, you needed to be seen dining and dancing at THE BLACKHAWK several times a month at the very least. It had a bandstand, a dance floor, and the best steaks in Chicago. Those good old days were long gone before I was knee-high to a grasshopper. Today, THE BLACKHAWK was still a pretty swanky joint with a main dining room and several private suites. We were escorted to one on the second floor —family reunion time.

"Uncle Grouchy, was you a'scared of those meany mean terriblists?"

"Dummy dumb dummy, you was supposed to say Uncle Groucho, not Uncle Grouchy."

"Poopyhead."

This heated exchange was followed by a round of raspberries and more inventive name-calling. Ladies and gentlemen, my nephew Samuel, age 12 and a quarter, and my niece Molly, age 'this many.'

I knew something like that was coming. Status Buttons are great for reading the people around you. Especially if all eyes are on you waiting for a response to this Briscoe family
in-joke, delivered innocently and with *certified-genuine* sincerity by my lovely red-headed niece, Molly Anne Briscoe.

"Molly dearest, we Briscoes aren't afraid of anything. Isn't that so, Uncle Teddy?"

"Fucking-A," answered Uncle T, who was two martinis beyond self-censorship.

"Julius, Edward. I wish you wouldn't use such language around the children."

"My apologies, Bermuda. How's come they call you Bermuda anyways?"

"My parents honeymooned on St.George's."

Wild Will Briscoe was a huge fan of the Marx brothers. He named Leonard after the oldest Marx brother, whose stage name was Chico. I was named for Groucho. I guess that BJ's parents had their own child-naming protocols. Her much younger sister is named Jamaica May. Their late brother was named Roman Augustus.

We each had a suite in the AMBASSADOR EAST courtesy of FLEMING, KIRKLAND, PORTER, AND BRISCOE. Despite Leonard's admonitions, someone had rummaged through our bags before bringing them into the hangar. All of our best clothing had been mishandled and were unfashionably rumpled. We sent them to the valet for pressing. We'd need our dress-up clothes tomorrow night for the public ceremony where my brother would become a made man in the FLEMING, KIRKLAND, PORTER, AND BRISCOE legal protection ~~racket~~ operation. The only difference between assholes like Droopy Pagano and most lawyers I know is their sense of style or lack thereof.

FKP&B, a white-shoe law firm, occupies the entire fortieth floor of THE EZRA KIRKLAND LEGAL ARTS BUILDING. The practice employs nearly one hundred and fifty attorneys. Twenty office in Springfield, and thirty were assigned to the Washington D.C. lobbying operation.

THE KIRKLAND LEGAL ARTS BUILDING, a forty-story black granite behemoth, dominates the corner of South Wacker and West Jackson. It was touted as the Merchandise Mart for legal and related services. There were nearly fifty law firms to choose from, ranging in size from your one-man bands to your symphony orchestras.

The KIRKLAND LEGAL ARTS BUILDING has its own zip code, is home to restaurants and coffee shops, FKP&B SAVINGS AND LOAN, two same-day delivery services, a telephone answering service, a dry cleaner, a bespoke tailor, half a dozen print shops, several notaries, meeting rooms for hire, private investigators, and, of all things, a gunsmith.

The entire 2nd floor was devoted to doctors' offices, daycare centers, a pharmacy, the original Studs Turkel's Snackatorium, whatever that was, and a Jack LaLanne's Health Club.

A gleaming white stretch Lincoln limo picked us up at the AMBASSADOR EAST at half past ten Wednesday morning. White limos often make me think of weddings. One of the things Gracie wanted for our wedding day was a gleaming white stretch Rolls-Royce to squire us from here to there and back again. Thoughts of Gracie are still painful. I guess they always will be.

We arrived at Leonard's building at the appointed hour. We were greeted in the lobby by Leonard and his assistant, the lovely Donna Coopersmith. Donna was a perky, blue-eyed bleach blonde bleached blonde by the same company that produced Doris Day's, Jayne Mansfield's, and Phyllis Diller's signature hair colors. Donna was in her mid-twenties. She gazed at me with concerned compassion brightened with a touch of desire. Leonard must have shared Gracie's story with her.

"Uncle Grouchy, I mean Uncle Groucho, why did those meanie-mean terriblists steal your hair?"

I took a hank of Molly's hair, converted my fingers into scissors, and pretended I was trimming her bangs. "No, sweetness, I got some goop in my hair and couldn't wash it out no matter how hard I tried, so snip, snip, snip." She giggled. We were riding an express elevator to the fortieth floor. Well, it's only express to the thirtieth floor, where it becomes a local.

"What color does your hair have, Uncle Julius?"

"Pretty much the same as yours, Sam, and your dad's or Uncle T's over there. But not the grey parts."

The elevator stopped on the thirty-seventh floor. Uncle T handed me the Zero Halliburton case and stood in front of me. The doors opened, there was a trio of guys wearing matching white Armani tracksuits standing in wait. The centerpiece of this gleaming threesome was good old Dr. Morgan Fields. Small world. Right?

Uncle T, in his darkest tones, said, "Sorry, fellas, this car is going up."

"So are we," answered the COO of ~~The Errand Boys~~, oops, Chicago Private Investigations.

"Edward Briscoe? Why am I not surprised to see you here?"

"I dunno, Fields. Maybe you'll tell me."

Fields didn't get the opportunity. Leonard chimed in and told us that Chicago Private Investigations (CPI) was a division of Fleming, Kirkland, Porter, and Briscoe and its go-to resource for all sorts of investigations. Reputable. Plausibly deniable, discrete. For security and public relations concerns, CPI kept an office on the fortieth floor. Lenny wasn't at all surprised that Fields recognized Uncle Teddy.

A building full of lawyers. Careful, guarded conversations that never declared, only implied. Genius. Fucking genius. This, sure as shit, explained where Fields obtained his murder-for-hire clients. The notion clicked into Uncle Teddy's head too. His Status Button was awhirl with new colors and the wildest textures. I blasted Fields and

Lenny with a timed release TRUTH® bomb. This was going to be one interesting afternoon.

By the time we reached the fortieth floor, Morgan Fields, a world-class investigator in his own right, discovered that we were in town for Leonard's coronation. That we ran into his man Lapin in Atlantic City. The last time we were in Chicago was for Leonard and Bermuda's wedding. And that Teddy promised Fields a sit-down for a Novichok update before we left Chicago.

FLEMING, KIRKLAND, PORTER, AND BRISCOE's offices reminded me a lot of the MILES GOLD DESIGN GROUP's showroom in the Z^2. But larger. Much, much larger. Muted neutral colors and plush carpeting, each division's walls were paneled with rare, exotic woods. What overhead lighting there was, was limited to accent duties. There were overhead speakers that filled the space with barely perceptible pink noise. Melvin Porter believed it helped with the productivity.

Lenny's private partnership ceremony was as unceremonious as it could possibly have been. Basically, we watched Victor Fleming run my half million through their Batdorf machine twice. I had overpaid by twenty-five thousand dollars, which was cheerfully refunded. Lenny put the money back into the Zero Halliburton case and handed it to me. "This money cannot change hands in this building, my brother. We'll take care of that at the house." Then there was the shaking of hands, peppermint schnapps, and Cuban cigars.

One of the requisite status symbols any self-respecting, prestigious white shoe law firm ought to have is a five-star chef. Theirs was Wellington Taylor, a direct descendant of

Zachary. His signature dish, the one he was world-famous for, was, well, you guessed it.

Lunch was excellent. The drinkers were approaching the legal limit. More cigars were lit, and all I wanted to do was go somewhere and fire up a joint.

"You don't look like you're having much fun at all," oozed Donna Coopersmith with *certified-genuine* false sincerity.

"I heard what happened to your friend. I'm so so sorry, Julius; if you need to talk, well, I'm a good listener. Any way I can help, sweetie, I'll help." Code for 'mercy fuck available, inquire within.'

"For sure?"

"Of course."

"Is there somewhere around here where I can smoke a joint without freaking anybody out? The roof? A storage room? A nearby park, perhaps?" She gave me a 'what the fuck' look.

"You mean right now?"

"If it's not too much to ask? Yes, please."

I wasn't surprised to find that the roof of the EZRA KIRKLAND LEGAL ARTS BUILDING was a world-class adult playground. It boasted a recently drained swimming pool still ringed by lounge chair frames, a natural grass putting green, and a workout area with state-of-the-art machines and free weights. On one corner of the roof was the meeting room. It was a twenty-foot yurt, just like the ones at Waverley. We went inside. It was carpeted floor to ceiling, had a big screen TV, an awesome stereo rig, and furniture upholstered with genuine Corinthian leather.

We sat on a five-place grand sofa that must have cost at least three times more than my Jaguar. I removed my cigarette case from my coat pocket. It held ten joints and a box of matches from MONGO MINGS CHINESE WEST. I offered Donna a joint and held the case so she could reach it. She debated which joint to choose. There was little difference among them. I was ranked Waverley's best on-campus doobie crafter three years running by *Waverley's Got Truth,* an unofficial underground broadsheet anonymously published by Eli Gold, or so I'm told. I had twisted them up back in Jersey from a bag I bought from Harry O'Hanlon, who knew a guy who knew a guy who had the best reefer on the planet. Be advised, bullshitters clutter every walk of life everywhere, my friends. Everywhere. Countercultures included.

"Oh, I just can't make up my mind, Julius. You choose." Her colors were going places I didn't want them to go. The next to the last thing I wanted to do was mess around with a sympathetic stranger. The last thing I wanted to do was to mess around with my brother's ditsy 'assistant.'

I lit up a joint and passed it to Donna. She was a virgin. Inexperienced pot smoker, that is. She had no idea. I walked her through the basics, and in no time, she had kicked off her heels, stood up, and started singing "Baby Love." A near-perfect impersonation of Diana Ross. I hit her with something I've been working on called BE COOL®. My way of discouraging unwelcome advances. It made Donna think it was her idea to not make a move on her boss's cute brother. Donna's advances caused me to think of Gracie. But so does most everything on the planet.

Donna's interest in me faded. She changed the subject, "My goodness, Julius, that's a really cool watch. May I have a closer look? Oh my gawd, will you look at the time? We'd better get back."

Chapter 4
new horizons in corporate espionage

"And if you don't underestimate me
I won't underestimate you."

Dear Landlord
~ Bob Dylan

CHICAGO PRIVATE INVESTIGATIONS' world headquarters was in a sumptuous suite on the thirty-seventh floor. Dr. Fields was eager to show off his operation and pump Uncle T for information about William Novichok.

It turns out that murder for hire wasn't Fields' primary source of income. His main sources of revenue were run-of-the-mill staples like divorces, background checks, and corporate espionage; assignments mostly from the law firms that infested the Kirkland Building. CPI employed a dozen investigators, their assistants, and a gaggle of geeky science wizards who staffed a forensics laboratory that was the envy of Chicago's law enforcement community. Fields escorted us into one of his small, secure conference rooms.

"Briscoe, what's with the bald guy?"

"This is my nephew, Julius. He had hair the last time you saw him."

"You sure you want him to listen to this conversation?"

"Fields, he's my consigliere."

"Julius, I meant no disrespect."

"Sure you did. You're forgiven. This time." I gave him a grin and a gangsta wink.

"So what's the story on Novichok? Did he really retire?"

"Maybe. Maybe not. The last time I spoke with him, he told me his grapes were infected with bunch rot. Whatever that is, it is bad. He has to plow everything under and start over. Novichok's vineyard will have a negative cash flow for the foreseeable future. So maybe he's not one hundred percent retired."

"That's good to hear. When will you be in touch with him again?"

"Can't tell you. He calls me and hasn't given me his number if he even has one. My wife and I will be out of the country until January. If he reaches out before I return, Julius will answer that specific phone. So if something should come up while I'm away, get in touch with Julius at our store on Spruce Street."

"Well, if he does want to go back to work, I'd like you to convince him to work with
THE ERRAND BOYS directly. No disrespect, Edward, but the fewer people with knowledge of these kinds of contracts, the better. It puts all of the parties at risk. If you can get him to agree, I'll give you a handsome finder's fee and a ten percent royalty for a year. How's that sound?"

"Make it fifteen percent and three years, and I'll pitch it to him."

"Done."

I checked my Rolex; we had just enough time to ply more corporate secrets from Fields before we had to return to the AMBASSADOR EAST to get gussied up for tonight's big shindig. Fields was already in TRUTH® mode, but to be on the safe side, I hit him with a low dose of ZOMBIE MODE®.

"Fields, how do you go about finding clients seeking men like the Pooles and Novichok?"

"Easier than you might think. Remember that job in Philly? The one in the hospital? That was financed by the vic's executive assistant, who was also the executor of his estate. Talk about a license to steal. These guys can charge the estate pretty much anything they want. That vic's estate was humongous, and the only living heir had gone missing. Cha Ching. That little shit Steverino Washbourne has the next seven years to drain the ten billion dollar estate dry."

"The client wanted the full-service hit. Not a whiff of poisoning or foul play. Degree of difficulty: Off the charts. Fucking impossible."

"Two days after Novichok accepted the assignment, the vic dropped dead in a hospital corridor in front of half a dozen witnesses. The coroner and several of the best cardiologists in the building ruled it a heart attack. Not a trace of foul play. None at all. I have no idea how Novichok pulled it off. I can sell the shit out of a guy that can do things like that, believe you me."

"But Fields, how do you get around the crime-fraud exception to the attorney/client privilege?"

"All the best lawyers always caution their clients to use the phrase 'hypothetically speaking.' As in, 'how does one arrange for my rich uncle's demise? Hypothetically speaking, of course?' That's when a well-connected lawyer hypothetically writes something on a business card and hands it to his client. The card might advise that the telephone number on the card would only be answered for the next twenty-four hours."

Chapter 5
lawyers, guns and dummies

"Everybody's restless and they've got no place to go
Someone's always trying to tell them
Something they already know
So their anger and resentment flow."

Mohammed's Radio
~ Warren Zevon

THE AMBASSADOR EAST provided its guests with nothing but the finest amenities a five-star hotel could offer. Even its most affordable suites reeked of luxury and exquisite good taste. Like all world-class hotels, THE AMBASSADOR EAST'S anchor restaurant was first-rate. The world-famous PUMP ROOM was a posh, upscale restaurant that served the world's best people the world's finest cuisine. It was at the legendary Table One, where Lorna McKay did the deals that made THE ERRAND BOYS the dominant force in Chicago's underworld ecosystem.

FLEMING, KIRKLAND, PORTER AND BRISCOE hosted their annual Thanksgiving Eve employee appreciation dinner in THE PUMP ROOM. All of its Chicago-based employees and their families were invited. Nothing more exciting than a room full of lawyers. Right? I had already planned my escape even before we entered the joint.

At the far end of the dining room was the head table. Seated there were the partners and their spouses. We Philadelphia Briscoes, accompanied by Sam and Molly, and their sitter, Deirdre DePalma, were assigned to the banquette closest to the VIP table. A bandstand just large enough for a quartet had been set up across the dance floor from us: piano, drums, a double bass, and a Shure microphone on a weighted stand and a pair of colossal Marshall speakers.

Molly, cute as a button in her frilly blue dress, sat in a booster seat at the apex of the semi-circle. "Uncle Grouchy," giggle, "I mean Uncle Groucho," giggle giggle, "does you has a dog?
I like dogs. Mr. Bosco has to go to the doggie hotel cuz we has too many company." She frowned. This is merely speculation, but I think someone has force-fed Molly on Shirley Temple movies. She has that same pouty way of speaking and that same hands-on hips imperious attitude. She's downright adorable.

"Molly, my dear, we used to have a dog. His name was Jack."

"Did Jack have to go away?"

"He did. A long time ago."

"What kind of doggie was he? Does you has his picture?"

"Jack was a mutt: a little bit shepherd, a little bit collie. I don't have his picture, but I'll bet your grandmother does. If you ask her real nice, I'm sure she'll show it to you." Mother was seated between her grandchildren. Mom always carried one of those genuine leather photo wallets that held a bunch of pictures in plastic sleeves. She never goes anywhere without it.

"Uncle Grouchy, your doggie was really cute. Does you miss him?"

"Always sweetness, every day."

Sammy nearly forgot his place. Like many boys his age, Samuel Briscoe began talking loud and squeaky before he realized his surroundings and took control of his vocal cords.
"ARE YOU kidding mee? Holy cow, Uncle Julius, is that really your car?"

"It is."

"Seriously? For real?"

"For real, Sam. For really real."

Mother had shown him that picture Nettie Gold took of me and Gracie standing by the Jaguar. We were about to go to the Sadie Hawkins Dance and were dressed up like Main Line hillbillies—a post-modern *American Gothic*. The sky was filled with heavy, dark rain clouds. A shaft of light streamed brightly through a gap in the cover and cast its glory on us. You couldn't buy better lighting. We each had a sly grin on our faces. Couldn't have been a happier moment. Now, thinking about that day makes me sad.

"When we come to visit you, will you give me a ride in it? Do you have the six or the twelve? Is it faster than a Porsche Speedster? Is that your girlfriend? She's really pretty. What's her name?" He lowered his voice to a whisper, "Are you two doing it?" My nephew, Sam Briscoe, spritzing in an adrenaline-fueled rush.

"Of course, I'll take you for a ride. It's the six. The twelve's are way too fussy and not as quick as the sixes. I've never run against a Porsche, so I dunno. Yes, that's

Gracie Gold. And if you promise me that you'll be nicer to your sister, Molly, I'll arrange for us to borrow her Grampy's Bugatti Atlantic. The coolest car ever made."

According to one of those complimentary magazines they litter your hotel room with, the one called NIGHTLIFE: CHICAGO!, Drexel Hills very own JJ Cross was performing at a club called THE GATE OF HORN tonight only. I called ahead, reserved a table for four with my AMERICAN EXPRESS, and mentioned that Jim and I go way back. It was all I needed to justify bailing from the ceremonies once Leonard was officially applauded for becoming an equity partner in the firm and gave a speech praising everyone in the room with specific mentions of Mother, Uncle T, Aunt Connie, and yours truly. I excused myself as soon as I could and went out onto North State Street, that great street. Donna Coopersmith and several of her cohorts were standing around smoking cigarettes and trashing their bosses' wives.

"Hey everybody, say high [*sic*] to Mr. Briscoe's hippie brother, Julius. Don't let his haircut fool ya.' He's very cool."

Thanks for the endorsement, Donna. She kissed me on the cheek and breathed something naughty into my ear. Damn, BE COOL® wears off much faster than I anticipated. Donna was turned on and ready to party. She had an all-is-forgotten look on her face. Her colors had that dangerous glow again.

Someone grabbed Donna by the shoulder and turned her his way. "Is he another one of your *'we're just friends'* friends, Donna? You fucking bitch." Delivered with a sarcastic, demeaning, mocking imitation of a whiny twenty-something woman. This was coming from Jimmie Bob Butcher, one of the guys I met at FKP&B that afternoon. He had a firm handshake and stood about five-seven. Butch Butcher had a permanent scowl and Cary Grant's chin or a reasonable facsimile. Just two years out of the University of Chicago law school, Butcher was already known as a fearsome litigator. He was wearing a nifty Sharkskin suit. Evidently, he believed that he owned Donna Coopersmith.

I asked him, "Are you fucking nuts?"

Butcher blanched. He finally recognized me. A confrontation with a partner's brother could very well cripple his chances for advancement in the firm.

"Sorry, man, I thought you was someone else."

"So, did they teach you to be a rude asshole in law school, or are you self-educated?"

"Look, man, I don't want no trouble with you. It's just that that bitch is always running around on me. It's humiliating, Briscoe. Fucking humiliating."

The thought re-infuriated him. Butch Butcher tightened his grip on Donna's shoulder and cocked his right arm, balled his hand into a fist threatening to blacken both of her eyes. There was no way I was going to allow that to happen. I hit Jimmie Bob Butcher with a full-strength dose of FEAR AND LOATHING.®

Please know that a full-strength dose of F&L is so powerful that it can divert a stampede of raging bulls, quell a riot, scare the shit out of Muhammad Ali, John Wayne, or even Elliot Ness.

The highly ill-educated asshole lost control of his bladder. The remains of a seven-course meal began to bubble in his bowels. Things were about to get worse for him. Butch angrily yanked a pack of Winstons from his coat pocket, shouted, 'You owe me a buck fifty and a blow job, you fucking whore,' and threw it at Donna. He disappeared back into the hotel, where he likely further embarrassed himself in the lobby.

"Want a smoke?" Donna shook the pack of Winstons, and one cigarette magically rose above the others. I declined politely and raised my arm to flag down a passing cab.

"Where you headed tonight, sugar? Got a hot date?"

I told her that I was going to see an old friend who was performing at THE GATE OF HORN.

"You don't need a cab, handsome; it's just up the street. Who's playing tonight?"

"JJ Cross."

"JJ Cross? *The Pied Piper of Drexel Hills?* (which is the title of his forthcoming second album.) You're fucking kidding me. I just love him. Mind if I tag along?"

"Not at all, Donna. It'll be my pleasure."

"So, how do you know JJ Cross?"

"We're from the same neighborhood. His kid brother Richie and I are about the same age. Went to Shawnee Elementary and the seventh grade together. Jim took piano lessons from my dad."

"You went to *that* school? The one where JJ rescued the teachers and the children. The one where the terrorists lynched some old lady and a couple of kids? That school?"

"The very same. One of the murdered kids lived across the street from us. Her name is Margie. Margie Lipshultz."

"Poor dear."

"She was a great kid."

Donna led the way to THE GATE OF HORN singing *Rescue Me,* JJ's first hit single. Donna was a pretty good singer. Just then, she was homing in on being legally drunk. A sip of beer or a sniff of brandy would probably push her over the legal limit. Normals.

Since it was Thanksgiving, the city schools and most of the suburban ones were closed for the rest of the week. Chicago area teens love to party as much as any other teens you will ever encounter. The moon was full, and the evening air was unseasonably warm. We approached a street corner where an octet of letter sweater-clad teeny boppers was crooning *a cappella* a Manfred Mann chart-topper. Fingers snapping with one hand, a bottle of Schlitz in the other. As we passed by, they were singing,

> "There she is just a walking down our street singing do wah diddy, dum diddy do."

Corey Lapinsky, the court jester of the gathering, believed that line to be an omen. He broke formation, hustled towards Donna, and began to serenade her while walking backwards. Barely inches separated their faces.

The singing continued, slurred and off-key.

"You look good. You look fine. I nearly-nearly lost my mind."

He gave me a 'what are you going to do about it' look. He gave Donna the 'I just want to fuck your brains out and what are you going to do about it' look. He was drunk and stupid.

"Buzz off, will ya kid?" Donna snarled at the fool. She planted the palm of her right hand in the middle of Corey's chest and pushed ever so gently. At that very same instant, I caused the drunk's legs to give out from under him. He fell to his knees and then to the ground. He still had the use of his arm and neck muscles, which he used to cushion the impact, preventing possible structural damage.

Nonetheless, his nose and forehead were bloodied. The sight of his own blood was more than too much for poor Corey Lapinsky. He passed out. Corey's crew was outraged. Not one of them could pass a breathalyzer test, yet they all swore up and down that it was me, not Donna Coopersmith, who had somehow laid their brother low. There were seven of them to deal with—a small audience but large enough for my purposes. Retaliation, lust, and fury flooded their Status Buttons. I hit them with a low dose of FEAR AND LOATHING,® transformed my left hand into a semi-automatic, and shouted, "Get the fuck out of here, you little low-life turds, or I'll shoot." They turned tail and scattered into the windy city.

Many say that THE GATE OF HORN was the country's first folk music coffee house. Some in New York City disputed, labeling such claims as ~~bullshit~~ outrageous misinformation—yet another salvo in the pissing contest between The Big Apple and The Second City.

JJ Cross was already a national hero, a household name long before anyone knew he could sing and play with the best of them. It gave the *Pied Piper of Drexel Hills* a head start in the music game. Even so, being booked to headline THE GATE OF HORN was a big deal. The house was packed. Patchouli, pot, tobacco, beer, and pizza. Pressed tin ceilings. Black and white floors. Bentwood chairs, red and white tablecloths. Mostly college-age types sporting well-worn jeans, corduroy jackets with leather elbow patches, sandals, and tie-dye. Both Donna and I were criminally overdressed.

"Why did you reserve a table for four if it was just you?"

"I own a couple of restaurants back home. If you call either of my places to reserve a table for one, you're going to end up seated in the back by the restrooms, the kitchen, or the pay phones. Not a great spot to watch the show."

"Do you really own a couple of restaurants, or are you just trying to impress a girl?"

"I inherited two MONGO MINGS CHINESE restaurants. One's in Center City, and the other is in the suburbs."

"I just love Chinese food. Do you do the cooking, or do you just own?"

"I'm not a chef. Shit, I'm still in high school. Well, not right now. I've taken the fall semester off."

"Why's that?"

"My fiancé was killed. There were things I had to deal with."

"I'm so sorry. I shouldn't have asked."

Our waitperson wore a name tag that said 'Pretty Peggy-O.' She smiled at us and said, "Hello, my name is Susan. What can I get you two tonight?"

A disembodied voice announced, "Happy Thanksgiving, Chicagoland. Welcome to the GATE OF HORN. Let's hear it for Capital Records' recording artist, the pied piper of Drexel Hills. Everybody's hero, JJ Cross."

The crowd rose to its feet as Jim sauntered into the spotlight. We were seated at the table directly across from the center-stage microphones. He winked at the bald guy wearing a three-piece bespoke suit seated next to a chain-smoking bleach blonde wearing a slinky blue dress and way too much makeup and opened his set with Jimmie Rogers' *"In the Jailhouse Now."* It was greeted and followed with enthusiastic applause, whoops, and whistles. Jim thanked the audience, and then he shaded his eyes with his right hand and swept his gaze from side to side. Finally, he said, "I'm told that an old friend from back home is in the audience. Damned if I can spot him. Hey, Julius, you out there?"

I had an idea of what Jim was up to and decided to play along. While I was debating what to do, JJ led the audience in a chant, "Julius, Julius, wherefore art thou Julius?" Classy crowd.
I stood up. JJ invited me to join him on the bandstand. We gangsta hugged.

"Would you look at this? The last time I saw this guy, he was wearing jeans and a grungy sweatshirt just like Maynard G. Krebs, and he had hair. Lots of hair. What's going on here, Julie?" He rubbed my naked scalp.

"I'm trying to start a trend." The audience laughed. Longer and louder than I would have expected.

"Rule number one, never upstage the guy with the guitar. Great seeing you, Jules. Now go sit down; I've got to get back to work."

"Hey, Jimmy, please play 'Draft Dodger Rag'."

For those unfamiliar, it's a song by Phil Ochs about a young pragmatist who explains why he's not Army material.

> "I'm just a typical American boy
> from a typical American town…."

It's a crowd-pleaser.

Jim's set was amazing. Performing with some of the top names on the folkie circuit sure taught him a lot. Most of his set consisted of traditional anthems that everyone in the audience knew by heart. His encore was an original about a badass gangster from the south side of Chicago.

The audience gave him a standing ovation and then charged the bandstand for autographs, memorabilia, and a friendly chat with an emerging star. Donna joined the mob. I needed to call the hotel and check in. I hadn't told anyone where I was headed nor when I might return. It was nearly midnight. Me, a stranger in a strange land. They'd be worried.

"Hello, Mother, it's me, Julius."

"Julius Truman Briscoe, where the fuck have you been?"

Whoops.

"Mom, Jimmy Cross is in town. I went to see him perform at this club called THE GATE OF HORN. I'm sure I told you and Uncle Teddy. What's going on? Why do you sound so pissed?"

"Connie's been looking all over for you. Edward shot and killed a man in the PUMP ROOM. He told her to find you right away."

"What?"

"I didn't see what happened. I was helping Deirdre put the children to bed. She likes you, Julius. She's very sweet and very smart. Deirdre's studying to be a psychologist."

"Focus, mother, focus. Where's Uncle T right now?"

"I think he's still in the restaurant talking to the police with fifty of the best lawyers in Chicago covering his fat ass."

"I'm on my way."

I found Donna Coopersmith in the congregation of JJ Cross worshippers and told her that I had to get back to the hotel. Family emergency. She could stay at the club or walk back to the AMBASSADOR EAST with me.

"Julius, Jimmie Bob was my date tonight, my ride home. I'm gonna stay here and talk to JJ some more. Isn't he just the ginchiest? You go on ahead, sweetie. I'm a big girl. I'll figure something out."

I slipped her a Benjamin, asked her to have JJ call me at the AMBASSADOR EAST if he had the time, and then I rushed back to the hotel.

Chapter 6
the Pump Room incident

"Pretty woman walking down the street
Pretty woman the kind I'd like to meet
Pretty woman, I don't believe you, you're not the truth
No one could look as good as you…"
Oh, Pretty Woman
~ Roy Orbison

So here's what you need to know about the fatal shooting in the PUMP ROOM. The trophy wife of one of the partners while an underclassman at Northwestern had a sophomore year fling with one Walter W. Walters, now an assistant junior associate at FKP&B. He tried to rekindle the flame while they were doing the Hully-Gully on the dance floor.

According to a reliable rumor, Walter beseeched her to meet him in the men's room for a quickie. He was advised that that would not happen and that, whilst she was thinking of it, he was "out of her league and therefore out of her life. Get lost now, shit-for-brains, or I'll tell Artie what you said to me. He'll fire your ass, just like that." And, for dramatic effect, she snapped her fingers up close to his face.

Walters was stung. They had often fantasized, post-orgasmically, about running off to one exotic location or another. He knew he had to have her again when he saw her seated next to that blowhard Arthur Kirkland. Walter was certain she felt the same. Pop. That bubble burst. Walter W.

Walters had a Saturday night special holstered in the small of his back. He thought that it was the best time ever to show it to her.

Uncle T had a similar interest in the elegant Bonnie Kirkland and had been keeping a keen eye on her throughout the evening. He knew a lot of guys like her current dance partner. He knew body language. And he knew a lot about handguns. Teddy also knew that that hothead was strapping, was left-handed, and too drunk to know better.

The fool must have said something the incumbent Mrs. K didn't much care for, and she slapped him across his face good and hard and reared back to slap him yet again. She also was a lefty. With her next swing, Walter caught her left arm with his right and grabbed it tightly. Walters went for his revolver. At that particular moment in time, he was standing directly across from Uncle T, who was seated on the outside edge of the banquette, watching the dance floor.

It was no contest. Before my niece Molly could even count to 'this many,' Teddy was on his feet and standing right next to the asshole, the muzzle of Aunt Connie's tiny pistol pointed at the dude's left temple.

"Drop it, or I'll drop you. If you knew who I am, you would not hesitate."

Walters kept his gaze on Bonnie Kirkland and snarled, "Fuck off, pal. This here is none of your fucking business."

"Right, you were. At first, it wasn't my business. But then you started giving this beautiful woman, this very beautiful woman, a hard time and even pulled a gun on her; well, then you made it my business. Ask around. I'm a very successful businessman."

The thing about Saturday night specials, the kind young miscreants might give to their attorneys for safekeeping, is that they are, invariably, single-action revolvers. The FKP&B associate cocked the hammer of the pistol and pointed it towards Bonnie Kirkland's left breast, and that was enough for Uncle T. He shot the asshole in the temple with that tiny 22 he took off of Aunt Connie. A heartbroken ex-lover boy dead and bleeding all over the dance floor wasn't even close to the biggest scandal THE PUMP ROOM had ever entertained.

As we have previously explored, a 22 caliber pistol makes more smoke than it does noise. That and the fact that the drummer and the vocalist of *The Chicago Cavaliers*, the evening's entertainment, had been feuding over a woman, the drummer's ex-wife. That evening, H. Barry Belsky invented Heavy Metal Drumming. He got every decibel out of that simple drum kit. Of course, that style of drumming and Handsome Harry Hart's vocal stylings were incompatible.

Midway through Harry's perfect cover of *'Oh, Pretty Woman,'* Handsome Harry lost it. Always a heavy hand with his cymbals, Belsky had launched into an ill-timed, unprovoked, inappropriate drum solo a la Ginger Baker. Handsome Harry swiveled to confront the demented drummer, tossing the microphone aside. It landed in front of one of those giant speakers. The feedback squeal was deafening. You wouldn't have been able to hear a 357 Magnum go off right then. Bonnie Kirkland, her hands covering her ears, knelt to see what had happened to Walters. Mere nanoseconds after the bass player pulled the microphone away from the speaker; Bonnie Kirkland let out a horrified scream at the same pitch and volume as the feedback—a seamless transition from chaos to terror.

A gleaming white ambulance arrived at the Ambassador East, lights flashing and sirens screeching a good twenty minutes ahead of Detective Sergeant Zalman Rutkowski and his team of forensic experts. After a thorough examination, they concurred that Walter Walters, an assistant junior associate in the law firm Fleming, Kirkland, Porter and Briscoe had died from a gunshot wound to the head sustained approximately one hour and a quarter earlier.

Detective Rutkowski attempted to interview the witnesses but had to run a gauntlet of attorneys who specialized in delaying tactics. It gave me enough time to return from The Gate of Horn and breech the loose cordon set up in The Pump Room's lobby.

"Whoa, pal, where do you think you're going?

"I'm going in there."

"No, you are not. That's a crime scene. It is off limits."

"Not to me, it's not; I'm their lawyer."

"Ain't you a little young to be a lawyer?"

"I'll have you know that I graduated from law school in less than an month. I'm a super smart prodigy. So cut the crap and Let Me Pass." Patrolman Scott Fedko apologized with forced genuineness and stepped aside.

On the advice of Arthur Kirkland, the head of the firm's criminal law division, Uncle Teddy and my brother were knocking back shots at the bar. This activity would make it impossible for the police to obtain a reliable accounting of the events leading up to the shooting. I brushed past a couple more cops to find Uncle T and Leonard shitfaced at the bar and damned proud of it.

"Uncle T, what the fuck?" He filled me in. Leonard explained that Uncle T's action in defense of another person's life was justifiable. All we needed was to convince Detective Sergeant Rutkowski. My specialty. Piece of cake.

As all of you must have surmised, Detective Rutkowski had little doubt that Uncle T acted in defense of another person's life and was all but certain that no charges would be filed against him. He asked Uncle T not to leave town until his superiors gave the okay. He took Uncle T's contact information and praised his courageous, heroic actions. Man crush?

Never leave home without it.

Chapter 7
thanksgiving at chico's

"You got mud on your face. Big disgrace
Somebody better put you back into your place"

We will Rock You
~ Brian Harold May

Leonard and Bermuda Briscoe and Jamaica May Leventhal own a three-story Queen Anne-style mini-mansion on a hill. It was on Lake Street in Evanston, Illinois, a block from Lake Michigan and a mile and a half from Northwestern University, where Bermuda June was a tenured professor of Post Civil War American Literature.

The gleaming white limo dropped us off at Lenny's house later than scheduled. Blame Teddy Briscoe. He had a hangover from all of his plausible deniability drinking last night.

It had taken Aunt Connie and me half an hour to get him off the bed and into the shower.
I zapped his nervous system with RAWPOWER® several times until it finally took hold. Once it did, he became, miraculously, his good old energetic self with a world-class hangover.

Lenny, on the other hand, seemed none the worse for wear. When we arrived, he was throwing a football around with Sam and a couple of the neighborhood kids on his expertly groomed, elevated front lawn.

"Yo, Julius! Go deep." I was street-level. Lenny was up on the terrace, six feet higher.

"Can you throw it this far? Seriously, Chico, you're old. Really old. Over-the-hill old. Can you throw it this far?"

"Groucho, stop ~~fucking~~ messing around. And just go deep."

"Hang on a second." I helped Mother and Aunt Connie from the limo. I left Uncle Teddy to fend for himself. I kept an eye on my big brother as I loped about quarter speed towards the lake. Seconds later, Lenny hit me in stride. Perfect spiral. I raced into an imaginary end zone, spiked the ball, and danced, fists held high in celebration. Philadelphia style.

Remember the date. On this Thanksgiving day in 1964, the brothers Briscoe played catch with one another for the first time in their lives. Someone should contact Guinness.

Up the hill and up the steps to the wrap-around porch on a glider sat Molly Anne Briscoe and Deirdre DePalma.

"Look, everybody!"

Molly was wearing her tap shoes and punctuated each utterance with a flourish of steps even the great Gene Kelly would admire.

"It's Uncle Groucho, I mean Uncle Julius!" Tap, tap, tap. "Hi, Uncle Julius," the tap-tapedy-tapping continued as she greeted each of us. "Hi Grammy, Hi Aunt Connie, Hi Uncle Uncle Teddy!" Molly's theatrically exuberant greetings alerted her mother, Bermuda June Briscoe, about half a dozen college-aged college students, and a pair of uniformed servers bearing appetizers and friendly smiles.

Following the hugs and knishes, we were given a tour of their new home in the best part of town where lived the best people in that part of town. We sure were impressed. It wasn't nearly as large as the Gold's, but it also had that stately English Manor vibe going for it. A suitable dwelling for a prominent lawyer, his distinguished Literature professor wife, and two precocious minor children. And lest I forget, according to Molly, a Golden Reliever named Mr. Bosco who was currently having a swell time at the Doggie Hotel on Popular Avenue.

Like Waverley Academy, many Northwestern students hailed from places too far from Chicagoland to make the expense and tedium of a roundtrip home cost-effective. Some friends who lived closer to Chicago invited some of them to spend the holiday with their families. Others remained on campus, deprived of warm company and a homemade Thanksgiving dinner. Many Northwestern faculty members invited several such afflicted students into their homes for a Thanksgiving dinner that couldn't be beat. Bermuda invited half a dozen stranded students to share the holiday with her family. Lenny and BJ were expecting 53 guests for dinner—men, women, and children.

No tour of Casa Briscoe West would be complete without experiencing Molly Anne Briscoe's pretty and pink bedroom on the second floor. It featured a big girl canopy bed and more frilly pastel decorations than one could count. Her bedroom was filled with stuffed animals representing every continent on the planet. Two of each species, naturally. Molly had a story to tell about each and every one of them and would have told them all to me, but again, my big brother Leonard came to the rescue.

"Hey, Julius. Are you ready?"

"Ready for what?"

"For some football. It's the annual Lake Street Thanksgiving touch football invitational. Evens against Odds." I gave him a blank stare free of charge.

He clarified, "Even-numbered houses versus the odd-numbered houses." That made sense. But it also made for a divided neighborhood that cultivated years-long rivalries.

"Sure thing. When and where?"

"Now and outside. We have the whole street to ourselves. The head coach of the Odds is the 'honorable' town councilman Leander Wolfe. Every Thanksgiving, I'm told, he has the police put sawhorses up on each end of the block. There will be no interruptions from inconsiderate motorists during the Lake Street Invitational."

"Let me warn you about Councilman Wolfe. He, also, is a lawyer. He works out of an office in his basement where his wife, Taffi, is his executive secretary. Second rate all the way. He's a spooky little guy, Julius. Envious and devious. Be nice to him. Just don't take any advice or shit from him."

I promised Molly that I'd come back later to hear all about her menagerie.

Lenny wasn't exaggerating about Leander Wolfe, the kind of man for which the word "shyster" was coined. Short and bulky, he was seedy in every way imaginable.

Wolfe wore flashy diamond rings on his pinkies and a long-sleeved T-shirt that read "Lake Street Oddities" across the chest. Wolfe's lovely wife, Taffi, wore a black and white striped blouse that provided delightful perspectives on her ample cleavage. She was this afternoon's referee and league commissioner. And right off, there was a dispute for her to rule upon.

This was the first year that the Briscoe family would be participating in this highly competitive event. Evidently, it was a big deal. Each home on the winning side of the street kept the Lake Street Touch Football Championship Trophy proudly displayed in a front window for six weeks or so before passing it over to the next-door neighbor. *The Lake Street Evens* gathered in Lenny's living room, talking strategy and pumping each other up for the challenge ahead.

According to rule number 7, also known as the anti-ringer rule, a list of all anticipated Thanksgiving dinner guests must be submitted to league headquarters no later than one week prior to kickoff. No college-level or professional athletes were permitted to participate. If there even was a rule book, neither the welcome wagon people nor the Wolves had provided Lenny with a copy. So when we tumbled from the house, all twenty-seven of us, good old Leander Wolfe, hit the ceiling.

"Whoa, there, Briscoe! Did you register any of these people with Taffi at the league office?"

"What the fuck are you blathering on about, Wolfe man?" Chico hadn't forgotten how to confront attitude with attitude. It led to an ungodly dispute about the rules, common sense, courtesy, and decency before resolving into a compromise. Since the Evens had assembled an NFL-sized roster and the Odds only numbered eight, it was agreed that the Evens would also only field eight players.

That wasn't even the weirdest rule. Like in volleyball, the players had to rotate positions at every change of possession. To give every member of the Lake Street Evens a shot at gridiron glory, one player would rotate in as another rotated out of the game.

It was my turn at quarterback. We were up three scores to 2. Sammy Briscoe is unbelievably fast for a kid his size. He routinely whizzed past his defenders only to drop blistering passes from his father and Uncle T. That was before I rotated to the rescue. The Oddities team was comprised entirely of adults with height, weight, and speed advantages over our squad's younger members, including Sammy and Traci Ianucci, the next-door neighbor. The first thing I did was hit the defenders with a low dose of PECKINPAH® just to even the odds.

Traci and Sammy were around the same age. Both attended Northwestern Prep and were deep in the throes of puppy love. Traci was maybe even a step faster than Sammy. It's good to have speedy receivers on a football team, whatever the level.

It was third and about five yards. We were at midfield. Both Traci and Sammy had burned Leander Wolfe for crucial first downs. He was frustrated and angry. Buttons do not lie.

We needed five yards for another first down. I had the kids run crisscross routes. Traci had already whizzed past Wolfe a time or two before. With the clock running out and the Oddities still down one score, I launched a perfect spiral in Traci's direction. Wolfe tripped her as she went whizzing by. Traci hit the concrete, knees, forearms, and chin. Bruises, scrapes, and fury. She bounced up, bleeding and angry. My perfect pass wasted. My QBR was certain to take a big hit.

Traci charged at Wolfe and knocked him to the concrete. He was shaken, nearly to tears. Traci must have clawed at the man's face. Scratch marks on his forehead and eyelids. He tried to push her off of him, his hands on her budding breasts. He was a lawyer. He knew how bad it looked.

"Can someone help me with this maniac? Please! I don't know what's got into her. She just went crazy for no reason. No reason at all."

"You tripped me, you cheater head. You're gonna pay. Asshole. You are so gonna fucking pay. My big brother Dominick's a cop in Denver. He's coming for Thanksgiving and maybe Christmas. Mommy and Daddy went to go get him at the airport. They should be home soon. You are so fucked, Councilman dickhead."

Feisty one that Traci Ianucci. I gave her my handkerchief, and asked Sammy to take Traci into the house and get her cleaned up. Wolfe was still lying on the street, waiting for a hand-up that never would come.

"What about you, baldy? You gonna give me a hand here or what?"

"Are you fucking nuts? I saw what you did. And so did a lot of other people. I don't lend a hand to scumbags like you. You're on your own pal. Where I come from, tripping little girls and copping a feel off an eleven-year-old is so very not cool."

"Best of all, everyone on the block watched Traci beat the shit out of you. A skinny little thing with those tiny little titties at that. Whoosh! There goes the reputation."

"So here's some free advice. Go home. Pack up your shit. Sell the house and land. Never show your fucking ugly face in these here parts again."

He gave me a questioning, spiteful look as he struggled to his feet, "If you had any idea who I am, you wouldn't have disrespected me. There will be repercussions; I can assure you of that, young Mr. Briscoe."

"You're mistaken, dipshit. I'm not a Briscoe, I'm William Novichok the baddest man in the whole damn town. I am not a person to be fucked with. Now run along home, little piggy." And so he did.

Chapter 8
the certified-genuine Julius

"Got the message this morning
The one that was sent to me
About the madness of becoming
what one was never meant to be."

The Groom's Still Waiting at the Altar
~ Bob Dylan

The 14th annual Lake Street Thanksgiving touch football event was over. The Lake Street Oddities had been disqualified, giving the Evens the coveted trophy. Perhaps not a win to celebrate. The fans and participants headed home for their holiday feasts.

Molly Briscoe was dressed up like a pilgrim: an ankle-length black dress and a white apron. One of those capotain hats (the things you remember from the sixth grade), complete with a brass buckle, was perched jauntily on her curly red hair. She was waiting for us at the top of the porch stairs.

"Which one of them meany mean Oddsies hurt my bestest friend Traci?"

Already hell on wheels, and Molly's only 'this many.'

"How's Traci doing?"

"She's being really, really brave. Mommy's putting owie stuff on her."

"Where are they?"

"They're in the powdery room."

"What's a powdery room?"

"It's like a bathroom, but you can't has a bath in it cause it doesn't has a tub."

"I see. Where is this unusual place?"

"I can show you."

She took my hand and led the way. Molly Anne Briscoe is four years old and looks like Gracie looked when she was that many. They stole my heart the moments we met.

The powdery room was towards the back of the house, between the dinette and the family room. Sammy and Deirdre DePalma were standing guard. Sam's arms were folded against his chest. A confounded expression on his face. His Status Button was glowing angry. He was, undoubtedly, thinking about good old Leander Wolfe and what he would do to the motherfucker if only Sam were a little bit bigger.

"Hey, kid. You holding up?"

"I'm good. Do you know if Uncle Uncle Teddy brought his gun with him?"

"He did not. The police have it. Why are you asking Sam?"

"Cause someone needs to shoot that asshole Councilman Wolfe."

"I wouldn't spend too much time thinking about Councilman dickhead. I'm guessing you won't be seeing him around here too much longer."

"You sure?"

"Pretty sure kid. Pretty sure."

I ducked my head into the powdery room. Traci was seated on the toilet lid. She had bandages on both knees, a band-aid on her forehead, and a thermometer in her mouth. BJ at her side.

"There's my favorite brother-in-law right now. Is he the handsome man who gave you his handkerchief?"

Traci shook her head yes.

Bermuda looked at her watch and retrieved the thermometer from Traci's mouth.

"You're normal. Good to go. So go already."

"If it's alright with you, Professor Briscoe, I'll take the children to the beach."

"Excellent thought, Deirdre. Please be back by quarter past three, or sooner if any of them should require a change of wardrobe.

Julius, Leonard's been asking for you. He's in his study. Do you know where it is, or shall I escort you?"

She took us the long way around. BJ wanted to know how I was doing. So much turmoil and tragedy in so short a time. She was amazed at how well I was bearing up. I said that I felt hollow inside, numb; that that kind of shock doesn't wear off quickly. It lingers. Then she told me that if I ever needed to talk to someone about anything, well, she's all ears.

Then BJ told me about her younger sister, Jamaica, a senior at Northwestern Prep. Jamaica's ambition was to be a teacher like her older sister. Later that afternoon, she would entertain the children in the playroom while her plus one would join us in the formal dining room. And, if you asked her, he was all wrong for her kid sister.

"Julius, he's studying to be a Rabbi. My beautiful, sweet, talented, darling baby sister Jamaica May is many wonderful things, but she is definitely not Rebbetzin material. That's all I have to say on the subject. Do me a favor; if you think you're up to it, please flirt with her tonight. Julius, she's very flirt worthy. I want Jaimie to see how Robert reacts. He's the clingy type."

I told her that I haven't had much success with flirting, but I'd try my best.

Leonard's study was just off the main dining room through a hidden door. Press down on a section of the chair rail that separates the wainscoting from the wallpaper, and abracadabra, a secret door springs open just like in the movies. When we arrived, the door was already open. Leonard and Uncle Teddy were watching the Chicago Bears play the Detroit Lions on the largest color television screen I'd ever seen. The Lions were up by four. The Bears had first and ten from their own twenty. Only thirty-two seconds remained to snatch victory from the jaws of certain defeat.

The walls of Lenny's secret study were lined with bookcases filled with hundreds of identically clad volumes —legal tomes, dark wood, area rugs—Neo old school everywhere I looked. My brother Leonard was sitting on a leather club chair, my Zero Halliburton case was his footrest.

"Come on in, Julius, and please shut the door behind you."

Leonard pushed a button on the remote control that muted the sound. He asked about my encounter with Wolfe. I was telling Lenny a version of the truth when suddenly he turned up the sound. The announcers were shouting; their voices had gone hoarse. The Bears had just come from behind to defeat the Lions 27 to 24 on a seventy-two-yard catch and run. Billy Wade to Mike Ditka. We missed it. Instant replay technology was still a year or two away. We listened to hysterical fans and announcers describing the miracle for another minute or so before Lenny turned the television off. He gave us a stern look and began a lecture one could never forget.

"So one of my partners, Arthur Kirkland, is as paranoid as they come. He personally scrutinized every single one of those hundred-dollar bills we had received for the Longstride job. Can't be too careful. If any of those bills had been marked, he would have lit a Monte Cristo with it. Thankfully, only one of those twenty five thousand hundreds was marked in any way, a telephone number underneath the name Toni. A heart dotting the letter 'i'."

"Arthur marked the bills destined for the Longstride contract. If you look at the back of a hundred-dollar bill, the lower right-hand quadrant, for instance, you'll see a column of horizontal hash marks between a set of vertical borderlines. What Arthur Kirkland and his assistants did was to darken the space between a pair of hash marks. Thinnest, shortest little lines. Easy to overlook. They'd darken one of those tiny spaces on each bill in the bundle in ascending order. When you flipped through it, you'd see a dark line rising from bottom to top. They had marked about half of Novichok's bundles before they ran out of quick-drying *hundred-dollar-bill-green* ink."

"Arthur says it's just a precaution. I just think he likes the smell of money, grime mixed with cheap perfume and cocaine."

Uncle T and I gave Lenny a puzzled stare as if to say what the fuck does this have to do with me or the price of tea in China?

"I know what you're thinking. You're thinking, what does this have to do with me or the price of Peking tea?" Lenny took his feet off the Zero Halliburton case, lifted it up, sat it on his lap, and opened it. He tossed each of us a stack of hundreds held together with a mustard-colored strap, with FKP&B Savings and Loan printed on one line and $10,000 on the line below. We, too, had scanned them for markings. I guess we missed the ones we had just learned about.

"Try flipping through these boys. Tell me what you see."

Whoops.

"What's going on here? Julius, how in the world did you wind up with these bills?" The air whooshed from the room. The only sounds to be heard came from the dining room where the caterers were setting up. I looked at Uncle T. His colors and textures were non-stop crazy. His mind was working on thousands of ideas at about a thousand miles per second. After a minute or two, he whispered into my ear, "Maybe you should just tell him?"

I asked Uncle T to hold that thought and mashed down on Leonard's pause button. Chico wouldn't be able to move a muscle or form memories until I released the pressure.

The major problem was that there was no way to explain how I had gotten ahold of so many hundred-dollar bills Arthur Kirkland and his team had converted into expensive flipbooks. One solution was to use my persuasive skills on Lenny and his partners. That might work. Uncle T stood up walked over to Leonard's chair to get a better look inside the Zero Halliburton case. All of the money, less the twenty grand, was still in it. Good news, they hadn't divvied it up yet. Most likely, they'd get around to it after supper.

"Alright, Uncle T, let's figure this out. Can I trust Lenny with the truth? I mean, I hardly know him. He's just a voice on the phone a couple times a year. Or should I feed him a version of the truth? One he can handle?"

I unpaused Lenny long enough so he could answer my questions. As soon as he had, I paused him again. I needed to know how they were going to divide the money. Would it be an equal split, or was the distribution more convoluted? Partner, I just then learned, did not necessarily mean equal partner. Seniority dictated that Fleming and Kirkland got 35% each, Porter thirty. This meant there were more than enough unmarked bills to keep Arthur Kirkland in the dark —a relatively simple task. Just ask any of his trophy wives.

I pushed Lenny's pause button again. He was back to normal. He picked up right where we left off.

"Little brother, are you fucking deaf? I'll ask you again; what's going on here? Answer me, Julius, how did you end up with these bills?"

"Leonard, are you really certain you want me to answer your question? I can assure you my response will be mind-blowing, life-changing. It will take some getting used to, believe you me. Keeping this secret will be a lifelong burden, just ask Uncle T."

"I need to know, Julius. The partners will be stopping by sometime after dinner to pick up their shares."

"Leonard, there are more than enough unmarked bills to cover Kirkland's cut."

Lenny relaxed and smiled. Problem solved. He went to his desk and retrieved three lockable bank bags. And began to sort the bundles.

"This still doesn't explain, Julius, how you got your hands on these bills?"

His colors were as crazy as Uncle T's. He was angry. At me. At Kirkland. At Fields. At himself for being unable to imagine how his long-lost little brother had acquired the marked money. "Julius, this is some serious shit. I need to know. I can't have this come around and bite me on the ass sometime in the whenever. Understand?"

"Understood. I'll keep it simple. Lenny, I'm Willie Novichok."

Leonard turned white. The blood drained from his face, and the terror in his eyes made me worry that he was maybe about to have a heart attack. I calmed him down with a thing I call DOLLY®. It's named for the chord I first used on Dahlia Gold at Eleanora's funeral and recently on Miriam Gold at Gracie's. I calmed him down. I offered him a joint. He gave me a look that said that I was full of surprises. He surprised me right back by grabbing the joint, firing it up, and taking a couple of huge hits before passing it around.

"Let me get this right? You're Morgan Fields' new wonder boy?" I nodded yes. "Then tell me how you did the Longstride job. The man had better security than the fucking mayor, for fuck's sake. Little brother, this is really good pot."

"Believe me when I tell you, Lenny, you don't want to know."

"Believe me when I tell *you,* Julius, I'm your older brother and need to know. Right now, young Mr. Briscoe. Right fucking now."

I said all right and stood up, removed the roll of bills from my pocket, peeled off a C-note, and handed it to Leonard.

"I'm hiring you to be my lawyer. That means I get confidentiality, discretion, plausible deniability, and triple green stamps. Right?"

"Correct."

Uncle T handed Lenny another hundred.

"Lenny, you'd best sit down for this."

He sat. Teddy sat. I sat.

"So, how did you pull off the Longstride hit?"

"Lenny, I can do things Normal people like you and Uncle Teddy here can't do."

"Like what?" he scoffed, "Leap tall buildings with a single bound? Shit like that?"

"Better."

"Better how?"

"Lenny, I'm parched. Could you please fetch me a glass of water?"

He tried to get up.

"What on earth is going on? Julius, I can't move a muscle. Don't tell me that you're doing something to me?"

"Of course I am. A demonstration is often better than an explanation. I'm what some of you Normals call psychic. I killed Leon Longstride by stopping his heart just as easily as I have paralyzed most of your body. He wasn't the first person I've killed that way."

Judging from the expression on his face, Lenny had questions—train loads of them.
I unpaused him.

"Before I tell you the whole truth and nothing but the truth, if, at any time, you decide you don't want to remember what I can do and have done, well, just say so, and I'll make it like you haven't heard an unusual word all afternoon."

Lenny's Status Button pinwheeled through all the colors that there are. Fast as a tornado. He was eager. He shook his head yes. "Lay it on me, Groucho baby." It really was really good pot.

I started at the beginning with the Gino Pagano encounter and got all the way up to Atlantic City when the phone rang. The guests would be arriving in a couple of hours—time to freshen up.

I told Lenny we'd pick this up later. I reminded him that he cannot discuss this with anyone, not even BJ. Anyway, I'd already seen to it that he would be unable to reveal my secret by any method of communication now in existence or might exist in the future.

Don't leave home without it.

Chapter 9
walking in the sand

"In a world that keeps on pushin' me around
I'll stand my ground and I won't back down."

I won't back down
~ Tom Petty

Of course, Leonard's secret study had a secret exit as well as that secret entrance. Pull on the volume entitled "Cook County Tax Court Records 1898-1915," and abracadabra, another secret door springs open to reveal a circular staircase leading down to the storm cellar/fallout shelter—just like in the movies.

Everywhere I looked, there were boxes of canned goods, bottled water, bunk beds, meals ready to eat, and all that good stuff. A steep set of stairs led up to the storm door and the backyard beyond. While we walked towards the front of the house, Lenny, as any proud homeowner might, pointed out all of the improvements he'd already made to the property and those he planned for the future. The three-car garage was brand new. Work on the swimming pool would begin in late April or early May. Tennis bubble the year after.

Lake Street was open for business again. The caterers provided their own valet parking service. While they were setting up in front of the house, Leander Wolfe, a Louisville Slugger resting on his right shoulder, stormed up to the unsuspecting valets demanding to know where the fuck was that asshole Ovalchick hiding? He was drunk. He was a loud drunk. We were approaching Wolfe from his blind side. He couldn't see me coming. No one can.

"Here's another demonstration for you, Lenny."

I hit Wolfe's pause button, walked down to street level, and stood nose-to-nose with the asshole. I unpaused him. From Wolfe's point of view, I appeared from out of nowhere, with me saying, "I thought I told you to get the fuck out of town? Hit the bricks." The shock of it all made his heart race, made his mind panic. He executed a near-perfect about-face, and that little piggy squealed all the way home. Again. And I didn't need to double dose him with FEAR AND LOATHING®.

The three of us smelled like frat party, so we decided that there was enough time before the guests arrived to take a walk on the beach for some fresh air and some fresh scents—sustainable deodorizing.

The first thing about Lake Michigan that took me by surprise was that it has waves, just like the Atlantic Ocean. I had never once in my life imagined that a lake would or wouldn't have waves or beaches. It's official, everyone, Lake Michigan, and probably some of the other ones too, have waves and beaches. Always did, whether I was aware or not. There's a lesson in there somewhere.

We removed our high tops and socks, tied the laces together, slung them over our shoulders, walked down the stairs to the beach, and turned south.

I've been thinking lately that maybe, somehow, I attract all this shit. Well, ever since the Gino Pagano incident, anyways. I wonder if I might exude some sort of pheromone that attracts trouble. Like this simple walk on the beach did.

Now, I can't go around day after day patrolling the mean streets of Philadelphia, Chicago, or even Atlas City, righting wrongs, keeping the peace, discouraging larceny, or curing City Hall of its many maladies. I haven't the time or the inclination.

On the other hand, if I see something, I have to do something. Mostly, nothing too drastic.
A shoplifter or a pick pocketer suddenly develops crippling arthritis. A stickup man gets the giggles. Shakedown artists get the shakes. Confidence men lose theirs.

What about your ordinary thugs and neighborhood bullies, you ask? Well, I CROSSWIRE® them. Signals meant for the right side of their bodies I reroute to their left and vice versa. Causing them to lurch unsteadily about like Frankenstein's monster or a toddler learning to toddle. It only lasts a few minutes, long enough for the asshole to never want to experience that terror ever again. Like I said, I don't go out of my way to be the righter of wrongs, but…..

A young woman in her twenties, let's call her Vicki, wearing a yellow bikini top and cut-off jeans, was playing frisbee with her dog down on the damp sand. The dog, who was called Rocket, made athletic mid-air catch after athletic mid-air catch that he promptly returned to his mistress. They were drawing an enthusiastic crowd.

Maybe it was a gust of wind off the lake or maybe just an errant throw, the Wham-O Professional Grade Frisbee hit Gerald F. 'Shadow' Merton, a disciple of Phil Spector's, squarely on the back of his head, knocking his shades and grape Popsicle to the sand. It lit his short fuse on fire.

Rocket and Shadow Merton's left foot reached the Frisbee nearly at the same moment. Rocket had just gotten a good grip on his toy when Shadow stomped on it. A tug of war ensued. Man versus beast. Both were tenacious. Both determined. Both growled menacingly. Without lessening the pressure on the frisbee, Shadow Merton managed to position himself to deliver a vicious kick to Rocket's ribcage. He swung his right leg behind him and would have delivered a devastating blow had I not intervened. Before he began his downswing, I paralyzed Merton's right leg and nothing else. It's a wonder he maintained his balance for as long as he had—two and a half seconds, according to my inner Rolex. Never leave home without it.

Shadow Merton fell face first onto the sandy beach after heroic, yet losing battles with gravity and inertia. His right leg was sticking up like a fuzzy street sign. I helped his girlfriend roll him onto his side, preventing likely suffocation.

"I can't move my leg, Mary. Why can't I move my leg?"

"I don't know, Shadow, honey. I just don't know." Mary, the great-granddaughter of the legendary gangster E.J. Weiss, was long and lean. The kind of girl guys go to the beach to meet. She cried out, "Is there a doctor? A nurse? A faith healer?"

"Mary, there's no need for shouting. My Uncle Edward is a prominent prognostician from Slibberdy, Pennsylvania, he is here on holiday. He's just over there playing frisbee with Vicki, my brother Chico, and Rocket. I'll go fetch him."

I briefed Uncle T on the mission. "Just calm them down. Give the clod a good once-over twice. Pretend to think it over for a while and then tell them that Merton has what is known in the medical community as premature chronic promulgation and that things should return to normal quite soon." To further ease their minds, Teddy asked for her phone number. He'd call after supper to check on ~~Shadow Merton's condition and~~ the smokin' hot Mary Weiss. I consulted my Rolex. We needed to get back. The dinner guests would be arriving any moment. We would be fashionably late, smelling like the Great Lake with beach sand in our hair and clothes.

Chapter 10
thanksgiving chicago style

"Seems I've got to have a change of scene
Cause every night I have the strangest dreams
Imprisoned by the way it might have been
Left here on my own or so it seems."

Feeling Alright
~ Dave Mason

When we returned to the house, there were casually dressed people everywhere. Down on Lake Street, half a dozen luxury cars were waiting on the understaffed valet service. A line of people was waiting to get into the house. More people chatted on the terrace while uniformed servers with appetizers and wine, roamed among them.

Teddy and I joined the queue, waiting to get into the house. Lenny waded into the crowd, greeting, back-slapping, hand-kissing, and glad-handling. I wondered why the line was moving so slowly. Uncle Teddy and I wanted to change into fresh, less informal, clothing before dinner. Were they carding everyone? No. It was worse than that.

I'm a little unclear about regional holiday traditions. Or if this one even qualifies as such. The caterer had set up a podium on the porch by the front door. The charming hostess, wearing an *Arbuckle's* West tunic and a name tag that said Alice Brock, stood behind it. She had a color-coded copy of the guest list in front of her. Also on a side table were three goldfish bowls, the kind you find in the five-and-dime store. Each one was about half filled with solid-colored gravel. Green, blue, or yellow, which corresponded to three of the four dining areas set up in the house. The fourth area was for the children who would be banished to the playroom in the basement come supper time. Each bowl also contained slips of matching colored paper.

These are the components of something called 'university-style seating.' Basically, you draw a slip of paper from your designated bowl. On that paper is the number of your assigned seat. Randomization being an effective social lubricant, according to a professor of Psychology at Northwestern. Uncle T and I were among the last in line and were directed to draw from the green bowl. I drew #22 and Uncle T #7.

People mingled in the foyer, on the wrap around porch, and on the terrace until the hostess Alice, remember Alice?, walked amongst them, playing a silver triangle to announce that dinner was about to be served. "Please take your seats. Thank you."

Most family homes do not feature dining rooms that can seat twenty-five with no scrimping on the elbow room. BJ and Lenny's does. The house was built back in the Roaring Twenties by the notorious gangster that even Al Capone feared, E.J. 'Hymie' Weiss. Which goes a long way to explain the secret entrances and the oversized rooms.

Seat #22 was on the far side of the dining room table, almost directly across from the secret latch that opens the secret door into Lenny Briscoe's secret study. Seated on my right was a woman in her early forties, maybe. She wore a black sleeveless dress, had a pair of those Pocahontas-style pigtails, and little or no makeup. She was rail thin and had an oversized head. The dour-faced woman had a detached manner and cold grey eyes.

"Hello. I'm Julius Briscoe. How do you know my brother?"

"I'm Theadora Perriman. Bermuda June and I are colleagues at Northwestern."

"And you, Julius, where do you attend school?"

"Waverley Academy in St. Davids, Pennsylvania. Although not presently. I've taken the fall semester off. I had personal matters to attend to."

Professor Perriman gave off that classic gunfighter vibe. Cold. Calculating. Status Buttons do not lie. It was clear she knew about my trials and tribulations these past months, Thea being chatty with my sister-in-law and everything.

When I mention someone's Status Button, feel free to think *aura*. From what I know about what Normals call *auras*, they seem to serve the same purpose as Status Buttons: to reflect,
non-verbally, a person's nature, current mood, and intentions. Theodora Perriman's Status Button/*Aura* said she was buzzed from the four glasses of Chardonnay she had at the reception and may be in an elevated mood. It's hard, most times, to read or influence buzzed strangers.

One component of a person's Status Button is its color cast. An overall tone that affects all of a person's 'colors.' Theodora Perriman's color cast was a sickly green, I associate with sadness. It's kind of what I imagine mine would look like if I had one.

The whirlwind, later identified as Vanessa, Arthur Kirkland's oldest daughter by his second trophy wife, the feminist novelist Julianna Robinson, stormed into the dining room muttering under her breath and juggling several upscale branded shopping bags and a slip of green paper telling her where to sit. There was only one empty seat at the table. The one on my left. She set her bags on the sideboard and sat right down. She smelled like lilacs, vanilla, and privilege. The girl was stylish head to toe. She turned to me and asked, "Did I miss it? Tell me, please, that I missed it."

"Hello, I'm Julius. What do you hope you missed? Tell me, and I shall endeavor to make it so. But only if you tell me your name first." I was thinking that she might be someone I could practice flirting with.

"How thoughtless of me, I'm Vanessa Robinson. You? You look familiar. Don't you go to Waverley Academy?" I shook my head yes. "You don't remember me, do you?"

"Sorry. One would think I should, you being so beautiful and everything." Too much? Maybe I should dial it down some.

"We met at that mixer at your school. I go to EXMOOR. I was calling myself Vanessa Kirkland back then. You sure you don't remember me?"

"Pretty sure. You strike me as being pretty unforgettable."

"My hair was darker and longer. That earnest Joan Baez look. Back then, I was always wearing plain Joan outfits from places like JC Penney or even, Coco darling please forgive me, Sears and Roebuck's. I wore lots of Canoe, but everybody did, even you, if I remember correctly. My clueless rebellious days."

"You told me about your girlfriend being in the hospital with a broken leg. I told you how sorry I was. Gave you a kiss on the cheek. And, well, one thing led to another, and the next thing I knew, we were making out in your Jaguar. Still don't remember me? Mister Julius Briscoe?"

She leaned over and French-kissed me. I remembered all right.

Chapter 11
pass the gravy

"Paranoia strikes deep
Into your life it will creep;
Starts when you're always afraid
Step out of line, the men come and take you away…"

For What It's Worth
~ Stephen Stills

Leonard stood up, holding Alice's silver triangle, and played a medley of old standards until everyone got the idea and ceased socializing randomly.

"Hello, and how are you? For those of you who don't know me and vice versa, I'm Leonard Briscoe. Welcome to our home, and Happy Thanksgiving. Bermuda June, and I thank you so much for coming. And now before we begin serving, let's each of us introduce ourselves and tell everyone what we're thankful for. I'll begin."

Vanessa punched me on the shoulder, and not at all lightly. "I told you my name, didn't I? You said you'd take care of it. Excellent job, Briscoe. Way to go."

"Give me a break. You never said what it was you hoped you missed. Believe me when I tell you that if you had provided adequate advance notice, I most certainly would have put a stop to this. Not now. It's much too late."

Around the table, people were thankful for coffee, vodka, John Wayne, Doris Day and Rock Hudson movies, TV Guide, da Bears, *Herzog*, hula hoops, their significant others, Chesterfields, transactional analysis, and chocolate milk. Then it was my turn.

"Hello, I'm Julius Briscoe. I'm gonna have to take the fifth. Believe you me, you don't want to know what I'm thankful for. And I don't want you to."

The room went quiet, and then it was Vanessa's turn. I gently tapped her truth button,
"I'm Vanessa Robinson, Arthur Kirkland's daughter. I'm thankful for daddy's money, Michigan Avenue, Maxwell and Rush Streets, and most of all for my old friend Julius Briscoe, and you should be too."

We hadn't had a serving of turkey, stuffing, mashed and sweet potatoes, cranberries, and all the rest, and it was already the weirdest Thanksgiving dinner of all time. Sitting across from us was Robbie, the almost rabbi, Uncle T, and FKP&B's recently widowed vice president of accounting, Marcus Smythe-Hawley.

As I remember, Robbie was most thankful for the Torah, red horseradish, the Yankees, and his one true love. Robbie was Jamaica May Leventhal's guest. Not yet having met Jamaica May, I already could see that he was all wrong for her. I vowed to double my efforts later on.

Robbie the Almost had a modest friendship ring in his coat pocket, a lump in his throat, and an elevated heart rate. He was concerned that I had been thankful for criminal behavior. And that I conveyed a sense of bitter anti-socialism, and if I wanted to talk things through, well he is a good listener. I thanked him for his input, hit him with a shot of BACK OFF®, and turned to Vanessa Robinson, who was knock knock knocking on my shoulder demanding my full attention. Again.

"So I'm really mad at you, Julius Briscoe."

"Why are you mad at me?"

"You know!"

"I don't know, and I'd be foolish to hazard a guess."

"You never called me. You said you would."

Good grief. She reminded me of Gracie in some ways. And of Norma Desmond in many others. I was struggling with how to tell her that it was still too soon for me even to consider getting into any kind of a relationship let alone an intimate one. It had only been three months since Gracie's death. I still feel her next to me, you know?

Theadora Perriman was tap, tap, tapping on my right shoulder. I turned and gave her my best-baffled look. "Yes?"

"Pass the gravy, please, Julius."

I did as she requested and started to turn back towards Vanessa, but Thea put her hand on my forearm and said, "Darling boy, I know what you've been through this past year—the deaths of your girlfriend and her cousin. You seem so calm, cool, and in control. You fascinate me."

Buttons don't lie, Theodora Perriman was a horny predator. A cougar. She was also a trained headshrinker.

"If you ever want to talk things over, well, Julius, my darling boy, I'm a professional listener whether I'm wearing clothing or not." She winked.

Be Cool. Never leave home without it.

◊◊

Chapter 12
promises to keep

"How does a girl like you get to be a girl like
you?"

North by Northwest
~ directed by Alfred Hitchcock
~ screenplay by Ernest Lehman

Our Thanksgiving meal officially ended when a squadron of sugar-buzzed little kids swarmed up from the lower level bearing crayon-embellished construction paper turkeys and ones made of milk chocolate. Bringing up the rear of this invading force were three young women in their late teens. Janie Dalton, Staci Feinberg, and Jamaica May Leventhal.

Vanessa and I were still chatting when the little kids poured into the main dining room. Cute. Cuter. And extraCuter. Nessa was telling me about the time, just last month, she almost missed breakfast because she couldn't open her dorm room door. That damn door knob wouldn't turn no matter how hard she jiggled it. Everyone else was already at breakfast. The halls were silent. She was starving. It was pure torture. It was nearly an hour before one of her dorm mates returned from breakfast and rescued her. By the time Nessa got to the dining hall, they were out of chocolate milk.

Before Vanessa could launch into another fascinating yarn, Molly Anne Briscoe climbed onto my lap and gave me a slurpy kiss on the cheek. "Hi, Uncle Groucho! Does I taste like grapes?"

I thought that meant 'gimme a kiss.' So I gave her a peck on the lips. "You do. You do taste exactly like grapes. That is amazing! Molly darling, tell me how did you do that?"

"Popsicles, you silly boy." She pinched my nose with one hand and thumped my forehead with the other. "Nyuk, nyuk, nyuk."

"Molly, you look very beautiful. How was your dinner?"

"Dinner was yummy."

"Molly, say hello to Vanessa. Vanessa, say hello to my beautiful niece, Molly Anne Briscoe."
I held up four fingers and whispered, "She's this many."

They said their hellos, and Molly, always the observant one, asked, "Are those your bags?" Nessa nodded yes. "What's in them?"

"Gifts, Molly dear."

"For me?"

"Hmmmm. Maybe. Could be. I can't seem to remember." Molly had a new bestie. I got the impression that Vanessa was auditioning a potential surrogate kid sister, either that, or she was trying to get into Molly's uncle's good graces.

"Listen, sweetie, I just remembered that there is something for you. But I don't have gifts for everybody in this room. It wouldn't be polite to open yours here. What do you say we take these bags and hide them somewhere together? And then you can open your gift."

"Yum, yum, yummy idea, Miss VanNessa. We can hide your bags under my bed, and then I can show you my stuffed aminals."

"Great. I love stuffed aminals. Can't wait to meet them." Vanessa focused on me and asked if I would be joining them. I thanked her for the invite but replied that I had already met the aminals and that I had promised to help my sister-in-law with something important, and that I'd catch up with her later. She gave me the evil eye and stuck her tongue out at me. Normals.

So I'd been thinking about how to flirt with Jamaica May Leventhal all afternoon. There were challenges within challenges to overcome—Normal and paranormal ones. Sure, I could hit her with something I call LOVE ME TWO TIMES®. I haven't used this on anyone since Monique, but I knew which buttons to push and when.

I think this is what is called performance anxiety. This could be an impossible challenge.
I mean, what if we don't make a connection? What if Jamaica May hates me? What if she's pimply with bad breath and wears glasses with Coke bottle lenses? This was dangerous, unchartered territory. I reminded myself that fear is the mind-killer, summoned my inner tiger, and went looking for Jamaica May Leventhal.

The wrap-around porch was crowded, mostly with strangers. Strangers to me and vice versa. I worked my way through the crowd to get a better look at Jamaica May 'Jaimie' Leventhal. Robbie Greenfield was hovering over her. They were chatting near the stairs at the northwest corner of the porch. Jamaica May was easy on the eyes, that's for sure. She reminded me a lot of Grace Gold.

Jaimie was calm, forthright, and outgoing. She had an incredible smile and bright blue eyes that darted back and forth whenever she spoke.

BJ was right. Jamaica was flirt-worthy at the very least. I hit Robbie with a PSYCHIC FLASH-BANG® and watched him try to deal with it. Jamaica was describing the San Francisco sound to the clueless Robbie when his eyes glazed over, and he began to teeter and sway. He would have tumbled down the porch stairs to an uncertain fate had I not grabbed him and stood him up straight. I told Robbie that he looked fucking awful and that he should drink some water and lie down.

Never leave home without it.

Sure I could use my skills and win Jamaica over instantaneously. But something within me wanted to win her over with my charm and sophisticated Main Line manner—the Normal way. Then BJ appeared out of nowhere, took me by the arm, kissed me on the cheek, and said, "I see Molly has already found you. Julius darling, this is my sister Jamaica May." Bermuda June was a wee bit tipsy. "Jaimie honey, this is Leonard's brother Julius. Believe it or not, you two have a lot in common."

"For instance?" Jaimie and I answered in unison, looked at each other, and smiled.

"Well, you're both late-in-life children. You both have a much older sibling. Jaimie's not so much. Both of you go to a private school. Each of you drives a European sports car. And you're both gorgeous. I've gotta mingle. Keep an eye on him tonight, little sister; them Briscoes is keepers." She gave us a wink and a wave and then dived into the crowd.

Jamaica wanted to know what kind of car I drive.

"I have a '62 Jaguar XK-E. You?"

"Nice! Those are so beautiful. I drive a '61 Porsche 356. A red roadster. Yours?"

"Also a roadster. Mine's BRG."

"BRG?"

"British Racing Green." I leaned in close to her and whispered, "Do you like to get high?"

"I sure do."

"Then why don't we take a walk on the beach?"

"Groovy idea, Julius Briscoe. You just might be."

"Be what?"

Chapter 13
inside Jamaica May Leventhal

"Do away with people blowing my mind
Do away with people wasting my precious time
Take me to a simple place
Where I can easily see my face."

3/5 of a mile in ten seconds
~ Marty Balin

Jaimie Leventhal and I indeed had a lot in common. We shared passions for movies, folk music, ee cummings, JD Salinger, fast cars, *The Fugitive,* killer weed, *America's Got Bandstand,* The Rolling Stones, Pepsi, pizza, and Chinese food. We were walking through the park towards Lake Michigan. It was late afternoon. We had maybe another 45 minutes of daylight before things turned dark and dangerous. We found a park bench a couple of yards from the stairs leading down to the beach. We fired up a joint and got to know each other the way only stoners can.

"Listen Julius, when we get back to the house, let's put on a show for Robbie, like we were down on the beach making out." Jaimie's way of breaking the ice?

"How come I didn't see you in the Pump Room last night?"

"A friend of mine is making a movie. I play the naive young country girl who takes up with a spoiled young aristocrat. Don't look at me that way, I didn't write it. We rehearsed until nine, then went to THE GATE OF HORN to see JJ Cross's last set."

"Really? I was there also."

"Wait, of course, you're the guy in the three piece suit! We arrived late and had to sit in the back by the pay phones and restrooms. Couldn't see the stage very well. Forgot my glasses. Saw JJ rub your head for good luck. Then he sang "Draft Dodger Rag," which is one of my favorites. So, how do you know JJ Cross?" I told her.

"So BJ tells me that you want to be a teacher?"

She scoffed, "Like when I was ten or eleven, maybe. No, I'm thinking I want to be a newspaper or maybe a television reporter. Northwestern has the Medill School of Journalism. It's one of the best there is. And since my sister is a tenured professor, I'm pretty much automatically in, and tuition is free."

"So what about you, Julius? What are your plans? Where have you applied? What did you get on the SATs?"

I told her that I hadn't applied to any colleges, hadn't taken the SATs, and owned a couple of restaurants and three or four dozen convenience stores with my uncle. That college was an unnecessary indulgence at this time in my life. And that I wasn't an 'Employee of the Month' type anyway. Then I asked her about Robbie Greenfield, who seemed to think that Jaimie and he were an item.

"I don't know. You're Jewish too, right?"

"Mainly because my mother's Jewish. That's how it works, I'm told."

"Me too." She punched my shoulder lightly, playfully. "So I was curious about Judaism and went to that Synagogue on Poplar Street with a couple of my girlfriends. It was a Friday night; it was crowded. We had to sit behind this lattice wall called a *mechitza*—the men in front, the women behind. We would have walked out, but we were already feeling too self-conscious.
We sat through the ceremonies (yawn) and accepted the invitation for free wine and cakes in the social hall."

"After blessing the wine, Robbie honed in on me. Right away he was too clever, 'Tell me I'm not experiencing early onset dementia, and this is your first time visiting our shul? I mean, how could I have forgotten a face as lovely as yours?'"

"We got to talking. I told him that I hadn't been raised Jewish. Didn't celebrate any of the holidays, not even Hanukah. He offered to teach me about Judaism if I'd like. So I met him a couple of times at the *Howard Johnson's* to talk about the Hebrews, you know, Moses parting the Red Sea, handing down the Ten Commandments, all that ancient ancient history stuff. Good news though, at least the strawberry malts at the Howard Johnson's are divine."

"No matter how enthusiastic Robbie was about our Jewish heritage, I just couldn't connect with it. He was from Hartford and was staying in town for the holiday, so like a dummy, I invited him to join us tonight. I think he might have gotten a wrong idea. Not that I tried to give him one."

Talking about Robbie, the almost Rabbi, and our overlooked Jewish heritage was bumming Jaimie out. She changed the subject.

"Did your teachers give you an assignment to do over-the-holiday too?"

"I dunno. I skipped a lot of classes this semester."

"Goodness! How many did you skip?"

"Pretty much all of them." Oh, the things you shouldn't say when you're stoned.

She gave me an appraising, leery look. "You don't seem like a fuck-up to me. So why did you cut so many classes?"

"I had personal matters to attend to, but I'll still graduate on time." I channeled Molly Anne and asked, "So what about you? What stupid assignments did your meany mean teachers spoil your vacation with?"

She laughed, "That's good, that's really good. You sounded just like Shirley Temple right then. I have to write a story about a newsworthy event that happened during Thanksgiving week. The parade is off-limits. Anything else is fair game."

"What are you writing about?"

"Nothing so far. I've been too busy to do much research. The only big story this week is United #505. Neither the Trib nor the Sun Times had much information. The FBI is being tight-lipped as usual. The airline won't release the passenger manifest, so I'm still snooping around. My journalism class doesn't meet until next Friday. I'll find something. I've got a news for nose!"

She was totally high. I was about to tell her about our experiences on Flight #505 when
I caught sight of three or four guys strolling on the beach in our direction. They were less than fifty yards away. A few seconds later, another three Status Buttons were hard-charging towards us from the park entrance. I guess I was about to experience Chicago-style crime up close and personal. They were still too far away for me to get any read off their Status Buttons or to dose them with anything lethal or not.

I looked at my watch and said that we should get going. Jaimie took hold of my arm to get a closer look at the Rolex.

"That's so cute! I didn't know that Mercedes-Benz made watches. I don't want to go back now, Julius. It's a beautiful evening. When we go back, I'll have to deal with the Robbie situation, and I don't want to. I really fucking don't."

"Seriously, Jaimie, we need to get going. We're about to have company, and from this vantage, they don't appear to be the kind of company you'd want to keep. Robbie won't be a problem, Trust Me."

I'll say this about good old Jaimie Leventhal: She was exuberantly high, the kind of high only experienced stoners can achieve so quickly. Wrong time. Wrong place. The three-pack was now on our left and no more than ten yards away. Their Status Buttons announced their hostile intentions. The beach bums had reached the stairs leading up to the park. They were close enough to determine that they were not a threat to anyone, anywhere, anytime.

"Yo. Hey man. You got any more of that weed? Smells awesome. I'm just saying."

"Sorry, dudes, I'm fresh out. There's maybe a baby roach over near that bench. Have a good one man. I'm just saying."

We headed towards the park exit at a casual pace. Jaimie was joyous, exuberant. She started singing that Dylan song, off key, at the top of her lungs, "come gather round people whatever you own." No question about it, Jamaica May was all wrong for Robbie the Almost. Our three friends on the left swooped in and faced us, walking backward, matching us stride for stride.

"So if you won't share your dope with me mother fucker, you're gonna have ta share your woman with me and me boys. I don't take no no's for an answer."

Without hesitation, he snapped both arms straight out towards us; a pair of official Yancey Derringer sleeve guns sprang from his ruffled cuffs, pointed right at me. His wingmen flashed their Bowie knives and toothless grins.

Shit.

My muscle memory couldn't decide which threat to eliminate first and sought targeting guidance from its superior, yours truly, Julius Truman Briscoe. I hadn't killed any of them yet, which was a good thing. I sure didn't want to have to zap Jaimie's memory. That often leads to unpleasant consequences. I hit all of them with a triple dose of PECKINPAH®, and then I escorted Jaimie home. It would be another thirty seconds or so before the leader of the pack would fire those Yancey Derringers, slightly wounding two of the frummer yids I had mistaken as threats. They were just returning home after an innocent stroll on the beach.

All of this street theater zoomed right past Jaimie, who was too stoned to grok the weirdness of the confrontation.

Never leave home without it!

Chapter 14
the zen of baize

"I'm empty and aching and I don't know why"

America
~ Paul Simon

Way up there on the wraparound porch, at the head of the stairs chatting, smoking, and smiling were the Kirklands, Arthur, Bonnie, and Vanessa, when Jaimie and I, arm in arm, pretending to laugh like lovers often do, came into their view as we ascended from street level to the terrace level. When we neared the porch, as scripted, Jaimie began kissing my cheek and my lips. Even stoned out of her mind, Jaimie Leventhal was a pretty good actress. This bit of melodrama was intended for Robbie the Almost but was intercepted by Vanessa the Possessive. Nessa's hackles went up, her claws extended. You could almost hear her think nasty thoughts.

Once again, my big brother saved the day. Leonard raced up to greet Arthur and Bonnie Kirkland, who had just arrived, having celebrated Thanksgiving with the firm's most very important VIP clients, Marcello and Fiona Washbourne, at their Kenilworth estate. He escorted them into the house and, presumably, to the bar. Vanessa had little choice but to follow a few steps behind Daddy and that bitch Bonnie Bramlett Kirkland, evil stepmother number four. Vanessa turned back towards us with fierceness in her eyes. She mouthed the words, 'I am so pissed at you, asshole.' My lip-reading lesson for the day.

Vanessa shot me the bird and then turned and stomped into the house just like Molly might.

We found Robbie the Almost flat on his back on a sofa in the west sunroom, an ice bag on his forehead, the weight of the world on his shoulders. "Jaimie, my one true love, where have you been? I've been so worried. There was a rumor going around that you ran off with this hiloni, this momser shaygetz Julius Briscoe and now I see that the rumor is true. What's going on with you two? I'll bet he didn't tell you what he's thankful for. Am I out of the picture already?"

"I hate to break it this way to you, Robbie. You're such a nice guy and all, but Julius gets my motor going, and you, you're, well, you Robbie, you're just boring." Robbie the Almost almost broke into tears. He began begging like one of those little annoying dogs. Mission accomplished.

Jaimie turned to me and asked if I knew how to play pool. I reminded her that I was from Philadelphia, and yes, I knew how to shoot some pool. She took my hand and led me to the library/smoking room up on the third floor. It ran the entire length of the house. Giant windows faced the back of the property and its proposed swimming pool.

"That's my bedroom suite over there." She pointed to a door at the far end of the hallway a peace sign-shaped evergreen wreath hanging on a mahogany door. "I live on campus when school's in session and here when it's not. Maybe later, if you play your cards right, I'll take you on the three hour tour."

The regulation-sized pool table sat in an alcove in the southwest corner of the library. Jaimie was a pretty decent pool player. She had the touch and the strategy down cold

—a challenging opponent. While we were playing nine-ball, I got to thinking about the color of the baize on Lenny's table. It was bright red. The baize covering Miles Golds' tables, the ones in the house, the penthouse, and the tailor shoppe was Waverley Blue. Up until this moment, I thought all of the pool tables in the world were covered with Waverley Blue baize. Guess what? Life gets more complicated with every step you take.

When I finally got over Lenny's choice of pool table coverings, I recalled the last time I had played pool. The memories of that day hit me hard. I stood very still, let my eyes defocus, and gazed blankly into the Graceless world.

"Julius, you zoned out. Where did you go?"

"I was thinking about the last time I played pool." I proceeded to sink the three, four, five, and six balls without saying another word. I didn't have a decent shot on the seven ball and played safe.

"Don't leave me hanging like that. When was the last time you played pool?"

I guess I really did have to tell her. "The last time I shot a game of pool was on the afternoon my fiancé was killed."

Talk about your buzz kills.

I told Jamaica May Leventhal the sad story, beginning with the *Miss America* pageant and ending with that ill-fated game of HORSE. I spared her the self-incriminating details and the feelings of hollowness. Nevertheless, Jaimie wept and offered up a hug—a pretty nice hug, but not the hug of all hugs. She whispered in my ear that she was a good listener if ever I needed to unload.

Across the hall, the doors to the elevator opened, revealing the four equity partners and Uncle Teddy. Lenny made a beeline to the pool table and slapped a Krugerrand down on the end rail.

"I've got next game. Listen, Julius and Jaimie. We have private matters to discuss. I hope you wouldn't mind waiting downstairs for a while."

We agreed, all smiley and cooperative. I wondered why Uncle T would be included at the partner's meeting. Only one possibility sprang to mind: *William Novichok.*

We were blindsided on the second-floor landing by Molly Anne, wearing bright yellow jammies and a Pepsodent smile.

"Hi, Aunt Jaimie and Uncle Groucho. Can you reads me a story? Please? Pretty please with sugar and a cherry on top?" The kid's as cute as a button. Who could refuse her? I have absolutely zero experience in this arena. I was the youngest child, effectively the only one, and until this evening, I had never read a bedtime story to a little kid. I may have told bedtime stories to Gracie, but I'll never tell you about any of those.

That evening, I learned about a Little Red Hen, Three Little Kittens, and a Pokey Little Puppy. Molly knew the stories by heart and word for word even though she couldn't tell a 'b' from a 'p.' Midway through the second reading of *The Pokey Little Puppy Joins the Navy*, BJ appeared from out of nowhere to inform me that our gleaming white limo was on its way and that Aunt Connie wasn't feeling too hot. Say goodnight, Molly.

"Goodnight, Uncle Jaimie," giggle. "Goodnight, Aunt Grouchy." Giggle, giggle.

Chapter 15
a message from the east

"There's too much confusion, I can't get no
relief"

All Along the Watchtower
~ Bob Dylan

"Why, Uncle Grouchy, do you have to leave so soon? It's not even nine o'clock? I'd drive you back, but my car's in the shop, and my sister and your brother won't let me touch their rides. Uncle Groucho? What's with that?"

I explained that Wild Will Briscoe named his sons after two of the Marx brothers. And how is that so different from how her parents named her and her siblings?

"I mean, you were born in February, BJ in March, and your brother in May. Right?"

"Right. Not only that, but we, the descendants of the world-famous dance team of
Hannah & Otto, are named for the popular vacation destinations where we were conceived."

"Listen, Jaimie, let's not spoil the buzz. My ride's here, but I'll be back tomorrow, so maybe we can hang out some more." I kissed her on the cheek. We walked down the stairs, all three sets of them, to the limo below. It was still gleaming white and looking sharp. Uncle T stood by the open door, awaiting my arrival.

"Jaimie, it sure was swell meeting you. Hanging out with you sure made it a Thanksgiving to remember. I'll see you tomorrow." She didn't take the hint and stood around, giving me the moony eye.

"Julius I had a great time, even if it was BJ that put me up to it."

"What do you mean? Tell Me The Truth."

"BJ said I should be nice to you because of what happened to your girlfriend. That's all."

Uncle T butted in, "Jaimie, I need to discuss something with Julius privately. Be a good girl and run along if you wouldn't mind."

She folded her arms across her chest, stood up straight, and gave him one of those looks that would cow lesser men than Teddy Briscoe.

"Listen up, Jaimie. Be cool. When we come back tomorrow, I'll give you a story guaranteed to earn you an A+ in your Journalism class. Deal?"

"What is it with you, Julius Briscoe, why do you always keep me hanging on?"

Jamaica May stomped her foot and breathed an exaggerated sigh, turned around, and scampered up the steps to the terrace and the wrap-around porch beyond, where she feared Robbie the Almost might be standing at the head of the stairs, a pair of stone tablets held high above his head, wrath and fury in his eyes.

"So, how's Aunt Connie?"

"Connie's fine. I didn't want you asking about the meeting with the partners in front of Connie and your mother. I've got news, Julius, but it's gonna have to wait until we get back to the hotel."

On the ride back to the AMBASSADOR EAST, the conversation was dominated by my mother's and my Aunt Connie's non-stop appraisals of Jamaica May Leventhal, Vanessa Robinson, and Deirdre DePalma. Which of those three was best suited for me? I maybe should have intervened, but my mind was all abuzz with speculation concerning the conversation Uncle T had with the FKP&B equity partners.

We stopped at the front desk to retrieve our keys and messages. Uncle T had a fistful; I had but two. Jimmy Cross called to thank me for my support (and Donna) and to let me know that he was off to Athens, Georgia, where he would begin his "Pied Piper" tour of Southern colleges. He'd be back home for Christmas. See you then. The other message was from Miles Gold.

"Urgent. Please call ASAP regardless the hour."

Since it was Thanksgiving, I called the number for the property in Gladwyne Falls. The answering service picked up immediately, and the operator said the number was not answering. Would I care to leave a message? I told her who I was and that I was returning Miles Gold's call. Would she please locate him? The message he left for me said it was urgent.

"I'll be happy to connect you, Mr. Briscoe. But I need to verify your identity. Your authorization code, please."

I replied, "I shot an elephant in my pajamas."

She responded professionally, her manner cordial, unamused, "Thank you, sir. One moment, please."

Miles came on the line a heartbeat or two later.

"Happy Thanksgiving, Julius. How was your holiday? How are you?" I filled him in.

He asked me about Flight #505. Did I have anything to do with thwarting the skyjackers? As if he had to ask. Then he got around to the concerning news.

"The chief of Police of Atlas City, Andy Mayweather, and an FBI agent named Raymond Krieger stopped by the shop yesterday asking the whereabouts of someone called Jeremiah Dickinson. I asked them who that was and why were they questioning me. They were surprised that I didn't recognize the name of one of the persons implicated in my granddaughter's death.
I reminded them that those names had never been released publicly. I assured them I had no idea where this Dickinson fellow might be. Then they asked me about you. They have been unable to locate Grace Gold's fiancé and that they have questions."

"I told them that you were out of town sharing the holiday with family and that I had no idea what your return plans were. They seemed to take no for an answer, gave me their cards, and urged me to pass them along to you as they really did have questions."

I thanked Miles and asked if he had been able to scrutinize either of them. He had. Miles can read *auras* as well as I can read Status Buttons. He calls *auras sutnists*. His visitors weren't showing any of the telltale signs of suspicious thinking.

I asked about his Thanksgiving and how everyone was doing.

"Miriam's in a bad, bad way. As bad as Dahlia was, but worse. You must visit her as soon as you're back in town. When are you returning?"

"I'm flying back Monday morning. I get in around two."

"Why don't you come straight to the towers? We've been staying here in town more and more often since Gracie. There are fewer reminders of her and Eleanora here. Did Edward give you a key to his penthouse? If he didn't, you're welcome to bunk in with me. It'll be good to see you."

"Miles, I have some very interesting things to tell you. Things we can't speak of over the phone."

There was a knock-knock knocking on the door. Uncle Teddy.

"Miles, someone's at the door—gotta boogie. Speak with you tomorrow. Give everyone my best. Goodnight."

"Goodnight, Julius." The mighty Miles Gold sounded weary, worn down by events he could neither foresee nor control.

Uncle T stood in the doorway, a bottle of bourbon dangling from his hand, a loopy smile on his face. His colors and his textures were dancing synchronously.

"What's going on?" We walked to the sitting room and sat.

"Why were you meeting with Lenny's partners?"

"They wanted to know all about Willie Novichok. They said Junior Poole the Second couldn't have done as perfect a job as you did on Leon Longstride. They think you're a wizard. If they only knew."

"The partners wanted to know whether or not I would be willing to be Novichok's handler. I told them that I would, but what about Fields? Wouldn't he get his knickers in a knot? And Victor Fleming said that Fields already had too much on his plate. And the way he said it implied a total lack of respect or confidence in Dr. Morgan Fields. Or maybe I'm reading too much into it."

"So all this time, Jules, I'm thinking, 'Whoa, wait a minute. Ain't you guys lawyers? Officers of the court and all that goody two-shoes shit?' So I asked them."

"They gave me a look that said 'grow up already.' Arthur Kirkland stood up; he actually stood up, Julius, and started pacing back and forth as if he was in court addressing a jury. He was wearing a three-piece pinstripe worthy of Miles Gold himself. So he stops pacing right in front of me and looks into my eyes for a long time, expecting me to flinch or some shit. I don't lose staring contests, Julius, you know this."

"So no more than a minute goes by when Kirkland graces me with a wink, a smile, and an attaboy and proceeds to give me the lowdown on how Chicago's most notorious outlaws became FLEMING, KIRKLAND, PORTER & BRISCOE, a prestigious white shoe law firm."

Chapter 16
ninety percent legit

"I was not caught, though many tried
I live among you, well disguised"

Never mind
~ Leonard Cohen & Patrick Leonard

Uncle Teddy complained, "Jules, that Arthur Kirkland is nothing but a big bag of foul smelling gas. He started like he would lecture me about the history of post-Industrial Revolution Chicago. Then he talked about the migration patterns of certain ethnic groups and how they interacted with each other in the new world. He talked about prohibition and how it led to gang warfare. Then, out of nowhere, he talked about his great grandfather who changed the face of the underworld forever."

"Two words. Diversification. Legitimization. They did the same thing Mo Stern did back in the day. Nowadays, the original fearsome Chicago Mob is as law-abiding as it gets. They're just like us. Private gambling clubs, by appointment only prostitution, money laundering, some blackmail, and influence peddling. They're mostly into Real Estate, lawyering, upscale car dealerships, cash businesses like nightclubs, banks, vending machines, juke boxes, and drive-through burger joints. They're just like us, ninety percent legit."

"Then Kirkland explained that the murder-for-hire jobs were fulfilled by Morgan Fields' ERRAND BOYS brand, which dominates the market. Near as they could tell, Poole went on a dozen or so non-murders every year. The Longstride hit was brought in by Arthur Kirkland himself on behalf of a VIP client of the firm."

"They thanked me, swore me to secrecy, told me that they'd be in touch, and instructed me to hit the bricks. That was pretty much it. Imagine that? Lenny's a gangster? And everyone calls me *the* black sheep of the family? Ain't that the way it always goes?" Teddy yawned, said 'Goodnight, Novichok,' and stumbled back to his suite at the other end of the hallway—time to get some shut-eye.

It had been a long, hectic day. Fun, tiring. I was going to need more than my usual four hours sleep. I was just about to drift off when the phone rang. Who the fuck would call me this late? I looked at my Rolex; I never take it off. It's waterproof to a depth of over three hundred feet. My way of keeping Gracie close. It was six minutes past one.

I picked up the receiver, "Yes."

"Julius, it's Leonard. Listen, we should talk. Privately. Meet me out front tomorrow morning, say around seven sharp? Wear your suit. I'll be driving a crimson Bentley Continental. See you then." He hung up without receiving a confirmation. Arrogant asshole. I called the operator and arranged for a wake-up call and to have messages left for Mother and Uncle T, saying that I would be having breakfast with Leonard and that they should proceed without me. Then I went back to sleep.

I arrived at the main entrance at exactly 6:57 the next morning. Shoes shined, tie straightened, teeth brushed, I was clean-shaven and had a promising crop of hair follicles neatly repopulating my skull. Leonard drove up at 7:00 on the dot and seemed surprised to see me standing there.

Some kind of chauvinistic attitude, I guess. Like my generation is too irresponsible to be punctual, I got in the car anyway. It's really nice. All genuine leather, polished wood accents. Posh. And quiet. Maybe the quietest ride I've ever had.

"This is a really nice car, Leonard. How long have you had it? Still smells like new car to me."

"It came with the promotion. The firm owns the dealership. Nice perk? Right?"

"So Julius yesterday you were telling me of your experiences. And as I remember, you had just killed Lance Longstride and dumped his body in the river. You said you went to Atlantic City, but you didn't get around to telling me why or what, if anything, happened whilst you were there."

"Put on your lawyer hat, my brother; this is where the bodies really begin to pile up."

Without trying to explain *pair*ing, I told Lenny about Ben Gold and Emma Sachs who was *Miss Pennsylvania* on her way to becoming *Miss America*. That we had all become members of Emma's team and drove down to Atlantic City for the remainder of the summer. I explained how we stumbled on another chapter of *Tabula Rasa,* which had plans to blow up Boardwalk Hall.
I gave him a behind-the-scenes accounting of the Leon Longstride job. Didn't mention *The Psychic Brotherhood of Greater Philadelphia,* but I did mention terminating the eight *Tabula Rasa* assholes in that Margate City rental.

Lenny stopped me to point out that what I did was called cold-blooded murder. I counter-pointed out that *Tabula Rasa* was plotting to kill 15,000 people on national television.

That would have been cold-blooded mass murder. I couldn't turn *Tabula Rasa* over to the feds because none of my fact-gathering techniques could be revealed or explained to anyone outside my circle of trust, which now included my long-lost brother Leonard, essentially a distant relative.

Lenny's Status Button looked like the inside of a cyclone. He was having a hard time processing the way I handled the *Tabula Rasa* situations. I worried he'd completely lose it when I got around to telling him about what I did to Atlas City, New Jersey. But before I could, we pulled into the parking garage in the Ezra Kirkland Legal Arts Building.

Lenny said, "Let's finish this after breakfast. Okay?"

"Sure."

"Tell me it isn't true, Julius. I can't fucking believe that you walked out on the Beatles."

Chapter 17
new challenges

"There's something happening here.
What it is ain't exactly clear."

For What It's Worth
~ Stephen Stills

Over breakfast in Sweet Marie's, a coffee shop on the ground floor, Leonard confessed his feelings of guilt about our relationship, which he categorized as distant, inadequate, and unfortunate. We were born almost twenty years apart and, all that time, lived nearly a thousand miles from each other. We rarely spoke on the phone, and when we did, we could barely recall what the person on the other end of the line looked like. Our weekly phone conversations were more like an obligation than anything else.

Things only got worse after Dad got murdered. Leonard flew in for the funeral and flew right back out. He was trying an 'important case' and needed to be in court the following morning. Leaving me to comfort Mother and Uncle Teddy, who was feeling guilty for having to have emergency surgery instead of watching the store that afternoon.

Leonard wanted to know how I felt about our relationship. I told him I'd let him know as soon as I thought we had one. That stung him. Maybe I set the bar too high. We finished breakfast in silence and didn't speak again until we were seated in the secure conference room in the executive suite on the fortieth floor.

"Julius, this room is certified to be free of listening devices. One of our electronics experts from floor thirty-seven checks it for bugs daily. It's safe to finish our privileged conversation in here." Leonard still seemed shaken by my confessions and attitude towards our tenuous relationship.

"So tell me, Julius, what happened after *Tabula Rasa?*"

I told him about killing the two suicide bombers and about Gracie's murder and the aftermath. He was stunned. "Jesus, Julius, I sure as shit did not need to know any of this. How does Uncle Teddy handle it? How do *you* handle it? How many have you killed? How many have you crippled?"

"Forty-five dead, nine I've let live limited lives. You must understand this one thing, Leonard, I am not a Normal, everyday, average person. I don't need society to punish the lawless, the discourteous, the greedy, the heartless Normals that cross my path every fucking day. I can and have done a much better job. Remember how I handled Wolfe and that dude on the beach? Plus, no one on this earth can lie to me successfully, making it a snap for me to decide guilt or innocence and to apply the appropriate disposition."

"Just look at the criminal justice system, Leonard. A person commits a horrible crime, like pre-meditated murder, and what does the system do? It locks that person up in prison for a period of time, feeds, provides free medical care and pretends to teach marketable skills and civilized behavior. Then, they send them back into the unsuspecting world with a degree in high crimes and misdemeanors. And what's the financial cost per prisoner-year? Last I checked, it's over 40K. Add in the cost of the trial and the appeals process to the price society has to pay because it has lost its way crime and punishment wise, and done the wrong things. The right thing is a swift, irrevocable disposition. Years at hard labor or a bullet to the head. Keep It Simple, Stupid."

"Now, Lenny, if you want, I can make you forget everything I've told you about my secret. All you'll remember is that we had a swell time hanging out and getting to know each other. Long lost brothers bonding and all that jazz."

Lenny stood up, went to the credenza by the door, retrieved a leather folio, a yellow legal pad, and a handful of pencils, and returned to the conference table. "Julius, I don't want to forget about any of this. In fact, I'd like a better idea of the things you can do and how we might be able to monetize them. If that's alright with you?"

I said it was fine with me and asked what he had in mind. He answered, "Tell me, Julius, have you ever considered going to law school?" I told him I hadn't and had no interest in the legal system or the lawyering business—too much effort for inadequate results. I went on to tell him about all of the buttons and techniques I have developed and used so far.

"What you can do, Julius, is dazzling. I know you're scheduled to fly back to Philadelphia Monday morning, but I'm wondering if I can persuade you to stay another week. I have two projects for William Novichok."

"Tuesday of next week, we are taking depositions in our class action lawsuit against Big Tobacco. As you well know, people lie. I'll pay you ten thousand dollars a day to sit in and point out the liars. We'll need to work out some kind of discrete signaling protocol. I'll need as close to instant feedback as possible."

I made the pinkie of his left-hand tingle and twitch. "Does that work for you, older brother?"

"Of course. What was I overthinking?"

"Leonard, the money's nice, but Uncle Teddy and Mother are taking the rest of the year off, leaving me in charge of the empire. The restaurants do fine without me. But I haven't gotten around to having my 'motivational conversation' with most of our BIG CORNERS employees yet."

Lenny looked confused, "What do you mean by 'motivational conversation'?"

"Last spring, I had a 'chat' with each member of the MONGO MINGS CHINESE staff, both east and west, while using TRUST ME! and BE HONEST WITH ME® to ensure that everyone was on the same page as far as workplace ethics and conduct are concerned. It's a long list of do's and do nots. Which can be easily summed up as 'do your very best every day, and you will be the most highly compensated restaurant employees in the area.' Our employee turnover rate is negligible."

"With Teddy, Connie, and Mother on vacation, the larcenous scumbags embedded in the Big Corners staff, the old-timers and the part-timers alike will try to pilfer us blind. Any chance you can reschedule the deposition?"

"Your personnel management techniques, Julius, are groundbreaking. You should consider working as a consultant or a motivational speaker. With skills like yours, you'd make top dollar and invaluable contacts." I told him I'd think it over but that I saw no way around my scheduling conflict.

"Julius, I just might have a solution. If I do, we'll know by supper time at the very latest. We're having leftovers. Imagine that? BJ ordered way too many turkeys."

"Listen, I need to make a few phone calls." He slid the legal pad and pencils my way. "Julius when you have a moment, please make a list of the things you can do to a person. "Here's the other assignment. This one needs to be executed ASAP." He slid the folio across the table with just enough force. It spun to a stop directly in front of me, ready to be opened. An omen? Or a telephone ringing in the distance? Leonard said he'd see me in a few and raced towards his office.

The folio contained a natural causes contract on that scumbag "Doctor" Morgan Fields in the amount of two million dollars and the contents of his safe. But before I dispatched Fields, I had to obtain specific information from him. Whatever that information was, it was too sensitive to be put down in writing. Should I accept the contract, that part of the assignment would be given to me verbally.

A two-million-dollar payday! I'm all in. I wondered why the partners wanted Fields dead.
I mean I wanted him dead too, and I've only met the asshole twice. I thought of dozens of likely reasons. I never came close to guessing the actual one. Unless he was out of town, Morgan Fields arrived at the EZRA KIRKLAND LEGAL ARTS BUILDING at 10 AM, plus or minus a minute or two every weekday. It wasn't yet 9 AM. So I went to work making that list Lenny requested.
I practically filled the entire page with the things I have names for and those I don't.

Leonard returned to the secure conference room, looking at his watch. He was in turmoil; his face and Status Button told the story.

"I see you've read over the contract. Is it safe to assume that you'll do the job?"

"It's safe. If you don't mind my asking, why?"

"Fields crossed the line, Julius. That's all you need know except for this one thing. Many of the natural causes assignments Fields received came, indirectly, anonymously from certain government entities. Fields represented those contracts to the partners as your standard murder for inheritance deals. No mention of the public servants willing to cross the line that might cause the partners to deny the contract. As if they would ever turn down serious cash money."

"Junior was also the world's greatest sniper. He had two verified kills from over a mile out.
I don't know all of the details. Let's just say Fields mistakenly submitted receipts for airfare to and lodging in Dallas last November and express shipping of two wooden crates to a George Kaplan in care of The Adolphus Hotel, Commerce Street, Dallas, Texas. By the time accounting red-flagged it, Poole was dead. Heart attack at a country club in your neck of the woods."

I pretended to cough, then took a bow. Lenny gave me a look and said, "You didn't?"

I nodded yes and said, "I did. That mother fucker killed Ellie Gold. Gracie's cousin. Miles' granddaughter. Frontier justice, brother. That's plenty good enough for me."
Lenny's face turned white. I think he finally realized that his kid brother was some kind of other being.

"Julius, Fields has been holding out on us for years. The partners don't trust him. Each of them had tried their best to rein in Field's arrogant behavior. None of them had been able to control him. I'm the low man on the totem pole, so it's my turn. They made me CEO of CHICAGO PRIVATE INVESTIGATIONS and THE ERRAND BOYS, the firm's perennial problem children. We've decided to eliminate Fields. Natural or accidental causes preferred. We have a hefty key-man insurance policy on the bastard. So Julius, what's your thinking?"

"First, I need to know what information I am supposed to squeeze out of Fields."

"Simple, what was Junior doing in Dallas last November? And who booked him? Julius, there's paperwork filed with the Bar Association that connects the firm to Junior Poole the Second as an independent contractor. We need to know what we don't know. Today would be best."

"What's in the safe?"

"Can't really say. None of the partners have ever seen its contents. I'm guessing booty and dirt on any number of millionaires, politicians, government officials, and probably even the partners and clients of this and several other prestigious, influential law firms."

"Uncle Teddy told me Fields informed him that natural causes and pristine accident contracts must be paid entirely in advance. The traditional half-now and half-after model doesn't work for kills that don't look like kills. All the money upfront. Results guaranteed."

Leonard scooped up the folio and the legal pad. He tore off the top page, folded it nice and neat and put it in his inside coat pocket. "Follow me."

The company safe was nestled deep in the rabbit warren that is the Accounting Department. Leonard knew the combination. He had already counted out my two million and packed the money into a pair of handsome brown leather briefcases. Lenny consulted his watch, tossed the yellow legal pad into one of the briefcases, and said, "Let's go store these in the Bentley. You wouldn't believe the alarm system on that baby."

Chapter 18
ramona

"My blood runs cold
My memory has just been sold
My angel is the centerfold."

Centerfold
~ Seth Justman

We reached the executive parking garage at quarter til ten and placed my two million in the carpeted boot. Lenny leaned against the Bentley, removed my list from his pocket, read it over several times, and finally asked, "Tell me about this ZOMBIE MODE. What does it do exactly?"

"It makes people do what I tell them to do. I'll dose Fields with it when we're on the elevator. It'll last long enough to get him to tell us what you need to know and to open the safe. Once the safe's open, I'll flip his off switch."

Lenny lit up an expensive cigar. I lit up a joint.

"Is that a good idea, Julius? Maybe you should wait until after to get high."

"I don't get high like Normals like you get high. It's different for me. Helps me control things I can't possibly explain to you. Trust me, brother, we're cool."

Morgan Fields pulled up in a bright yellow '38 DUESENBERG SPEEDSTER and parked right next to Lenny's

Bentley. What a car, right up there in every category with Miles Gold's

'37 BUGATTI ATLANTIC. Fields was wearing a tracksuit the identical shade of yellow with a matching messenger's bag slung over his shoulder. He looked at the two of us smokers, waved, and gave us a laugh.

"Good morning, gents. What brings you here on this lovely holiday?"

"My brother Julius has to sign some documents. Morgan, do you have family? Brothers, sisters, mothers, fathers? That sort of thing? Or is it true that you were raised by wolves in the Yukon?"

Fields laughed and asked if he could have a hit. I passed him the joint, but before he could take a toke, I put him into ZOMBIE AND TRUTH MODES and told him to give the joint back to me. The last thing I wanted to do was to try to kill a stoned asshole.

"Dr. Fields, I'd like to make an offer, do you have the pink slip handy for this beauty?"

"I do not own this classic. I leased it from the partners' dealership, BENNINGTON'S FINE MOTOR CARS on Lincoln. They have this program much like The Book of the Month Club. You get to lease as many as four different vehicles a year. Many of them classics like this baby."

"What do you drive, young Mr Briscoe?" I told him. He was impressed. We talked cars for a minute or two before I had to tell him to stop talking. It was either that or kill him on the spot. Fields was a mind-numbing bore.

Usually, the Status Button of a person in ZOMBIE MODE is tranquil. They're not doing much thinking. Fields' was different. His textures were still animated but sluggish. He was still thinking or at least trying to. One for the memoirs, that's for sure.

We arrived at the thirty-seventh floor unseen. The building was all but empty. I had Fields lock the glass doors behind us and instructed him to take us to the safe and open it. Lenny gave me another questioning look. I told him that something was off. That this was the right move. It sure was.

The walk-in safe was only accessible from Fields' office. It opened to reveal an arsenal of the latest in lethal weaponry. Not what we were expecting. Lenny asked, "Where's the rest of it?" Zombified Fields just stood there. When I asked the same question, zombified Fields took a nasty-looking vintage Tommy Gun off a shelf, revealing another combination lock. I told him to unlock it, and he did.

Wow. We hit the fucking jackpot. Just like in the movies, the rear wall of the gun safe swung open to reveal Fields' treasure trove. There was cash. Dollars. Pounds. Swiss Francs. Rubles and Yen. There was a pile of 24-karat gold bars. Each one was worth a bundle. And there were precious stones, works of art carefully wrapped in heavy brown water-proof paper, and Pendaflex expanding files. Dozens of them. We decided to divvy up the haul in Leonard's secret study after we finished with Fields.

Morgan Fields was where we left him, sitting on his Herman Miller chair, watching Newton's balls swing back and forth. Lenny stopped the science demonstration and said, "Ask him about Junior Poole the Second and Dallas."

I asked, "Dr. Fields, why did Junior Poole go to Dallas last November?" Fields started to answer, angrily, "What the fuck do you think he was…." He broke into a sweat; his hands began to tremble, his eyes glazed over, and he shrieked in agony every time he tried to say another word. His colors and textures swirled and whirled and disappeared into something like a miniature black hole. Dr. Morgan Fields was dead as a doorknob at twenty-two minutes and eighteen seconds past ten in the morning, according to my Rolex chronometer. How about that? I'm the guy who killed Junior Poole the Second, the guy who actually killed President Kennedy. Someone should give me a medal.

"Julius, what the fuck?"

"Un uh Lenny, it wasn't me." I made a note to be thankful for that 'payment up front policy' for the next time Thanksgiving rolls around.

I was reviewing the curious death of Morgan Fields in my mind when the doorbell rang. Lenny said that he'd see to it. I told him it would be best if I did because I could deal with whoever was out there better than Lenny could. He agreed.

You always remember your first. Right? Well, my very first boner introduced itself while I was watching the matinee at the Waverley Theater in downtown Drexel Hills one rainy Saturday afternoon. Ronnie Cartwright's mom drove the five of us ten-year-olds in her maroon Volvo station wagon.

The thing about Saturday afternoon matinees was that you got a lot for the price of admission: 35 cents. They showed a bunch of cartoons of varying quality, newsreels about soldiers, politicians, and celebrities. More coming attractions than you cared to watch, one or two chapters of your favorite movie serials like *Flash Gordon Conquers the Universe* or *Don Winslow of the Navy*. All that and a couple of bonus B movies were added to extend the popcorn-selling window. One of those movies starred Ramona Ransom, a famous Olympic swimmer turned famous B-movie actress. The temptress that opened the floodgates.

Poseidon's Dream was actually pretty boring until Ramona's character *Amytis*, wearing a flimsy toga, swam across a pool of water to get closer to the camera. As she exited the pond, her toga clung tightly to her otherwise naked body. My first glimpse of an adult woman's anatomy. Shwing.

And there she was, just standing in the hall smoking a cigarette. Ramona was about to ring the doorbell again when I came into view. She was older and blonder than I remembered but she brought back those good old days in living Technicolor. BOING. Fucking muscle memory.

I hobbled up to the door and said, "We're closed for inventory. Can you please come back on Monday?"

"But I have an appointment with Dr. Fields. Artie Kirkland said to meet him here."

I unlocked the door. To be on the safe side, I dosed her with REAL TIME AMNESIA®. Our conversation would be short and sweet and soon forgotten. I introduced myself as Jimmie Bob Butcher, Dr. Fields' assistant and said, "I regret to inform you that Dr. Fields has had a family emergency and had to leave the city early this morning. I apologize for the inconvenience."

"If you don't mind my saying, I'm a big fan."

"*Poseidon's Dream*. Right?"

"Yes, ma'am. How did you ever guess?"

"You ain't the first, honey. Tell me this, do I still get you hard?"

I gave her a 'the-customer-is-always-right smile and asked, "Is there something I can help you with, Miss Ransom?"

"Why, that is so sweet. But no. It's quite confidential. Arthur said to only speak with Dr. Fields."

"Then I'll be sure to leave Dr. Fields a note. Does he have your numbers?" She said he did.

"Please have a good day. Again, my apologies. And yes. Yes you do."

Before Ramona Ransom turned to leave, I restored her memory functions to normal.
I watched her enter the elevator and waited until her car reached the lobby.

While I was entertaining Ramona Ransom, Lenny went to the mailroom, procured shipping boxes of various sizes, and was packing up the loot when I returned.

"Who was at the door?"

"Lenny, you're not going to believe this…"

Before I could get to the headline, Lenny interrupted, "After everything you've told me so far, I'll probably believe anything you say."

"Ramona Ransom, Lenny. It was fucking Ramona Ransom at the door." Lenny's Status Button told me that he was trying to remember who that was.

"*Poseidon's Dream*, Lenny. She was Miss Wet Tee Shirt of 1949."

"Oh yeah, now I remember. Why was she here?"

"She had an appointment with Fields. Arthur Kirkland set it up." I explained how REAL-TIME AMNESIA® works to my older brother. He seemed stupefied.

"What's with you, Julius? You seem to stumble upon turmoil wherever you go!"

"Get outta my face, Lenny." I looked at my watch. "Right about now, Ramona has forgotten all about our encounter. She probably believes that she had another senior moment. With Fields out of the picture, I think Kirkland will hand her over to you."

"But Julius, what the fuck happened to Fields? If you didn't do anything to him, was his death just a bizarre coincidence?"

"I wish it was. I believe someone had hypnotized Fields, a stage magician, a shrink, a doctor, or perhaps someone like me and told him never to answer questions about Dallas, Junior Poole, Oswald, Ruby, or President Kennedy. And when I asked him about Junior Poole and Dallas, remember Fields was in TRUTH® mode and could not lie. The conflict was too much for the man, and his brain went haywire and short-circuited his nervous system, which caused his heart to cease working properly."

"That's what I'd do if I didn't trust someone to keep a secret; I'd plant a booby trap in his mind, set to go off if he attempted to be truthful about a specific matter like the assassination of a courageous President. But it's just a theory."

If I was correct, the mandate to honor a secret would probably extend to a written document as well, like what I did to Lenny. In that case, the best we could hope for was an appointment book or an address book. Even if we found one, what would it prove? I told Lenny that Dr. Fields should be cremated as soon as possible. Legality and ethics be damned.

Our best course of action was to proceed as planned. We packed everything except three too large paintings, a life sized marble bust of the Greek philosopher Aristotle, and Fields' corpse. We brought the loot down to the garage, and stowed it in the Bentley. Our way of saying Willie Novichok was here. Plausible deniability.

◊◊

Chapter 19
the fast food rendezvous

"…I never lost one minute of sleepin'
Worryin' 'bout the way things might have been."

Proud Mary
~John Fogerty

"Julius, let's take the elevator back up to forty. I want to check my messages. I'm concerned that you now have too many things to lug back to Philadelphia. Two or three more suitcases you don't want luggage handlers handling. And now you have three briefcases and those paintings to shlepp through two airports."

"How about that, my brother? You've read my mind. I'm not in a big hurry to get back on an airplane. Maybe what I'll do is buy a set of wheels here in Chicago and drive home. So, have you come up with a solution to my scheduling conflict?"

"Hopefully. It's why we're going to check for messages on my phone."

When we reached Lenny's office, his direct line was ringing. The caller was Red Henderson, the third chair for the defense in the Big Tobacco class action lawsuit— Lenny's opposite number. There's a protocol in these matters. The way Lenny explained the pecking order to me was that third chairs interacted with opposing third chairs, and so on and so on. If one side had a proposal to pitch, it was done so by the lowest-ranked member of the team to his counterpart, who would either pass the idea up the food chain or not—the most powerful member of any legal team. Lenny had pitched a deposition delay to Henderson, and it was hit out of the park. Their first chair accepted the proposal (as usual, he wasn't ready) and offered dates in late May to conduct the depositions. Lenny said that that wouldn't do and to meet us at BIG AL'S in an hour. Bring your calendars.

Then Lenny opened the safe in the credenza behind his desk. He handed me a locked small canvas bank deposit bag. "What's this?"

"This is the evidence of Poole's trip to Dallas. It's circumstantial at best, but it might just come in handy some day. Julius is that old chifforobe still in the basement. It was next to the oil tank as I recall."

"It is."

"Did you know that the carved crown piece hides a secret compartment?"

"I didn't. Why?

"I want you to stow this evidence in there. That way, only you and I will know where it is. Just in case it's needed someday. Just be careful there's a semi-automatic and several clips, a bayonet and some French money in there as well."

"Why not just put this shit in a safety deposit box in ZOLOTO SAVINGS & LOAN? I mean the house could catch fire and mom is looking at houses in Florida. It could easily get lost in the shuffle."

"What if something happens to you? How would I retrieve it?"

"No worries, I'll have the bank send you a signature card."

The route to our junk food rendezvous took us past BENNINGTON'S FINE MOTOR CARS. Prominently displayed in the front window, on an elevated platform, was my ride home, a brand-new snow white FERRARI 500 SUPERFAST coupe with a bold Waverley Blue racing stripe bisecting the car end to end. Lenny read my mind again and pulled into the dealership without me asking or prompting.

It was Black Friday, yet not a soul was browsing the lot or the showroom. You'd think a luxury automobile would be atop everyone's Xmas wish list. The salesmen raced out to greet and glad-hand Lenny. The Executive Sales Manager was named Brian Linden. He took charge of the brown-nosing with practiced officiousness. Lenny introduced us. I asked, "How much is that *FERRARI* in the window?"

Linden gave me a look that said, 'If you have to ask, you cannot possibly afford it.' And he told me that this baby was loaded with features that nearly doubled the standard sticker price. He ticked off the features in great detail and concluded; "It's as luxurious as your brother's Bentley. But faster. Much, much faster." His Status Button told me that he was an envious asshole. I asked him if BENNINGTON'S accepted cash. They did. Lenny assured

Linden that I had the funds and that we'd settle up after lunch. The car would be ready in about an hour and a half.

Philadelphia has its cheesesteaks. Boston has its grinders. And Chicago has its Italian Beef sandwiches. In each city, there are those that favor one competitor over another. In Chicago, according to Lenny, the Italian Beef to beat was BIG AL'S. There was a long line to get in most afternoons and evenings. Being the day after Thanksgiving, BIG AL'S was anything but jammed.

It's a good thing that I hadn't tried to visualize Cheyenne 'Red' Henderson. I probably would have imagined someone looking like Clint Walker in a fringed calfskin get-up, saddle bags slung over a massive shoulder, and been totally wrong. First of all, Red Henderson was a woman—young, early twenties. Auburn hair cut short in the latest fashion. Cheyanne was barely five feet tall, and still was a perky weekend tomboy, fresh out of law school, and extremely beautiful. Her Status Button was bright and vibrant, as was her smile. And she had a huge crush on Lenny Briscoe. That devil.

This afternoon, she was all business what with her being opposing counsel and me being the kid brother. It got me thinking that maybe Lenny was getting some nookie on the side. Maybe I'll put him in TIME LIMITED–TRUTH MODE on the way back to BENNINGTON'S.

Now, for those unfamiliar with the Italian Beef sandwich, let me tell you that it's worth the risk of a trip to Chicago. Simply put, BIG AL'S signature Italian Beef sandwich is to die for. Basically, it's a French Dip sandwich with several significant differences. One is that the gravy goes in the sandwich, and another is a spicy, crunchy relish that gives it its kick.

The original Big Al was working the counter as he always does on days following national holidays. He recognized Lenny and Cheyanne and greeted them with a great big, genuine smile. He seemed puzzled by my presence. Lenny introduced us and mentioned that I owned a pair of restaurants in Philadelphia. We ordered BIG AL'S signature Italian Beef sandwiches with all the fixings, the world's greatest French Fries, and Al's award-winning fresh-squeezed Lemonade. Lenny and Cheyanne went to a secluded booth to negotiate. I stayed behind at the counter and talked shop with BIG AL.

The rest of the morning whizzed by in a blur. The sandwich was awesome. Big Al was open to franchisees in the Philadelphia market. He gave me his lawyer's card. Buttons don't lie. Lenny was having an affair with Cheyanne and vice versa and who could blame them?

Doing the paperwork for the *FERRARI* was the most time-consuming part of the morning. Sign here. Sign there. Initial this. Initial that. Count the cash twice and a third time to be sure. Then, a check ride with Brian to go over the features. "Keep it under five thousand RPMs for the first 300 miles, then let her rip." This baby can hit one hundred miles per hour in fewer than ten seconds. It'll tame Turtle Creek Trail in record time. Can't wait.

I drove the *FERRARI* back to the hotel in fairly heavy traffic. Wow, that sales guy wasn't exaggerating. The *SUPERFAST* is super cool. A four hundred horsepower V-12 engine, built-in AM-FM stereo radio, air-conditioning, power windows, five-speed manual transmission with overdrive, built in dual-port radar detectors, Connolly leather seats, a pair of cupholders and a set of luggage custom-made to fit perfectly in the boot and on the aft bench. Plenty of room to stow my share of the haul.

Machines aren't people. What buttons they do have are mechanical. All the same, I could feel the car's frustration. All that horsepower reined in. I pulled into the AMBASSADOR EAST'S driveway at quarter past noon. I slipped the doorman a fifty and instructed him to keep the car handy and to have a bellboy bring the luggage up to my room. I'd need but a few minutes to change out of my suit.

When I pulled up to Lenny's house, he, Sammy, Traci, and Deirdre were playing touch football up on the terrace with some of the neighborhood kids and some of BJ's strandees. Let's just put it this way: a *FERRARI 500 SUPERFAST* doesn't look or sound like your everyday Caddy, Buick, Ford, or Chevy; it draws a crowd wherever it goes.

"ARE YOU kidding Meeee? Holy cow, Uncle Julius, is that really your car? I got first dibs on a ride. Traci, that's a fucking two-hundred-mile-an-hour supercar. And my favorite uncle owns one." It drew a crowd. I walked up to the terrace to watch everyone ogle my new pride and joy.

Chapter 20
scoops

> "I've always lived by this golden rule
> Whatever happens don't blow your cool
> You gotta have nerves of steel
> And never show folks how you honestly feel."
>
> *But I was cool*
> ~ Odell Brown

"Uncle Groucho, what kind of car is that? It looks like a super fast rocket ship. Does it zoom-zoom really really fast?" Molly and Deirdre had joined me at the head of the terrace stairs. Molly was wearing a purple jumper over a stained Mickey Mouse sweatshirt. Her red hair had been swirled into an incongruous beehive style.

"Can I has a rides in it? We could go to the zoo and see all the real aminals. Let's go now, Uncle Groucho, I mean Uncle Julius. Daddy knows a shortcut, and I memberized it."

"Molly, maybe we could go to the zoo tomorrow. That copacetic with you, pumpkin?"

"I guess?"

"Young Mr. Briscoe, if I knew you better, I'd say you were over-compensating. But I don't know you at all, so I couldn't have said you were over-compensating." It was the first time Deirdre said anything other than 'Hello, young Mr. Briscoe' at me. She was off to a snooty start, that's for sure. As if her age, post-graduate status, and undeniable hotness made her my superior. Deirdre DePalma was from Bayonne, New Jersey. She had that accent and that attitude. DeeDee DePalma had droll down to a science. She was tall and skinny—about five seven. Maybe ninety-two pounds soaking wet. And she was probably the culprit responsible for Molly's uncanny ability to channel Shirley Temple at the drop of a capotain. Dr. Pavlov. Paging Dr. Pavlov.

"What exactly do you not think I'm compensating for? Certainly not for my looks, intelligence, or prospects. Not any of that. So what is it? Tell me, what do you think I'm compensating for?"

Deirdre deadpanned, "I'd say it's your lack of modesty."

So it was like that.

"Tell me, Deidre DePalma, is baby sitting your life's work? Or maybe you're doing it to earn tuition money for Dental Hygienist school."

"Don't be such a wise-ass young Mr. Briscoe. I'm just helping with the children for the holiday. I'm Dr. Perriman's full-time graduate teaching assistant."

That made sense. Once I thought about it, I could see that Deirdre was a much younger version of Theodora Perriman. Buttons don't lie. Maybe not yet a full-grown cougar, but Deirdre was old enough to be on the prowl for boy toys. And she was.

Jaimie Leventhal parked her Porsche Speedster behind my *FERRARI*. The top was down, and a king-sized Golden Retriever, presumably the legendary Mr. Bosco, was on the passenger seat. Jaimie was torn. There, parked in *her* space in front of *her* house, was a super-rare, super-expensive super-car. It had to be a hallucination; there were only so many in the world. What were the odds that one would be parked on Lake Street right here in Evanston? Who belonged to this beauty? Probably one of Leonard's degenerate associates.

If nothing else, Jaimie's subconscious was aware that at that very exact moment, Deirdre DePalma was stalking yours truly. Jaimie was torn. She worried that if she stopped drooling over that dreamy car to address the Deirdre situation, by the time she reached the terrace level, the Ferrari would have disappeared into the never was.

Meanwhile, Mr. Bosco barked three deep husky woofs. Molly scooted down the stairs to greet her best friend. Deirdre and I had no choice but to follow.

Jaimie had somehow rigged a restraint to prevent Mr. Bosco from leaping from the car to chase after a passing rival—a squirrel, a cat, or perhaps another dog. Molly's best friend was understandably excited to be back on his home turf and began to do the only thing he could do: prance excitedly with his forelegs and claw at the genuine leather seat he was on. Reupholstery would be required if something wasn't done like right away.

I've never experimented with other species, but their buttons, especially dogs, are very much like Normals. So I hit Mr. Bosco with a quarter dose of PECKINPAH®, which gave Jamie enough time to free the dog from his constraints so he could celebrate a joyous reunion with Molly Anne Briscoe, cute as a button. There was laughter, hugs, and species-appropriate face-licking. Grape popsicle.

"Hey, Julius Briscoe, good to see you again." Jaimie walked right up to me, kissed me on the cheek, and gave me a look. "Do you know who owns that *FERRARI*? Please don't tell me it's that scumbag Morgan Fields."

"Jaimie, no, it's not his, it's mine."

"Yours?" I showed her the keys.

"Mine. Lenny and I were going to a joint called BIG AL'S to get brunch. We drove past this dealership. The *FERRARI* was in the display window. It was love at first sight. I had to have it. It had to have me. So I bought it. Nice, right?"

"It's very nice. But I can't help but wonder, Julius, what you're compensating for?"

"Jaimie, I'm not compensating for anything. Why do you chicks always play the C card when a guy does something without seeking their wise counsel first?"

"That's one expensive machine. Will you be able to keep up with the payments?"

"It's all mine. I paid cash. Maybe I haven't mentioned this before, but Jaimie, I have my own money. Lots of it."

"I do too, sort of. Are you going to take me for a ride?"

"Of course, but I must advise you that you're second in line. Sammy called first dibs already. So Jaimie, are you still stuck for a news story, or have you come up with one?"

"No. I haven't run across anything spectacular—just the usual boring stuff. You said you might have something special for me. Give it up, handsome."

"My family and I were on United Airlines flight #505, and we've all agreed to do an interview with you."

Her eyes lit up. She smiled a wide smile. Jaimie's Status Button shone so brightly that it came close to being visible to Normals. She flung her arms around me and once again attempted to give me the hug of all hugs. I'll just say this about that, she's starting to get the hang of it.

Jaimie raced into the house and up the stairs to her bedroom suite. She came running back about three minutes later with a Speed Graphic camera, a spiral notepad, and several ballpoint pens. She had changed into a revealing blouse with the word 'PRESS' stenciled across the back. Jaimie also wore a frayed old fedora cocked back off her brow. It was a souvenir from her family's visit to the set of THE ADVENTURES OF SUPERMAN, a gift from the actor who played Clark Kent.

We gathered in the dinette, which featured a twelve-foot-long picnic bench that sat under a skylight that gave the room a warm, glorious glow. Jaimie wanted to start the interviews by taking photos. I reminded her that she agreed not to reveal our names in her article, so photography really wasn't an option.

She got the whole story from our perspectives. Each of us told her that one of the Mummers in coach was the true hero of Flight #505. Uncle T had Sheriff Hermann's numbers in his little red book. He went to the kitchen phone to see about setting up an interview.

"Max. It's Ted Briscoe. Is this a good time?"

"Good as any. They put me on desk duty because I killed that puke. Turns out he was a trust fund baby from Long Island. He wanted my dearly departed grandfather's Bulova, a bloody family heirloom. I told the fucker no fucking way, so he pointed his pistol at me. This fool was so dumb that he didn't see that I was armed to the teeth. I shot him in the chest. Self-defense. So Teddy, why are you calling?"

"My nephew Julius is trying to get into this girl's pants. Max, I gotta tell you, this hottie is worth the effort. She's a journalism student at Northwestern. So Jules tells her what we witnessed in the first class cabin, and she'd like to interview someone who flew coach. I thought of you. Are you willing to talk to her? She's a sweet kid, Max, you'll like her."

"Don't you remember Briscoe? The Feds told us not to talk to anyone about the hijacking—some shit about national security and an ongoing investigation. You can't believe how full of it those guys are. It can't get back to them that I talked to the press."

"Don't worry, she doesn't know your name. And she won't hear it from me."

"Good. Then tell her my name is Socrates Simpson."

"Whatever floats your boat. Let me bring her in. The next voice you'll hear will be Jamaica May Leventhal's. Thanks again, Max. Julius and I owe you."

Following her interview with 'Socrates Simpson.' Jaimie raced up to her rooms on the third floor to start work on her exclusive story about the hijacking of flight #505 by the notorious terrorist group *Tabula Rasa*. An exclusive she would later sell to the CHICAGO SUN TIMES for enough money to pay off her Porsche.

I met up with Leonard in his secret study to divide the booty from the late Morgan Fields' secret safe. There was

something like sixteen million in dollars, foreign currency, gold bullion, and precious stones. There were half a dozen paintings expertly wrapped in heavy brown paper.
I saved the unwrapping for Miles Gold. He's quite the art expert.

Lenny and I studied Fields' files, which consisted of calendars dating back to 1939. One pattern emerged pretty quickly. The initials J P followed by a four-digit number appeared regularly throughout the calendars. No more than a day or two before every entry with the initials J P, there were entries bearing the identical four-digit number seen in the J P block preceded by a different set of initials. Over half of them were W D. I'm pretty sure that J P was none other than Junior Poole. Who or what was this W D? Neither of us had a clue.

The phone rang. Lenny picked up and listened for nearly three minutes without saying a word. He nodded every so often as if the caller was somehow magically watching his every move. Finally, Lenny said, "Arthur, this is terrible news. I had no idea Morgan was in such poor health." Leonard listened again. Seemed even longer this time. Finally, he said, "Off the top of my head, no. Did you check his Rolodex?"

Lenny listened some more. "He's right here. I'll be certain to tell him. The partners should meet soon, don't you agree? You're more than welcome to join us for dinner. BJ has a way with leftovers." He listened some more and then said, "Well, check with Bonnie and let us know. I'll reach out to Victor and Malcolm. Of course. Speak with you soon."

Lenny hung up the phone. "That was Arthur Kirkland. Morgan Fields is dead. Heart attack, they think. I need to set up a partner's meeting. Oh yes, Julius, before I forget, Arthur wanted to let you know that Vanessa has transferred to Waverley Academy and is looking forward to seeing you on campus."

So it was like that.

◊◊

Chapter 21
the Ferrari dialogues

"Well, I'm not bragging babe so don't put me down
But I've got the fastest set of wheels in town....."

Little Deuce Coupe
~ Brian Wilson, Roger Christian

So, the first official passenger in my brand new *FERRARI 500 SUPERFAST* was Samuel L. Briscoe, my nephew. He just turned 12. Can you believe it? I have a nephew and a niece. They live in Evanston, Illinois, in a cool-looking house a stone's throw from a Great Lake that has waves, beaches, and, so I'm told, popsicle vendors.

Sammy is in the seventh grade at Northwestern Prep. It's within walking distance of his family home on Lake Street.

"Uncle J, this is so cool! Will you let me drive it when I get my learner's permit?" I grunted noncommittally.

"I've read all about the *SuperFast* in ROAD AND TRACK. Zero to sixty in like six seconds flat, zero to a hundred in less than nine seconds. And it's more expensive than Father's Bentley. Uncle J, you need to turn left at the light. We'll be on Sheridan Road. If there's no traffic, you can open her up and see how fast she goes. Let me have your watch. I'll time you."

I handed it to him.

"Wow, Uncle J! Is this a real Rolex?"

I nodded yes and told Sam that I had to break the engine in slowly. Keep it under 5000 rpms for the first three hundred miles. Sammy studied the inscription on the back of the watch. "Grace Gold, she's the one in that picture Grammy showed me, right?"

I confirmed with a slight nod.

"Wow, Uncle J, she must really love you. Rolexes are super expensive. Gary Mermelstein's super-rich grandparents gave him one for his Bar Mitzvah. Did you know you could throw a Rolex into Lake Michigan, and it would take a licking and keep on ticking? Here, let me show you." He leaned forward and began to lower his window. I muttered 'fuck it' under my breath. I downshifted, popped the clutch, and floored it. The *FERRARI* leapt forward with tremendous force, throwing Samuel L. Briscoe abruptly back into his seat. I followed up by hitting my wise-ass nephew with a short burst of PSYCHIC FLASH-BANG®, a more effective deterrent and much easier to tote around than a hot stove.

"Don't fuck with a man's watch, boy. Bad things happen to people who do."

"Uncle J, Uncle J. I was just goofing around. I would never do that for real. How come Grace Gold didn't come with you for Thanksgiving?"

"Because she's dead, Samuel. d e a d—DEAD. Didn't anyone tell you? Your father? Your mother?"

"No. We only talk about Philadelphia people at dinner when Father's home. And I don't remember him ever talking about you, or Grace Gold. Dad misses dinner a lot. He's so busy. And they wouldn't talk about stuff like people dying in front of little Molly. She's too young. So I'm really sorry, but I just didn't know. What the fuck happened?"

I told him about the Atlas City massacre without naming names or telling him what I did to the bastards. Sammy's Status Button went haywire. Anguish, fury, vengeance, and righteousness dominated his display. He's a Briscoe, all right.

"So what happened to those assholes? Did they go to jail?"

"No, since they were minors and star athletes, they had to pay a small fine and do community service. The judge sealed their records. And that was that."

"That was that? Didn't you want to kick the shit out of them and watch them die a slow and painful death?"

"Yeah. I did."

I turned onto the Northwestern campus and drove around like a tourist, under the speed limit, windows down, radio blasting the blues. The campus was a mixture of architectural generations. There were a lot of green spaces, trees, flowers, fountains, and fancied-up traffic signs. I enjoyed the admiring glances, returned the waves and smiles from the pretty co-eds that dotted the walkways.

Sammy was something of a motormouth, and it wasn't long before he broke the silence right in the middle of Howlin' Wolf's *Killing Floor*. That boy's gonna need an education. Good thing I came along when I did.

"Uncle J, what do you think? Should I get Bar Mitzvahed? A lot of my friends got Bar Mitzvahed already or are going to soon. Father told me that as far as he knew, none of the Briscoe men ever had one. But if I wanted to, he'd find a synagogue that accepted lawyers and sign me up for lessons. Uncle J, did you get Bar Mitzvahed?"

"No, Sammy, I didn't. But you need to be your own man. Make your own choices. The old schoolers say that getting Bar Mitzvahed tells the world you're now a man's man, and everybody should stay out of your way."

"Whether you have a ceremony and a fancy party or not, you're on your way to being a grown-up, and you're gonna have to learn to deal with a whole bunch of stuff you won't see coming until it knocks you on your ass. And the first thing you should do is learn to be nicer to people, especially little Molly. She's just a kid. I don't have a younger brother or sister. You're lucky to have such a cute one."

"Yeah, I know I need to tone it down. Sometimes it's just hard. Molly says the dumbest things."

"Sam, try to imagine what people eight years older than you think of some of the things that come out of your mouth?"

"So Uncle Julius, do you believe in God?"

"I don't kid. I know you think I'm cool, and I am. But that doesn't mean you should do like
I do."

That gave him pause. About thirty seconds' worth, "Good point, Uncle J. I'm happy I finally got to meet you. So, some of my Christian friends are always telling me that because I don't believe in Jesus, I have no shot at getting into heaven. Should I be worried? And how come there are so many religions anyway? Should I join one? And, if so, which do you recommend?"

It was clear that Samuel L. Briscoe had found a trustworthy, tolerant, interactive role model in me and was milking the opportunity nonstop for information, guidance, and inspiration. Lenny was too busy being a prominent white-shoe lawyer to spend much quality time with his only son.

"I'm not the guy to ask about religions, Sammy. I don't know any more about them than you do. What I do know about religions is that they're just like the movies."

"The movies? How do you mean?"

"Sam, are you familiar with the term 'suspension of disbelief'?"

"Kinda, yeah, I think. Isn't that when you go to the movies and the good guys shoot the bad guys or vice versa, they don't die for real? They just pretend die. But while you're watching, you believe the good guy did kill the bad guy or vice versa."

"That's exactly it, Sam. Well put."

"So how's a religion like a movie?"

"Well, because they both expect you to believe their bullshit going in, even though they know that you know that their bullshit is bullshit. That's how."

"Dude, Uncle J, that is so deep. So okay, okay, I'm not supposed to, but I need to tell you this; Aunt Jaimie totally has the hots for you. I overheard her telling mother this morning. How about that Uncle Julius? Aunt Jaimie is smokin' hot, don't you think?"

What I thought was that whatever I thought about Jamaica May Leventhal, I couldn't share with my naive chatterbox nephew. Quicksand.

I parked right in front of the terrace stairs where Jaimie, Deirdre, Molly and Mr. Bosco were playing hopscotch on the sidewalk. Jaimie Leventhal had her Leica camera and took photos of the car. Sammy bounced out and declared, "That *FERRARI* is super amazing, Aunt Jaimie. Uncle J is a great driver." He gave her a wink and ran into the house to call his crew and boast about his Uncle's supercar.

Jaimie slipped into the passenger seat. She was wearing bell bottoms, a white embroidered peasant's blouse, RAY-BANS, LONELY MOON PERFUME, a lavender choker, pigtails, and a cheerful smile. She gave me a wink and a kiss on the cheek, fastened her safety harness, and said, "Howdy, handsome. Got any more of that killer weed?"

I told her to look in the glove box and that she was to be my navigator, and to light up when we were well away from the house. She took me on the same route as Sammy had. We talked cars and the many joys of driving fast ones. Jaimie's scenic tour of the Northwestern campus took us to the bookstore, where she was hoping to buy some out-of-town newspapers. She wanted to see what the Philadelphia and New York City rags reported about the flight #505 foiled skyjacking. The campus bookstore was closed for the remainder of the holiday. It always comes down to a Plan B doesn't it?

Jaimie directed me to downtown Evanston. I parked nose first in a diagonal space in front of WOODBINE'S, a bookstore. It was having its grand opening. WOODBINE'S is a Philadelphia-based chain owned by the Sullivans, whose ancestors (the Tsolomonskis) were founding members of the *vhagonzug* along with the Zolotos (Golds), Briscoes, and Burgers. WOODBINE'S stocked a wide selection of out-of-town newspapers from as far off as Peking and Buenos Aires and as many books as the building could legally hold.

Centered in WOODBINE'S spacious lobby, on a semi-circular platform, was a pretty young woman wearing a slinky backless evening gown with a white sash across her bodice, which read *"Miss Evanston"* in large purple letters. *Miss Evanston* wore a fake gold crown encrusted with fake rhinestones. She was handing out leaflets to passersby, flashing expensive dental work with a smile that did not disguise her boredom. Her eyes lit up, and her Status Button brightened when Jaimie and I walked into view.

"Jamaica May Leventhal, girlfriend, I am so glad to see you!"

"Judi? Who crowned you *Miss Evanston?* When?"

"Shush....Jaimie....shush." She looked left and right before continuing, "That asshole Mr. Terrence 'I'm so cool' Sullivan hired me to be a greeter, you know, smile, wave, and pass out these coupons. Here, take one; they'll think I'm working. He made me wear this horrible outfit. Who's your handsome friend?"

"Forgive my manners, Judi, this is Julius Briscoe. Julius meet Judi Mazurski. We're both in that movie I told you about. She plays the jealous ex-girlfriend."

Judi Mazurski gazed into my eyes and offered her hand, expecting it to be kissed gallantly.
I took it with both of my hands and shook it. We smiled at each other. She winked. Jaimie's Status Button went dark and envious. She told Judi that it was great seeing her but that we were in a bit of a hurry and that maybe we'll talk again on our way out. And do you know where they keep the out-of-town newspapers?

The entire northwest wall of WOODBINE'S was done up like those old sidewalk newsstands you can still find in the big cities. Mainstream magazines clipped to sagging wire clotheslines framed the outer wall. Girlie magazines like *Playboy*, only their mastheads visible, hung in a similar fashion on the back wall, behind the counter, out of reach of the young 'uns and the pervs. The out-of-town newspapers were stacked in green wooden milk crates sitting on a genuine, weathered, city sidewalk rescued from a recent gentrification project on the south side of Chicago. Authentic nostalgia.

Jaimie rifled through the stacks of Philadelphia, New York City, Boston, and Washington D.C. newspapers. The Wednesday editions all had front-page coverage of the attempted skyjacking. Not one of them identified *Tabula Rasa* as the culprits or explained how they came to be subdued.

The front cover of THE PHILADELPHIA DAILY NEWS Thanksgiving edition featured three black and white photos and a headline that read "LBJ TO DEDICATE JFK MEMORIAL STADIUM" in big bold letters. The photos were of President Johnson holding a beagle up by its ears, an aerial photograph of Philadelphia Municipal Stadium, and Emma Sachs's official *Miss America* portrait. Emma would sing the national anthem before as many as one hundred thousand football fans at the Army-Navy game tomorrow evening.

Manning the register at this newsstand mock-up was none other than Terry Sullivan, a junior at Waverley Academy. I recognized him right away. I could see he was struggling with the incongruities. A guy that looks like an upperclassman at Waverley. A guy no one has seen since Gracie Gold was killed who was with a girl that looked a lot like Gracie Gold. But it couldn't be Julius Briscoe with a bunch of out-of-town newspapers and a hundred-dollar bill standing right there in front of him right here in Evanston, Illinois, a thousand miles from home. No, it could not be. Of course, it was.

"How ya doing, Sully?" He stood there dumbfounded—his mouth agape.

"Julius Briscoe? Is that really you?"

"So it would seem. How have you been, Terrence?

"I'm doing well, Jules. What's with the buzz cut? Don't tell me you joined the Green Berets or some shit?" SOS. Same old Sullivan.

"Nah. Nothing so drastic."

Jaimie walked up next to me and deposited a pile of magazines on top of our pile of newspapers.

"Silly me, I forgot to bring my wallet. Can I pay you back when we get home?" I didn't even get a chance to nod my head yes. "Look, Julius. I thought you might like to get this one." She showed me the latest issue of MOTOR TREND, with the actor Peter Sellers sitting on the hood of his *FERRARI SUPERFAST* on the cover. She kissed me on the cheek. Jaimie turned the magazine towards Sullivan and said, "Julius just bought one of these today. His is bright white. It's parked right out front." Terry Sullivan totally freaked out. He gasped. His colors melted into a goopy mess.

"Terry, this is Jaimie. Jaimie, this is Terry. We both go to Waverley Academy back east."

Things were already too much for Sullivan to process when an assistant manager type rushed up to the newsstand window, pardoned himself, and said, "excuse me Mr. Sullivan, but your father's on the line and needs to speak with you urgently, and there is a crowd gathering in front of the store waiting for the three o'clock signing event with Saul Bellow. The crowd is starting to block the sidewalk, the neighbors are restless."

Terry glanced at the stack of periodicals we had assembled, took my hundred-dollar bill, and gave me a fistful of twenties and two nickels in return. He said he had to go and that it was great seeing me and stuff. He changed places with the assistant manager and zoomed towards the front of the building.

The crowd wasn't for Saul Bellow; it was for the *FERRARI*, more or less. A group of enterprising young thugs had formed a wide perimeter around my car. If you wanted a closer look, it would cost you to enter the inner circle. Defiantly, I escorted Jaimie, keys in hand, towards the passenger side door.

"That's five bucks a head, buddy. But for you and your lady friend, it'll only run you ten."

I smiled and asked, "How much have you made so far?"

The pseudo-gangster thought about it some, then decided to oversell the attraction's popularity. He proudly announced that he'd collected a hundred and ten dollars so far.

I whistled, "I must tell you, I'm quite impressed. Very much so. Now, I'll take my cut." I hadn't hit him with anything yet. I wanted to see how that fool would react.

"Why the fuck would I do that?"

"Because it's my car. And I want my cut. And my cut is one hundred dollars."

It's safe to conclude that the Northside Nightmares hadn't collected a nickel from the Black Friday shoppers who weren't about to pay even a penny to gaze at an expensive foreign car parked on Davis Street. In that part of the world, *FERRARIS* and their ilk were a dime a dozen. So far, the scam had only resulted in a foot-traffic jam that blocked access to the shoppes on either side of WOODBINE'S.

"How do I know that that's your car?"

"Well, Einstein, for one thing, I have the keys. See?" I dangled the key fob with the prancing stallion on it before his very eyes and told him to get the fuck out of our way. He had no choice but to stand his ground, look as tough as he possibly could, and snarl, "Make me, motherfucker. Make me."

I did.

Never leave home without it.

The *Ferrari 500 Superfast* is a 2+2 grand tourer. Built to seat two luxuriously and two more, knees on chest, uncomfortably in the aft seating/storage section. It was, however, perfect for Molly Anne Briscoe-sized passengers. It was her turn for a ride in my super fast rocket ship. She was miffed at me because I wouldn't let her bring Mr. Bosco along. Deirdre urged Molly to be more understanding while she fastened my niece's seatbelt. She slid onto the passenger seat, buckled her safety harness, and gave me a wink and a smile. DeeDee was wearing skinny jeans, a bright red tank top, a dark brown leather vest, John Lennon-style sunglasses, a bright red beret, patchouli, and a surplus Army field watch. I advised her that she was to be my navigator. She said to turn left onto Sheridan Road and keep going until she said otherwise.

"Young Mr. Briscoe, I gotta tell you this is one sweet ride. Set you back much?"

I answered, "Not really, no."

Deirdre DePalma stared at me disapprovingly, "Now, young Mr. Briscoe, I do believe you *are* overcompensating.

Turn left at the light. If you don't mind, I'd like to stop by my dorm to check my mail. I won't be but a second. You and Molly can chill out, listen to the radio, and bond. I believe young Molly Anne Briscoe has something very important she wishes to discuss with you."

Deirdre's dorm was named Bobb Hall, an older granite building that reminded me of Shawnee Elementary. But larger, much larger. Gloomy and imposing. She gave us a wave and disappeared into her home away from home.

"Uncle Grouchy, does you like DeeDee?"

"Sure. She's nice."

"Does you like VanNessa?"

"A little bit."

"Does you like Aunt Jaimie?"

"I like her too."

"Is she your girlfriend?"

"No silly. We just met yesterday."

"Does you like me?"

"Of course, Molly dear. You and I, we're related. We're family."

"Family? Related?"

"Your father is my brother. That's how we're related to each other."

"Well, I told DeeDee that I am going to marry you when I'm all growed up. And DeeDee says I can't marry you 'cause we're in the same family. Is that real? Or is she just fibbing 'cause she wants you for herselfs?"

"It's real."

"So then you could marry DeeDee, but you couldn't marry Aunt Jaimie?"

"I could marry Jaime if we both wanted to. Jaimie and I are only related by marriage but not by blood. She's from your mother's side of the family, the Leventhals. I'm from the Briscoe side of the family. See?" She gave me a cross Shirley Temple-like frown and said, "No."

With exaggerated leaps and bounds, Deirdre DePalma raced from Bobb Hall towards my car. She was waving several sheets of paper above her head, and uncharacteristically shouting and whooping—just like one of those sweepstakes winners you see on late-night TV. She had a joyous smile and a twinkle in her eye. I thought about hitting her with a dose of PECKINPAH[®] to, you know, embellished the scene. But before I could, she whooshed into her seat, buckled up, kissed Molly and me, gathered her breath, and gave me a million-dollar smile.

"Good news?" I asked.

"Best news ever." She was still out of breath from the excitement and her headlong rush back to the car.

"Last month, a paper I wrote about *synesthesia* was published in the Illinois Illustrated Journal of Modern Psychology. The head of the Psych Department at the University of Pennsylvania read it and wants to speak with me about becoming an associate professor at UPenn and assist him in his research into such phenomena. UPenn, young Mr. Briscoe, that's the Ivy League. I'm going to call him as soon as we get back to your brother's house. He has unlimited long distance."

"Synesthesia? What's that?"

"It's a condition that some people have that affects their sensory perceptions. Some of these people," Deirdre made an air quote sign, " *'see'* brightly colored shapes when they hear sounds. Other people *'see'* words, individual letters, and numbers with specific colors. The letter A could be orange; a B could be yellow. The word JULIUS, red, white, purple, green, white and blue."

"Synesthesia varies from person to person. For some people, certain sounds trigger specific taste sensations. Piano sounds might taste like raspberries—Sinatra, like marinara sauce. This one guy told me that it tastes like a gin and tonic when he hears Billie Holiday sing. And those are just some of the types of synesthesia we know about. There is so much that we don't know."

"Why's that?"

"Most often, *synesthetes* don't realize that they're neurodivergent, or if they do, they are reluctant to discuss their condition with just anybody. Embarrassed, superstitious, or fearful of becoming outcastes, it's hard to say. Makes it very difficult to find these people. Especially those in the general population, but here on campus, it's much easier to locate and interview synesthetes. All you need is a talented silkscreen artist, a bunch of telephone poles, and access to the seven hundred and eighty-two bulletin boards on campus where you can put up eye-catching recruitment posters."

How about that? I just learned there *are* more people kinda like me and the Golds in the world than we had imagined. Buttons do not lie. I asked Deidre what she meant when she said that synesthetes 'see' colors and shapes when they hear certain sounds. Deidre summarized what had been described to her as overlays—abstract imagery integrated into everyday experience— supernaturally generated hallucinations. She could have been describing Status Buttons or *sutnists*. I'll bet Pablo Picasso was a synesthete.

It seemed to me that synesthesia just might be a distant relative of my and the Golds' paranormal conditions. I wondered if there were any synesthetes in our family trees. I asked Deidre if she had encountered or ever heard of synesthetes that were able to influence other people's behavior. Deidre gave me a studious look, mixed with concern and contempt. "Why would you ask something like that?"

"It seems a possibility."

"Well, to be truthful, and please don't tell anyone that I said this, but I believe that the likelihood of there being people with paranormal abilities here on earth is just as, if not more likely than there's life on the other planets in our solar system."

"That makes sense," I said.

"What makes sense to you, young Mr. Briscoe?"

"That those people wouldn't know that they were 'different.' Unless someone wasn't born that way but got that way after being, say struck by lightning, having a weapon pointed at them, or something traumatic like that. One day, you're a Normal. The next, you're not. Otherwise, how would that person know he was 'different?'"

"Exactly. How would they know? Of course they wouldn't. So tell me this, young Mr. Briscoe: you're not taken aback, you're not skeptical. Most people I know think that my stories about synesthetes are bullshit. Conversation starters, nothing more. But you, you get it. Maybe from personal experience?"

"No such luck DeeDee, I'm just a typical American boy who reads a lot of science fiction, you know? What about you? Do you have this synesthesia thing?"

"I don't either. Julius you're a Philadelphia boy right? I know this is a long shot, but have you ever heard of a Dr. Erskine? Professor Klaus Josef Erskine of the University of Pennsylvania?"

"In fact, I have. He gave a lecture at school last year. Waverley has these weekly assemblies where they bring in all sorts of people to give presumably inspirational talks about this and that, as well as demonstrations of CPR, self-defense, square dancing, yodeling, stuff like that. So this one time, it was your Professor Erskine. He talked about Psychology and why it's an important field of study for young privileged minds to consider. Basically, phony-ass recruiting propaganda. He had pretty much put all of us to sleep. Then he started talking about people with paranormal gifts, which perked everyone right back up."

"Professor Erskine said that he had worked with a genuine psychic, a remote-viewer, during WWII. They had used him to spy on the Nazis with limited success. Although this man could indeed 'remote-view,' he could not 'remote-hear.' He had, however, trained himself to read lips. Unfortunately, he did not know a word of German other than gesundheit, frankfurter, and strudel, which weren't commonly used by the Nazi High Command when it was plotting its nefarious campaigns."

I could have told Deirdre that the remote viewer Erskine spoke about was Max Gold, Gracie's father. Of course, I did not. I wonder why Chancellor Gold let Professor Erskine indoctrinate the Waverley Academy's student body with his tales of the supernatural. I made a mental note to ask him about that and several other things that have been troubling me.

"So, young Mr. Briscoe, if I'm lucky enough to get Dr. Erskine on the telephone, and if I'm lucky enough to receive an invitation for an interview, could I maybe catch a ride to Philadelphia with you?"

So far, I've only packed all of the stuff I needed to bring home into the *FERRARI* as a thought experiment. That large custom suitcase could hold all of my clothing with room to spare. All of the currency, foreign and domestic, the gold bullion and gemstones would fit in the *FERRARI-RED* leather travel cases which were sized to fit perfectly on the aft bench.

There just might be room for Deidre. Even so, would I want her as a passenger? She would be this close to the booty we looted from Fields' safe. Including several, works of art, expertly wrapped in heavy brown paper. I was planning to stow them in the aft footwells. She'd for sure want to know what was in the custom made luggage. Not a good idea. I hit Deidre with a dose of TRUST ME!® and told her that, unfortunately, I had been tasked by my mother to bring a couple of her cases back home with me. The passenger seat has been spoken for.

When we returned to Lake Street, Uncle Teddy, Aunt Connie, Lenny, and Bermuda June were playing cut-throat hopscotch, which involved physical contact and the drinking of spirits. Too complicated to describe. Take it from me, it was bizarre. BJ and Lenny came over to the car and helped Deidre unfasten Molly's seatbelt.

"How was your ride sweetie."

"Mommy, Uncle Groucho's car is so super fast. We went all the way to Canada and back home in time for dinner. We woulda gone all the way to the North Pole so I could visit Santa, but DeeDee needs to use the phone, so we came back."

BJ scolded, "Molly dearest what did I tell you about fibbing? Do you remember?"

"You said that there is good fibbing and bad fibbing. I was good fibbing mommy. I really, really was. Uncle Groucho told me so."

Chapter 22
the great unknown

"Sure as night will follow day
Most things I worry about
Never happens anyway"
Crawling Back to You
~ Tom Petty

Of we three Briscoes, Lenny is the smallest—thin and wiry. Just like Dad. Still lean and athletic. He volunteered to ride in the plus two section and was able to lounge on the back bench, seemingly at ease. Uncle Teddy settled into the passenger seat and was befuddled by the safety harness. He wasn't one to reach out for a tutorial. It took him a minute and a half before he was safely strapped in. Lenny took charge of the navigational chores and directed me to follow a meandering route through tree-lined residential streets while we talked all things ERRAND BOYS.

Lenny said, "I hadn't anticipated having to run the non-murder-for-hire business so soon after becoming an Equity Partner. But here we are, the Briscoe Crime Family tooling around in a fancy Italian sports car trying to figure shit out. I do know for a fact, that Fields hadn't allowed any of his subordinates anywhere near THE ERRAND BOYS product line. Those were Fields' accounts exclusively. Profitably. Problematically, as things turned out."

"Now I've gotta worry about the people that hired Junior Poole the Second, through our firm, god-dammit, to assassinate the President of the United States for fuck's sake. I can see the headlines now, **"PROMINENT CHICAGO LAW FIRM MURDERED JFK!"**

"Julius, Edward, I don't need anymore *tsuris* in my life. Certainly not scrutiny from those powerful enough, ruthless enough to hire fools like Fields and Poole to kill Jack fucking Kennedy."

Uncle Teddy to the rescue. "Calm the fuck down Leonard. Fields died what, seven, eight hours ago? Heart attack. Natural causes. Right? There's no reason that those invisible men, whoever they are, would know that Fields is dead and won't know until the next time they need to contact THE ERRAND BOYS. They may never reach out to you again. Who's to say? But if they do, you'll be prepared to deal with them."

"I will? How?"

"That's what we're going to figure out now. First I gotta guess these people, whoever they are, don't rely on just one service provider. If anything, it's likely they have decided that Junior Poole, Morgan Fields and your Law Firm are no longer on their A list. Oswald wasn't their only patsy. My guess is they are holding Fields and Poole in reserve in case some enterprising journalist catches a whiff of something Pulitzer worthy. So far, Lenny, your firm has plausible deniability. You caught a break this morning when Fields had his heart attack. Julius did you have anything to do with that?"

"I did and I didn't." I filled Teddy in about our exploits in the EZRA KIRKLAND LEGAL ARTS BUILDING this morning. Uncle T enjoys irony as much as the next guy. He asked, "You're keeping the money, right?"

"And a lot more." I told him about Fields' walk-in safe and promised that he had a nice tribute headed his way. More than enough to pay for his European holiday.

"So I'm saying right now there's nothing to worry about. Odds are pretty good you'll never hear from that client, Lenny. To be on the safe side, you shouldn't take any contracts from walk-in strangers. I don't think that you have anything to worry about from those nameless suzerains. Their secrets died with Fields and Poole. There's no reason to think that Fields told you or anyone else about the Dallas project. But to be on the safe side, don't take contracts on or from politicians."

"Good talk Uncle T. Good talk. I think you're right. None of the equity partners knew any of the details of Fields' ERRAND BOYS operation. They'd receive a cash dividend every so often that tempered their curiosity and kept them off of the thirty-seventh floor and out of Fields' shit. Thanks Uncle T, I'm feeling better. But you're right. No contracts with political types. No hits on kids either."

Lenny turned the conversation to the many issues of arranging non-murders for hire over great distances.

"Phones are too easily tapped," lamented Lenny. "Couriers too unreliable. The classifieds are too slow."

Teddy already knew, and Lenny is family, after all, so I explained our relationship with Miles Gold without mentioning *sicht* or his participation in the dismantling of Atlas City, New Jersey.

"Lenny, Miles Gold is the majority stockholder in the phone company. He gets all the cool gadgets before anyone else. He told me they were working on a handset that scrambles your voice on one end of a call and unscrambles it on the other. No one in-between, not even the fucking FBI, can make any sense of a scrambled telephone call. I'm pretty sure Miles can get us a pair. I'll discuss it with him when I see him tomorrow."

"Tomorrow?"

"Lenny, I'm going to drive home tonight. Miriam Gold still is overcome with grief. I did what I do and it helped for awhile. But then Ben and Emma went home for the holiday. And Lenny, I must tell you that Emma Sachs and Gracie Gold looked so much alike that you'd think they were identical twins. Miriam took one look at Emma and freaked out. Miles said it was heartbreaking to watch. He begged me to rush back as soon as I could. He even offered to charter a private jet. I told him about the *FERRARI* and the cargo and that I'd be back in town Saturday afternoon."

"That's crazy, Julius. Just fucking crazy. That's like, what? Almost a thousand miles. How you gonna do that?"

"I'm going to drive my fast car fast, Lenny, you know, *SUPERFAST*. Weren't you paying attention at the dealership? Your sales manager made it a point to point out that port and starboard, dual-band radar detectors come standard with every *FERRARI* shipped to the States. Not only that, don't forget my ability to convince any state trooper that managed to catch up with me that I wasn't speeding. Must be something wrong with your radar gun, officer."

"So what I'm going to do is drop you two back at the house. Then I'll drive to the hotel, pack up my things; grab a couple of hours of shut-eye, and then I'll swing back here and pick up my loot and then I'll head home."

Lenny started thinking out loud about the litigation potential surrounding modern innovations such as radar detectors, voice scramblers, Valium, and Slurpees. That's my big brother, Lenny, always with an eye on the prizes.

Chapter 23
departures

> "I'm sad to say, I'm on my way
> Won't be back for many a day
> My heart is down, my head is turning around
> I had to leave a little girl in Kingston town."

Jamaica Farewell
~ Lord Burgess

When we returned to Lake Street, there wasn't a parking spot to be had. Lenny told me to turn into the private alley that led to his detached three car garage. Jaimie's Porsche was missing, so I parked behind the Bentley just in case she was simply late to the party. Lenny's Status Button was finally trending towards normal. Teddy and I assured him that there was nothing to worry about. Yet.

We strolled towards the house. I couldn't get away with leaving Chicago without saying my farewells and expressing my gratitude for a wonderful visit. Deidre DePalma and Theadora Perriman were passing a joint around with several other university types as we approached the wrap around porch.

"So, DeeDee how did it go with Professor Erskine?"

"He's in New Mexico visiting his grandchildren. Won't be reachable until January. I don't know if I can handle the suspense."

"What suspense? He wrote you that nice letter. Be Cool DeeDee, you have nothing to worry about."

When Uncle Teddy, Lenny and I entered the house, the dining room was nearing capacity. The Briscoe's post-Thanksgiving dinner was nearly as well attended as its predecessor. BJ had reserved seats for us at the head of the table. Lenny's partners, their wives and minor children, Donna Coopersmith, and Amanda Rice, BJ's teaching assistant, were socializing less randomly than the evening before.

My path to my seat at the table took me past both Donna Coopersmith and VanNessa Robinson-Kirkland.

"So Julius did you get my message?"

"I think so. You're transferring to Waverley. Why'd you go and do that?" I should have known better.

"Julius, I love the setting. The campus is so beautiful. And it has a tennis bubble. Do you play?" She kept right on going, "The women's dorm is modern compared to Exmoor's. The teaching staff is outstanding and Waverley's Ivy League acceptance rate is exceptional. And, of course, we'll get to see each other more often. I'm so looking forward to that."

Donna Coopersmith jumped into the conversation as if she were defending a fresh kill on the veldt. "Julius, your niece Molly tells me you own a super fast rocket ship? She's quite the adorable little fibber, that one, isn't she?"

"It isn't a rocket ship, Donna, it's just a car."

"What kind of car?"

"A *Ferrari 500 Superfast*."

"*FERRARI?* I thought they made race cars."

"They do. Street legal ones also."

"Will you give me a ride in it after dinner?"

"I don't think I'll be able to tonight. I'm going to say some quick farewells and then I'm going to drive back to Philadelphia in time for the big game."

"Big game? What big game?"

"The Army-Navy Game. First night game in the history of the rivalry. A friend has front row seats on the fifty yard line. Emma Sachs is singing the national anthem."

Dropping Emma's name didn't spark recognition from either Donna or VanNessa. However, they were familiar with Emma's title and wondered aloud why I was so interested in blonde beauty queen types. I didn't feel like going into it, I excused myself and went to join the gathering of Briscoes at the head of the table.

As I've often observed, gossip travels somewhat faster than light does. My mother, Aunt Connie and BJ Briscoe greeted me with their arms folded across their chests, reeking of self-righteousness.

"What's this I hear you're driving back to Philadelphia tonight?"

That was Mother, but the question could have easily come from Aunt Connie or Bermuda June. The three of them greeted me with icy stares and indignation. I did my best to explain, but they weren't buying any of it until I played the grieving-mother-of-my-late-fiancé card. Mother was the first to acquiesce. She knew how close Nettie Gold and I had become since Gracie and
I have been together. I said my *mea culpas,* explained that I

really must be going, but wait, I need to say my farewells to Molly Anne and Jamaica May. Sammy was attending a post-holiday mixer at his school.

Molly Anne was holding forth in her pretty and pink bedroom on the second floor. There was an assortment of future movers and shakers, progeny of the incumbent movers and shakers, seated cross-legged on the floor, they were paying rapt attention to Molly's dissertation on the care and feeding of stuffed aminals.

"I call this one Razzle Dazzle. He's a Sumatran Tiger. They're the meanest tigers in the whole wide world. This big bad boy is Tony the Tiger, he's from India which is on the whole other side of the world. He's great. And look over there, that's my favorite uncle. Uncle Grouchy. He has fast cars, is very very handsome and he can beat up any old tiger with one hand tied behind his back. Ain't that the truth Uncle Julius?" She gave me an exaggerated wink. She really was a good little fibber.

Somethings in life that seem they'd be easy enough to do, are the hardest things you can actually do. Saying goodbye to Molly in front of her friends and associates was harder even than that.

"But you said we was going to the zoo tomorrow. Remember?"

"I do sweetness. I really really do. But a dear friend of mine is very very sad and the sadness is making her sick. And I have to try to help her. We're very worried that she might…" I fumbled for a word other than die. Molly came up with the right one right away. "You're worried she might die?"

"That's right, yes. Molly this is a very grown up question I have to ask you. Do you want me to ask it?"

"Yes, Uncle Julius, I know how to keep a secret." Shit. The kid has buttons, she shouldn't be, but she seems to be able to read my mind as does her father.

"That's good. Can you promise me to keep a great big secret?

"Yes I can, I'm a big girl now."

REAL TIME AMNESIA® to the rescue.

"Well Molly sometimes I can take the sadness from a person and make it go away forever.
I need to do that for my friend back in Philadelphia."

"What's your friend's name?"

"Miriam Gold. But most people call her Nettie."

"Nettie? That's the silliest name ever."

"Tell you what, I promise not to tell Nettie that you think her name is silly. If you were to tell any grown up that you know Nettie Beachum, they would be very impressed. Nettie was a very famous tennis player back in her prime. So do we have a deal to keep my secret?"

"Okay we have a deal." I gently restored her memory function to normal. "But when am I gonna see you again?"

"I'm thinking maybe I'll fly out for Christmas or maybe you and your family will come to Philadelphia some day soon."

I gave Molly Anne a kiss on the forehead, made a mental note to add the Evanston Briscoes to my Christmas list and went downstairs in search of Jamaica May Leventhal.

Jaimie was nowhere to be found. BJ, on the other hand was not. She told me that there was yet another emergency on the set of *Ramona in Chains,* a Brent Culpepper film. The cast and crew, including Jaimie were huddled up in a rehearsal space on campus trying to salvage the production. It wouldn't do for me to drive off into that dark and gloomy night without one more attempt at a hug-of-all-hugs. BJ scribbled the address and directions on an abandoned seating chart and handed it to me.

The rehearsal space was in the Armitage/Beatty Little Theater on the Northwestern campus. To me, it looked like a fully functional, somewhat tiny, venue for modest stage productions, lectures, musical performances and poetry readings. I entered the theater from the lobby. There were eight or nine people up on the bare stage. They were arguing intensely. Was it a scene from *Ramona in Chains* or something more spontaneous? Pretty sure it was the latter. Just to be on the safe side, I started stockpiling doses of BE COOL®.

I walked towards the stage and sat in the best seat in the house, front row center, and watched the drama unfold. It seemed that the argument, over creative differences, was between the director, a skinny over achieving, over compensator, and the lead actor, a skinny under-achieving, untalented clown according to Culpepper, a snotty prick if ever I saw one.

Culpepper removed his wallet from his jeans, pulled a newspaper clipping from the wallet, unfolded it and read, "According to Ronald Segal of The Chicago Sun Times,

'Brent Alan Culpepper, that's me, is a promising young director one should keep one's eyes on.' And you Tony Rosenberg, you are a talentless hack. You have no future in acting. Anyone off the street could do a better job than you, that guy over there for instance."

Culpepper skipped and stumbled his way from the stage to the auditorium floor all slapsticky and Charlie Chaplin like. He rambled up to me and said, "Look here Rosenberg, this one's perfect. Stand up my man. Let's have a good look at you."

You know me and pushy Normals, "You talking to me, shit for brains? People like you don't talk to people like me like that. Not if people like you want to keep breathing and retain all of your teeth, that is."

"See what I mean Rosenberg? This one's a natural sadist. You're a sodding oaf by comparison."

Rosenberg leapt from the stage just like Errol Flynn might have, unsheathed an imaginary rapier, ran Culpepper through with it, and exited stage right.

"Julius Briscoe? What are you doing here?" Jamaica May Leventhal leapt gracefully from the stage and seemed to float towards my location. Culpepper struggled to his feet, both hands on his midsection as if he had actually been skewered by that irate actor.

"Jaimie, darling, do you know this gentleman?" Culpepper asked between grunts, "I believe he'd be a magnetic Percy Rutherford. Can't you just see it?"

"Not really, no, Brent. Besides he lives back east. You can't afford to transport him." She turned her attention to me, "Julius Briscoe what's going on? Couldn't stay away could you?"

"I need to drive home tonight. I didn't want to leave without saying goodbye. Didn't want to hurt your feelings that way. I'm still not over what happened to Gracie. To life without her. But if there is one, it'll be with someone like you." She gave me a hug-of-all-hugs and a pretty good kiss too.

Chapter 24
on the road

"…I'm always alone
And my heart is like ice
And it's crowded and cold
In my secret life…"

My Secret Life
~ Leonard Cohen, Sharon Robinson

The Indiana Toll Road connects to the Ohio Turnpike which connects to the Pennsylvania Turnpike. It is nearly one hundred and sixty miles long. It posts a speed limit so absurdly low that it was easily mistaken as a minimum by people driving high powered road cars like mine. The toll road skirts the border between Indiana and Michigan and thus serves as Indiana's first line of defense against invading Wolverines should they ever bother.

I reached the toll booth just around midnight. There was a State Trooper and his trusty, black and white cruiser, light bar flashing red, white and blue parked on the other side of the zebra striped gate. He was talking to the driver of a horse trailer. I was maybe ten minutes ahead of a downpour. The man in the ticket booth was wearing a yellow slicker with a matching hat. He was in his thirties and whistled when I pulled to a stop.

"That's one fine looking motor car you're driving young fella. A *FERRARI*, ain't it?"

"Yes sir it is. So what's going on up there? One of those state-wide manhunts they always have out here in the boonies?"

"No son, it's nothing like that. Trooper Magnusson up ahead will explain everything. Where are you headed?"

"Philadelphia."

The horse trailer rolled away. It was my turn. The ticket booth guy handed me a ticket, pushed the button that raised the gate so I could be updated by Trooper Magnusson, who wore an olive drab slicker, a clear plastic liner over his campaign hat. He was a tall guy, probably a blonde headed Scandinavian type. He seemed affable, friendly. Buttons don't lie.

"What's going on officer?"

"How far are you traveling this evening young fella?"

I told him. He leaned down and looked into the car.

"That is one fancy ride. I'm wondering if you might be good enough to take the gentleman sitting out of the rain in my cruiser up to the service plaza just past the LaPorte exit?"

"I'd rather not. What's going on?"

"Well sonny it seems there has been a train derailment north of LaPorte. It was a circus train. The Grimshaw Brothers Fabulous Three-and-a-half-Ring Circus. You familiar with it where you're from?"

"Never heard of it."

"Well this here train was the one that carries all of the animals and props. The tents and the bleachers. Things like that. Well some of them animals, well, they got loose and they're roaming the countryside, frightened, and dazed. They don't feed them until they get them to their destination. So we're talking hungry-hungry lions, tigers, and bears, oh my. Mary Louise Freiberg rang up Chief Chesterton and told him that a tiger, a fucking tiger, was eating one of her calfs. The gentlemen in need of a ride he's an animal trainer with the circus. His car broke down. He needs to get to LaPorte yesterday."

"He's already sitting in your cruiser. Why don't you just take him there yourself with sirens screaming and lights flashing?"

"I'm here to advise motorists of the possible wild animal hazards ahead. I cannot leave my post."

"Dude, why can't the guy in the ticket booth over there advise motorists of the 'animal hazards ahead?' I mean it doesn't seem to be such a difficult task?"

Trooper Magnusson ditched affable and summoned up authoritative, "It's the responsibility of the Indiana Highway Patrol to protect motorists. Toll booth personnel are not sufficiently trained to perform such duties. So will you take him? I mean you're going that far anyway. He seems like a good enough fella. You should be advised that he does use salty language. And keep an eye out for them elephants. They're very difficult to spot in the darkness." Trooper Magnusson had a forthright manner which gave him just enough credibility to change my mind.

The animal trainer was the sporadically famous Charlie Dupree. I saw him one time on the Tonight Show. He's one of those crazy people who sticks his head in a lion's mouth for non-dental purposes. He has souvenirs from some of those encounters: One hundred and twenty six stitches and a prosthetic right ear. So far.

Charles *Catman* Dupree was in his late thirties, average build and height. He had a thick Brooklyn accent, wore a brown leather bomber jacket over pale green pajama tops with black piping. The waist-band of Dupree's pajama bottoms spilled over the waist-band of his cargo pants, its pockets bulging with who knows what. A silver whistle dangled from a leather thong around his neck. Dupree was sporting a bullwhip, long and short barreled tranquilizer guns and a starter pistol. He removed his utility belt, tossed it on the floorboard, sat down, strapped in and said "What's the fucking holdup boy? Get going. There are dangerous animals on the loose out there. And I'm the only man on this continent who can bring them back alive."

Not exactly. *What the fuck? Chuck?* I thought it was only fair to cut the asshole some slack. My reaction to his self-aggrandizing declaration was unvoiced. Some of his menagerie were probably dead or injured. Others might be roaming the Indiana countryside, foraging for anything to satisfy their hunger for free-range flesh. Good old Charlie was worried sick about his co-workers.

I checked the odometer. It read 237.22 miles. Close enough. I revved the engine a couple of times, merely for theatrical effect, before speeding into that dark and soon to be stormy night.

"I want you to drive as fast as you can for the next thirty miles. After that you'll need to drive more slowly. These animals are accustomed to artificial lighting and are actually drawn to it. So caution is highly recommended."

As fast as I can? Or as fast as I dared? The road wasn't yet ten years old. It was in good repair, with little or no hills or curves to slow down for. I hit one hundred miles per hour in the nine seconds flat Sammy Briscoe had predicted just this afternoon. Wow, what a car. Rock steady. Limitless power. No shake. No shimmy. I could have gone faster, but, aside from the lighted interchanges, the Indiana Toll Road was pitch black. Super dark on an overcast, moonless night. Never drive faster than your headlights *they* always say.

"I apologize for being so curt with you, young fella. I am so very worried about my cats, the bears and elephants too. I'm Charles Dupree. Call me Charlie if you like."

"I'm Julius Briscoe, Charlie, good to meet you. How did you get into the lion taming business? Are you available to speak at my school on career day?"

"I'll need to check my calendar. As to my lion taming journey, well that's a long, long, boring story Julius. One I'm not fond of telling. One you wouldn't enjoy hearing. I hope you won't mind my asking, but how does a fella as young as yourself get to be driving around in something like this? *Ferraris* don't come cheap."

I wasn't in the mood for chit chat. My plan, for the long drive home, had been to come to terms with my feelings of loss, anger and guilt over Gracie's death. And the things I did to avenge her. The trip to Chicago had taken my mind off of my troubles. I actually had a good time. But, I needed to complete the process. So, I took my frustration out on good old Charlie '*Catman*' Dupree. Nothing more fun than bullshitting a bullshitter.

"I won it in a card game."

"Get the fuck out of here."

"Straight flush. Can't help it if I'm lucky."

"Seriously kid, you expect me to believe that?"

"I don't give a fuck what you believe. Do you know how many animals survived?"

"I haven't been given a final accounting. Last I heard, two of the tigers, the females, and three lionesses and a male lion ran away and may be injured. They're even more dangerous when they're wounded. One of the elephant survived the crash and fled the scene. That's as much as I know. Not a good situation at all, young Mr. Briscoe. No, not at all."

"The news about the derailment leaked out right away. I'm guessing that, right now, most of Michiana's brave young men are stalking these woods looking to bag some big game right here on their home turf. Someone's going to get himself shot or mauled tonight. I just feel it."

The radar detectors started beeping, adding to his foreboding.

"Hey hey what's that sound?," questioned Charlie.

I slowed down and pushed the button that silenced the irritating noise.

"It's the radar detectors, Charlie. State troopers must be up ahead, I reckon." I hadn't sensed any Normal Status Buttons on the drive so far. And I wasn't certain which had the greater range; a radar gun or a Status Button. In fact, the only Status Buttons in range, other than Charlie's, belonged to critters out there in the wilderness that were no larger than Mr. Bosco.

"I wouldn't be surprised if they're using radar detectors to locate my animals. They're all wearing these newfangled collars that give off a signal that shows up on the radar. Might be what you picked up or it might be the coppers. Either way, you ought to slow down. Keep it under forty. What I'd like you to do, Julius, is scan the road ahead and the forest to your left. I'll keep a sharp eye on the right side. Be ready to stop when I say."

"Roger that." Yippie! I've always wanted to say 'roger that.'

I was creeping along at thirty miles per hour or so. We were ten miles west of the LaPorte Service Plaza. There, a hundred yards or so ahead, trotting down the grassy median strip that separated the East bound and West bound lanes was an elephant. A baby one. Cute and snuggly. Made me think of Molly Anne and her stuffed aminals.

"Yo *Catman*, are you missing a baby elephant, or is that critter over there indigenous to northern Indiana?" I pulled a little closer to it and stopped the car. Dupree scooped up his utility belt, before he ventured forth, he turned to me and said, "keep the high beams on and turn on your flashers. Elephants have excellent night vision, they react to bright lights just like deers do. They stand still and look stupid. Pay attention young Julius Briscoe, this is something you're gonna want to tell your grandchildren about."

Catman Dupree raced out of my car and shot a baby elephant in his pajamas with a tranquilizer gun. He got back in the car, peered into the aft cabin and said with a straight face, "you know, young Mr. Briscoe, if you got rid of all that junk, I'll bet Ella could fit back there nice and snug."

Dupree was expecting a reaction. I didn't make an effort.

"So Julius, did you, by any chance, happen to notice a mile marker?"

"We just passed mile marker 32."

Catman glanced at the clock on the dashboard, compared it to his watch and then said "We're close now. Let's get going. Keep an eye out young Mr. Briscoe, we ain't out of the woods yet."

◊◊

Chapter 25
tiger, tiger

"I want to ride, ride the tiger
It will be black and white in the dead of night
Eyes flashing in the clear moonlight
I wanna ride, ride the tiger…"

Ride the Tiger
~ Beyong Yu, Grace Slick, Paul Kantner

The Knute Rockne Memorial Service Plaza sits on a bluff between the highway and the forest. If you were an apex predator from another hemisphere, that stand of white oak and brush was as good a killing ground as any.

The Service Plaza consisted of several structures, parking for a couple hundred cars, trucks and tractor-trailers. It had a large central building that contained several fast food joints as well as a middle of the road sit-down restaurant, a gift shop, a shoe shine stand, restrooms and a tourism center.

The plaza was lit by floodlights mounted on thirty-foot poles, just like at the mall back home. There were filling stations for gasoline and diesel powered vehicles. The first responders to the circus animal crisis were deployed on the picnic area next to the ramp leading back to the highway. They had a 9,000-watt searchlight with a dedicated generator sweeping the northern horizon. There was a garishly painted Grimshaw Brothers panel van, its roof-mounted horn speakers blaring out circus music. Every so often, a pre-recorded announcer would declare, "The

Fabulous Grimshaw Brothers Circus is coming to town. Get your tickets now at your conveniently located CIRCLE K." Seemed Grimshaw Brothers management believed that their very valuable show animals might be homesick and would come trotting towards the familiar sounds. What are the chances?

I drove Charlie to the staging area. He thanked me as sincerely as any New Yorker can, shook my hand and pressed a couple of fifties into it. He also handed me a pre-autographed post card with a color photo of *Catman* Dupree, his head in a lion's mouth, and a business card. "That's my agent's information. Give Betsy a call and she'll help you set a date for that career day thing. Thanks again kid, you're aces in my book."

He turned to open his door. I said, "Charlie, stay put. One of your critters is inbound. Must be a music lover."

There were three very large buttons, red, purple, and yellow—that's all jungle cats seem to have—charging towards the encampment. I couldn't tell whether it was a lion or a tiger. But I could tell that it was moving fast. If *Catman* Dupree were to get out of the car just then, well, he'd likely be *catfood* Dupree in no time. The buttons sprung from the tree line, snarling and drooling. It was a lioness, the most fearsome predator in all the world, except for armed Normals, of course. She took every one of those fearless adventurers by surprise, let out a mighty roar, and leapt towards the throng of confused neophyte big game hunters. I hit her pause button while she was midair. Three, maybe four, tranquilizer darts struck her left flank. Only one successfully. She hit the ground with a thud and did not move a muscle until I was a hundred miles further east, and that big cat was safely re-caged.

`"Young Mr. Briscoe, how the fuck did you know Sheena was in the area. That one is fucking untrainable. She was born and raised in captivity but acts like she's the queen of the fucking jungle. I've been working with that cat for two years now. She's still not ready for the big tent. So tell me, young Mr. Briscoe, how did you know she was about to attack?"

"I had a hunch."

"A hunch?"

"Yeah. A hunch. I get them all the time and they're usually mostly always right. Nice meeting you *Catman*. I have a hunch we'll meet again someday soon."

Charlie '*Catman*' Dupree laughed and exited the car. I never saw him again.

The Indiana State Toll Road Commission mandates that every Service Plaza on its toll roads provide 24 hour service to travelers in need of food and fuel and restrooms. My next stop was the Esso station. Just like in Pennsylvania, motorists in Indiana are not permitted to operate a gasoline pump. Not sure why that is, but it is. I rolled over the signal hose and a bell chimed twice. Once for each axle. I stopped perfectly aligned with Pump #2, high test, 31.9 cents a gallon. I waited exactly two and half minutes before I used the horn. Three nice, polite beeps. No one answered the call.

I got out of the car and started filling the gas tank. As it turned out, it wasn't that difficult a task to master. The night-turn attendant shuffled barefoot out of the garage rubbing his eyes and muttering something under his breath.

I hit him with a low dose of RAWPOWER®, just enough boost-juice to get him through the night.

"What's this shit? So you pull up here in a fancy-smancey foreign car, wake me up and then start pumping the high octane on your own? You know it's agin the law for civilians to take matters into their own hands. Give it over now."

"Give what over?"

"The nozzle. You can't be seen doing that. My fucking boss hears about you working that gas pump, he'll throw a tantrum worse than the one my little boy Nicky Jr. threw when we ran out of chocolate milk yesterday morning. What's wrong with you man? Where's the humanity? This is my night job and it don't pay shit."

"Well then Russ, fill her up, wash the windows and check under the hood please, and no more bitching or there will be consequences."

He gave me a nasty look. A really nasty look. He was a large guy. Six two. Six three, maybe. Bulky, but fit. He wore grease stained ESSO branded overalls that were too small for him. *Russell Tomkins* embroidered on his left breast pocket. He clenched and unclenched his fists a couple of times in an effort to appear menacing. "You do know that we charge a ten dollar minimum this time of night." A fucking lie if ever I saw one. And I've seen a lie or two in my time.

"That's only fair. I can afford it. Now, I've got a twenty-six gallon tank here that's only a quarter full. Get moving. I've got a long way to go this evening. Don't waste any more of my time, putz."

The windows were sparkling, the crankcase, radiator, and the gas tank were all topped-off and I was out of there. I received no further complaints and observations from Russell who also worked as an apprentice free-lance carpet installer during daylight hours. FEAR ME.® Don't leave home without it.

One thing Lenny's ride had over my *FERRARI* was a premium thermos jug the same shade of crimson as the Bentley's custom paint job. It could hold a half a gallon of coffee and keep it piping hot for six and a half hours according to the manufacturer. Lenny gifted it to me after we finished packing the *FERRARI*. He couldn't process the foreign currency or the bullion without being called into question by his partners. So I ended up with the bulk of Fields' treasure. Thirteen million and change. Enough to finance the expansion of BIG CORNERS, MONGO MING'S and the successful launch of BIG AL OF CHICAGO'S, AUTHENTIC ITALIAN BEEF, PHILLY-STYLE, soon to have a major impact on South Street, Overbrook Park and Roxborough.

I parked next to the brightly lighted entrance to the SENATOR BLAKE CAPEHART HOSPITALITY CENTER. I'd be able to keep an eye on the FERRARI from the empty booth in SWEET MARIE'S where I planned to get a bite to eat and half a gallon of piping hot black coffee to go.

The building was all but deserted. There were no other cars parked nearby. There was a bank of telephones in the vestibule. I used the calling card Miles gave me and placed a call to Jamaica May Leventhal.

"What?" She sounded sleepy, maybe a bit hung over.

"Jaimie, it's Julius Briscoe."

"Hey Julius, it's been awhile."

"I know. I know. Sorry to be calling so late but I have another hot news story for you."

I told her everything I could remember about the circus train derailment and the efforts to recapture the wild animals that were terrorizing the Indiana countryside.

"Julius that's an amazing story. I'm going to call it in to the SUN TIMES. May I mention your name?"

"I'd rather you didn't. Just call me an anonymous source close to the situation. After all,
I did help capture a baby elephant, and a dangerous lioness. Or you can attribute it to Charles 'Catman' Dupree, he'll love the publicity. Jaimie, I've got to get going, I'm way behind schedule."

"Julius, that's what you get for being such a good samaritan."

"Thanks Jaimie. I'll give you a call when I get home. Good night, good luck and, good news tomorrow."

There was a "Hostess Will Seat You' sign partially blocking the entrance to SWEET MARIE'S OF INDIANA. A call bell sat next to the cash register. I rang it. Twice. I was about to go for three when a perky looking waitress all done up in pink and looking like a million bucks walked up to me, gave me the once over twice and finally said, "How you doin' sugar? Something I can get for you?"

"Well yeah, I'd like to get something to eat."

"Sure thing sugar. Hope you don't mind sitting at the counter tonight. Billy Ray's getting ready to vacuum the floor in the dining room. Once he finishes up, he's free to head home. Everybody's worried they might run into one of those escaped prisoners and get murdered."

"I prefer to sit in that booth over there. Tell Billy Ray I'll make it up to him. And to you too." Ivy, that's what her name tag called her, escorted me to booth number 12. She handed me a three fold laminated menu. I thanked her and gave her a wink. In return, I got a dirty look. Dirty bordering on nasty. Her Status Button boiled and bubbled. Was it something I said? Before I could open the menu, Ivy said, "Georgie, he's the night cook, he went home to protect the wife and kids from those heartless escaped convicts, so now it's just me, Ralph the security guard, and Billy Ray working tonight. I ain't much of a chef, but I can put together a nice sandwich if that's oakle-doakle with you."

"That'll be great. What do you recommend?"

"If I was you, I'd go with the club sandwich."

She came on all sweet and flirty, but her Status Button said she was still pissed and insulted.

"You seem to be angry with me. I need to sit back here so I can keep an eye on my car. I just bought it and I don't want anything to happen to it. The guy at the ESSO station and I didn't hit it off. He's not too fond of Italian cars. Gave me the finger as I drove away. I don't trust that guy."

"Ivy darling, all I want to do is to get something to eat, fill up this thermos and get back on the road. I don't believe that's a good enough reason to be cross with a notorious big tipper like myself." I tapped her TRUTH button, and waited for her to come clean.

"Why is it that guys like you think you can charm your way into a sister's pants just because you is handsome, white, can wink and be charming?"

So it was like that.

I took a moment to look her up and down before responding. Ivy was very good-looking. Probably been fucked over a couple of times by guys like me. You know, young, rich, handsome, and careless. She was wearing her hair in an Angela Davis-inspired Afro, had coffee-colored skin, two creams, lotsa sugar, a dazzling smile, and bright blue eyes that saw everything. Ivy was slender, tall, and athletic. She reminded me a lot of Ellie Gold.

I apologized even though I hadn't intended to insult her. I explained that I wasn't trying to get into a sister's pants. That I was currently celibate. That it was too soon after Gracie's tragic death to even consider flirting with a beautiful woman like her. That soothed Ivy's Status Button right quick.

"You said something about escaped prisoners on the loose? Ivy what's going on?"

"Well, 'bout an hour ago, Chief Chesterton, he stomped in. That man's a stomper, all right. Just ask my brother-in-law, and sat down at the counter like he always does and whispered something to Miss Lucy. She's the night manager. Not that that's unusual or anything. She's been doing him long before I came to work here. It'll be two years next Thursday. So the Chief, he has his apple pie à la mode and black coffee, gives Lucy a wink and a nod, and leaves without paying or tipping like always. As soon as that cracker walked away, Miss Lucy tells everybody not to worry, but there was a prison break up there in Jackson,

Michigan, and three or four known criminals were on the loose and might or might not be headed our way. Which is why all them cops are on the lookout down by the on-ramp. Do you really think I'm beautiful?"

"More so every moment I share with you."

"You just sit tight handsome, I'll be back with your dinner in no time."

"Do you really think I'm handsome?"

"Nah, I say that to all the guys. But you are kinda cute. For a white boy, that is." She gave me a wink, grabbed the thermos, balanced it on her head and waltzed towards the kitchen singing 'God Bless the Child.' She was no Billie Holliday, but Ivy still was a pretty good singer.

She was back in a flash or two with as finely a crafted club sandwich as there ever has been. She told be to slide over. I did. Ivy slipped in next to me and said, "I don't think I ever got your name."

I said, "take a guess," and took a bite of my sandwich. It was pretty tasty.

Ivy gazed out the window as if deep in thought while I finished half of my sandwich. Still pretty tasty. Finally she said, "Nicky."

"Really? You think I look like a Nicky?"

"You don't. You're probably a Reginald or a Cooper. No, that's Nicky Hopkins from the Esso. He's coming this way and he's sporting a crowbar. I cannot imagine why."

The rain had let up about five minutes earlier, a temporary respite from the storm yet to come. Nicky, wearing Russell's too small uniform, was still too far off to get a detailed read of his Status Button. From this distance all I got was angry and irrational. The closer he got, the clearer his intent. He was afraid to confront me so he was targeting my innocent and defenseless imported luxury sports car. Well not exactly defenseless.

I hit Nicky's pause button moments before it began to rain again. He was about to get pelted. Serves him right. My timing couldn't have been better. The would-be vandal stood aggressively poised, a crowbar held defiantly in the air, just like one of those slasher movie posters. All that was needed to complete the composition was a bolt of forked lightning illuminating the scene. Things were getting hairy. Just in case, I gave Ivy a dose of REAL TIME AMNESIA®.

Here's a fascinating thing Charlie Dupree told me: tigers usually stalk and attack their prey from behind. If I didn't do something quickly, Nicky would become frozen food. Seems that one of the tigresses had been stalking the disgruntled service station attendant from a discrete distance, and now that he was stationary, quickly closed ground and was about to pounce. Good old Nicky Hopkins was an asshole all right, but he didn't deserve such a fate.

I paralyzed the three-hundred pound cat before she could attack. My timing wasn't as precise as it had been with Nicky. The tigress, the one they called Lily, was off balance when I hit her huge yellow button. She toppled over and was down for the count, or at least until I crossed the Ohio state line.

Ivy gasped, contained a smile and said "I tawt I taw a puddy-tat. A great big mean old puddy-tat." I wasn't sure what to say. Then it came to me in a flash.

"You did. You taw a puddy-tat."

"You have the gift, don't you?"

"The gift?"

"You. You. I was beginning to actually like you and here you go bullshitting me?"

"Ivy, I haven't known you long enough to have to bullshit you. What makes you think I did?"

"Some one or some thing turned Nicky from the Esso and that tiger, that fucking tiger, into stone, and it wasn't me sugar. That leaves Ralph the security guy or Billie Ray or you. I've known those other two for almost two years. They ain't got no gifts. They hardly have any presence. That leaves you. Tell me I ain't right."

"Nuh uh, Ivy, it wasn't me. Trust Me sugar. One of those circus guys probably shot them with a tranquilizer dart. First dart missed the tiger, but hit Nicky. The second dart knocked the tiger on its ass."

I returned her memory functions to normal. It disoriented her big time. If you've ever dozed off accidentally and abruptly snapped awake before drifting into the oncoming lane, then you know what dear old Ivy was going through.

I speculated aloud that Chief Chesterton probably lied to Lucy, the night manager. I guess he figured folks would stay at home and not take up arms against escaped convicts, but for bragging rights and trophies suitable for taxidermy, everyone with a rifle and true grit would be out there shooting at anything that moves and drinking Wild Turkey and shooting at anything that moves.

It began to thunder. Roiling thunder. Deep, loud and threatening. Loud enough to rattle the windows. That following storm was catching up pretty darned quick.

"So it's not Cooper and it's not Reginald. So is it something like Kent or Darby or maybe Archer or Chatsworth? Am I hot or cold?"

"Frozen solid."

"Give me a hint. That's only fair."

"All right, I'm named for a famous star of stage and screen."

"Well now, that's more like it. So now tell me this, mystery man, how old are you?"

"Sorry love, only one hint per charming contestant."

"I'm just thinking out loud here sugar, you're about, what, nineteen, twenty, more or less. Means Mommy and Daddy did the nasty sometime in the mid 1940s, be my guess. So I'm thinking movie star names, Henry? Orson? Errol? Clark? Or maybe Humphrey? Tell me, handsome, am I even close?"

"Any closer and we'd be going steady." She got the hint and slid a couple of inches away from me. She was still pretty close. Ivy smelled nice, and she was good company. I didn't mind at all.

More lightning. Brighter than before. Thunder just a couple of seconds after. Play time was over, I needed to hit the road. So I gave it up.

"I'm named for Groucho Marx whose given name is Julius. My brother is named for Leonard, whose stage name is Chico."

She gave me a 'what the fuck? Who is Groucho Marx?' look. By the time I finished explaining the Marx Brothers to Ivy, it began to rain. Hard rain. Wait-it-out rain. Lightning flashed again and struck the crowbar still tightly gripped in Nicky Hopkins's clenched fist. At that moment Nicky was standing barefoot in a good sized puddle that he shared with the tigress named Lily. They didn't stand a chance. Lily was insured by Garden State Life, Auto and Casualty for five million dollars. Poor old Nicholas Hopkins Senior was not.

The storm transitioned from raging to tolerable in twenty-two minutes according to my Rolex. Ivy and I spent the time talking about our families and our lives so far. Our different lives in our different worlds were, in actuality, pretty much the same. I told her about Gracie. How much we loved each other. And how Gracie died.

Ivy's boyfriend, Marvin, a genius, was months away from his Master's Degree in Applied Mathematics when he was drafted into the Army, sent to Viet Nam where people would try to kill him and vice versa. There wasn't a day that went by that Ivy didn't burst into tears thinking of the unfairness of it all. Ivy Lincoln was another person I've met this week that I could trust enough to tell a redacted version of my story. It's a start.

The rain finally let up. We said our goodbyes.

"Now you be careful driving tonight. And don't you go picking up any hitchhikers. You hear me?"

"Roger that. Loud and clear. Over and out."

Ivy gave me a hug of all hugs and a pretty excellent kiss too. I can't help it.

I rolled slowly down the on-ramp, high beams on, alert for jungle cat buttons that might be lurking in the shadows. It was late and rainy. There wasn't another vehicle in sight. Every part of me said 'punch it.' I didn't.

It was almost too late when I remembered what *Catman* Dupree said, "Them tigresses, Lily and Toni, they'll sneak up on you from behind and bite you on the ass and worse. Way worse. So don't you go around telling people that I didn't warn you."

The tigress named Toni lay still in the drainage ditch near where the on ramp intersects with the highway. She had positioned herself there, presumably, to have an equal shot at east bound prey to the left and right of her. She had lowered her heart rate which had the effect of dimming her buttons.

My approaching headlights alerted her. Toni's buttons lit up like Christmas tree lights. I drew even with the big cat, gunned the engine, those 12 cylinders sounded a mighty roar, then I popped the clutch, put the pedal to the medal and swerved ahead. Toni ran onto the ramp behind me and charged. I hit the brakes and she leapt right over the *FERRARI*, landed ten yards beyond me and skidded another couple of feet on the wet asphalt. I hit her yellow button as she lifted her head to roar. A genuine Kodak moment. Never leave home without it.

◊◊

Chapter 26
the ferrari monologues

"I was just a lad, nearly twenty-two
Neither good nor bad, just a kid like you
And now I'm lost, too late to pray
Lord, I've paid the cost on the lost highway."

Lost Highway
~ Hank Williams

It took me almost eighteen minutes to catch up with the storm which was headed due east at about 20 miles an hour. I had to slow down to the minimum on the speed limit sign. Any faster and the car would start to hydroplane. The premium AM-FM radio was useless in thunder-stormy weather. I shut it off and focused on the road ahead and my life since Gracie was killed.

So typical American kids from typical American towns usually have their first turning points, the very first line of demarcation between their current, cozy lives and the unknowable territory called grammar school. Year after year, a life changing event after life changing event, until they slip the bonds of compulsory education and move on to discover the wonders of young adulthood.

My very first inflection point came earlier even than that, it was at Annabelle Gold's funeral. The way father explained it, Annabelle Gold was the wife of the richest man in the world and an important member of the *undzer shtick*. But not the boss. Moses Stern is the boss and will always be the boss.

"Stand up straight boychik, don't you fidget, don't pick your nose, and keep your mouth shut."

I was doing good. I really was. Until. Until the ceremony ended and the family escorted the casket to the burial ground. It rested on a shiny black catafalque drawn by a mare called Edwina.

At the end of the procession were the grandchildren, Benjamin, Eli, Eleanora and Grace Gold. I had never seen anything like Gracie Gold before, not anywhere. Not on the playgrounds, not on the television, not in the movies, not at the grocery, not in my dreams, or at the five and dime. That girl with the golden hair and blue blue eyes was magical, unique. I couldn't get her out of my mind. Not then or ever since.

"What's your name?" I asked, my finger pointed towards her.

She whispered 'Grace.' She put her forefinger to her lips. "Shush." Then she smiled at me. I'm not sure, but I think we might have set the world's record for being the youngest couple to experience 'true love at first sight.' I was almost five. Grace was too.

The funeral procession disappeared into the woods. Grace looked back at me and smiled.
I started to follow but my father grabbed ahold of my shoulder and said "Stay put Julius. She's out of your league, little man. Way out of your league." I didn't agree.

Over the years, Grace Gold and I saw each other, off and on, at get togethers on national holidays, a meager few hours per visit. One stands out as a before and after, life changing event, when things between Gracie and me got soulful, mystical, serious, intense. It was at Uncle Teddy's and Aunt Connie's combination Fourth of July picnic and my twelfth birthday celebration.

Mort, Max Gold, and Uncle Teddy grew up together in Center City, Philadelphia, way back in the days. They've remained close friends and business partners ever since. That year, Mort brought his wife, Dahlia, his twins, Eli and Ellie, and his sister-in-law, the famous tennis star Miriam 'Nettie' Gold, his nephew, Ben, and his niece, Grace, to the party. Turned out to be the best birthday ever.

You know how it is when you meet someone and hit it off right away? Well, it was like that with Gracie and me times a million. We wandered away from the organized activities into the forest behind Uncle T's house. We were walking side by side on the path that leads to my secret hideout. Gracie asked me, "Julius, what's it like to always have a huge party on your birthday? I mean everywhere you go, people are partying, shooting off fireworks to celebrate the day of your birth. Does it get into your head and make you all puffed up inside? Or is it humbling?" She looked me in the eye. Every part of her smiled at me. It was overwhelming. I wanted to feel like that forever.

"I dunno, I never thought of it that way. Why would I? I'll have you know that I do understand the difference between a person's birthday and a national holiday, and which is more significant."

"Well, tell me, which is more significant Julius Briscoe?"

"My birthday, of course." Back then, I had no idea how right I was.

"Race ya?" I took off into the forest. My hideout was about half a mile ahead. Gracie had no choice but to let me take the lead, kept about two paces behind, safe from a possible collision, close enough for taunting. Gracie was an expert.

"Can't you run any faster? I want to get home before Christmas."

"Really? That's your top speed?"

"I have a curfew, don't forget."

"Did you just poop your pants?"

"My Aunt Lizzie and my Mother run faster than you."

"Mister turtle foot please move aside."

I did. She turned on her jets and whizzed right past me. It took all I had to keep up with her, but I sure was glad that I did.

We were both pretty winded and leaned against this giant boulder and caught our breaths. Finally, Gracie smiled, giggled and said, "Yes."

"Yes?"

"Yes I'll marry you Julius Truman Briscoe." She leaned over and gave me a kiss on my cheek. And that was that. From that moment forward, it was settled. Gracie Gold and I were to be married someday in the future.

Grace's essence, not the memory of her, but the experience of her is at the foundation of my being. Every act of memory storage or retrieval has a Grace Gold component to it. What would Gracie think? What would she do? I don't see how I ever get past that.

Which brings me to my visit to Chicago and the bonding with my brother and his family and the encounters with VanNessa Kirkland-Robinson, Deidra DePalma, and

Jaimie Leventhal. The first women my age I've interacted with since Gracie's murder. My mother favored Deidre DePalma, mostly, I think, because DeeDee was the first contestant for my attentions that Mother met. VanNessa disqualified herself at the Thanksgiving dinner. And Jaimie? Well Jaimie is pretty special, I must tell you. She's bright, witty, talented, friendly and any other positive attributes you may have inferred from earlier passages. Jaimie's about five foot six, has blue eyes, strawberry blonde hair, a nervous tic that causes her left eye to blink at the most compromising moments. I liked her all right. I think I'd like to keep in touch with her if she's amenable.

This whole Novichok Situation is totally in a state of flux. Right now, on the one hand, I'm thinking Willie Novichok isn't going to see too much work from now on. Morgan Fields is dead. Lenny's new at the job, Uncle T is worried that my brother doesn't have the chops to vet and sign THE ERRAND BOYS' clientele. It's just now occurred to me that that I'm the most qualified to scrutinize potential clients. I am, after all, a walking talking infallible lie detector. The whole thing with Poole and Dallas? Shit, that could fade away or turn into the nightmare Lenny feared. Only time will tell.

On the other hand, it was just as likely that THE ERRAND BOYS would continue to do a modest natural death business. If you're someone tired of waiting on your rich mother/father/aunt/uncle/spouse/siblings/business partner/ rival to give up the ghost and kick the bucket, then you start to hear rumors and you hypothetically ask your lawyer about them. Well then, William Novichok at your service. Hypothetically.

Lenny questioned the morality of the whole undetectable murder-for-hire business. How could someone kill another person for money and then return home to his wife and family just like nothing at all unusual happened on his business trip?

Well, right now, I don't have a wife or family. My position is clear. If someone is willing to pay someone to kill someone else in a way that no one would call murder, well, someone will be willing to kill someone else in a way that would not arouse suspicions. Might as well be me. Functions in capitalist and Marxist economic theories equally well.

We don't take out full-page ads in major newspapers or commercials on late night TV or anything. People in the market for my sort of service find their way to people like me one way or another. Water seeks its own level, right? Besides, it's a cash business. Cash being the factor that motivated Lenny to be named salesman of the year after year after year by the CEO of THE ERRAND BOYS. Lenny needed off-the-books capital to fund his off-the-record activities.

I've killed people by accident, in self-defense, to prevent terrorist attacks, to avenge, and for money. I haven't needed to kill anyone since SHANGHAI SAL'S. And there is little doubt in my mind that sooner or later, for one reason or another, I would kill again.

I've already decided that for every contract job, I'll do a public service hit. Sorta like Junior Poole's fetish killings. Just not twisted or as random. My plan is to sit in the gallery of a criminal trial wherever a contract has taken me, and pass judgement on the defendant, letting his Status

Button determine his fate. I haven't done this yet, but will as soon as I go on an out of town assignment.

Then there is the matter of my brother Lenny, my niece Molly Anne and Ivy Lincoln. Like all Normals, they have buttons, yet somehow they seemed to have read my mind. I could read their Status Buttons as clearly as any I have ever encountered. Which means, according to previous assumptions, they should not possess paranormal abilities. No way that little kid could have come up with her answers otherwise, same with Lenny. Was Ivy's a wild guess, or the only conclusion she could reach that made any sense of what happened to Nicky from the ESSO station and that fucking tiger? Ivy gave off an earth-mother vibe of all encompassing acceptance. Maybe that was key.

I'm not one to worry, but I must admit that I think about *Tabula Rasa* at least twice a day, each and every day. I had single-handedly thwarted their initial attack on middle class sensibilities with its undertones of greedy profiteering. They had taken an elementary school building hostage, killed the Principal and two students before I could stop them. But stop them I did. The Shawnee Elementary terrorism incident generated national news stories for months, and turned JJ Cross, Special Agent in Charge Jasper Sexton and Chief Abe Polonski into household names.

The next *Tabula Rasa* target was in south Jersey. Atlantic City. They planned to blow up Boardwalk Hall at the crowning moment of the *Miss America Pageant*. I happened to be in Atlantic City with Gracie and her family. Her brother Ben had recently *pair*ed with Emma Sachs, *Miss Pennsylvania* the odds-on favorite to win the crown. We were all working on her team. Gracie and Nettie were

Emma's stylists. Dahlia was her singing, dancing and stage presence coach. Ben, Eli, Mort, Miles and I were her psychic body guards. And we were needed. Urgently so.

As it turned out, Emma and Gracie inadvertently identified one of the stagehands working the Miss America show. He was a member of both *Tabula Rasa* and the *Submariners.* We tracked him down to a three story rental in Margate City where I eliminated the threat. All eight of them. And sure enough, just last Tuesday, four *Tabula Rasa* assholes tried to hijack our flight to Chicago. What the fuck? What are the chances? Who's stalking who?

I often speculate on these issues. Am I attracted to terrorists or vice versa? I've checked at the Free Library and the *Bulletin's* newspaper morgue for stories about *Tabula Rasa.* All that came up were articles about the Shawnee Elementary tragedy. The FBI kept a lid on *Tabula Rasa's* failed plans for the *Miss America* pageant. As far as most people know, nothing happened. So far, I've dispatched fourteen *Tabula Rasas.* If it weren't for the armed Mummers on United flight #505, I probably would have killed four more. Do I feel any remorse? Regrets? Fuck no.

According to Special Agent in Charge Sexton, *Tabula Rasa* has chapters on college and university campuses all over the planet. Hundreds, if not thousands, of well ~~educated~~ indoctrinated, crazy firebrands with no shot at a productive life, and nothing better to do than to either sit around and bitch about the unfairness of it all, or go forth into the world and kill little kids and blow up municipal buildings. The kind of people that have tormented Normals, under one banner or another, since before ancient times. Maybe that answers the 'why me?' question. What caused me to have these abilities? Was there an enigmatic wizard/ master/sensei in my future to prepare me for a mythic adventure against the forces of evil in the coming years, or was I just running out of gas and coffee?

I crossed the Ohio State line about half an hour before daybreak. I was low on gas, had to take a leak and was hungry. There was a full service plaza twenty minutes to the east. I wasn't five miles into Ohio when the radar detectors started chirping. I obeyed the speed limit all the way to the JAMES R. GARFIELD SERVICE PLAZA. It was laid out like the two I'd stopped at before and the three I would visit afterwards. The gas station attendant was in his too-late twenties, artificially cheerful, jaundiced, shifty-eyed, yet obsequious idiot named Warren Malloy, if his name badge was to be believed.

"Goodness gracious! What on earth are you driving, boy?" Malloy was one of those guys whose father was a defective alpha male who always challenged his son and always bested him. Gloated about it. Rubbed it into his fate. What was a boy like Warren to do? He took it out on the rest of the world. That's what guys like Warren do. A serial criminal offender in the making.

"Fill her up, check under the hood, don't forget the tires and wash the bug carcasses off of the windscreen, please good fellow. Snap to it, I haven't all day." I did my best to sound like good old Milton Armitage, with deliberate, genuine, earnest condescension. A preppy stereotype, if there ever was one. It got under Warren's skin. Good. I'm tired of Normals like him. I've been working on this new chord I call FEAR ME®. Which is sorta like FEAR AND LOATHING® minus the vomiting and/or soiling of one's undergarments. Worked well enough on poor old Nicky, didn't it?

"So what's a thing like this cost?"

"I have no idea, I won it in a card game."

"Don't be a prick, man. It ain't everyday a guy like me gets to see a car like this. How about you let me take it for a spin? You could get the breakfast special at the BOB EVANS, and I'd be back before you finished your grits."

There was, of course, no chance I'd let a Normal drive my car, what with millions and millions in cash, jewels, and maybe valuable artwork stowed in the aft cabin. I hit Warren with about a half dose of FEAR ME® and told him to stop wasting my time. I can be a real prick when necessary. Warren wanted to give me a dirty look, a threatening scowl, spit in my face. Anything. Every time he tried, he chickened out, which fueled his self-loathing. FEAR ME® works great and seems to be scalable. It's gonna be a valuable weapon in my arsenal, that's for sure.

I took a booth in the BOB EVANS restaurant in the ULYSSES S. GRANT HOSPITALITY CENTER. I had a clear line of sight to my car which looked beautiful in the morning light. My waitress was named Babs and reminded me of Deidre DePalma, demeanor wise. Droll and sarcastic, capable of extreme cruelty.

A skinny guy dressed up like Brando in *The Wild One*, slid onto the bench across from me and just sat there and tried to stare me down. I knew this game, it's a variation of FLINCH, one of those childhood games that usually gets incorporated into more sophisticated ones. Every once in awhile, you encounter a throwback. Think I'll call this fella

'Cro-Magnon Mike.' I hit his pause button. My meal would be here any minute.

As expected, Babs returned with my breakfast, a pot of piping hot coffee and an apology. "I'm so very sorry young man. We've tried every kind of spray there is, but they just keep coming back. Law enforcement's no help either." She turned to Cro-Magnon Mike and said "Malloy, you low life piece of shit, get your ugly ass out of here. Stop bothering my paying customers."

"Be Cool, Babs. He was just leaving."

I unfroze Cro-Magnon Malloy and munched on my bagel as he tried to overwhelm the disorientation with bravado. Never works. I chewed slowly between grins. Malloy was entertaining. Then he got around to being stupid, "That your car out there, the white *FERRARI?*"

"Yes it is. There's twenty or more people of driving age having their breakfast in here just now. So why single me out?"

"Well 'cause my cousin Warren called me up and told me all about you and your car. You don't seem so bad-ass to me. No offense."

"None taken. So what the fuck do you want?"

"I just want to know if it is as fast as it looks."

"Oh, I'd say it's faster than that."

"No shit? Mind if I see for myself. Gimme the keys and let me take her for a spin while you enjoy your breakfast."

"You can't be serious."

"Deadly serious, my man." He put his left hand into the pocket of his motorcycle jacket and pointed his forefinger at me.

"You dumb asshole. Get The Fuck Out Of Here."

He did.

There are approximately two thousand one hundred and sixteen overpasses between the James R. Garfield Service Plaza and the Center City exit from Interstate 76. Each one was a reminder of Atlas City and the punks that killed Gracie. Each under passing served up the same course of emotions; anger, heartbreak, loss, emptiness, fury, wrath and vengeance. Exactly the therapy I needed. Each transit beneath an overpass helped me confront the feelings of guilt for not staying with the caravan that horrible afternoon.

We hadn't gone six miles on the Atlantic City Expressway when Gracie's caravan pulled into the Pleasantville service plaza. I had filled my tank the day before and neither Miles nor I were hungry so we drove on ahead. I had more than enough gas for the rest of the week. Grace died before we crossed the Ben Franklin Bridge. Would've it mattered if I had stayed in formation? Yeah, a solid maybe. Maybe I would have spotted the fools on the overpass, maybe I would have been able to read their intent, and maybe I could have stopped them cold. If I was in range and standing still, most definitely. At seventy-five miles an hour? No fucking way. That morning, it took me over fifteen hundred encounters with overpasses to reach that conclusion.

Hitting a target while operating a moving platform requires practice.
A skill I hadn't thought was necessary to hone. Most of the Status Buttons
I observed on the overpasses were in an automobile or truck. Few, if any, were pedestrians. So miscreants like the Atlas City Three would have stood out like a buffalo fart in a crowded express elevator.

I've come to realize, even with 20-20 hindsight, that there was little or nothing I could have done that would have saved Gracie Gold from her fate. If it was Gracie's fate to die young, then it must also have been her fate to not marry me and to not bear our children. That must mean that I am either destined to live a life of solitude constrained by my abilities or someone even more amazing than Gracie Gold was in my future. What are the chances?

◊◊

Chapter 27
look who's back in town

"Some days I feel like my shadow's casting me
Some days the sun don't shine."

My Dirty Life and Times
~ Warren Zevon

There was another new guy manning the Z^2's parking garage ticket booth. He stepped out, a time-stamped ticket in hand and announced, "It's fifty cents an hour, five bucks a day, forty-five bucks a month. Tell me, what kind of car is that?"

"It's a FERRARI. I'm Julius Briscoe, Vice President of Personnel with UNIVERSAL IMPORT-EXPORTS on P-10. We own six or seven parking passes. Please Respect Me and let me through." He thought for a moment or two, then reached into a hip pocket and withdrew a well-worn hip pocket-sized spiral notepad, leafed through the pages, found what he was looking for, replaced the notepad, went into the booth, and retrieved a three-ring binder, the one that contained the names of the tenants with parking privileges. "What did you say your name was again, young fella?" I retold him. He apologized for his error. It was only his second day. Or so he said. Normals.

"Here's a sticker to put on your windshield. Have yourself a wonderful day Mr. Briscott."

I drove down to level P-10 and parked next to my Jaguar. Uncle Teddy had given me the keys to his kingdom. I'd be staying in the penthouse until they came back from Europe. I went into UNIVERSAL IMPORT-EXPORTS, retrieved the Armadillo Wagon, loaded my booty into it, locked the *FERRARI* and wheeled the wagon into the building.

The elevator across the hall from our office door chimed. I focused on it. As near as I could tell, it was descending but not transporting anything threatening. No one at all was inside that car. Then why stop here? The elevator door opened to reveal Miles Gold, dapper as always, amused by the not-so-coincidental timing of his arrival to P-10. In case you've forgotten, the Gold men do not have buttons; they're kinda like me. They're remote viewers. They can see what another person sees, which is handy enough in a card game, but the Golds also can affect a person's vision, causing their victims to experience temporary blindness, which often causes a loss of balance and, occasionally, of life.

"So a trusted source eagerly told me that someone in a rare Italian sports car just pulled into my building, and that it was something to see. I'm here to see it. You as well, young Julius Briscoe, if I must. Welcome home young man." We laughed and gangsta hugged.

"Good to see you Miles, you're looking sharp this morning. Before I show you the car, let me show you what I've got here in the Armadillo Wagon. I led Miles back to my office, it actually has my name and title painted on the door. *'Julius Truman Briscoe, Vice President, Personnel,'* something Uncle T had done as a surprise.

"Your own office? Julius you are moving up in the world quite rapidly. It's heartening to learn young man, overwhelmingly so. You're an inspiration to us all." He winked.

I motioned Miles to walk ahead of me into my office. I followed leading the Armadillo Wagon to the safe in the northwest corner. I unlocked the safe and the wagon and we began to unload and catalog. Miles is an experienced, astute, businessman. He took charge of evaluating the foreign currency, when he finished he said, "Julius all that foreign money is worth roughly eight or nine million US, the gold bullion about five hundred grand. But don't liquidate it right away. Hold on to it for as long as you can. Gold always increases in value. The dollar does not. Keep it as a hedge. The jewels easily are worth a couple of million if one is patient about fencing them. The art, well I haven't seen the art yet, have I?"

We finished loading the safe. There wasn't any room left in it for the two million from the Morgan Fields contract. I guess I was gonna need a bigger safe sooner than later. I closed and locked it, closed and locked the office doors and led Miles to the garage.

"That is something alright. How's it to drive?"

"Well it was designed for high speed driving on European roads, and it performs well. I can't wait to take her to Turtle Creek Trail and see how she handles a challenge like that."

"Turtle Creek Trail? I'm not familiar."

I keep forgetting that Miles Gold is somewhere in his seventies, maybe even his eighties. He looks much younger. No one, not even Miles knows exactly how old he might be. Myron Zoloto was born in a cave in southeastern France towards the end of the century. The nineteenth one. His appetites for the crazy challenges of youth were never quenched when they should have been. When Miles Gold could have been exploring the winding back roads of Montgomery County in an automobile designed to master them, he was hard a work starting a business and a family in the new world. He's a genuine American success story. Rags, well very nice ones, to riches just like it says in all of the promotional brochures.

"Turtle Creek Trail? Miles, it's just off Upper Gulph Road in Radnor Groves. There are dozens of double and triple switchbacks. Plenty of twisty and hairpin turns. All of them are unbanked. It's way fun to drive. I can't wait to see what my *Ferrari* or your Bugatti can do on a road like that.

I unlocked the car and carefully removed the paintings. Each had been wrapped in heavy, brown, waterproofed paper when we found them in Fields' safe. I didn't want to take the time to unwrap and rewrap them. I had no idea what I had. Maybe dogs playing poker with velvet Elvis? We brought them back into the office and set them down on the conference/lunch table and carefully unwrapped them. My first look at what I took from Fields' safe as an afterthought. The partners had expected William Novichok would empty the safe after he finished with Dr. Fields. I needed to live up to their expectations, hadn't I?

"Holy shit, Julius. You ought to sit down. Blimey, I ought to sit down myself."

I'd never seen Miles Gold like that. Miles does not produce a Status Button so I've learned to read his moods the old fashioned Normal way. It was like he had shed thirty maybe forty years in seconds. Miles Gold was excited, elated, energized. I imagined wheels spinning triple-time in his head.

Miles Gold is a talented artist himself. His drawings and sketches are excellent in their own right. He also is a major donor to the Philadelphia Museum of Art and is on its board of trustees. When it comes to works of art, it's safe to say that Miles Gold totally knows his shit.

"Julius, these paintings are worth millions, hundreds and hundreds of them."

"Are you serious?"

"Very. This one is the van Gogh that disappeared shortly before WWII. It was thought to have been destroyed. If it were put up for public auction, it would likely bring a quarter of a billion dollars at the least. That Raphael is easily worth a hundred million. Also said to be stolen by the Nazis. This Picasso disappeared from a museum in Paris five years ago, if I remember correctly. There's a generous reward for its return. I believe those pastels were painted by Claude Monet. And this landscape, I can't believe my eyes, is a Rembrandt. Julius you just fell into a giant pot of money. How does it feel? You're gonna be as rich as Rockefeller. Perhaps more so."

"I'm at a loss for words, Miles. My first reaction was 'I can't wait to tell Gracie,' you know? And I can't tell Gracie, now can I? It'll probably sink in later."

"After the Longstride job, Miles, I thought I had more than enough cash to last us a lifetime. Gracie's idea of heaven was to buy a cabin cruiser and sail around and around and around the world. Those paintings could buy us a fucking fleet. The irony. The fucking cruel irony."

"Jules, you really cannot put any of these up for auction. Too many questions to answer. Your paranormal gifts can't help you produce provenances that are either long lost or were never generated. These are best suited for the black market. And I happen to know a thing or two about that. Julius, let me make you a fair offer for the Van Gogh the Raphael and the Rembrandt. Please give me a couple of days to do the research and to have the paintings authenticated in our presence, of course, by an expert from the museum."

Miles went out to the elevator lobby and retrieved a luggage cart from one of the elevator cars. We loaded it up with my brief cases and the custom suitcase and the six re-wrapped paintings and wheeled it onto the first available elevator.

The state-of-the-art express elevator takes fewer than two minutes to travel from the ground floor lobby to the sixtieth floor. I asked Miles one of the questions that has been dogging my mind since I met Jaimie Leventhal, "Miles, I hope you don't mind me asking, but after your wife passed, how come you didn't *pair* with someone else?"

"Well I don't know for certain, but I do have a theory. My guess is that because Annabelle and I had brought gifted sons and grandsons into the world, all of them have the *sicht,* we had fulfilled our supernatural purpose. I never again experienced anything close to *pair*ing. But I did come to love again. I had ordered an engagement ring to give to Corrine. But before it was ready, before I could ask her for her hand, she was gone. Murdered by that scumbag Lloyd Longstride."

"But you Julius, you and Gracie, I don't believe you ever *pair*ed. At least not in the way we Zolotos have *pair*ed. As I remember, you told us about the time when you were both twelve years old and felt an energy pass between you. Maybe it was a pre-adolescent *pair*ing, most likely it was a communal sugar high. I believe that if you're destined to have a *pair*ing-like experience it will happen in the near future. The universe is probably just waiting for you to heal."

Uncle Teddy and Aunt Connie's penthouse apartment faces southwest, has three bedroom suites and was furnished with the kind of bulky pieces that Connie Briscoe adored. They could have come from some long-lost ancient eastern European castle or something, they were ornately carved, massive, heavy, dark and domineering. They were hidden in a forgotten corner of one of Mo Stern's warehouses that had been transferred, for tax purposes, to Sandra Showalter. Mrs. Showalter studied the collection, thought of Aunt Connie who loved such pieces. And the rest, is natural history.

I moved all of my stuff into the guest bedroom suite and carefully placed the paintings on the boot shelves in the walk-in closet. I slipped the briefcases under the bed. The evidence against Junior Poole and Dr. Fields and the two million would be placed in my safety deposit box in ZOLOTO SAVINGS AND LOAN first thing Monday morning. I unpacked my suitcase, sorted my dirty laundry just like all of the women in my life taught me to do which resulted in eight unequal piles. I rearranged them into something more workable and then took a nice hot shower.

I carried my laundry to the utility room where I discovered that Aunt Connie and Uncle T were fresh out of Oxydol. Just a sprinkle of powder on the bottom of the box remained. I doubted that Miles Gold stocked any laundry supplies in his penthouse, so it was either knock on Mort and Dolly's or Nettie's doors or take the elevator to the lobby and visit MARTINELLI'S a posh, upscale grocery store on the ground floor of the ZOLOTO ARCADE.

The Golds are all able to switch *sicht* on and off whenever they want. Which is something I greatly envy. I cannot turn off whatever *IT* is I have. I've never given *IT* a name, mainly because I've always believed that *IT* was a temporary thing. Soon to be lost in a stream of shimmering memories. I now believe *IT* is not temporary. Believe I'll call *IT slam.* Status Buttons from this moment forward I will think of as *SB's*.

The doorbell rang. I was far enough from the front door that all I could tell was that I had a visitor. As I approached the entryway, the *SB* resolved into Emma's. Could Ben Gold be far behind? I willed myself to be brave, strong and noble and opened the door.

Two out of three ain't bad. There was nothing noble in my thinking. Emma Sachs was as beautiful and as Gracie-like as I remembered. I flashed on an entire sequence of events that led to the violent death of Benjamin Franklin Gold, me consoling the distraught Emma Sachs, dosing her with LOVE POTION NUMBER NINE® three times a day. Where did that come from?

We smiled at each other and I invited them in.

"So Julius, how was Chicago? What's your brother like?"

"Well Ben, Lenny reminds me of father. He looks a lot like Dad, has a wife and two kids. They live in a cool house near the lake. Ben, do you guys have any laundry soap? Ted and Connie ran out."

"I don't know, probably. You know mother, she never runs out of anything. Well except for her sanity. Jules all she does all day is seethe and grieve. When we're in Gladwyne Falls, she walks to Eli's shooting range behind Mort and Dahlia's three times a day to practice firing rifles and sidearms under different lighting conditions. Eli told me that he saw her toting a crossbow to the range one day last week. Julius, I'm worried that Mother might be planning a hunting trip to the Pine Barrens. We need to talk her out of it.

Ben was doing his best to avoid saying anything that would cause Emma to pick up on the subtext.

"Maybe I can cheer her up. Nettie's like a second mom to me. I'll bet I'll have a smile on her face in no time. So Emma, are you psyched for tonight?"

"I am Jules. I am. Once the White House announced that President Johnson was attending, it turned into this huge big deal. I'd call it a cluster fuck, but use of that expression is specifically prohibited in the official *Miss America* Handbook and Spiritual Guide. All of a sudden, everyone and I do mean everyone wants to be part of the dedication. All of the Kennedys are attending as well as the Mayor, the Governor, Pennsylvania's senators, Hugh Scott and good old Joe Clark, Lloyd Bridges, Frank Sinatra, Johnny Carson, Groucho Marx and Walter Cronkite. And there's sure to be more by the time we get to the stadium. They keep changing things around. They just now called to tell us that we're going to enter from the east side instead of the west. So now President Johnson and Lady Bird are to my left and the Mayor and the Governor are to my right. Julius, it ain't easy being *Miss America*." She was buzzed on something. Ben and I know many of the same people.

"Why the all of a sudden switcheroo?"

"For the television cameras. They're all set up to shoot the game from the west side of the stadium. I don't know why it took them so long to figure that shit out? So Julius, how was your trip to Chicago? You weren't on that plane, were you?"

"We were. Most of the passengers in coach were law enforcement and all of them were armed. Only one person was killed. One of the skyjackers. The other three were captured and we landed in Chicago sooner than advertised. My visit was fine. I hadn't seen my brother Leonard since our father was murdered. I met his wife and children for the first time. Check it out, I have a niece and a nephew. And, I bought a *FERRARI*."

"Seriously? A *FERRARI*. Which model?" I told him. Ben said he couldn't wait to see it and then looked at his watch, "Jules we stopped by to offer you lunch, mother ordered deli. She's eager to see you."

To be frank, Nettie Gold looked like shit. Miriam Beachum-Steenbeck Gold has lived long enough to lose her parents, her husband, Georgia and Ben, Annabelle Gold, who was her mentor and best friend and mother-in-law, her niece Eleanora, and her beloved daughter Grace Edna. Each succeeding loss reminded her of previous losses and how much each person meant to her. A whirlpool of melancholy nearly impossible for Nettie to escape. It was my mission to rescue her.

We were in Miriam's office/trophy room. There were photos of Nettie with celebrities from all walks of life. Gold-plated trophies from long-ago victories.

I *slammed* Nettie with a cocktail of REAL TIME AMNESIA®, TRUST ME!®, and DOLLY®. She won't remember the details of our conversation, but she will totally believe that Gracie's murder has been properly avenged. All of that pain, anguish, and intolerable sadness would soon be locked in an internal drop-safe designed to hold such unpleasant memories.

"So Nettie, Ben tells me you're taking target practice on the back forty. You going after big game? I heard that the circus animals roaming around northern Indiana have all been captured or killed, so there no longer is a need for so much target practice."

"No Julius. I'm going to kill the sons of bitches that murdered our darling Gracie."

"You're too late for that Nettie, those sons of bitches are already dead."

"How can you know that Jules? Those high muckety-schmucks in Atlas City won't tell me shit."

"I know that because I'm the one who killed them. You didn't think I'd let anyone get away with killing our darling Gracie? Did you?"

"But how Julius, when?"

"It took me most of October. I didn't just kill those three assholes, Nettie. I wiped out their entire families, their school teachers, the judge, the lawyers and the cops that looked the other way. They either died a painful, horrible death or they're now confined to a nursing home. Deafened, blinded and muted. The last thing they remember, the last thing they saw before their world went dark was my face. The last thing they heard was my voice whispering, "This is for Grace Gold. Rot in hell mother-fucker."

Nettie began to laugh and to weep silently. Tears ran down her face and splattered onto her collar bone.

"Mother Gold why are you crying?"

"Because Julius, it is so sweet of you to create such an elaborate fable for me. It just doesn't make any sense. How could anyone murder so many people in so short a time in a small town and get away with it?"

"Nettie dear, I'm thirsty. Would you mind fetching me something to drink?"

Never leave home without it.

Chapter 28
tabula redux

"Look what's happening out on the streets
Got a revolution, got to revolution."

Volunteers
~ Marty Balin, Paul Kantner

Philadelphia Municipal Stadium was built in the 1920s to be the centerpiece of the Sesquicentennial celebration to be held in 1926. It had a regulation clay track surrounding an infield large enough for baseball, and soccer or American football games to be played simultaneously. It helped make Philadelphia a contender to host the 1928 Olympics. Unfortunately, Philly was out politicked by the Netherlands. Municipal Stadium could seat a hundred thousand in the stands and another hundred thousand on the infield. It would go on to host some of the biggest rock and roll shows of all time.

The stadium was too large for the Phillies and A's and the Eagles regular season games. Too many seats to fill. Not enough fans to fill them. Consequently it was only used sporadically. Maybe half a dozen events a year including the ARMY-NAVY GAME.

Mort Gold and Uncle T own a black car service called THE CENTER CITY CARRIAGE COMPANY. We rode to the stadium in their flagship limousine, a gleaming white, stretch Rolls Royce Phantom V. The very same one Gracie had her heart set on for our wedding day.

The 75th Army-Navy Game was not sold out. When we arrived at our seats, the stadium was already about half full. The early birds are the most dedicated fans of their favorite team or of public intoxication or of both. Without having said a word to one and other, we began scanning the stadium using our paranormal abilities. All the way across the field on the Army side, directly opposite us, straddling the top three rows and four seats wide, was a television camera platform. It was not in use for tonight's game due to budgetary and continuity concerns. It was constructed with two-by-fours and two inch plywood and painted municipal green and was covered by some kind of tarp. Any shot of the field from that position would show the players moving in the opposite direction from what the main cameras showed. Not only that, but the cost of deploying high bandwidth triaxial cable from the production truck to that location was, at five dollars a running foot, prohibitive.

From this distance, I could make out a hostile *SB* underneath that platform. Every so often, one of those stadium vendors, an insulated box containing perhaps hot or cold beverages or hot or cold snacks, slung over his shoulders, walked to the landing at the top of the stairs and disappeared behind the camera platform and stayed put for about two minutes or so. Then he'd head down the opposite set of stairs as another vendor was heading up. I needed to get closer to that platform. I had one of my celebrated hunches. Seemed to me that it was very likely that these people had smuggled a sniper rifle or worse past the Secret Service in *'Get your Ice Cold Beer'* refrigerated with dry ice boxes. Beneath that dry ice was a secret compartment containing one piece of a stripped down high powered weapon. Just a theory. But a good one. One worth investigating.

I huddled with Miles, uncleDad, and Eli and explained the situation. Then Eli and I walked to the top of the stadium and made our way around to the opposite side of the field. Hopefully in time to foil what looked like to me to be an assassination plot. Whoever those guys were, they clearly hadn't received the memo about the change of entrance plans. From that side of the stadium, the shooter wouldn't have a clear shot at the President until he reached the middle of the field.

Lyndon Baines Johnson is tall all right, but his Secret Service guys are probably taller. Add to that the Cadets and Midshipmen standing at attention on either side of the pathway. The shooter wouldn't be able to correctly identify the target until LBJ began speaking. I checked my Rolex. We had plenty of time for us to reach the shooter's position and neutralize the mother fucker.

I wasn't planning on killing him. I was going to *slam* his Truth button, paralyze him and leave him for the authorities. He'd sing like a canary and give them every thing they needed to track down and destroy whoever was behind this operation. Deep down, I already knew.

It took Eli and me ten minutes to walk to the opposite side of the stadium and take a position behind the camera platform. For privacy, the sides of the platform's superstructure had been covered with olive drab canvas, likely requisitioned from a decommissioned Army tent. There was a rectangular window covered with a black see-through mesh facing the field, made the whole thing look like a low-rent skybox. We were now close enough for Eli to *connect* to the shooter's *eyestream.*

The shooter was seated on the back row eating an apple and surveilling the stadium with military spec field glasses. His weapon, similar to the one Oswald purportedly used, was resting on the back of the seat ahead of him. My reading of the shooter's *SB* told me that he was calm, focused, intelligent and delusional.

Eli observed, "he can't make any kind of a shot from his position. Once the ceremonies begin, everyone's going to be up on their feet and our pal isn't going to have a shot on anything except people's backsides. So either he's going to climb up onto that platform to get a clear shot, or maybe there's something else going on."

"Can you see anything that might be a transmitter, a remote detonator or a walkie talkie?"

Eli closed his eyes and stood very still. "Right now he's watching the crowd through binoculars. Julius, he's scanning the stands and the entrance ways on the opposite side of the stadium and every so often quickly returns to the podium on the platform at midfield. Looks like he's going to shoot the President when it's his turn to speak. So what do you think we should do?"

"Let's piss him off." We climbed onto the camera platform, yelled and chanted "Go Army Go." We stomped our feet on the wooden deck mimicking the steps I learned from Molly Anne. Tapedy, tap, tap, tap. "Go Cadets Go." Tapedy, tap, tap, tap. Etcetera.

Eli remained *connect*ed to the shooter who put the binoculars into a ditty bag and retrieved a silenced semi-automatic, checked the chamber then nothing. The shooter stopped moving, stopped seeing, hearing, remembering. "Julius what the fuck are you up to?"

"Well, you know I talked about handing him over to the feds, but the more I thought about it, the more I realized it was a bad, no, make that a terrible idea. First of all, I am a much better interrogator than any FBI guy, and second of all, there's no way the FBI would share anything they might get out of this asshole with anyone. And I really need to know who the shooter's working with and what else they might be trying to pull off tonight. After the game may be way too late. And I really didn't want to get shot in the foot. Let's go have a face-to-face with that asshole."

We climbed down off the platform and stood by the entry flap and strategized. "He has accomplices, at least two that I saw smuggling the rifle parts up here. So there could be more, and you can bet your ass they're all dangerous. So be on the lookout for someone that might be checking on the sniper." Eli looked down towards the field. Up there in nosebleed heaven there were no assigned seats. Just first come, first seated. Being the least desirable of all the cheap seats, no one was seated closer than twenty rows downslope from us. Eli *connect*ed to the *eyestream* of the Army fan seated on the aisle seat of row EE. Then we entered the assassin's lair.

We found the paused shooter, a silenced forty five automatic in her right hand pointed towards the ceiling. My would be killer was a young woman whose *Tabula Rasa* title was *Aristotle Friedan.* Her slaver name was Meredith Carver-Bradford of the Andover Carver-Bradfords. A bona fide Boston Brahmin, an ordained *Have,* ministering to the downtrodden *Have Nots* of the world.

I relieved her of her weapons and personal items and checked for tattoos and needle marks before unfreezing her. She had the beginnings of a tattoo on her left wrist, probably a Lady Rolex. The words *'Sic Semper Tyrannis'* were tattooed in an arc on her left deltoid. She was wearing a school ring from Phillips Academy, class of 1960. A good sized ruby in a 24 carat gold setting. The most exquisite class ring I've ever seen.

One thing that's absolute, the longer you're paused, the more difficult the recovery. Relatively speaking, five minutes isn't a terribly long time to be in suspended animation. Some of my patients had been frozen for hours. Usually I'm not around for their re-awakenings. I had little choice but to deal with whatever Meredith Carver-Bradford's reaction might be like. It was pretty unusual. I was nose-to-nose with her when I abruptly unfroze her. The paranormal equivalent of ripping a grimy band-aid off of a skinned knee. She screamed. Loudly. ZOMBIE MODE® to the rescue. ZMODE® is not all that different from being paused. The subject can move, but only when instructed to do so.

"Please be quiet. You've probably noticed that you can't speak even if you want to. And it seems to me that you might have something on your mind that you'd like to share with Eli and me. Am I correct? You're free to shake your head yes or no." She shook her head yes. I'm Tom. Tom Farrell, by the way, thanks for asking"

"Here's the deal, I'll allow you to speak your mind after you've answered my questions and not before. Is that clear?" She indicated that it was.

"Tell me your name and where you're from." She complied. What choice did she have?

"I know that there are people working with you. Where are they now? What are they up to?"

She told me. I didn't like what she told me. Forced a change of plans. I froze her solid. Which means that I pushed her central yellow button as well as those on her body that govern specific muscle groups. She cannot unfreeze without my assistance.

JFK Memorial Stadium has forty entrances/exits evenly distributed around the horseshoe shaped structure. What the fiendish *Tabula Rasas* had in mind was gruesome. They expected that once the President had been shot, the crowd would stampede towards the stadium exits which would be coated with home-made napalm and ignited at the decisive moment. Those that chose to remain inside the stadium would be *Aristotle Friedan's* to toy with.

There were six members of the Center City chapter of *Tabula Rasa* stationed around the Stadium prepared to spray the exits with a potent homemade concoction that burns hot enough to melt steel and concrete in seconds. It would be *Tabula Rasa's* contribution to the anti-war effort. Fucking idiots.

Our plan was to race down to ground level and try to locate and neutralize the assholes before they started to spraying the exits. I handed the gun to Eli. He would need it more than I would if things got ugly. He unscrewed the silencer and put it and the 45 in his leather jacket pockets. "If I have to shoot someone, the silencer isn't going to matter. The shit will hit the fan either way. And you can't fire any more than two rounds through one of those things. They heat up too fast and they negatively impact accuracy and even could blow up in your hand. Good for one shot up close and then you gotta shitcan it. Good thing I brought my gloves."

We raced down the stairs to ground level and walked out onto the arcade with its concession stands, restrooms and pay phones. I found the first terrorist right away. He was stationed two exits north of us. His SB was tranquil. Maybe he was stoned, maybe he was meditating, visualizing the pain about to come, hearing the screams that would quickly follow, and anticipating those smells. I slammed him with TRUTH and ZOMBIE modes. He gave up the locations of his co-conspirators. In next to no time, Eli and I assembled and disarmed a flock of zombified *Tabula Rasas* and had led it back to its camera platform clubhouse.

I used the walled in sniper's nest as an interrogation room and started with *Aristotle Friedan's* worker bees. All six of them told a similar sad sad story of growing up nerdy, scorned and ridiculed; science whizzes with full scholarships to the Drexel Institute of Technology where they learned to make super-napalm and perfected the revolutionary delivery system they weren't going to deploy that evening.

They were all proud members of *Tabula Rasa,* who worshipped Meredith Carver-Bradford and would do anything to please her. Anything. Other than that, none of them knew shit. Mistress Meredith said do this. They did this. Mistress Meredith said do that. They did that. Voluntary Zombie mode. Ain't those anarchist Normals just the cutest?

The napalmers sounded earnest enough, their SB's told me that they were truthful. Their only motivation was their devotion to *Aristotle Friedan.* Too bad fellas, you conspired to murder hundreds maybe even thousands of red blooded American football fans. All the best demographics; men and women eighteen to fifty four and their minor children. For that you shall receive no mercy.

I've named my latest concoction after the terrorists that keep crossing my path. I call it TABULA RASA®. You might have already figured out what it does. TABULA RASA® is a complete, total, irreversible memory wipe. After the game, those six would be shaken awake and screaming by the stadium clean up crew. They would have no idea who or what they were or where they belonged. It was a toss up about whether to let them retain language and other rudimentary skills like toileting and grooming. I flipped an imaginary two headed coin, and let them keep the fundamentals. I'm such a softie.

Kick-off was scheduled for 6:09 on the dot. Television people are sticklers for punctuality. All of the speechifying would be done before the 6 o'clock airtime except for President Johnson's. He had but one whole minute between six o two and six o three. Fresh from winning the election, one minute was not enough time for LBJ to reminisce about and to lionize John Fitzgerald Kennedy with ample time remaining for some good old fashioned politicking. Lyndon Baines Johnson would go five minutes and eighteen seconds over and would have gone far longer had not one ambitious assistant director cued the Marine Band…

From the halls of Montezuma to the shores of Tripoli…

The network cut away to a commercial break. The field was cleared and ready for kickoff in fewer than two minutes and twenty eight seconds.

And now, for the main event. Julius Briscoe, truth giver and irresistible force, versus Meredith Carver-Bradford, degenerate liar, seductress, murderess, pamphleteer, revolutionist, heiress and charter member of the Mayflower Society. She was still frozen-solid. Without going all techie detailed about it, frozen-solid cannot be undone by any of the world's greatest physicians, bio-weapons experts, faith healers, snake oil or energy drink salesmen. It can only be undone by me. Don't know what the long term effects might be should something unpleasant happen to yours truly. Fortunately for Meredith nothing happened that would prevent me from defrosting the perpetually icy debutante.

According to the 1962 Bryn Mawr College Yearbook, *Merrie* loved, "men who aren't afraid to cry, long solitary walks on deserted beaches, reading Shakespeare by a roaring fire, a Saint Bernard slumbering at her feet and a Siamese cat reading over her shoulder, Jacquline Susann novels, Betty Friedan and that sexy David Bowie."

Did I mentioned foul-mouthed bitch? Forgive me I should have. Most people when they're unfrozen, act out, often violently. Meredith sat stock still across from me staring into my eyes and breathing slowly. Her *SB* wasn't giving anything away. Her textures were a standing wave, her colors were pastels, it was as if she hadn't a care in the world.

She was, of course, the first to speak, "Who the fuck are you? Who the fuck sent you? Do you fucking know who I am?" It was getting pretty boring. I interrupted, "who I am isn't all that important. What I can do, what I'm willing to do to you, that's what is important."

I hesitated. Memories of what happened to Morgan Fields sprang up and left me with doubts.

I didn't want to do something that might end up killing her before I could get answers. Was *Tabula Rasa* as sophisticated as those unknown suzerains behind the Kennedy assassination? Could they have done something to Meredith that could kill or incapacitate her should she try to speak the truth? Only one way to find out. I hit her with a Truth® bomb and after giving it a thought or two added Real Time Amnesia® to the mix, which would, theoretically, bypass any booby traps embedded in her mind. Meredith wouldn't be able to lie to anyone and would believe everything I said without question and forget all about it when we finished chatting. And, on the plus side, she'd still be able to remember her name, address, and phone number. Some femme fatales have all the luck.

I asked her non-threatening questions about her personal history. Where she grew up, where she went to school, who her friends were, favorite movies, songs, tv shows. Normal chit chatty stuff. She was good. She kept her defenses up. It was time to fight dirtier.

One thing about Normals from Meredith's side of the tracks was their self-consciousness. From day one, they're told how, when and where to eat, poop and sleep, to stand up straight, and how to behave, especially in front of grandfather Bradford.

"Meredith Carver-Bradford, you look a terrible fright. Like a common commoner. Hard day?"

"The fucking worst."

At that very moment, LBJ began his speech, "My fellow Americans, we gather here in Philadelphia, the birthplace of America, of Freedom and dignity for all mankind….."

"That fucker. That dumb ass Texas goat fucker. I'm supposed to kill that son of a bitch." She lunged for the rifle on the row below her. Somehow she lost her balance, fell forward and slammed her head into the top of the seat back in front of her. Cut a half moon shaped gash in her forehead. She rose stunned and woozy. "Sit down. Do it now." I hit her with a double shot of OBEY®. No more Mr. Nice Guy, time's a wasting.

The good news was that there were no more active threats from her *Tabula Rasa* cell. Which I took to mean that there might be other assholes out there tonight. And if there were, she might not know nothing about it.

Her handler was named *Aristotle Gutenberg*. He taught her procedures, how to acquire weapons of terror on a sticks and stones budget. She received her assignments from a coded message posted on the Community Bulletin Board inside the MARTINELLI'S MINIMART down the block from Meredith's townhome. She was given her current mission months before President Johnson's participation had been announced. There was much prep work to be done before kickoff.

I prodded her for more information about *Aristotle Gutenberg*. All she would tell me was that he was in his late forties, no taller than her, in good health—her SB displayed a fleeting image of a shirtless man, presumably *Aristotle Gutenberg*, with a romance novel quality six-pack and biceps, a hammer and sickle tattooed on his left forearm, the Statue of Liberty on his right. A determined scowl on his ruggedly handsome face. He would be watching the carnage at home on his brand-new color TV.

What to do about the debutante with poor taste in men? There weren't any limits to my options. There wasn't any doubt that the upper ranks of *Tabula Rasa* would be interested to learn why their carefully laid plans went askew. They would come calling, and I wanted to be there when they did.

I asked Meredith that since the project was initiated long before President Johnson's participation had been announced, if *Tabula Rasa* might have had a different target in mind initially. She told me that their target was symbolic, not political: *Miss America,* Emma Sachs, Gracie's doppelgänger.

I did a whole bunch of stuff to her mind and arranged for us to meet for a late dinner at her townhouse in Society Hill. Then Eli and I rushed around to our seats on the Navy side of the stadium, where their superstar quarterback was already having a bad game.

The back cover of *The Philadelphia Daily* News, serves as the front page of its sports section. The headline said it all in big bold letters: "**BORING.**" Army and Navy had played to a butt-numbing 7-7 tie in the longest game in the history of the match-up.

If you were to inquire about the rumor going around that there was an assassin targeting President Johnson at the Army-Navy Game, well, you'd be lied to.

◊◊

Chapter 29
inside the belly of the beast

"When you bite off more than you can chew
you got to pay the penalty.
Somebody's got to tell the tale,
I guess it must be up to me."

Up to Me
~ Bob Dylan

I had the limo drop me off at Third and Lombard. Even in this part of town, a gleaming white stretch Rolls Royce in sluggish Saturday night traffic draws a lot of attention from pedestrians and motorists alike. It was good cover for me to walk unnoticed to Meredith Carver-Bradford's townhouse on Delancey Street.

One would think that an exclusive neighborhood would not allow anarchists anywhere near or, certainly not, within its trendy borders. Nonetheless, there lived Meredith Carver-Bradford, plotting the overthrow of everything imaginable from the basement of her three story terrace in the heart of Society Hill, where all the best people lived on cobblestone streets dating back to colonial times.

I knocked on her front door and waited. It occurred to me just then that she may not have made her way home yet. For all I knew she was walking from the stadium. I waited half a minute and knocked again. A voice behind me said, "I'm not there." It was good old Meredith Carver- Bradford holding a couple of shopping bags, "Do I know you? You're pretty handsome, I think I would remember. Have we fucked? I've been so scatterbrained lately." I told her that we met at the stadium earlier this evening. And she had not yet had the pleasure. But if she behaved herself she still might. She handed me the brown paper grocery bags from MARTINELLI'S MINIMART on Two Street and fumbled in her pockets for her house key.

"Have you eaten? MARTINELLI'S makes the best lasagna. I just need to heat it up for a few minutes. It'll give us time to get to know each other. You know I don't think you've told me your name?" She led me to the kitchen in the back of the house. It was long and narrow. The house, the kitchen, and her mind. Way too narrow by my standards.

"I'm Thomas Farrell, pleasure to meet you….I don't think I got your name either."

"I'm Meredith, but you can call me Merry if you like and if you behave yourself, of course." She winked.

I don't think I've mentioned it yet, but Meredith Carver-Bradford is hot. Smokin' hot. She stood about five foot five in her official Dale Evans cowgirl boots. Five two in her stocking feet. Merry had dark red hair cut short, plain and simple. She had the greenest green eyes I've ever seen on a Normal. Merry had a delicate mouth set in a permanent frown.

If you're born into lots of money, then you're likely to have inherited good genes, benefitted from exceptional medical care, gone to all the finest schools, and rubbed shoulders with all the best people from the Redwood Forest to the New York Island.

I watched her unpack her groceries. A large, covered tin containing the lasagna, a loaf of Italian bread, a can of pitted black olives, a pack of CHESTERFIELD KINGS, a deck of Bicycle playing cards, a head of lettuce, a quart of milk, and a can of Maxwell House. I asked her if there was a coded message from *Aristotle Gutenberg*. She told me that there wasn't one and she didn't figure to find one until Monday afternoon at the earliest. Coded messages on the bulletin board in MARTINELLI'S MINIMART could be expected on Mondays, Wednesdays, or Fridays before noon. Nor did she know how much time it would take before instructions from top management reached *Aristotle Gutenberg*. Or how much time it would take the apex Aristotle, let's think of him as *Aristotle Rex*, to decide when, not if, to kill Meredith Carver-Bradford who had failed *Tabula Rasa* so completely and had given him the clap.

The lasagna was pretty tasty. We sat across from each other at the dining room table, a family heirloom made from planks salvaged from the Mayflower. Unsurprisingly, Meredith was an adrenaline junkie, and, at that very moment, incredibly horny. I didn't want to put an end to my celibacy streak with the likes of her. The only reason she was still alive was because I needed her to lead me to this *Aristotle Gutenberg* and, hopefully, further up the food chain of command. She was giving me a come hither look, her *SB* was whirling sensuously. She slid halfway down her chair so she could reach my crotch with her bare foot. "Wanna go upstairs and play?" She whispered. "I can't wait to show you what I've done with the bedroom."

Merry was already loaded down with the alterations I had made to her psyche but I needed to add one more ingredient to the mix. Halfway up the squeaky staircase, I commanded her to go lie down, she'd need plenty of rest if she planned on fucking with me. I told her that I needed to leave and that I would stop by tomorrow evening and take her to dinner at *Arbuckle's*, so be sure to wear her best dress and to put her make up on and fix her hair up pretty. Seven PM on the dot. She looked surprised and flattered. "Nighty Night. Don't let the bed-bugs bite."

There was a spare key to the townhouse hanging from an empty cup hook in the cupboard containing Meredith's everyday tableware. I wondered what had happened to that poor cup. Was there an accident? Knocked off the counter inadvertently? Or hurled towards one of her careless lovers?

I pocketed the key and explored the rest of the townhouse. Meredith would be sleeping soundly until noon Sunday. The basement had that basement-musty smell, accented with printer's ink and volatile chemicals. It had a low ceiling with overhead fluorescent lights. I'm nearly 6'1" and had to scrunch down when I walked or risk smacking my head into one of those fixtures.

There was a print workstation with a four-color silk screen machine and an old fashioned letter-press, just like the ones at Hazen High, and there was a small desk with an electric typewriter on a roll-away stand. A vintage Grundig multi-band radio lived atop a ten drawer map cabinet that sat beneath a casement window which opened into a well with a plot of grass and an herb garden. Antenna wires sprouted from the back of the radio up to the security grate covering the window well.

The map cabinet contained a variety of posters. In the top two drawers were ones that said ***"Tabula Rasa Wants You!"*** in big bold letters and featured a stylized image of Meredith Carver-Bradford wearing an Uncle Sam outfit complete with stripes and stars, cleavage, a top hat, a fierce scowl, a finger pointed right at you. The next five drawers contained similar militant messages over images inspired by the downtrodden, yet noble workers of the 1930's school of art. The lower drawers contained commercial work. In-store posters and shelf-talkers for MARTINELLI'S MINIMART, Grand Opening posters for a Buster Brown shoe store on Locust Street and a series of posters and one-sheets for *Poor Richard's,* a souvenir shop on the Independence Mall.

On the west wall was a do-it-yourself bomb-making lab. The same kind of set-up that you see in all those mad scientist movies. There was a folding table in the middle of the room with four folding chairs around it. Coffee stained, professionally written marketing scripts masking taped to the table in front of four dial telephones. A cold-calling center for terrorists? What will they think up next?

> Check this out: "Hello this is (SAY YOUR PSEUDONYM.) I'm calling on a recorded line from *Tabula Rasa* world headquarters in an undisclosed location. Did you know that you're being fucked over? Like so many Americans exactly like you? Your generous donation of five dollars or more will help in our battle against those that would be our overlords."

Anarchy, it seems to me might just be a tough sell.

I locked Meredith's front door and started walking towards Zoloto Towers. I hoped to recruit Miles and Mort, Eli was a lock, to help me track down and interrogate this *Aristotle Gutenberg*. There's nothing like a remote-viewer or two on a stakeout. If unwelcome eyes had eyes on a target, they would easily be spotted by any of the Golds who would do the temporary blindness thing on them—which was usually good enough for me to locate and deal with the individual.

I was thinking of ways to identify and track *Aristotle Gutenberg* who, according to Meredith, was the mastermind behind the Shawnee Elementary incident, the plot to blow up *Miss America* and the assassination attempt on LBJ at JFK Memorial Stadium.

A chance to capture and interrogate a *Tabula Rasa* Field General was too good of an opportunity to rely solely on last minute improvisation. I needed to consult with the *Psychic Brotherhood of Greater Philadelphia*. Bounce ideas around and to think up new ways to use our skills to deconstruct *Tabula Rasa*.

The air was turning colder. I was glad to be wearing my black leather coat. It was cold enough that I could see my breath. It was near midnight. I was walking through a restaurant district when a voice from across the street called out my name.

"Hey Julius. Julius Briscoe. Is that you man? Remember me? I'm Scotty. Scott Armstrong? Cobbler's Way? Shawnee Elementary? Remember?"

I looked around. Scotty was standing on line with a young woman. They were waiting to get into HYMIE'S FAMOUS DELI for a midnight nosh. I crossed the street while bringing my memories of Scott Armstrong to the fore. He was a year or two older than me, hung out with the older kids. Was a pretty good shortstop and point guard. I never saw him once during my brief time at Moses Hazen High. Even up close, I hardly recognized an old friend from my old neighborhood.

Scott invited me for a late-night snack in the best deli in Center City with him and his fiancée, Silvia Sangello. I knew her to say hello; she was backyard neighbors with Margie Lipshultz. I thanked him but said that I really needed to get going. He tried to look disappointed and handed me a business card: Vice President of Sales, Guy Armstrong & Sons Motors, a used car lot on East Lansdowne. "So Julius, tell me what are you driving these days?"

"Well Scotty I own a Jaguar roadster, and I just bought a *FERRARI 500 SUPERFAST* in Chicago. What about you? What are you driving these days?" Scotty was flabbergasted. Not the answer he was expecting. He stuttered and stammered as he fumbled for an appropriate response. Right about then he'd settle for an inappropriate one. Which is what he did. "Get the fuck out of here Julius? For real?"

"Scott, why would I lie? Good seeing you again man. Silvia, girl, you're looking mighty fine tonight. Gotta be going. Next time?"

◊◊

Chapter 30
turtle creek trail

"…(you) complain about the present and blame it on the
past
I'd like to find your inner child and kick its little ass.…"

Get Over It
~ Don Henley, Glenn Frey

Somehow for some reason everyone wanted to hang out with me in Aunt Connie's and Uncle Teddy's penthouse that Sunday morning. Their pantry was seriously low on canapés and assorted delicacies on account of the fact that they were out of the country for the next six weeks. So why here? Possibly it was Uncle T's giant screen color TV and the twenty foot dining room table. Ample space for a smorgasbord.

"So Julius did you do anything interesting in Chicago, meet any interesting people?"

"I sure did, Nettie." I stopped as if I'd said everything there was to say on the subject of 'interesting people.'

"That's it? 'I sure did?'"

"You do know that my mother, Uncle Teddy, Aunt Connie and I were on flight #505 last Tuesday, the one famous for the lamest skyjacking attempt of all time. It was, Emma, a cluster fuck start to finish." Wink. wink.

I told them all about Lenny, B.J., Sammy, Molly Anne, white shoe lawyers, Lenny's elegant neighborhood, Lake Michigan with its ocean-like waves, hidden rooms with secret entrances and exits, THE BLACKHAWK, THE PUMP ROOM, THE GATE OF HORN, JJ Cross, Rocket the Wonder

Dog, random socializing, a Thanksgiving dinner that couldn't be beat, Italian beef, and buying the FERRARI.

Dolly asked, "So did you meet anyone special?"

"Yes, no, I don't know. It's too hard to even think about people that way. You know?"

The game came on, your Philadelphia Eagles at their Cleveland Browns for a shot at the title in the championship game in two weeks. We drank beer and wine, smoked marijuana that came all the way from Afghanistan, ate our fill of imported foods, prepared by famed chefs and watched the Eagles' season spiral into oblivion.

At half time, Nettie, Dolly and Emma went back to Mort and Dolly's place to put the finishing touches on the dessert, which was still classified as a surprise. While they were out of earshot, I called a meeting of the *Psychic Brotherhood of Greater Philadelphia.* Eli knew most of the story, Miles, Mort and Ben did not. I brought them up-to-date as succinctly as possible. They all reacted to the plot to assassinate the President, with anger, revulsion and indignation. When I told them who the original target was, well, let's just say they went all in.

After I described the message drop in the MARTINELLI'S MINIMART on Two Street, Miles excused himself and went to his penthouse. He returned a couple of minutes later with a leather bound book that listed all of his and the *undzer shtick's* real estate holdings. It was as thick as the Drexel Hills phone book, yellow and white pages combined. He leafed through it until he found what he was searching for and said, "We own a building not a hundred yards from MARTINELLI'S MINIMART. There's a Pharmacy on the ground floor and two furnished apartments on the second. Both, according to these records are unoccupied."

There you go. MARTINELLI'S opens at six a.m. sharp every morning. Except on Sundays when it opens at eleven fifty-nine a.m., a feeble middle finger to the blue laws. The basic plan called for the Golds to keep watch from as many vantage points as there were people inside MARTINELLI'S at any given moment. *Sicht* is really cool that way. *Connect* to one set of eyes and you can access every set of eyes nearby. It's hard to imagine, but Eli says it's really cool. He says it's like being in a TV control room with a lot of monitors showing images from a lot of different viewpoints. Our hope was they would eventually *connect* to someone's *eyestream* as he thumbtacked a canary yellow three by five index card to the Community Bulletin Board. I'd be waiting for him when he exited MARTINELLI'S ready to Zombify his murderous ass and escort him back to the apartment over the Pharmacy.

Nettie, Dolly, and Emma returned bearing beignets and chicory. They wanted more details about my trip to Chicago. I was surprised to learn that none of them knew about the incident in the Pump Room and Uncle T's contribution to Shakespeare's remedy for a troubled civilization: "First thing we do, let's kill all the lawyers."

We spent the rest of the afternoon on Turtle Creek Trail testing our cars and our reflexes. Mort Gold finally broke down and gave Eli the practically brand-new red Corvette that someone had traded in for a *Cadillac 60 Special*. Ben was an automatic transmission guy and, instead of driving the Jaguar like I planned, rode with me in the *FERRARI*. Mort rode with his son, and Miles stayed behind to confirm the status of the apartments above the Pharmacy on Two Street.

Turtle Creek Trail runs between Upper and Lower Gulph Roads in Radnor Groves. It's about three and a half miles long with a string of switchbacks and hairpin turns that would challenge even the best cars and drivers in the world. There were no crossroads, stop signs, or stop lights to slow you down. The only problem was that it was zoned for two-way traffic. What good is a shortcut to or from the Mall if it isn't bidirectional?

I'm not clairvoyant. I can't see the future. And I'm trying to not live in the past. But I can see a time when Eli Gold becomes a world class race car driver. He's that good.

Turtle Creek Trail is one of those roads less traveled. It is far too challenging for Normal people driving their bulky, understeering, sluggish vehicles to and from the Mall. All we needed to do was to barricade the Lower Gulph Road intersection with the zebra striped police sawhorse barriers that, during the Cuban Missile Crisis, Zack Crosby stole and stashed in the woods under a waterproof tarp. We took turns trying to beat my personal best which was approximately twelve minutes and thirty seven seconds. That afternoon, Eli in his little red Corvette set the unofficial new record; a blistering nine minutes and eleven seconds. Congratulations Eli. The trophy's in the mail.

"Julius, one of these days, can I get you to teach me to drive a stick?" asked Ben Gold. We were heading back to town in the *FERRARI*. "Sure thing Ben."

Ben Gold is three years older than Gracie and me. As protective a big brother as you might expect. Our friendship was slow to develop on account of the fact that I was sleeping with his kid sister sans his explicit approval. But he got past that while he was hospitalized as a result of the road rage incident on the Ben Franklin Bridge. Just like we all got past the realization that we are immune to each other's paranormal skills. The Golds can't see what I see. I can't mess with their nervous systems.

Ben was the head of security for Emma Sachs, *Miss America.* She was one of the most popular *Miss America's* of all time. She is movie-star pretty, talented, accessible and TV
talk-show-guest funny. In fact, her entourage had swollen to an even dozen. If things had gone differently, Gracie and I probably would have been a part of Emma's crew.

"So kid, how are you holding up?"

"I'm getting there Ben. And I will get there. What about you, Ben? How do you handle it? Emma looking so much like Gracie, I mean."

"You know Jules, I never saw Emma that way until you remarked, what was it? 'Holy fuck' Gracie, why didn't you tell me you had a twin sister?'" We laughed at the memory. Ben lit up a joint and switched on the radio which was tuned to an FM station that only played the hippest sounds. We smoked some more amazing shit and sang along with the Rolling Stones' cover of Chuck Berry's 'Carol.'

We returned to Zoloto Towers with just enough time for me to take a quick shower, put on a suit and tie and catch a cab to Society Hill for my date with the smokin' hot Meredith Carver-Bradford and an opportunity to question her further. Making it so someone can only tell the truth only solves part of the equation. You need to know what questions to ask and in what order. 'Tell me everything' doesn't work. It only produces rivulets of guilt. I was certain I could extract more information about Merry's band of anarchists by asking the right questions.

I arrived at Meredith's doorstep one minute past early. I knocked on the front door and waited for her to open it. I didn't want her to know that I had 'borrowed' her spare key. I waited another minute before knock, knock, knocking on her front door. And again she didn't answer. By my calculations, she should have awakened fresh as a daisy, ready to conquer the universe at noon or half past at the latest. I began to doubt the cocktail of behaviors I had given Meredith. Had I miscalculated? Had she awakened miraculously free of my programming and wandered off into the moonlight alone?

I waited another minute and then tried again. Still no response. I looked up and down the block. No pedestrians. No cars. No *SB*s peering from the neighboring windows. I unlocked the door and stepped in.

Holy shit. Her place had been robbed. The living room had been ransacked. The exposed brick walls had been defaced with vulgar drawings and the words "DEATH TO PIGS" were written in big bold red letters above the fireplace. Expensive antique furniture had been slashed open. All of the doors in her china cabinet were askew. Her irreplaceable heirlooms had been ripped asunder and strewn everywhere. There was a felt-lined mahogany box fitted to contain silverware lying open on the dining room table. It was empty.

Evidently the thieves were an illiterate bunch. The engraved badge on the inside of the lid read: "Crafted for

Eudora Williamson Bradford by Paul Revere, Silversmith, Boston Massachusetts. May 4, 1772."

I checked the kitchen. It was, if possible, an even larger mess. Her everyday dishes lay shattered on the floor. Boxes of food had been ripped apart their contents added to the clutter. Cans of foods and soups had been opened and emptied into the clogged kitchen sink. What a fucking mess. I called out for Meredith. No reply. I feared the worst. The worst was worser than I feared.

I walked slowly up the stairs, keeping my feet on either side of the treads to avoid any telltale creaking. There were no sbs within my range. And there should have been at least one; Meredith's. When I had left last night, her bedroom door was wide open. Now it was shut.
I considered two possibilities. Either latent paranormal abilities had come to the fore and she no longer produced a Status Button. Or? Or Meredith Carver Bradford was dead. And that's what she was, all right, she was dead. Strangled from the looks of it. She was lying face-up on her bed, naked as the day she was born. Scrawled in lipstick on her abdomen was the symbol]O[. The O had been drawn raggedly around her naval. The calling card of the serial killer Junior Poole had been channeling the night he murdered Ellie Gold. I killed Poole that very same evening. An official BUSTER BROWN AND TIGE electric clock had been ripped from the wall at one minute past one and was now covering her lady parts.

I had told Meredith just yesterday that my name was Thomas Farrell, the same fake name Poole was using on his mission to make Lucille Kittridge's murder look like an accident. Ellie Gold's brutal slaughter was his dessert. Was the original]O[psycho still alive and killing? Or was he being scapegoated yet again?

Meredith's bedroom had been disrespected as brutally as her body had been. Dresser drawers ripped out of the frames, clothing thrown everywhere. Her jewelry box had been emptied. Anything hanging on her walls, photos or works of art, were askew as if someone was looking for a wall safe. Meredith hadn't bothered to provide me with an inventory of her prized possessions nor her Dun and Bradstreet rating or anything like that. She would have, had I asked. Other than the jewelry, the sterling silver, and probably a silk pillowcase or two, I had no idea what else might be missing.

I was sure that the medical examiner would conclude that Meredith's body had been raped and probably sodomized by a crew of necrophiliac home invaders. I needed to be gone.
I returned to the kitchen. The cupboard that had contained her everyday dishes was empty. There was no reason to think that the spare key would have survived the onslaught, so I tossed it on the floor in the general direction of the broken dishes and went to see what damage had been done to the basement.

The basement level was relatively free of chaos or debris. They had wheeled the typewriter stand to the foot of the stairs where they left it. An IBM Executive typewriter weighs nearly forty-two pounds and would seem conspicuous if wheeled down Delancey Street at any time of day. They left it where I found it. They broke all of Dr. Frankenstein's glassware and littered the tiled floor with the shards. The letterpress and the silk screen machines appeared to have been moved slightly from their moorings.

Far too heavy for these wimpy ass bad guys to knock over or to carry. I was turning to head back up the stairs when I noticed that the bottom drawer of the map cabinet was slightly ajar. I investigated. The drawer was empty. As I remembered, it had contained posters, one-sheets, and stationery for *Poor Richard's Souvenir Shoppe* on Independence Mall. The other nine drawers still contained the commercial and revolutionary artwork I had observed last night.

I slipped out of Meredith's back door and walked down to Two Street to check the Community Bulletin Board in MARTINELLI'S. There wasn't a single canary-yellow index card with or without a secret coded message pinned to the bulletin board. I'd check again tomorrow.
I bought a tin of lasagna, a loaf of Italian bread, a can of black olives, the Sunday Inquirer, and the Sunday Times. I walked over to Spruce Street, caught a cab, and went back to the **Z**2 to deliver the bad news.

Chapter 31
arbuckle's

"I felt so helpless, what could I do?
Remembering all the things we've been through."

Leader of the Pack
~ Ellie Greenwich, G.F. Morton, Jeff Barry

The Blue Laws of the Commonwealth of Pennsylvania and the City of Brotherly Love mandate that only restaurants, grocery stores, filling stations and pharmacies were permitted to be open for business on the lord's day. Despite those restrictions, the Zoloto Mall was pretty busy.

Each of the five floors held at least two popular restaurants serving a wide range of cuisines and budgets. A couple around my age, Paul and Paula Hildebrand, were coming out of MAMA SWEETIES AT THE Z^2, hand in hand, happy in love. I hit them with TRUST ME!® and REAL TIME AMNESIA®.

I instructed Paul to call the police from that pay phone over there and tell them there had been a murder at 314 Delancey Street in Society Hill. If they asked his name he was to tell them 'Thomas Farrell' and hang up. I instructed Paula to call the Philadelphia Inquirer, the morning paper, and to ask for the City Desk and tell whoever answered the same thing I told Paul to say with important additional details; the victim's name and an accurate description of the legend scrawled on Meredith's abdomen. If they hurried, their photographer could get to the crime scene before the police. The back door was unlocked. Afterwards, I restored Paul and Paula's memory functions to normal and gave each of them a Benjamin and told them to have a nice evening.

I was gratified that someone would. Only one of those anonymous tips was taken seriously.

If I had my way, Meredith Carver-Bradford would have lived long enough to lead me to *Aristotle Gutenberg*, watch me interrogate and kill him, then I would turn my attention to her. I'm no Saint, okay? I'm no Mike Hammer, I'm no Joe Friday or Sherlock Holmes. But I have watched them on TV and read a bunch of detective novels. Even without their expert advice, it was clear to me that *Aristotle Gutenberg* killed Meredith at around one o'clock this morning. Which meant that *Gutenberg* probably wasn't an out-of-towner, but most likely a local, possibly, given Meredith's pedigree, a prominent obscure Philadelphian. Perhaps the proprietor of a trendy gift shop on the Independence Mall? He shouldn't have taken the posters. That's the thing about murderous criminals, one way or another, they always find a way to fuck things up.

I walked towards the residential tower toting my evening meal in a brown paper bag. I was about to overtake a woman pushing a baby carriage built for two. I swung out to my left and picked up my pace. I was half past her when she shrieked, "Oh my gawd, Julius. Julius Briscoe is it really you?"

"It would seem so. How are you, Brenda? How are those little guys doing?" I resumed walking towards the residential lobby. She kept pace.

"We're doing well Julius, thanks for asking. What about you? You doing okay?"

"I'm hanging in there Brenda. Good days. Bad days. Mostly in-between days."

"Well Julius don't be shy, if you need to talk things through, I'm always here for you."

"How about you Brenda girl? You still with Tommy? Seems like every time I turn the radio on, one of Tommy's hits is playing. I won fifty bucks this one time betting Harry O'Hanlon that one of Tommy's tunes would be playing when he turned on his car radio. He was always wary of me before. Now he's terrified."

"It's off and on. Tommy's not exactly a one woman man. But I'm handling it." Her *SB* told another story.

"Julius, have you heard the big news?"

"What big news?"

"Donnie Clarke is producing and hosting a New Year's Eve television special, *"Keep on Rockin' in the New Year."* Tommy's the headliner plus all of Philadelphia's finest will be performing: Frankie and Annette, Chubby, Fabian, Jimmy Darren, JJ Cross, Bobby Rydell and Dolly Gold and her tributarians. It's gonna be a hell of a show."

"Wow. What a lineup! Where's it gonna be? How can I get a ticket?"

"Get this. It's gonna be in Tommy's old high school gym. Can you believe it?"

"Moses Hazen High?"

"You've heard of it?"

"I went to seventh grade there. It's a long, very boring story, Brenda."

"Julius, your name is already on the VIP list. Just show up. You can bring a date if you're up to dating again."

We reached the elevator banks. Brenda turned towards the parking garage elevators, I turned towards the express elevator alcove which was velvet roped off and guarded by a burly attendant who moonlighted as a semi-professional wrestler. Bobo Berkowitz was a villainous thug type, invariably bested in the ring by a Gorgeous George type. Win. Lose. What did Bobo care? They paid him with cash and cocaine. Women he had to get on his own.

"I gotta get going. I'm starving." I held up the grocery bag. "Good seeing you again Brenda. Hope things work out with you two. Tell Tommy I said yo."

"Thanks Julius, where you headed?"

"We have a penthouse up on sixty. Well it belongs to the business, but my Uncle Teddy and Aunt Connie live there most of the year. They're flying to Paris right about now. I'm house sitting."

"Well color me impressed. Would you mind showing me the penthouse? I read in *Philadelphia's Got Style* that they are magnificent. I'd love to see one. Would you mind?"

"Brenda, I cannot. The floor is restricted to the owners and their authorized guests. I can't authorize you yet. Problems with the paperwork. My Uncle Teddy could if he weren't riding in a big old jet airliner right about now. So a raincheck maybe?"

"Okay. I'm gonna hold you to that. Tell me Julius, you coming back to school next semester?"

I told her that I was. The express elevator returned to the lobby with a loud ding. I pointed out that her son and brother looked like twins and that it was great seeing her and thanks again for helping at Gracie's funeral. Then I got on the elevator.

You have to have a key to operate the express elevator to the sixtieth floor. If you turn the key to the right and then back to the left and then back to the right again and push the button, the elevator would whisk you to your floor without alerting the residents of its impending arrival. However, if you were to just turn the key and push the button, the elevator would elevate you and sound a chime in all of the penthouses on the sixtieth floor. I turned the key to the right and pushed the button.

The elevator parked on the sixtieth floor in exactly one minute and twenty one seconds.
I removed the key, the doors opened and everyone was standing in the foyer, stern looks on their faces. Curlers, babushkas and housecoats on the women. Jeans and tee shirts on the barefoot men.

"Julius, I thought I taught you the elevator protocols."

"You did Miles." I whispered, "Turns out my date gave me cold shoulders, cold arms, hips, thighs, everythings. Meredith's *dead tired*, in bad shape Miles, really bad shape. I need your advice. And the *Brotherhoods'*." I crossed myself and asked in my normal voice, "Have you eaten? The MARTINELLI'S MINIMARKET on Two Street makes the best lasagna in town. I bought the large tin. Do you have any Chianti? Teddy and Connie are fresh out."

It turned out that Nettie was taking everyone to *Arbuckle's* for dinner. Emma had yet to be introduced to Lizzie Wallace-Stern Gold who ran the legitimate side of the late Mo Stern's empire from her offices above the restaurant. It was time for Emma to kiss the ring.

Nettie said, "Girls we better get going, our Limo will be here soon. That means you gentlemen as well. Julius, you're welcome to join us. Lizzie will be delighted to see you. She thinks you're 'super-fine."

"Well I would, but I just bought this nice lasagna and I don't want it to go to waste."

"For goodness sakes Julius, put it in the fridge and have it tomorrow, it'll keep. And look at you, you're all dressed up and ready to go. So what happened? Your hot date give you the cold shoulder? What kind of extra dumb bimbo would stand up a young man as handsome as you?" The dead kind Nettie, the dead kind. Guess I was going to *Arbuckle's* tonight after all. It would be good to see Lizzie Gold again.

Miles got the hint that a meeting of the *Psychic Brotherhood of Greater Philadelphia* was necessary. He said, "Mort, Eli, Ben, may I have a minute or two?" He led us into his penthouse, where I gave them the sad, sad news about the dearly departed anarchist socialite, Meredith Carver-Bradford.

The Golds all but lost it when I told them about the markings on Meredith's naked body:]O[. Same as the ones Ben and Eli found on Ellie's body.

"Julius, what on earth does that mean? You dispatched Farrell, so this couldn't have been his doing. I've not read anything in the papers about a series of murder/rapes in quite awhile."

"The police never released the information about the killer's signature. They didn't want copycatters like Junior Poole out there leaving bogus clues that had them chasing their own tails all around town. So maybe the real killer's been active all this time.

"It seems to me that this was a hit, not a home invasion. There was no sign of forced entry, not that I was looking for one. Meredith was sleeping soundly, thanks to something I call NIGHTYNIGHT®, and wouldn't have been able to hear a bomb going off, let alone the doorbell, or even been able to walk down the stairs to answer the front door. That means someone had to have a key. And it's not too much of a stretch to think that this *Aristotle Gutenberg* was the one to have a key to Meredith's place. She had a thing for him. That's for sure."

"But why trash her place?" asked Eli.

"To throw the police off. I think the asshole would have hauled off all that print and bomb making gear if he could have. But they weren't prepared to do any heavy lifting so he chose to make it look like the work of crazies. But he may have left a clue anyhow."

"What do you mean?"

I told them about the missing posters for *Poor Richard's Souvenir Shoppe* and suggested that had they been left in that drawer, sooner or later, a police detective would come knocking on *Poor Richard's* door asking questions and expecting the whole truth and nothing but the truth.

Miles excused himself and went to his office. He returned with a leather bound binder that contained biographical, financial and often incriminating information about the movers and shakers of the greater Philadelphia area. Similar to J. Edgar Hoover's steamy files on the world's otherwise high and mighty.

"*Poor Richard's* is owned by Elbridge Ross the Seventh. He's a direct descendant of George Ross a signer of the Declaration Of Independence. Elbridge Ross is upper tier high society, hardly the type to be advocating anarchy, one would think. Although, he's considered quite the eccentric from what I've heard over the years. I don't believe Ross could have killed Meredith Carver-Bradford with his bare hands. He's much older than me, barely five feet tall, portly, dresses up like Benjamin Franklin when he's in his shoppe, right down to the bifocals and waistcoat."

Elbridge the Seventh, as described by Miles Gold, wasn't anything like what I saw in Meredith's *SB*. I'm seeing images in Normals' Status Buttons more and more often. These images appear for milliseconds at best. Flashes so vivid, so hyper-real as to defy description. My own personal theoretician speculates that Normals with eidetic memories would most likely be able to generate an image of someone or something significant in their lives.

Lizzie Gold is a living legend. The biological daughter of Georgia Wallace and Benjamin Stern who died tragically in a night club fire when Lizzie was just three years old. Annabelle and Miles Gold had been designated to be Lizzie's guardians should anything bad happen to Ben and Georgia. They adopted Elizabeth Alice Wallace-Stern two months before Mort and Max Gold were born.

Lizzie Gold had been classified as 'problematic' by every 'Admissions Consultant' at every private school Miles and Annabelle attempted to enroll the child in.

"She just wouldn't be a good fit."

"I'm sorry to say, but I don't believe Elizabeth would thrive here."

"She's not Sillington Academy material."

On and on and on went the rejections. Not to be deterred, Miles founded Waverley Academy on the third floor of the original Zoloto Towers the following Autumn. Lizzie Wallace-Stern-Gold its first graduate.

There's a portrait of the Golds and the Sterns hanging in the great room of Gold Manor. It showed Miles Gold and a pregnant Annabelle holding hands. Standing next to them were Ben and Georgia Stern holding a three year old Lizzie between them. They were cheek to cheek to cheek and smiling. You couldn't look at that painting and not smile yourself. Lizzie Gold still has that infectious aura. When we arrived at *Arbuckle's*, she greeted everyone with hugs and kisses. She has a way about her. It's impossible to not feel energized when you're hanging with Lizzie Gold.

"Julius Briscoe, you young rascal, where have you been? What have you been up to? Daddy tells me you took the semester off because of what happened to Gracie. I understand young Mr. Briscoe, I truly do. Just remember I'll always be here for you. If you need to talk things out, I'm a good listener. But you need to finish your schooling young man. You'll never know when some of that bullshit might come in handy!" She winked.

I wanted to tell her that I was already financially set for life. All of my paintings had been authenticated by the museum's expert. Her father offered me three hundred million dollars for the van Gogh, the Raphael, and the Rembrandt. Which I accepted immediately. Even with Lizzie's status as the godmother of Center City's underworld high society, I couldn't tell her about the adventures of William Novichok, my misadventures in Atlas City or my interactions with *Tabula Rasa.* If I wouldn't tell Gracie about such things, why would I tell her aunt?

Lizzie Wallace-Stern Gold's *Inside/Out–A Tale of Identity* topped 1936's best seller lists for four months running. It's an autobiography of a young mulatto woman, adopted at an early age by her late parents' best friends, who were Caucasian agnostics. Elizabeth was raised in an upper upper crust community but always felt isolated, unwelcome despite the phony smiles and invitations to every exclusive social event between Society Hill and West Devon. Lizzie Gold is intelligent, athletic, cheerfully attractive, kind and good.

It was at the University of Pennsylvania where she majored in Journalism and was captain of the Women's Track and Field and Cross Country teams, that Lizzie encountered people like her ethnically and intellectually. It was life-changing. Mind expanding. The burden of her uniqueness finally relieved.

Things were going super fine for Lizzie in the spring of '36. Her autobiography was climbing up the best seller lists, she had qualified for the US Olympic team, the New York Times was sending signals, everything was glittering and shining. Joy overwhelmed her world. Then? Then she ruptured a tendon in her left knee at a meet in New Haven. Poof. She'd be on crutches until October. She went to the Olympics anyhow.

THE PHILADELPHIA EVENING BULLETIN hired Lizzie to report on the US Track and Field and Cross Country teams at the 1936 Summer Olympic Games in Berlin. Her candid interviews with the black Americans on the US team about competing in the openly racist Nazi Germany earned her a nomination for a Pulitzer Prize and launched her career as a celebrity journalist and syndicated columnist.

She had it all. Until. Until Jack Wheeler, a pompous gossip columnist unearthed Lizzie's relationship with the rumored notorious gangster Moses Stern, her PoppaMo, alleged godfather of Philadelphia's so called Jewish mafia. Lizzie was branded as a heartless mob boss who handed out death sentences every single day of the week except, in accordance with the Blue Laws, on Sundays. Lizzie's syndicator dropped her faster than Lucy dumped Desi.

A couple of weeks later, Wheeler tripped and fell down four flights of the steep back staircase in the TIME/LIFE BUILDING in New York City. His neck, several ribs, pelvis and both arms were broken in multiple locations. He died from internal bleeding. The fact that Miles & Mort Gold were in the same building finalizing an ad buy with the General Sales Manager of Time/Life was probably coincidental.

◊◊

Chapter 32
fennario's

"I've been around this whole country, but I never yet
found Fennario"

Pretty Peggy-O
~ Bob Dylan

A Philadelphia police captain, who shall remain
nameless, for a donation to his favorite charity, namely his
children's college fund, would turn all of the traffic lights
green on North Broad Street from City Hall to Ridge Avenue
between three and five a.m. He would also station his fire
engine, red & white squad cars, souped-up Pontiac GTOs, at
critical intersections to prevent possible collisions with the
crosstown traffic. A thousand bucks an hour per vehicle. A
price Eli Gold and I could easily afford. Here's the bottom
line: Eli's little red Corvette is about a second faster to 60 mph
than my gleaming white FERRARI SUPERFAST. To 100 mph?
Well, that's another story.

We raced up and down North Broad Street until 5 a.m.
on the dot. Then we headed back to the Z^2, parked our
racers in the garage, and took the armored Cadillac over to
Fennarios for a hearty breakfast with that down-home
counterculture vibe which is so hard to find in most parts of
this town without pity. We needed to kill a couple of hours
before heading over to MARTINELLI'S MINIMART on Two
Street to see if *Aristotle Gutenberg* had left a secret coded
message for the late Meredith Carver-Bradford. Highly
unlikely if he was the one who killed her, wouldn't you
think?

The so-called folk music revival began to build momentum following WWII and gained steam in the late fifties and early sixties as the intelligentsia's preferred alternative to the never-ending stream of pablum on your favorite top forty radio station.

By the end of the baby boom, coffee houses featuring folk music artists had sprouted up all across the country. As we know, Chicago has the *Gate of Horn*, the Big Apple is home to *Gerdes Folk City, Cafe Wha?*, and *The Bitter End* among others, Boston was famous for *Club 47* and Philadelphia had *Fennario's Folk Arts Center* on Sansom Street. Each of these venues attracted humble, thoughtful audiences who appreciated authentic folk music played on acoustic instruments by earnest, committed, authentic young men and women who believed in equality, liberty and the brotherhood of man.

Weekend evenings, *Fennario's* is the place to be entertained and educated by folk artists like Rambling Jack Elliot, Buffy St.Marie, Lightning Hopkins, JJ Cross, Spider John Koerner, and Reverend Gary Davis. Since half of its potential clientele were underage and obtaining a liquor license was a futile exercise in ass-kissing and bribery, *Fennario's* only served non-alcoholic beverages, crustless sandwiches, and other alternative comfort foods.

During daylight hours *Fennario's Folk Arts Center* was this free-form hangout for local artists, poets, one man bands, singers, dancers, mimes, non-conformists and what have you's. No better place to sample a wide range of rare and unique SBs. It hosted an all you can eat breakfast buffet that somehow managed to serve something for every taste bud. And that's not all. For $15, you could purchase fifteen minutes of fame and glory on the world renowned

Fennario's main stage. Sign up with the lovely hostess and wait your turn. Eli eagerly signed on the dotted line. I asked him what he was up to and he said 'wow.'

We found a table in the Alan Lomax Gathering Hall and sat down for a hearty breakfast and to read the morning papers.

The Philadelphia Daily News

19 Arrested for Murdering Mississippi Civil Rights Workers

By Allison McDowell - United Press International

Philadelphia, Mississippi- This quiet little town was rocked awake this morning by the news that the FBI had arrested nineteen suspected Ku Klux Klan members and charged them with the murders of missing civil rights workers Michael Schwerner, James Cheney and Andrew Goodman.

-continues page 4

The Philadelphia Inquirer

Prominent Socialite Found Slain in Luxury Townhome

By Louise Lancaster. Photographer Jerome Oliver.

Society Hill- Police were dispatched to a town home on Delancey Street in response to an anonymous call to emergency services at approximately 9 p.m. Sunday evening. The elegant townhome had been ransacked and defaced with crude drawings on its lovely exposed brick walls. Prominent socialite Meredith Carver-Bradford's naked body was found in her second floor bedroom. A cryptic inscription had been drawn on her abdomen with lipstick. (See Jerome Oliver's photo essay on page 6.) ***<u>WARNING!</u> SOME PEOPLE MAY FIND THESE IMAGES HIGHLY DISTRESSING.***

The article went on to describe the conditions inside with disturbing, candid photographs of Meredith's body and townhome. The photographer even took shots of the recruiting posters, the printing press and everything else in the basement. There was a sidebar editorial decrying the corruption of America's best and brightest by subversive ideologues.

Eli reacted "Wow, Jules. How do you think the Inky got that story?"

"Well Eli, last night, I might have 'persuaded' a young couple to call the cops and the paper.
I guess the Inky got to Meredith's place before the cops did. Imagine that? I forgot to tell you about it, sorry.
Remember? I did the same thing in Atlantic City. Had some random stranger call that task force and tell them about *Tabula Rasa's* plan to blow up Boardwalk Hall."

Someone was tap, tap, tapping on the microphone. It was our lovely hostess, Gwinnette 'Gwinny' Rutledge. Wow. "Eli Gold, boyfriend it's your time to shine! Come on up and impress the shit out of us."

Eli stood up and took a bow. There were like eight other people in the room. He turned to me and said, "Julius I'm gonna need you to play the piano. I have to impersonate Chuck Berry in mother's New Year's Eve show. I can't do a proper duck walk while playing the piano, now can I? Come on Julie, it's just like riding a bicycle."

It's a good thing that Eli doesn't have buttons. At that particular moment I might have killed him. I hadn't touched a piano since my dad was murdered. Go figure, upright pianos and pool tables bring up my worst memories.

William Briscoe was a self-taught honky-tonk pianist in the mold of the great Jerry Lee Lewis. He taught me and a bunch of neighborhood kids including JJ and Richie Cross, Margie Lipshultz and Aunt Connie how to play the piano with enthusiasm and wild abandon. I gave Eli a look that

would kill your average Normal. He said to me, "Come on Julie. It's fucking Chuck
'C-F-G' Berry. Piece of cake. I need to practice my duck walk." Eli ran upstage and strapped on a well worn acoustic guitar, probably abandoned by some broken hearted Dylan wannabe. Eli needed it as a prop. I sat down on the piano bench and stared at the keys.

It's not exactly like riding a bicycle, but it all came back to me before I started to panic. Chuck Berry's tunes are simple enough. Which doesn't mean you should consider them simplistic rock and roll dance tunes. Charles Edward Anderson Berry, of the St.Louis Berries, is a great song writer. A poet. Brilliant lyrics swaddled in basic rock chords and rhythms. Eli pulled the microphone up close and stage whispered:

> "Oh Carol, don't let him steal your heart away.
> I'm gonna learn to dance if it takes me all night and day."

Eli swiveled towards me, pointed a finger and shouted "Hit it Julie!" I unleashed my inner Jerry Lee and let loose. The piano needed tuned and I needed practice. Other than that it went as good as it could. Eli's a dynamic singer, the son of a dynamic singer. His infectious vocals saved the day. Eli's 'duck walking' had everyone in the sparse audience up on their feet and cheering him on. A good time was had by all.

An hour later, we rolled past Meredith's place. There was yellow police tape crisscrossed over her front door, and a large sign that said "CRIME SCENE. DO NOT ENTER" staked into the postage stamp sized front yard.

Unsurprisingly, there wasn't a canary yellow three by five card pinned to The Community Bulletin Board inside MARTINELLI'S MINIMART. Essentially, the MINIMART is a BIG CORNERS with fancier trimmings and inflated prices. I introduced myself to the manager. He was stocking the cereal aisle with Sugar Corn Pops and Shredded Wheat. His name tag said M. ANTHONY. He was in his early thirties, had a premature bald spot, a skinny mustache and ambitious energy.

"Excuse me sir. I'm Julius Briscoe. My partners and I will be opening a sporting goods store up on Chestnut Street next March, if everything goes according to plan, that is. I greatly admire your posters and shelf talkers. If you wouldn't mind, I'm hoping you can put me in touch with the designer that produced them. They're quite striking."

"I'd love to help you, young man," he walked over to the checkout counter and removed a copy of the *Inquirer* from the wire rack and handed it to me, "but she's the one that got murdered last night. Such a shame. She was the friendliest person. And if you don't mind me saying, Miss Bradford was smokin' hot."

I pushed his appropriate buttons and asked, "have you ever seen anyone posting a yellow index card on the bulletin board?" He thought for a second or two and then said, "yeah sure, that's the guy that comes in here dressed up like Benjamin Franklin. Arrogant asshole, if you ask me. He works in that souvenir shoppe on the mall."

I restored his memory functions to normal, thanked him and might have mentioned that BIG CORNERS was on the lookout for a regional manager. If interested, he should get in touch with Edward or Julius Briscoe at the O, 18th and Spruce.

Poor Richard's Souvenir Shoppe has entrances on Chestnut Street and on the Independence Mall. I parked the Caddy two blocks to the west. *Poor Richard's* is on the ground floor of a colonial style duplex that was built following the revolution by Elbridge Ross II. Back then, it hosted an upscale dry goods store with living quarters on the second floor. It has remained so configured and in the family ever since.

We really didn't have much of a plan. We'd just tell good old Elbridge that we were looking for cool presents for our friends and families. *Poor Richard's* was famous for its Revolutionary War-era styled gifts; Betsy Ross flags, Revolutionary War-themed chess sets, jigsaw puzzles, revisionist versions of Monopoly, Candy Land, Chutes & Ladders, and Parcheesi. There were plastic muskets, fake flintlock rifles and pistols, freshly printed copies of *Common Sense, Poor Richard's Almanack*, the *United States Constitution,* and, of course, *The Declaration of Independence*. For an additional $25, your name would replace John Hancock's on that much-desired number one slot on the replica. I was thinking about getting one with my Julius T. Briscoe on it. Would make a swell Xmas gift for Mother, wouldn't you think?

Right there, smack dab in the middle of *Poor Richard's* display window, was a life-sized mannequin done up to look like Benjamin Franklin dressed up like Santa Claus. Gift-wrapped boxes at his feet. And a great big hand-lettered sign plastered in the window that said,

WE ARE CLOSED DUE TO A FAMILY EMERGENCY.
WILL REOPEN AS SOON AS POSSIBLE.
SORRY FOR ANY INCONVENIENCE.
JOHAN MANES, PROPRIETOR

Well don't that beat all? According to Miles, Elbridge Ross VII was the owner. Guess Miles' records weren't up to date.

The other half of the duplex was home to *Aunt Abigail's Gunpowder Tea Room.* A stout woman in her late forties, early fifties maybe, was sweeping the concrete in front of that side of the building with a witch's broom. She was dressed up in a lovely blue gingham frock with a matching bonnet. She also wore a white apron and wire-framed spectacles. She was puffing on a corn cob pipe. Whatever she was smoking sure didn't smell like tobacco to Eli and me. Aunt Abigail finished sweeping and called out to us, "You young fellas interested in some nice warm cocoa? It's on the house. Come on in. You two look so down in the dumps, my cocoa's guaranteed to cheer you young bucks right up. Wait'll you get a look at my crullers."

We thanked her and followed her into *Aunt Abigail's.* It smelled wonderful. I tapped her blue Truth button as we walked on by.

December isn't the Independence Mall's busiest time of year. Which is to say we were her only customers at the moment. Auntie Abby sat us at a glass-topped café table in the Chestnut Street window. She said, "You lads sit right here and look handsome. I'll be back in a jiffy with something yummy." She sped off towards the kitchen. Like my dad used to say, 'there's no such thing as free cocoa.'

She returned in a jiffy and a half with a tray holding a carafe of hot chocolate, two mugs, and a silver serving dish full of fresh crullers topped with a variety of icings.

"Why aren't you two handsome lads in school?" It was Eli's turn to lie. "It's Flounder's Day, so we came to town to do some holiday shopping and maybe get laid."

"And where do you young men attend school?"

It was my turn. "We attend EXMOOR ACADEMY in Haverford. Your shop smells amazing, and these crullers are to kill for. How long have you been a baker, and would you be available to speak at our career day next month?"

She told us the shop had been in her husband's family since before the Civil War. And that she learned how to bake at her grandmother's knee long before she got around to studying reading, writing, and arithmetic. If you were to ask her, fancy schoolin' don't get you that far these days no how. And, she gave an emphatic '*no thank you*' to career day. I asked her if she knew why *Poor Richard's* was closed this near to Christmas.

"Ain't that the most peculiar thing? Elbie must be tossing and turning in his grave. He always sells a boatload of those expensive Swedish wooden toy sets this time of the year. *Poor Richard's* brings a lot of business our way. Now I don't know what'll happen. No, young fella, Johan up and took off early this morning with that wacko friend of his, the one that looks like Joe Stalin.
I can't seem to remember his name right now. He sat right there where your sittin' and drank my tea and ate my crullers. He had an unfamiliar accent and I asked him what it was. And he said 'Greek.' Which caused Johan to laugh

like it was the funniest thing ever said on God's green earth."

"What else do you remember about this guy?"

"It just now came to me. His name. Johan called him Rex."

"Rex?"

"Yes, Rex. You know like 'Rex the Wonder Dog.' You know Rex means king, don't cha?"

"So did Manes tell you when he'll return?"

"No, didn't even bother to tell me he was leaving. Saw them loading up some fancy foreign-looking car early this morning. One of those jobs that has shiny pipes on the outside. Seemed to me that they were arguing. Couldn't tell you what they were saying."

"So *Auntie Abbie*, do me a huge favor, will you? When Manes opens up shop again, please call my service and leave a message. There's big money in it for you."

"How big?"

"Say 20 bucks?"

"I like the sound of that. That's $20 US cash money, right?" I nodded yes, "sure sugar write down your number and I'll call you soon as he returns."

"Thanks so much. So are you the original *Aunt Abigail*?"

"No, no, dearie. I'm Pam. Pamela Peterson. My Jonathan inherited the place back in '49. It's been a good business for us. We've done quite well with it."

Eli said, "My grandfather told me just last week that an old friend of his owned *Poor Richard's*. Elbridge Ross is who he said owned the place."

"Sure. Sure. Old weird Elbridge used tah own the place. Until. Until he was shot through the heart just like my poor dear Jonnie. According to the police, a no-good degenerate stick-up man, high on God knows what, probably robbed and killed my Jonathan and Elbridge Ross one Wednesday night when all the shoppes on the block stay open late."

"So did this Johan Manes buy the place from the estate?"

"No, dearie. That dreadful Johan is Elbie's grandson. That's one angry young man, I don't mind sayin'. I told the police that I wouldn't be surprised to learn that it was that Johan Manes that did the murders. The way I see it, that greedy bastard Johan killed his grandfather for his fortune, then my beloved Jonathan, when he went out to investigate the gunshots. Police said Manes had an airtight alibi and that it was likely that one of those no-good homeless men that have been robbing the stores in this part of town that did the deeds. No. If you ask me, it was that piece of filth, Johan Manes. You can never trust a tattooed man. They're all no-good degenerate fornicators."

"Tattooed?"

"Yes, that Johan has a tattoo of the Statue of Liberty on his right forearm and that communist symbol on his left. You know the one I mean?"

"The Hammer and Sickle?"

"Yes, that's the one."

"What's this fella look like?"

"Not too very tall. Stocky. But pretty darn handsome, I must tell you." She giggled politely, coquettishly.

Pam's *SB* said she was truthful and had something like a crush on Johan Manes, aka *Aristotle Gutenberg*. I checked my Rolex. I had to get going. I needed to officially enroll in the winter semester and be academically advised and sociologically and psychologically evaluated. My first appointment was in about two hours. I thanked her for the snacks, bought a dozen crullers and some gunpowder tea bags to resell at the **O**, and reminded Pam to call me as soon as Manes reopened *Poor Richard's Souvenir Shoppe*. It was time for me to rejoin the real world.

◊◊

Chapter 33
the same old same old blues again

"You can't always get what you want
But if you try sometimes
Well you might find
You get what you need…"

You Can't Always Get What You Want
~ Keith Richards, Mick Jagger

How about that? There really is an Aristotle Rex. Thanks, Pam. My latest hunch suggests that both of the Aristotles, Rex and *Gutenberg*, wanted to watch the chaos following LBJ's assassination from the safety of Manes' study above Poor Richard's; Tabula Rasa's fury unleashed in living color on Johan's brand-new Zenith giant screen TV. One problem with that: The Army-Navy game had been blacked out in the Philadelphia television market. Not enough tickets to the event had been sold prior to the deadline, and the game would not be televised live. It would be aired at midnight thanks to the miracle of videotape technology.

It's a good bet that Aristotle Rex booked one of the swanky meeting rooms in the Waldorf Astoria and convened a conclave of Aristotles from this side of the Mississippi to meet in the Big Apple and drink spirits and marvel at the greatest terrorist achievement of all time unfolding on the big-screen TVs that encircled the room. Until. Until LBJ was not assassinated and thousands of people were not burned to a crisp in a napalm inferno. Humiliated, the angry-angry Aristotles presumably hopped the next train back to Philly and made a beeline for Delancey Street. We probably missed running into each other by mere minutes.

Eli and I rode back to the Z^2 in silence. I really wasn't looking forward to returning to the Waverley campus. Other than Eli, Brenda Burger, and Terry Sullivan, I hadn't seen any of my classmates, instructors, or office personnel since Gracie's murder. Too many people who would want to offer their condolences and share their memories of Grace Gold with me, triggering all of those furies within yet again. It was inevitable. Time to grin and bear it.

I needed to officially enroll for my final semester and be counseled by wise advisors. Who were certain to be ambitious, ambiguous Normals brought in by the new administration. Maybe Miles took Gracie's murder harder than anyone. He often mentioned how much she reminded him of his Annabelle. Now they're both gone. I believe that his memories of Annabelle and Gracie cling to the campus like ghosts. Eli thinks that's the main reason Miles turned the reins of the day-to-day operations over to some guy he hired away from The Collins School in upstate New York. According to Eli Gold, Vice Chancellor Herbert Hawkins was a first-class asshole.

I grabbed a quick shower, shaved, put on clean jeans, and a well-worn Waverley Academy sweatshirt. The phone rang.

"Briscoe residence."

"Edward, it's Max Hermann."

"Sheriff, this is Julius Briscoe. Teddy's out of town."

"When's he due back? I'm calling in a favor, and it's time-critical."

"Not until next year, Sheriff. Is there something I can help you with?"

"Are you involved in the BIG CORNERS operation?"

"Yes. Uncle T and I own the company."

"Can you get word to your store managers?"

"Of course."

"What do you need?"

"Julius, I've just been appointed to head up a task force looking into the serial killer that murdered the socialite Meredith Carver-Bradford. Maybe you read about it in the Inky. She was the most recent victim of a madman that has been operating for years now. The son of a bitch preys on young, attractive women. Strangles the life out of them. Rapes them. Sodomizes them. Scribbles hieroglyphics on their bodies. Sick mother fucker that one. Since it was one of their own that got murdered, the people that matter finally organized a task force faster than you can say Jack Robinson. You familiar with the story?"

"Sure, it was all over the news. How can we help?"

"Julius, what I'm about to tell you must be kept on the QT. I need you to instruct your store personnel to be on the lookout for someone purchasing certain products. Evidence sweeps of over twenty crime scenes, Julius, have turned up a bunch of disgusting stuff that's for sure. But every sweep has also found the same items scattered within a hundred yards of each scene. Some in trash cans. Some in the gutter. I'd like your people to be on the lookout for anyone buying a pack or carton of Chesterfield Kings, a bottle of Frank's Black Cherry Wishniak, TastyKake Butterscotch Krimpets, a tube of red lipstick or a red magic marker, a pack of Trojans, and a pair of rubber gloves. We have reason to believe the perp buys that stuff on the day of each murder. It is important, Julius, that your managers share this information with as few employees as possible. The press must not catch wind of this operation. Should any of your people happen to spot this character, and it's a long shot at best, they should call this special hotline number. Do you have a pen?"

"I'll get one. Give me a minute, Sheriff."

I wrote down the phone number and guaranteed Sheriff Hermann that my employees will not tell anyone about

his project. Then I went down to Universal Import-Exports and typed up the ghoul's shopping list, made copies, and drove the FERRARI to St.David's. Normally, I'd park on the student lot in the southeast quad. This day, I did not. I parked in an unmarked slot on the parking lot adjacent to the *Georgia Wallace-Stern Administration Building*. It sure looked beautiful in the afternoon light. I entered the building at half past noon, when most of the staffers would still be at lunch.

The lobby of the *Georgia Wallace-Stern Administration Building* was as beautiful as any of the lobbies in any of the five-star hotels in the country. Smaller, of course, but no less impressive. Minnie Schönberg was still the receptionist. She was always cheerful, and with her, it wasn't ever an act. She genuinely loved her job, her co-workers, and most especially, the students. She relished following our journeys from adolescence to young adulthood. She was everyone's favorite 'Auntie.' Buttons Don't Lie.

I guess you could call it sucking up or brown-nosing, but Minnie Schönberg adored Gracie Gold, the fair-haired daughter she never had. It put me right up there in Aunt Minnie's pantheon. She raced around the front desk and gave me a granny hug of all granny hugs and a judgmental, stern look.

"What have you done to that gorgeous head of hair of yours, Julius Briscoe? And most importantly, where on earth have you been, young man? You had us all worried sick. Seriously, young Mr. Briscoe, many people around here thought that you had done yourself harm. But not me, I know you much better than that."

It was my turn to lie. "Aunt Minnie, I tried lots of times to come back to school. Trust Me.
I just couldn't. Every time I thought about going to class, I thought about Gracie. Every time
I thought about Gracie, I thought about what happened to her. Every time I thought about what happened to her, I got angry. It was safer for everyone if I stayed away. So I holed up in Lizzie Gold's place down in Florida until I got my mind right. Then I went to Chicago and visited my brother Leonard and his wife and kids. So how about you? How's your family?"

The Schönbergs were all present or accounted for, in good health, and thriving in the LBJ economy.

"What brings you by, Julius? Did you miss me? Aren't you going to compliment me on my new look?"

I told her she looked beautiful like always and that I was here to enroll for next semester. There's forms to fill out, fiery hoops to leap through. The usual bullshit. Also, I needed to get a parking sticker for the *FERRARI*, and I'm supposed to meet with my advisors. Please point me in the right direction."

She said, "I'd be delighted. But I must caution you, these new people are, well, let's just say that they're an acquired taste, many of us haven't gotten around to tolerating."

As if summoned by the mysterious forces of the Universe, a lanky, ambitious bureaucratic type stormed into the lobby, soiling the mood. He was wearing pleated chinos, a pale blue button-down shirt, a clip-on bow tie with a stars-and-stripes motif, desert boots, and he had a cable-knit tennis sweater draped artfully over his shoulders. This insecure clown demanded loudly to know who had parked a *FERRARI* in his highly desired space. The unmarked one that everyone knows he parks his powder-blue Karmann Ghia cabriolet in every day. Ladies and gentlemen, my academic advisor, Clive Dearborn. An unreasonable guy if there ever was one.

"Dude, I cannot tell a lie. That *FERRARI* belongs to me."

"You need to move it, young man, like right now."

"No way. I haven't the time. I'm already late for my appointment. And besides, that space is unmarked. Maybe you should Back Off pal."

"Oh. I see. I'll wager you're my 1:30. Briscoe is it?"

"That's me, all right. Julius Briscoe at your service." He sized me up and down and seemed to reach the erroneous conclusion that he could beat the shit out of me without breaking a sweat. Buttons Don't Lie. He said, "Walk this way," then he strode towards the administrative wing like Gary Cooper with lumbago. I did my best to mimic his style, turned back towards Minnie, and did the eyebrow thing. She covered her mouth with her hands and giggled politely.

I didn't need a course in Personnel Administration to tell me where Dearborn stood in the Waverley Academy's hierarchy. Lowest man on the totem pole. Hind teat. Bottom of the barrel. Dearborn's somewhere down in there. He led me to his tiny, but tidy office on the lower level.

"Before we get down to business, young Mr. Briscoe. One question, please. How is it that a full scholarship student drives a $60,000 sports car? Enlighten me, please."

"I won it in a card game. Caught an inside straight flush. Can't help it if I'm lucky."

Dearborn's *SB* went wacky. His sense of order had been derailed. Back at Boise State, when he was still introducing himself as Clyde Phillipson, he had been the class of '59's resident wise-ass. Clive had worked through that and now considered himself a rising superstar in the private education racket and believed himself to be above such tomfoolery.

"Do you really expect me to believe that, Briscoe?"

"Doesn't make a difference to me what you believe, it is what it is. Won it fair and square from one of my brother's business associates. They're all high-holy-roller lawyers in Chicago. In my experience, playing cards with guys like that is like taking a parking space from an academic advisor. Piece of cake. Know what I mean?"

I thought about sticking my tongue out at him, instead I hit him with that old standard,
FUCK YOU®. It always does the trick. Good old Clive was shocked by my effrontery. Someone from his childhood years ago had taught him to count to ten in his mind before responding to something that might someday offend him. This was one of those days. And it was about to get worse.

Dearborn remained silent for three mandated ten-counts. Then he spoke up as authoritatively as anyone of his kind could: "After reviewing your course of study for the upcoming semester, young Mr. Briscoe, I felt compelled to make certain changes. No self-respecting Ivy League Admissions Officer would ever consider a student with"Business Administration" or "Business Accounting:An Overview" on his transcript. No sir-ee Bob, they would not."

"I've withdrawn you from those abominations and enrolled you instead in POLITICAL SCIENCE:POST-WAR PROGRESSIVISM, which I happen to teach, and AMERICAN REVOLUTIONARY LITERATURE. Not only are these challenging subjects for advanced students such as yourself, they are also the sort of things those college admissions people keep a keen eye out for. Not only that, but you won't have to journey off campus. And yes, you'll still be playing racquet sports daily all semester. No need to thank me."

I felt disillusioned, disheartened, dispirited. Another feckless role model had crashed and burned before my very eyes. At that moment, I felt alone. Cornered. After thinking it over, I realized that I was only a pawn in the famous pissing contest between Waverley's academic advisors to see who would place the most students in the most prestigious colleges and universities. There was big money in it for the winner.

"You did what? Who the fuck are you to go changing shit around without my consent?"

"I'm your academic advisor, young Mr. Briscoe. I'm just doing what I believe is best for you."

"What's best for me is that you put my schedule back together exactly the way I had it. You have ten minutes." I looked at my watch and said, "Starting now." I know. I know. There's no way I could get away with attitude like that at a public high school.

"Don't take that tone with me, young Mr. Briscoe. I'll not stand for it. Your hostile attitude reminds me to remind you to see Vice-Chancellor Hawkins once we're through. Perhaps he'll be able to teach you some civility."

"You're down to nine minutes and twenty seconds. You best get on the horn to EXMOOR. Like right now, asshole."

He gave me his best intimidating glare. I countered with a double dose of FEAR ME®. He checked his Rolodex, picked up the phone, punched in the numbers, and prayed it wasn't too late. Fortunately for him, it wasn't.

I'll summarize. THE WAVERLEY ACADEMY does not offer courses in Business Administration or Accounting but has reciprocal arrangements with the other private schools in Montgomery County. My previous academic advisor, Cinderella Miller, had made the necessary arrangements with EXMOOR ACADEMY last spring. It offered the knowledge I'd need before taking on more responsibility in the BIG CORNERS empire. Thirty-eight stores and counting. EXMOOR required a fifty percent deposit, which I paid in cash. Chancellor Anton Smith walked me through the EXMOOR campus and the paperwork, shook my hand, and said he'd be looking forward to working with me next year, and all that. Oh, by the way, only my mother, Uncle Teddy, and Miles Gold were authorized to make academic decisions on my behalf. The power of paperwork. Dearborn looked deflated. He had but one more card to play in this pissing contest.

"Briscoe, where the fuck were you last semester?"

"Well, Clive, old chap, old buddy, old pal, I drove to New Jersey and killed or disabled the twenty-seven people who were responsible directly or indirectly for the death of Gracie Gold, my fiancé. You know, Chancellor Gold's granddaughter? As you might surmise, processing so many people is quite time-consuming. When I was finished with Atlas City, the first semester was well underway. So I went to Alaska, where I bought a log cabin, smoked a lot of weed, and devoured a bunch of Jack London and Ian Fleming novels."

"Clive old poop, I guess I had you figured right all along. Lazy, insecure, ambitious, a dumb brown-noser. You didn't do your due diligence on me, did you? Had you bothered, you would have learned that I am the co-owner of BIG CORNERS. Since you're from not around here, let me tell you that BIG CORNERS is a chain of successful convenience stores. When I graduate, I'm going right into the family business, which is why I signed up for those courses. You are such a dumb asshole, asshole."

Before making my 'confession,' I had dosed Dearborn with a combination I'm calling FORGET ABOUT IT®. Basically, the same thing I did to my brother and Nettie Gold. Dearborn would remember everything I told him but would be unable to share it with anyone. Now, that's what I call torture. Also, I installed DOCFIELDS® a potent mental booby-trap, just like the one that killed Morgan Fields. Never leave home without it.

My Academic Advisor and close personal friend, Clive Dearborn, insisted on escorting me to my appointment with the Vice-Chancellor. Herbert Hawkins was cut from the same cloth as Clive Dearborn or vice versa. He had a corner office on the first floor, right down the hall from Chancellor Gold's much larger suite. He stood six-two or six-three, was rail thin, in his late forties, had a buzz cut and a toothy grin. He wore a short-sleeved white button-down shirt and a crimson "I LIKE IKE" bow tie. The inventor of *gravity's* portrait was centered on the perfectly knotted tie. He introduced himself and invited me to take a seat. Vice-Chancellor Hawkins handed me a leather portfolio that contained the paperwork I needed to review and sign.

"Chancellor Gold tells me that you are a remarkable young man."

"Miles is being generous. The Golds and the Briscoes go back centuries." I leafed through the paperwork, signing this and signing that. There was a small issue: "I'm going to need a parking sticker for my new car."

Hawkins looked through my file and said, "When did you sell the Jaguar?"

"I haven't sold it. I won a *Ferrari* in a card game when I was in Chicago last month. The tie? Is it a clip-on?"

Hawkins outed himself as something of an expert when it came to cars. Especially exotic ones. He asked the usual questions. I was surprised to learn that Vice Chancellor Hawkins was unfamiliar with Turtle Creek Trail and that he owned a '52 Morgan +4 and a late-model Mustang fastback.

◇◇

Chapter 34
vice president of personnel

> "But I'm just a soul whose intentions are good
> Oh Lord, please don't let me be misunderstood."

Don't Let Me Be Misunderstood
~ Bennie Benjamin, Sol Marcus, Horace Ott

According to a majority of Hollywood screenwriters, it takes a minimum of three murders to be classified as a serial killer. Technically, then, I am not a serial killer. I mean, after all, my 'victims' all died of 'natural causes.' The Shawnee Six's deaths were officially ruled unexplained by the Delaware County coroner. I'm not a psychopath with a burning thirst for blood, and I don't wander from town to town looking for my next victim. When I kill, it's out of necessity. Just wanted to clear that up.

I began my tour of our western region stores armed with my motivational agenda and Christmas bonus money for every full or part-time employee. It takes me about an hour per store per shift. I greeted every employee with a handshake, a TRUTH BOMB, and a dose of SVENGALI®. People can't lie to me and will take everything I tell them as fundamental, self-evident truths.
I compelled the staff to do their very best every single day to make their individual BIG CORNERS the best darned convenience store in the whole wide world.

I took each shift manager and cashier aside to tell them about Sheriff Hermann's top-secret assignment with one important alteration. If anyone with that peculiar shopping list should turn up, they were to call me immediately and to only call the task force if my service reported that I was unreachable. I gave them the special code phrase, "Yes, we have no bananas," that verified that I regarded their call as a high priority and that YOU RANG® was to track me down post-haste.

I realize that those of you that have only known cell phones may not understand the restrictions of the primitive telephone service of the twentieth century. Telephones back then were connected to one another by wires and complicated switching machinery. So everywhere I went, I had to call my service to let them know where I was and how long I'd be there.

When explaining company policy, I draw heavily on the Golden Rule, the law of the jungle, the Ten Commandments, fair play, and common sense. Following these guidelines will earn BIG CORNERS' employees job security, much better than average wages, and the envy of their counterparts in the rapidly expanding convenience-store industry. And remember to always do whatever your supervisors, Ted Briscoe or I, instruct you to do, unless, of course, it would violate one of Asimov's laws.

This approach has been 100% successful so far. Based on six months' worth of data from both MONGO MINGS restaurants, employee turnover has been negligible, our repeat customer rate has been phenomenal, our wait staff receive tips of, on average, 30 percent, and the cash registers always balance. Happy employees, happy customers, happiness all around. Can't wait to see how well the highly motivated BIG CORNERS team performs now and into the future. I think Lenny's probably right. I could make a fortune in the personnel brain-washing business.

It took me the rest of the week to visit all thirty-eight stores twice. Day shifts, night shifts, swing shifts. I got to know our employees and they got to Know, Respect, and Revere me. Never leave home without it.

I got back to the O at 4:30 Friday afternoon. I had whittled down my presentation to about eight to ten minutes per employee, depending on how much time the Q&A took. I went down to Uncle Teddy's office and began to type up my notes. I have a pretty good memory, but putting things in writing seems to cement the information into my brain.

Margot poked her head into the office; she looked flushed, nervous. "Julius, there's some FBI guy upstairs asking for you." She handed me his business card:

FEDERAL BUREAU OF INVESTIGATION
SPECIAL AGENT RAYMOND KRIEGER
FB4-5555 EXT. 215

I found Special Agent Krieger standing by the magazine rack. He was leafing through the latest edition of MOTOR TREND. He stood about six feet two, with a slender build. He was wearing an off-the-rack grey suit from Gimbels or Lit Brothers. A solid middle-class Normal from his crew cut right on down to the bottom of his shiny black rubber-soled shoes.

"Special Agent Krieger, I'm Julius Briscoe, how can I help you?" We shook hands. His SB was in sharp focus. He was likely thinking of me as a suspect, not as a source.

"I'm not one to believe in coincidences, but ain't that a *Ferrari 500 Superfast* parked right outside your store, just like the one in this here magazine?"

I walked over to the front window and looked out onto Eighteenth Street and exclaimed, "Golly gee willikers, would you look at that? I guess you FBI guys sure know all about foreign cars and shit. Don't that beat all?"

"I'm Special Agent Raymond Krieger, nice to finally meet you. Is there somewhere we can speak more privately?" Before leading him to the conference room on the lower level, I asked him if he'd like a cup of gunpowder tea and a tasty cruller from *Aunt Abigail's*. He declined politely and mentioned that many in the bureau would consider my offer an attempt at bribery. I hit the feeb with a double shot of Fuck You® and a Truth Bomb® and led him down the stairs.

"What's on your mind, Special Agent?" Thanks to Miles Gold, I already knew. Best not to share that tidbit with a highly trained investigator like Special Agent Raymond Krieger.

"We're looking into the disappearance, probably the kidnapping, of Jeremiah Dickinson from a youth home in Atlas City, New Jersey. Briscoe, do you own a red Ford pickup?"

"No, I only own sports cars. That's my *Ferrari* out there. Who is Jeremiah Dickinson and why would you think I'd know anything about his alleged abduction?"

"Jeremiah Dickinson is the fourteen-year-old boy who threw the kettle weight that killed Grace Edna Gold this past September. You do know who Grace Edna Gold is, don't you?"

"Of course I do. But I've never heard of this Dickinson fellow until just recently."

"How recently would you say?"

I consulted my inner Rolex, "About thirty seconds ago. Give or take."

Krieger poked and prodded for another five minutes. He came away convinced that I had nothing to do with Jeremiah Dickinson's alleged kidnapping and that, considering the enormity of my loss, I was holding up remarkably well. If I needed to talk to someone, the federal agent advised me that I was qualified, under several government programs, for grief counseling sessions free of charge.

I escorted Special Agent Krieger back upstairs. Margot, wearing her best winter coat, greeted us, her eyes flashing with impatient anger. I had agreed to be her escort when she took her 'niece and nephew' to sit on Santa Claus's lap this afternoon. Thanks to Special Agent Krieger's unscheduled visit, we were running a little late.

Margot had become something of a local celebrity following the publication of a series of articles in The Philadelphia Inquirer called *'Savage Destinies: Innocent Lives Destroyed'* by the paper's star investigative reporter Loretta Lewis. The series recounted horror stories about innocent men and women ground up and spit out by the system.

Margot's tragic tale generated the most public outrage and sympathy. Not only had she been victimized by her boyfriend and railroaded by the justice system, but she had been irretrievably damaged while an inmate at the Industrial School for Women in Muncie, Pennsylvania. As a result of unspeakable savagery, Margot was unable to bear children or to engage in sexual intercourse without severe physical and emotional pain. The series concluded with these words: "Despite the horrors, the indignities she survived, Miss X remains, to this day, hauntingly beautiful and serene."

The Inky knew when it had a winner. It plastered Margot's image on billboards all over the Delaware Valley, on the side panels of its delivery trucks, and in a banner ad above the masthead for weeks and weeks. If it were not for Uncle T's and Miles Gold's intervention, the Inky would have printed the chapter about the ironies surrounding Margot's current employment. The **O**, of course, is co-owned and operated by Edward Briscoe, whose son, Victor, was killed right out there on Eighteenth Street by the Buick Roadmaster operated by Margot St James, who was, at that time, under the influence of a massive overdose of chloral hydrate, a hypnotic date-rape drug she mistakenly thought was aspirin.

So here's the thing about stalkers: they're all fucking nuts. Obsessive, delusional, unbalanced bat-shit crazies. Even before the publicity, Margot had attracted them daily on her way to work. We routinely chased them off. Uncle T and I had little choice but to promote her. So we kicked her downstairs, out of the sight of the lunatic passersby. Now, she's Uncle T's executive assistant.

Margot had learned all about logistics while working for Dr. Michael DeBocca, the director of production at *PhillyMint*. With 38 stores, inventory distribution and internal communications are ongoing, inefficient facts of BIG CORNERS' life. Margot rolled up her sleeves and streamlined those parts of the operation in a little less than a month.

Chapter 35
meet youse at the iggle

"…wander through a forest
where the trees have leaves of prisms
that break the light into colors
that no one knows the names of…"

I Wasn't Born to Follow
~ Carole King, Gerry Goffin

Nadine O'Hara has been Margot's best friend since they were both four-year-olds. Way back then, Nadine had been a Brodsky, and Margot had been Margaret Jameson. Nadine stood by Margaret during her troubles at Fairmount High and all the way through Margo's imprisonment and eventual release. During that time, Nadine had given birth to two children by different fathers: a boy she named Banjo and a daughter named for her husband's late grandmother, Melody Bradford O'Hara.

Banjo's biological father was a multi-instrumentalist in a blue-grassy, old-school, new-wavy roots music ensemble calling themselves *The Raucous Troubadours*. Roscoe Rodgers had a girlfriend in every town the *Troubadours* played. In Philadelphia, his consort had been Nadine Brodsky, who, at that time, worked at *Fennario's* as a hostess/short-order cook and sometimes backup singer. It was lust at first sight.

The Raucous Troubadours were more of an opening act than they were headliners. The unpolished type you endure while patiently waiting for the star to take the stage. Following a disappointing, somewhat hostile reaction to their disastrous first set, the *Troubadours* eluded the boo-birds by high-tailing it back to Fall River. Hours later, their

VW microbus was pulled over by Officer Stewart Judee, a Connecticut State Trooper.

During a possible probable cause search of the psychedelically painted microbus incapable of speeding, Officer Judee discovered six kilos of marijuana, eleven pounds of magic mushrooms, a liter of a clear liquid suspected to be lysergic acid diethylamide, and a ream of laboratory-grade blotting paper. The *Troubadours* were charged with possession with intent to sell and were sentenced to five years in the MacDougall-Walker Correctional Institution, a maximum security facility. No safer place to keep those degenerate hippie drug dealer types away from the goodly citizens of Connecticut.

Roscoe, a natural-born smart-ass, didn't survive his incarceration intact. The resident alpha males didn't take to Roscoe's brand of humor and reminded him of his shortcomings each day. By the time he was paroled, Roscoe had lost many of his teeth and his good looks. His fingers and thumbs had been repeatedly broken and left untreated and were irretrievably malformed. Since he could no longer play an instrument, Roscoe got himself fitted with dentures and was booked steadily as a lounge singer doing covers of the top forty songs on your Hit Parade.

It is widely known that the Center City Santa's Village is home to the real, actual, *certified-genuine* Santa Claus. The one and only, gift-giving, jolly old good-natured St.Nick. Modern parents have grown up believing such fairy tale propaganda and couldn't imagine taking their sweet little darlings to any other Santa in the whole wide world.

Every Philadelphian knows exactly where to find the *certified-genuine* Santa Claus in the days leading up to Xmas; he'll be sitting on his throne on the eighth floor of *John Wanamaker's*, where, by appointment only, for a generous honorarium and a donation to Santa's favorite charity, he'll entertain your sweet little darlings and their extravagantly unrealistic wishes for a minute or so, smile for the photographer elf, and then shoo your runny-nosed brats off of his lap with a bundle of made-in-Japan-cheap Santa souvenirs for them to cherish forever and ever.

Right smack dab in the middle of its Grand Court, *John Wanamaker's* has this two-and-a-quarter-ton bronze statue of an eagle called Durana. Ever since the roaring twenties, it has served as a rendezvous point for thousands and thousands of people. The invitation, "Meet youse at the Iggle," has a fond place in the heart of every Philadelphian above the age of fifteen.

Margot had arranged for a limo and a motorcycle escort to rush us to *Wanamaker's* the moment I finished washing Special Agent Krieger's brain. We arrived at the Iggle, right on time, to find Nadine O'Hara, her husband Darrell, their two kids Banjo and Melody, and Darrell's sister Cara gathered around the big bird.

Cara O'Hara was earnestly trying to explain the historic significance of places like *Wanamaker's* to her brother's kids and getting nowhere quickly. "You two have to imagine what the world was like in the 1860s. That's a long, long time ago, when this place was built. Back in those days, people didn't have too many entertainment options. So places like this had to be more than just a big store."

"We want to go see Santa."

Cara looked at her watch and said, "Here's the thing, kids. Our appointment with Santa, he's very, very busy, you know, isn't for another forty-two minutes. So I thought you'd like to learn about this great big bird and this amazing super store. They're very famous."

"We want to go see Santa."

Allow me to make the introductions. Nadine Brodsky O'Hara is the prototypical, ordinary looking, side kick to your prototypically smokin' hot neighborhood femme fatale. If Margot's still a 10, and she is, then Nadine's a seven and an eighth. She's married to Darrell O'Hara, an up-and-coming junior officer in the 9th District of the Philadelphia Police Department.

A third-generation cop, Darrell O'Hara, is tall and dashing, and as outwardly straight-laced as they come. He gave me his best intimidating stare, which was pretty effective, I must admit.
I read his SB as hostile, suspicious, and threatened. I countered with a friendly grin and a half dose of PSYCHIC FLASH-BANG®. Knocked the piss and vinegar right out of him. Sergeant O'Hara was still able to give me a firm handshake, an insincere smile, and a clichéd warning, "I'm onto all you kikes. Watch your step, Briscoe. Especially around me sister." For emphasis, he pointed to both of his eyes with the index and middle fingers of his left hand and mouthed the words 'I've got my eyes on you, motherfucker.' Just like any politically ambitious junior-officer-on-his-way-up or down would.

Banjo Brodsky was almost six years old, stood nearly four feet tall. The boy was Dennis the Menace incarnate. A living, breathing, wisecracking whirlwind straight out of the comic books. A blonde-haired, blue-eyed, ruddy-faced perpetual motion machine. Banjo's SB was nearly impossible to make sense of. His colors were out of order and distorted. I hit him with a bespoke dose of CALM THE FUCK DOWN® which worked like a charm.

Melody O'Hara, like the majority of four-year-old girls worldwide, was sunny and adorable. Right up there with Molly Anne Briscoe in every way. Melody knew most of her ABGs. Had a Siamese cat named Lester, a Chihuahua named Spike, and a yellow parakeet named Tweetie. Melody was almost three feet tall, had dark curly hair, all of her baby teeth, and deep, dark brown, studious eyes. She took an instant liking to me, gripped my hand, looked up, and asked, "Mr. Uncle Julius, do you know where Santa Claus is hiding?"

Neither William nor Charlotte Briscoe had much use for religions. Not the one they were born into (Judaism) or any of the other popular religions available to them in this popular sub-division of spacetime. Which is how I came to be raised as a culturally Jewish agnostic. We didn't celebrate any of the Jewish or Christian holidays. Not Chanukah, not Christmas, Easter, or Passover. Nonetheless, I have been force-fed all things Christmas ever since kindergarten.

Every December, we had to learn and sing Christmas songs when Santa Claus himself visited Shawnee Elementary with his ho-ho-ho's, free copies of *Scholastic World, McGuffey's Reader, and The National Geographic.* He also handed out candy canes, chocolate bars, cap pistols,
yo-yos, Frisbees, and big round campaign buttons that said

"Official Santa's Helper." The sixth-grade teacher pretending to be Santa didn't seem to care much that I didn't believe in Santa Claus, Jesus, Buddha, Elvis, or Harry S. Truman. He just sat me on his lap and posed for our souvenir photo and sent me on my way.

A couple of my friends had been Bar Mitzvah'd, so I have clocked a few hours of ~~nap~~ synagogue time trying my best not to react immaturely to the strange language and the strange rituals.

Some communist guy once said that religion is the opiate of the masses. But if religions are really like opium, why aren't Normals more peaceful and respectful, and honest? Inquiring minds want to know.

Some of the numbness caused by Gracie's death was starting to wear off. It's safe to say that I am no longer able to so easily resist the invitations, subtle or blatant, coming from most of the females I meet every day. Cara O'Hara was way up there on the irresistibility scale. She was a senior at *Sacred Heart Academy* and had already been accepted by *Villanova* and *St.Joe's* into their pre-med programs. She was waiting to hear from *uPenn, Temple,* and *Bryn Mawr* before making a commitment. Cara's SB was intense. Her colors were bright and rich, her textures were like these concentric circles spinning in opposite directions at various speeds.

Cara O'Hara stood around five feet five, had bright red-orange hair, a galaxy of freckles that flowed from her forehead, across the bridge of her nose, and onto both of her cheeks. Her eyes were probing and a brilliant green, and she had a sardonic smile. Her Status Button said, and I'm quoting, "Julius, if we weren't in *Wanamaker's* and my brother and his family weren't here, I'd drag you to a secret place I know and fuck your brains out." Or words to that effect.

I can't help it.

Picture a crowded department store at Christmastime. Shoppers are slowly moving to and fro, resigned to the sluggishness, the constant, yet inadvertent, bumping and pushing. The irritating closeness of strangers. A young, well-dressed couple, a team of pickpocketers, were feasting on the listless crowd. I might have mentioned something to Sergeant O'Hara, and I might have hit him with a dose of PECKINPAH® before he went off to apprehend those dangerous felons and get himself another commendation. His dedication to duty freed me to openly flirt with his kid sister without his disapproving presence.

I know that most people in the Delaware Valley have shopped there often, but I had never set foot in *Wanamaker's* before that afternoon. What can I tell you? My parents failed me in the department store department. I was grateful for Cara O'Hara's dissertation on the history of *John Wanamaker's,* the country's first department store, the first to use electric lights. It was home to the world's largest pipe organ, and, among other things, the world's first indoor monorail known as *The Santa Express* this time of year, and *The Rocket Express* from mid-January to Thanksgiving week. It circled above the toy, camera, and music departments up on the eighth floor.

I was surprised to see that nearly all of the kids on the express elevator to Santa's Village were wearing their Halloween costumes. Some kind of tradition I reckon.

Banjo was dressed up like the movie cowboy, Hopalong Cassidy. He was wearing a black kid-sized ten-gallon cowboy hat, a black shirt, black high-tops, black jeans, and a pair of cap pistols holstered on the gun belt strapped to his waist. Melody was dressed like Wonder Woman, complete with a magic lariat and a sparkly tiara.

We rode the designated elevator up to the eighth floor. It was operated by a cheery young woman, Stella by name tag, who was dressed up like one of Santa's elves. The extra-large car was filled to capacity with eager youngsters and their indulgent parents. There was a chitter-chattering of excited young voices jabbering on about their Xmas wishlists and their favorite TV shows and Beatles songs. Just like in the *Wizard of Oz*, the dull gray elevator doors opened onto the vibrant, spectacular eighth floor. Wow!

The SB's of every single kid on our elevator car swirled into exactly the same pattern. Everyone was dazzled. Mesmerized by the splendor. As was I. Margot looked at me and began to chuckle, "Well look at you, Julius Briscoe! Just look at you! You look like all these little kids here. Girls, don't you think Jules looks really cute?" Nadine, Melody, and Cara nodded their heads in agreement. Cara embellished, "I'd say extra cute, if you don't mind me saying."

"I minds you saying," shouted an indignant Melody, "Auntie Cara, I called first dibs on Mr. Uncle Julius. Isn't that right, Banjie?" Banjo shook his head no and yes alternately. I guess that meant something to people of a certain age, but I'm not sure what.

John Wanamaker's eighth floor is amazing, incredible, mind-bogglingly cool. We stepped out of the elevator onto a power aisle done up like the Yellow Brick Road. It led to Santa's elevated throne far off in the distance. There were intersecting aisles and aisles of brightly packaged toys and games. We saw dolls and stuffed animals imprisoned in cardboard packaging. Row after row of unicycles, bicycles, tricycles, scooters, ice, and roller skates. Everything was neatly arranged by size and color. Everyone was overwhelmed by the cornucopia before them. A garish feast for their eyeballs.

There were jugglers, fortune tellers, and street magicians impersonating cheery elves, wandering about, entertaining the shoppers. Obsequious Santa's helpers were passing out coupons or directing confused shoppers to their destinations.

While in uniform, Sergeant Darrell O'Hara stopped into *Wanamaker's* one day last week to buy or otherwise obtain tickets for rides on the Santa Express and a reserved place in Santa's VIP queue. Before racing off at quarter speed to apprehend the pickpocketers, Darrell had the good common sense to hand the complimentary tickets to Nadine.

Although Banjo Brodsky was tall enough to ride the monorail unsupervised, he was not exactly considered trustworthy by his mother. Last year, the not so little rascal was also tall enough to ride solo. That time, he had smuggled a squirt gun filled with something vile-smelling and mixed with India ink onto the ride. Banjo's first and only victim was one of Santa's helpers, Amber Rose Braun, who ran backstage in tears, looking like one of those Rorschach ink blotter test things, and smelling like 'rhinoceros piss' according to Santa's agent Henrietta Underhill, who was keeping an eye on her randy superstar client from the wings.

Sergeant Darrell O'Hara had been scheduled to ride next to the little menace, but duty had called. As a result, I was assigned to keep Banjo out of trouble. I confiscated his cap pistols and gave them to Cara, who stowed them in her shoulder bag. Cara and Melody took their seats behind the monorail operator's cockpit in the first car. Banjo and I were directed to the Naugahyde bench in the last car.

Since Nadine was afraid of heights and somewhat claustrophobic, she and Margot took the escalator up to the 9th floor and a secluded booth in the *Crystalized Tea Room*. We agreed to meet at the gate to Santa's Village in forty-five minutes or so. And, if for some strange reason things go awry, meet up at the Iggle.

The cute teenager operating the monorail that afternoon was Jeannie O'Doyle who was, until yesterday, Santa's 'extra special' helper. Their torrid relationship flamed out when Jeannie discovered him in his dressing room with Nita Murphy happily bouncing on his lap instead of her.

Winston Carmichael has been Philadelphia's premier Santa Claus since '58. He was discovered by Henrietta Underhill of the UNDERHILL/FRANKENHEIMER MODELING AGENCY. Winston Carmichael was built like a svelte Santa minus thirty years or so. He was well over six foot tall, broad shouldered, had a permanent five o'clock shadow, dark curly hair, handsome, rugged features.

Despite all of his positives, Henrietta had a difficult time booking Carmichael on fashion shoots. He was too large. Most trend setting designers didn't produce their creations with Winston's proportions in mind. On the plus side, Winston was able to get steady work as a model wearing items from his personal wardrobe in shoots for non-high-fashion jobs.

UNDERHILL/FRANKENHEIMER maintained an exclusive wardrobe rental service to help their clients land those 'bring your own wardrobe' gigs. Among the garments gathering dust in storage was a bespoke Santa suit, crafted by a skillful but desperate tailor in 1894, for a giant of a man who died before paying for the outfit. With a few minor alterations, it fit Winston perfectly. He wore it to his audition at *Wanamaker's*. They put Winston on their list and told him that they would be in touch.

The rest is an age-old, but tawdry tale of self-indulgent greed, political and actual backstabbing, that helped Winston become Philly's favorite Santa since '58. And, yes, in and out of costume, Winston Carmichael was a consummate ladies' man. Evidently, making it with Santa Claus was something of a popular fetish back in those days. Ho-ho-ho.

◊◊

Chapter 36
dead man's curve

"Well the last thing I remember, Doc, I started to swerve
And then I saw the Jag slide into the curve."

Deadman's Curve
~ Artie Kornfeld, Brian Wilson,
Jan Berry, Roger Christian

Just sixteen years of age, Jeannie O'Doyle was as sweetly naive as it gets, and had totally taken Winston Carmichael's bullshit as a heartfelt proposal of marriage and love everlasting. When she found her handsome fiancé doing it with her former best friend forever, more than her heart was broken. Everything she learned in Sunday School, every promise to abide by the teachings of the church were forsaken in that instant. There was blood in her eyes and a hunger for revenge in her broken heart. Jeannie was also a certified monorail operator and was covering that afternoon for her cousin Bridey, who was down with the sniffles, or so she said. Just the opportunity the vengeful teenager was praying for all night.

The security guard at *Wanamaker's* employee entrance was this old timer named Hal Ashleigh. Everyone called him 'Ash.' He was friendly and affable, happy to have a steady job, a spiffy uniform, and a generous employee discount. Ash had a good memory for names and faces, especially the young women. And he secretly had a major crush on Jeannie O'Doyle. So despite her sour mood and furtive mannerisms, Ash let her enter the store without checking her handbag like he was supposed to do.

That afternoon, Jeannie had, in her handbag, a Colt Peacemaker that once belonged to her grandfather, who fought in the Spanish-American War alongside Teddy Roosevelt. Before he died, Mickey O'Doyle had taught his golden-haired Jeannie, the apple of his good eye, everything she needed to know about sharpshooting and the care and maintenance of the legendary hand cannon. Standing upright with a two-handed grip, Jeannie could shoot Dixie Cups off of a fence post from fifty yards out with the best of them. Shooting that bastard Winston Carmichael between his shifty eyes from an elevated position while advancing towards him at ten miles per hour didn't seem like a difficult shot to her at all.

Jeannie's plan was as simple as it was diabolical. She was also smuggling two boxes of ammo and several hacksaw blades in her handbag. The Santa Express had a crude, but effective, speed-limiting device; a steel band bolted to the console that prevented the throttle from being pushed to the maximum. Thus hobbled, the four-car monorail train could not exceed the speed limit, which was about ten miles an hour. Full-throttle, the Santa Express could reach its maximum speed in twenty seconds, when it would certainly derail at Deadman's Curve. After she killed that no-good two-timing bastard, Jeannie intended to push the throttle to the max and then shoot herself.

Not that I was a big Santa Claus fan or anything, but you can be certain I wasn't going to let things go according to Jeannie's plan. I've had some experience with gun-toting Normals in the past. Made Jeannie's angry, twisted SB easy to recognize and to read her anti-social intentions. Oh, you say, 'stopping her is a piece of cake for guys like you. Just push her red button, young Mr. Briscoe, and be done with it. That'll stop her dead in her tracks. Not so fast, Einstein.

Between my location and Jeannie's location sat about thirty kids and a smattering of adults. All of them had buttons.

I need to remind you that what I refer to as buttons aren't exactly symmetrical objects. They're more like regions and points in Normals' brains and bodies. Thinking of them as 'buttons' helped me to first make sense of *slam.* Give me a break, I was thirteen then, 'button' was the best explanation my subconscious could come up with considering some walrus-shaped *Royal King* wannabe was threatening to kill me with a switchblade. Of course, I don't actually push these 'buttons.' It's more like this beam of invisible energy that shoots out of my head towards the target.

Considering the number of people I've either killed or fucked with using *slam,* you'd think this wasn't the first time I had to deal with this problem. In every case, I've always had a clear shot, no other Normals between me and my target. So what to do? If I were to try to hit Jeannie's red button, I would most certainly hit any number of Santa Express riders' red buttons as well. Which was unacceptable. Same issue with all of the other buttons.

I was still trying to come up with a plan when the monorail doors closed. The train left the station. Jeannie greeted us with a well-rehearsed, but unenthusiastic-sounding speech about *Wanamaker's* groundbreaking monorail, the *Crystalized Tea Room*, the famous eagle, the world's largest pipe organ, and, of course, Santa's Village. Her droll dissertation was timed to mention Santa Claus as the train rolled past him, and Jeannie would have a perfect angle on that no-good heartbreaker, Winston Carmichael, who was, at that very moment, on a potty break. Only an empty throne in Jeannie's sights.

The official ~~Rocket~~ *Santa Express Users Manual* dictates that in the event Santa is not on his throne when the monorail first rolls past, the operator must take it around again so that the passengers would get what they paid their 9 cents for, an effusive ho-ho-ho from the *certified- genuine* Santa Claus.

It's called *Dead Man's Curve* because it sounds scary, and the monorail track passes over *Deadwood City,* where all the cool cowboy and cowgirl gear was now on special. Ten percent off and triple green stamps for the next twenty minutes. The monorail track curves just enough to the left, so by leaning my head against the window, I had a clear line of sight to the deranged teeny bopper in the first car. I hit her, only her, with triple doses of CALM THE FUCK DOWN®, DO NOT KILL SANTA®, and PECKINPAH®. Which seemed to do the trick.

The next time around, Santa was back on his throne, six-year-old twins with pigtails bouncing on his lap. Everyone waved and cheered. Jeannie wept silently as she retrieved the Peacemaker from its hiding place and shot herself in her broken heart. She slumped over onto the console. Her momentum and body weight were more than enough to push the unconstrained throttle to the max. An unintended consequence. The Santa Express rocketed forward with a sudden lurch. Beyond loomed *'Dead Man's Curve'* and certain tragedy. Everyone screamed and shrieked in terror. Which made it easy for me to push their central pause buttons almost simultaneously. All except for Cara, who was our last, best, and only hope. And she was way ahead of the curve.

A wire mesh wall with a skeleton key-locked door stood between Cara and Jeannie. When she realized what

Jeannie was doing with the hacksaw blades, Cara, a highly trained former monorail operator herself, wrestled Banjo's cap guns and extra caps from her shoulder bag and began to scrape the gunpowder out of each cap into the cover of her favorite lipstick, 'Georgia Peach' by Maxx Factor.

Within seconds, Cara had collected enough gunpowder to defeat the lock on the gate. She poured the gunpowder into the keyhole, used a length of Melody's Wonder Woman lasso as a fuse, and lit it with a vintage Zippo. As intended, her efforts produced a powerful enough explosion to spring the primitive lock. The door flew open, and Cara rushed into the cockpit, pushed Jeannie's limp body aside, and pulled back on the throttle. She was about half a second too late.

So there's this thing called *inertia*. It was invented by this guy Isaac Newton way back in the sixteen hundreds. According to Newton, *inertia* is the tendency of a moving object, say an out of control monorail train, to remain moving unless something, say a patented emergency monorail braking system, suddenly prevents it from moving. Which is what happened when the first car, traveling way too fast, triggered the sensor. The experimental prototype device cut the power to, and locked the wheels of only the first two cars.

The emergency braking system was designed to safely stop a two-car train that was traveling no faster than twenty miles per hour. Not a four-car train going nearly twice that speed. All that forward momentum had to go somewhere. It ripped the last car, the one containing yours truly and about a dozen paused kids, off the monorail, which left us swinging from the third car coupler like a pendulum or a wrecking ball. Before slowing to a stop, our car demolished accurate kid-sized reproductions of the legendary *OK Corral, John the Blacksmith's*, and a burger joint called *Rose of Alabama's*.

Once our car stopped swinging, gravity took hold and pulled the first three cars off the rail, causing all four of them to land onto the sales floor right side up and to rip the electrified rail from its moorings, which caused a short circuit that knocked the power out. All of Center City went dark minutes before the official start of the weekend rush hour.

Someone amongst the top high-management muckity-mucks at *Wanamaker's* had the good common sense to have state-of-the-art emergency floodlighting installed on each floor. They came on all harsh and contrasty mere seconds after the power went out.

The doors to the Santa's Express monorail cars were hinged along the port-side roof line and opened like Gracie's gull-wing Mercedes-Benz used to do. The impact had jarred them open on all four cars. I unpaused everyone and ushered them away from the wreckage.

Holy shit. I've never seen anything like it. By actual head count, I had paused and now just unpaused 36 kids ages 4 to 12 and, not counting Cara O'Hara, five women. Thanks to the padded interiors of the monorail cars, no one was injured too badly. Bumps, bruises, scrapes, and a few minor cuts. No broken bones, no shell shock, no life-threatening injuries. All of them had been rag-doll limp during the entire incident and had no recollection of the terrifying events.

One moment things were going along great. Everyone was angling to get a look at Santa Claus when Jeannie shot herself, and the monorail rocketed forward. The next thing they knew, they were scattered around what was the remains of *Deadwood City,* totally disoriented but otherwise none the worse for wear. They shuffled from place to place, trying to reconnect with their loved ones.

Fortunately, no one shopping on the eighth floor had been injured by the catastrophe at Deadman's Curve. Many of the shoppers flocked to the wreckage, eager to help or to gawk. Jeannie's Peacemaker, along with Cara's shoulder bag containing Banjo's gun belt, among other items, flew out of the car and, during the shuffling, were kicked towards the remains of *Rose of Alabama's.*

I'm not sure how old you have to be before you're able to tell the difference between an official Hopalong Cassidy cap pistol and a Colt Peacemaker. I can tell you from experience that almost six years old isn't that age. Banjo made a beeline for the shiny weapon, said 'golly gee,' picked it up, and pointed it in the general direction of his baby sister who was holding my hand. Banjie's extended arms could not hold the two and a half pound lethal weapon steady. His eyes were lit up with excitement, there was mischief in his heart.

We were standing by what was left of the OK Corral, a good ten yards from Banjo. He shouted "Hey smelly Melly, see what I got!" Then he pointed it in our general direction, and
I had little choice. Muscle memory screamed 'danger Julius Briscoe. Danger. Punch his red button.' Common sense prevailed. I hit his pause button, and, unavoidably, the pause buttons of eight other kids and two grown-ups, well-meaning do-gooders who had been trying to do good things when I inadvertently paused them.

I took the weapon from Banjo's hands, emptied the cylinder, pocketed the bullets, and stuffed the Peacemaker in my belt, badass gangster style. Then I unpaused all of them. It hit me just then how strange that was. I've always thought of *Slam* as a line-of-sight thing. A focused beam, not a wave. It seemed unlikely to me that all ten of those yellow buttons, each a different size, shape, and elevation, could have aligned so perfectly. A wave and a beam? Or something different?

They were frozen for all of ten seconds and seemed to be recovering well enough. Then Melody asked me a question that knocked me for a loop.

"Mr. Uncle Julius, how did you do that?"

"Do what, sweetie?"

"Make everybody stop moving. You didn't say 'Red Light' out loud, but everybody stopped walking when you thinked it. Then everybody started walking again when you thinked 'Green Light'."

I made a snap decision to enroll in a Parapsychology class should one be available. Shucks, I'd have to interact with my old pal Clive Dearborn again.

Here's the nice thing about REAL TIME AMNESIA®, it can be retroactive. If you use it soon enough, your victim wouldn't have had the time to form lasting memories of a recent experience, like Melody almost being shot by her half-witted half-brother who got to play *'Red Light/Green Light'* with Mr. Uncle Julius, the handsomest mind-talker in the whole wide world.

Never leave home without it.

◊◊

Chapter 37
escape from Wanamaker's

"Fear is the mind-killer. Fear is the little-death that brings total obliteration.
I will face my fear."

Dune
~ Frank Herbert

For good reason, most members of the animal kingdom fear the dark. So take a city-wide power outage, a couple of inches of unpredicted snow, and throw in a dash of claustrophobia, two cloves of xenophobia, a splash of phobophobia, and add in the sudden, horrifying realization that you have a roast in the oven and it was going to take three hours, at the very least, to get back home, and you have all of the elements necessary to organize a stampede, incite unchecked looting, and foment savage rioting. And here I was stuck on the eighth floor of *John Wanamaker's* with two little kids and their sexy aunt trying to figure out what to do about getting everyone home safely and how to prevent an impending catastrophe should the holiday shoppers lose self-control and go mental.

Cara O'Hara, a practicing pragmatist, reminded that we were to wait by the gate to Santa's Village for Margot and Nadine to return from the *Crystalized Tea Room* with the children's winter coats and something like an escape plan. We were pretty far from Santa's Village; there were hundreds of people racing in one direction or another, trying to find their way in the harsh lighting, screaming and shouting their loved ones names.

I was experiencing one of those moments, some would categorize as an epiphany. It seemed to me that all those

Status Buttons, every single one of them on all twelve floors, had synchronized. Colors, textures, rotation exactly the same. Then every multi-colored Status Button glowed pearly white. Thousands of them. Not just the Normals inside *Wanamaker's,* but everywhere I went from then on, Normals each have one, just one, cranium-shaped, pearlescent button. I thinked BE COOL® and watched as a confidant calmness soaked into the crowd of holiday shoppers. No unruly behavior when Julius T. Briscoe is in the building. Thanks for the tip, Melody. Can't wait to tell Lenny and Uncle T!

A man claiming to be a descendant of John Wanamaker himself came on the public address system, "Ladies and Gentlemen, I urge you to remain calm and orderly. Please stay where you are at the moment as we conduct a systematic floor-by-floor evacuation, beginning with the shoppers on the first floor. Be advised that the telephones are not working either. So there is no need to fight over them."

"Thank you for your cooperation, and please know that looters will be ~~shot on sight,~~ pardon me, prosecuted. My associates will be standing by at the exits handing out coupons for a twenty percent discount on your next same-day purchases. Again, thank you for your patronage and your civilized behavior."

Everyone was unsurprisingly compliant, yet it still took almost an hour for us to reach the front door.

We want to see Santa!

When we finally escaped from *Wanamaker's*, we spotted Sgt. Darrell O'Hara directing traffic. He was wearing a bright yellow safety vest over his mock leather full-length coat. He had an official police department whistle and a flashlight. Darrell O'Hara was wearing a pair of white gloves and a police officer's hat, all requisitioned from a red and white squad car that was mired in the traffic jam of all traffic jams. I'm not accepting credit for it, but the instant we stepped out onto Market Street, the power came back on. Then it went back off for a minute and a half, then back on to stay. Center City lit up just like a Christmas tree. Festive chaos.

Melody was riding on my shoulders and easily spotted her father demonstrating his leadership abilities at 13th and Market.

"Look, there's me Daddy. Hi, me Daddy, it's me, Melody." Darrell O'Hara was in his seventh heaven and too far from his adorable daughter to hear her greeting over the traffic noise and the frustrated motorists and pedestrians.

Only a few of my friends are Irish. That doesn't mean I think poorly of Irish people or anything, but it does go to explain why it took me so long to reach the conclusion that Sergeant Darrell O'Hara had it coming. I'm told he's had it coming for the better part of the decade. So much for the benefit of the doubt.

Everyone is a product of his environment, right? Since we all don't live in the same part of the environment, it takes some time, say, for the Irish and the Brits, the blacks and the whites, the Christians and Jews, and the *haves* and *have-nots* to holster their weaponized xenophobias and find sacred common ground. Each side must be willing to make an effort to understand that those strangers' customs and beliefs may, on the surface, appear to be incompatible with your own, yet, they fundamentally solve similar problems and serve similar purposes as do your equally strange customs and beliefs.

Sergeant O'Hara was standing dead center on the intersection, his right hand palm forward, signaling the westbound traffic to stay put. Your turn will come. It was snowing. Heavy wet snow. The kind that piles up and sticks around for weeks. O'Hara's SB was unsteady, jittery, probably from all those angry horns and the dozens of middle fingers disrespecting him. I'm no doctor, but Cara planned to be one and recognized his symptoms. She said, "Julius, will you go out there and rescue my brother, please? The engine fumes are getting to him and are making him woozy. Please? Pretty please? By the way, sometimes me Darrell can be a great big asshole, and he's likely gonna be combative."

"I've noticed that about him."

"But I loves me big brother just the same."

"Don't worry, I'll be gentle. Cara, Believe Me, you can Trust Me."

I've learned the hard way that I've got to be extra careful with Normals operating motorized vehicles. They're unpredictable enough on their own two feet, behind the wheel of a two-ton delivery van? Unpredictable times a million.

A while back, a road rager had nearly killed Gracie and her brother. I tracked down the irresponsible driver, studied his SB for almost an hour before I permanently blinded the son of a bitch. Rage adds a certain intense color cast to a person's SB. If it were an actual visible color, it would be bright, bright, glow in the dark, fire engine red.

The status button of the mover and shaker driving a brand-new Ferrari GTO was about to reach critical mass. If he was armed, and he probably was, he was going to take his frustration out on that strange guy wearing a policeman's hat and a good-looking black leather coat under a filthy day-glow yellow safety vest. After all, thought the driver, that dirty copper wannabe was deliberately keeping him from his date with a woman who called herself Harmony just so that asshole bogus traffic cop could drool over his new supercar for a few minutes longer.

I walked over to the Ferrari and signaled the driver to roll down his window.

"Hey man, sorry to bother you, but I just bought a *Ferrari 500 Superfast* myself and I really like the look of yours." That's what they tell the hostage negotiators: seek common ground. His name was Wilson Trendmore. He ran a brokerage firm out of a converted town home in Old City and was late for a very important date. I told him to Be Cool and went to save Darrell O'Hara from himself. Easier said than done.

"Briscoe, you dumb Jew bastard, did you know I'm clairboyant. That means that I can see the future. And one fine day not so far from now, I'm gonna kick your ugly Jew ass from here to next Tuesday."

How about that! It *is* actually possible to get loopy high on engine fumes. Maybe that explains why so many people live in big cities. Smog intoxication is just like any other form of intoxication. Sergeant O'Hara was as drunk as a skunk and twice as smelly.

We huddled on the corner trying to reach a consensus about where to have dinner while waiting out the traffic. The O'Haras lived in Devil's Pocket. Margot had a nice two-bedroom in Zoloto Towers. Nadine and Cara were going to stay over at Margot's that night. Also on their agenda was Christmas shopping in the Zoloto Mall and a girl's night out tour of Center City's most happening scenes. Mainly swanky bars in swanky hotels.

It was going to take hours to get to Catherine Street where three generations of O'Haras lived in a three-story row house. The children had stopped complaining about missing their audience with Santa Claus and switched to bellyaching about being very hungry. We were two and a half blocks from MONGO MINGS CHINESE. I asked, "Does everyone like Chinese food? I know a swell place not three blocks from here."

"Does they have fortunate cookies in there?" asked Melody with eagerness in her eyes. I told her that MINGS has the best fortune cookies in the whole wide world. And that MINGS fortunes are always true.

Everyone was more than fine with MINGS except for the contrarian Darrell O'Hara, who launched into a diatribe denouncing the Chinese people and their food, the MSG conspiracy, Jews, Presbyterians, Italians, Polacks, Spics, Spooks, Wall Street, Broad Street, fluoridation, hippies, flower power, street punks, folk music, rock and roll, the cop shows on TV, the fucking Redskins, and all politicians except for his cousin, State Senator Paddy O'Toole.

I was reluctant to hit O'Hara with even the mildest downer from my menu. His textures were fragmented, and his colors had desaturated to the point that his SB was a swirling blend of shades of gray. It was possible that I could inadvertently kill him while trying to just sober him up. I resorted to violence. I slapped him hard across the face. "What the fuck is wrong with you, O'Hara? You dumb mick bastard mother fucking shit-eating goon?" Then I hit him in the solar plexus. Hard. Knocked the wind right out of that blowhard.

Darrell was one tough mother fucker though. He recovered his breath and his asshole demeanor and was back on his feet in no time, bouncy bouncing on the balls of his feet. O'Hara's eyes and SB lit up like downtown.

"That's all you got, Briscoe? You slimy rat-faced Jew cunt, tell me that wasn't your best shot?"

"You should be thankful that it wasn't."

That perked him up, SB wise. Now I could do my thing to him with very little risk. I hit Darrell O'Hara with BE COOL®, BE NICE®, and SHUT THE FUCK UP®, and led everyone to MONGO MINGS CHINESE.

We were treated like royalty, and not just because it was the boss and his hungry friends on a slow and snowy night. I hadn't visited the Chinatown MINGS since before Gracie was killed and CiCi Cavalière finished remodeling the dining room. The wait staff and kitchen staff rushed to greet me. They all wanted me to know how sorry they were for my loss and to let me know how much they all loved and missed Gracie.

I made the introductions, and we were ushered into MINGS CHINESE'S one and only private dining suite, which was behind a door covered in red leather and an inscription on the lintel that read 仅限授权人员. CiCi had managed to create a 'nothing worth stealing in here' vibe with plain, simple, but sturdy furniture, a masterpiece of understatement. The 仅限授权人员 dining room could feed an even baker's dozen. The fine imported linens, crystal goblets, lacquered bamboo chopsticks, and authentic Shang Dynasty porcelain soup ladles made for a striking place setting. I instructed the head waiter, Jin Van Pelt, to bring whatever everyone wanted and the bill to me; that I'd pay cash, and by the way, how's his brother Wu doing?

Nothing jeopardizes a relationship more than violence or calling someone's loved one a dumb mick bastard. Especially if the victim of said violence and verbal abuse is Cara O'Hara's older brother, Darrell. Despite his myriad flaws, Cara has been devoted to Darrell O'Hara all of her life. Her SB always sparkled when she talked about her sainted brother. Hardly a saint, more like an arrogant bully with a badge, if you were to ask me.

I didn't think it was such a big deal. Just like any other drunk, the fool was out of control and running out of ethnicities, institutions, and celebrities to slander. He was lucky. Too many witnesses for a proper comeuppance. He remained calm through the rest of the evening and didn't require further interventions from yours truly. But the damage had been done. Cara's rating of me plummeted from 'irresistible' to 'only if hard-up and blackout drunk.' Buttons do not lie.

"You shouldn't have disrespected me brother Darrell in front of his family like that. Julius, that was just plain cruel. Can't ya see that?"

"Cara. Trust Me, your brother and I were just sparring, a pissing contest that's all." I was hoping to smooth things over and move from a minus one back to a ten on her desirability scale.

I believed I had met someone to put an end to my chastity streak with. She was pretty, smart, friendly, and, as I was learning, totally fucked up.

Many people will tell you, always in private, that women are inherently stubborn, and that Irish women are many times more stubborn than the stubbornest outsider woman that ever was. It seemed to me that Cara's and my budding romance was doomed. And maybe that was for the better.

Our relationship, Gracie's and mine, was effortless. We got each other. We were intimate before we were intimate. If you know what I mean. I don't think that I'll ever have a relationship like that again. Unless. Unless Miles Gold is right, and I'll *pair* with someone as soon as the Universe was good and ready.

Nadine took charge of the group and the menu and ordered for the table. She stood and brought the room to order. Then she told us there were but two rules for tonight's dinner. Rule number one: when it came time for dessert, everyone must wait their turn to read their fortune out loud for everyone to hear. The other rule was "Have fun and please remember to thank Mr. Uncle Julius who's treating us to this wonderful dinner.

Maybe Cara had lost interest in me for good, but her sister-in-law hadn't. Cougars, cougars everywhere you look. And, guess what? Nadine's a good listener with an available shoulder to cry on. I should write a book. Cara's sisterly love for Darrell O'Hara was everlasting and a bit creepy. Nadine's feelings for her husband? Worse than creepy. Buttons do not lie.

Jin Van Pelt brought a tray of appetizers to the table and advised me that my brother Leonard was on the telephone and that I could take it in the office. Down the stairs, through Charlie's infamous stealth kitchen, and into the office, which was a tribute to ordinary. There was an old fashioned candlestick phone sitting on a beat to shit wooden desk.

"Lenny, what's up?"

"Julius, I had a visit this afternoon from our movie star friend." Lenny paused while he thought of non-self-incriminating ways to proceed. "And?"

" And, Julius, she has a project for our friend Dr. N."

"I see. I believe Dr. N is tied up until after the New Year. Has she mentioned a start date? An end date?"

"The 'sooner the better' was how she put it."

"Send the details to the office, and I'll relay them to Dr. N and give you an answer by Tuesday at the latest."

"All right. Were you ever able to talk to your friend about that gizmo you told me about? Really would be helpful to have right now, wouldn't you think?"

"I expect to take delivery sometime this week. I'll ship it out along with everyone's Christmas presents. You'll get it no later than Friday. Should I send it to the house or the office?"

"The office is better. Be sure to give me a heads up on a delivery date so I can alert the mail room. And wait a minute, didn't you promise Molly you were coming for Christmas?"

"I told her maybe, but I sure didn't promise. Lenny, there's no way I can get away Christmas week. Most of our people are Christians, and Christmas Eve is a big deal for some of them. Family traditions. So we close most of the stores at sundown and don't reopen them until the morning after. We do keep a handful of high-traffic stores open til midnight. I'm probably going to have to manage one of them. Have you decided where you are going to put your gift?"

"I don't feel safe leaving it here in my office. Too many snoopers. Not one of them trustworthy. No, it's going into my study at home and into a locked desk drawer."

"Listen, Lenny, I'm at dinner with some people. Can we talk tomorrow?"

"Sure, that'll be fine. Your phone service mentioned an authentication phrase, something
I know nothing about."

"It's to verify that you are a trusted caller. Next time, tell the operator "Mom always liked me best.""

Dinner went as well as it could considering that Cara, Nadine, and Margot were all the time grilling me about Darrell's uncharacteristically civilized table manners. What did you say to him? What did you do to him?

◊◊

Chapter 38
just dessert please

"If I had to do it all over again?
Babe I'd do it all over you."
All Over You
~ Bob Dylan

Nadine Brodsky O'Hara stood up and did the chopsticks and wineglass thing and got everyone's attention.

"Tell me that wasn't the best dinner ever!"

"Mom," answered Banjo earnestly, "That wasn't the best dinner ever." The room gasped into a mock-stunned silence and remained mock-stunned for about five whole seconds before…

"PSYCH. Got you, Momsie." He giggled. "I really got you good," snorted her darling little brat as he pointed a scolding index finger at his mother. Nadine responded by sticking her tongue out towards her only son. Everyone laughed at the precious family interaction.

Nadine regained control of the gathering by singing, "Hey. Hey. It's fortune cookie time." She sang the line twice more, then returned to her normal speaking voice, for which we were all grateful. "And because it's a family tradition and because we need him to go get the car, Darrell gets to read his fortune first." She led the polite applause, then the still artificially civilized Darrell O'Hara rose, crushed his fortune cookie to death in his mighty fist, retrieved the slip of paper, and read, "He who throws dirt is losing ground." Darrell excused himself and left to retrieve his ride, a retired squad car, a red and white Pontiac GTO.

The children squabbled:

"My turn."

"No it isn't. It's my turn."

"Poopy head."

"Cry baby."

"Dumb, dumb, dummy!"

"Mommy's boy!"

They made faces at each other, blew raspberries, and used their armpits to simulate farts. Childish stuff like that. Nadine, with Solomon-like wisdom, pronounced that the readings would continue oldest to youngest. Which meant that she was next up.

Nadine, while looking directly at me, read her fortune: "You have a secret admirer."

Then it was Margot's turn: "If you look back, you'll soon be going that way."

My fortune cookie advised: "Focus on the magic of things."

Cara's predicted: "An old love will come back to you."

Then it was Banjo's turn. Nadine asked him if he would like her to read it for him, and Banjo declared that he could read really good and gave it a go,

"Your days will be filled with adventure, your evenings also."

You gotta hand it to Banjie, he gave it his five-year-old best before accepting his defeat and handed the fortune to his mother to read and explain. Then it was Melody's turn. She freed the cookie from the cellophane daintily, and with a practiced flourish, slammed the cookie into the polished silk tablecloth that came all the way from China, and unfurled the slip of paper. Nadine said, "Melody, sugar, let mommy read that for you."

Melody glared at her mother and said, "I can reads better than Banjie. I really really can." She cleared her throat, took a deep breath and a sip of water, and announced in her best grown up voice, "My fortune says, 'You will marry the handsomest man in the whole wide world, Mr. Uncle Julius." She shot me a wink.

I can't help it.

◊◊

Chapter 39
cochise

"Yeah, he big and dumb as a man can come
But he stronger than a country hoss
And when the bad folks all get together at night
You know they all just call…him boss."

You Don't Mess Around With Jim
~ Jim Croce

By the time Darrell returned with the car, the roads and sidewalks had been ground into slush. Crusty frozen slush, as most Philadelphians can attest, makes for some treacherous driving and walking that's for sure, especially for those wearing high heels or driving on balding tires. We squeezed into the GTO, and Darrell was gracious enough to drive us to the 9th Street subway station. We retrieved Nadine and Cara's overnight bags from the trunk, kissed and hugged the kids, then trundled down to the platform level and waited for the next train.

We had the westbound platform all to ourselves. Across the tracks from us on the eastbound platform were four or five guys around my age and size, smoking cigarettes and Phillies Blunts. They were clowning around, playing grab-ass, defacing billboards, or running their mouths about one thing or the other. They were too far away from us in the echo-ey chamber to make out what they were jabbering on and on about. One of them recognized Margot and changed the subject and their focus.

The Inquirer's article had referred to Margot only as Miss X. She had some avid fans right there across the tracks from us. They declared their everlasting love and devotion and shared their sexual qualifications. They heard the approaching westbound train, held a brief pow-wow, then bolted up the stairs and raced through a gauntlet of creaky revolving doors and turnstiles to scramble down the steep stairs that led to the westbound platform. You gotta hand it to those guys; they were fast enough to catch the last car moments before the doors closed. We were safe and sound in the first car. Or so we thought.

This time of night, the *PRT* was supposed to be running three-car trains. Thanks to the power outage, a crush of delayed commuters, and overtime considerations, they chose to not disconnect six of the cars. Margot's fan club was a couple of hundred feet behind us. A good five-minute walk through crowded, swaying subway cars. They were not yet close enough for me to get a solid read on their status buttons and their intentions. Innocent or not? Too soon to tell. To be on the safe side, I was planning on pausing them as soon as they got close enough.

I'm not a big fan of subways and Els, and I can afford not to be. But I've ridden them often enough to be familiar with what happens when your subway car moves across a gap in the electrified third rail. The car's lights blink out and stay off for a couple of seconds or so, and sometimes even minutes. I had forgotten about this feature until I was reminded somewhere between 11th and 13th Street. The brief blackout caused me to lose track of Margot's fan club. There were too many other passengers in the cars behind ours. So when the lights came back on, there, right in front of us, stood five members of the notorious Strawberry Mansion outlaw youth organization, the West Arizona Avenue Black Apaches. Red and white war paint on their game faces.

The chieftain of the Black Apaches is always addressed as Cochise. The Cochise du jour was fifteen-year-old Lorenzo Howard. He stood directly opposite me, his right hand resting on the butt of a pearl-handled pistol stuffed into the waistband of his Levi's. The kid was a fucking giant. 6'6" at least. Which was his only qualification for the leadership position of this fearsome band of brave urban warriors.

"Yo whitey, I wanna fuck Miss X's brains out. You gonna have a problem with that?"

"No, I'm not going to have a problem with that. But you will if you lay a finger on her. You don't want to tangle with me, Tonto. No, you fucking don't."

I'm not taking credit for this one either. Just then, the subway car's lights went out with a sudden sideways lurch, and nanoseconds afterwards, Cochise's gun went off. I can't tell you exactly how Cochise Howard managed to shoot his dick clean off, but that's what he did all right. Must have hurt like a mother fucker. Blame it on the blackout, a hair trigger, or the Bossa Nova. Honest kids, it wasn't me.

When the lights shrugged back on, Cochise's tribe had unsheathed their weapons and had them trained on me. Guns, knives, and machetes, oh my. It was not a good situation. Whatever I did to neutralize those thugs would be witnessed by Margot, Nadine, and Cara. Given everything that's happened since we hooked up at the Iggle, they were bound to have their suspicions.

The lights blinked out again. When they blinked back on, the remaining gang-bangers had fled the scene. GET

THE FUCK OUT OF HERE® works like a charm. Never leave home without it.

Cochise Howard was writhing on the subway floor as his life oozed out of him. Not only had he shot his manhood off, he also managed to nick his femoral artery. Lorenzo Cochise Howard died in agony before we reached the City Hall terminal. None of us wanted to wait around to be questioned by the cops, so we shot out of the subway station onto Broad Street and caught a taxi to Zoloto Towers.

That thing people say about Chinese food is kinda true. What with all the running around and close encounters, the four of us were hungry again. Margot and I briefed Nadine and Cara on their Zoloto Arcade late-night options. One thing the Jewish and the Irish people have in common is their appreciation of corned beef. And MURRAY'S DELI on the third floor of the arcade has, according to an article in *Philly's Got Style*, the best damn corned beef in Center City, if not on the planet.

Even for a Friday night, the line to get into MURRAY'S was pretty long. People, most of them Zoloto Towers residents, who had been delayed hours by several 'acts of God' before getting home, were too stressed out to cook and were lined up to dine at every restaurant in the arcade. Hungry-hungry, self-important VIP types in their bedroom slippers were queued up, and running out of patience.

The hostess was Mrs. Zelda Bergman, Murray's better half, going on twenty-five years.
Mazel Tov, kids. I should mention that good old Zelda Bergman has a matronly crush on yours truly. It sure came in handy that night. She told us, with a wink, that she could seat us immediately at separate tables for two, on opposite

sides of the deli. And if anyone complained, she'd let them know that we were regulars with reservations. So we paired off. Nadine and Margot at table number twenty-one way in the back near the pay phones and restrooms. Julius Briscoe and Cara O'Hara at table number three. A handsome power couple in the front window.

All kinds of thoughts were racing through my brain. The issue getting too much of my attention was "what's the story with Melody O'Hara?" Is she really a mind-reader? Seems like she must be. Yet, she has buttons. Is she capable of sending and receiving? Or will her gift fade as she grows older, like it does with most children around that age?

Then there were the other three O'Hara's. It was clear to me that Darrell and Nadine were headed nonstop towards splitsville. Darrell was a *certified-genuine,* bigoted, asshole bully. Can't help but wonder what I'd learn after hitting him with a Truth Bomb. I wasn't sure I could handle his version of the truth.

Nadine wasn't happy in her marriage, and one could hardly blame her. Darrell was insufferable, inattentive, and unfaithful. Both of her children were abnormal handfuls. Banjo was hyperactive and slower intellectually than his contemporaries. Melody was sweet but had an otherworldly aura about her. The child was moody, seemed to be able to read minds, and was as smart as Banjo was not.

I also wondered how you're supposed to convince a teenaged girl overdosing on hormones, that guys, even that one special guy, will say almost anything to get laid and she should be extra careful, especially with the older men who had seduction down to a science. Someone should have explained these matters to Jeannie O'Doyle.

Mostly I pondered *slam* itself. Buttons, it seems, have become old school. The use of different colored buttons to control a Normal has given way to a sleeker, more efficient way to get them doing what I need them doing. Now, post epiphany, Normals' skulls serve as an antenna/button, receiving and sometimes sending information to and from people like me. I mean, if there are other people like me. So when I *think* something, the targeted Normal does something. How cool is that? The Status Button has been upgraded. I still think of it as an SB even though Normals' foreheads have become a widescreen movie, and more and more Normals are able to project images onto them.

"Cara, that was some quick thinking back there on the monorail. You saved a lot of lives, mine included, for which I thank you." We were seated at table for two number 3. I was leafing through the jukebox pages hoping to find something suitable to the situation. I dropped a dime into the record machine and punched in B-17. "(I Can't Get No) Satisfaction" by the Rolling Stones.

Cara glared at me and declared, "Your false, flattering words don't work on me no more, Julius Briscoe. You cannot unring the bell. You said what you said, and you meant what you meant, so don't you go denying it. Makes me want to punch you in the face. You Christ-killing bastard scum you. Let me ask you this, Julius, is the corned beef here any good?" So it was like that. I hit her with a Truth Bomb and quickly came to regret it.

Cara's life story was long and ugly. I can't imagine what kind of person could do things to little children like her Daddykins, both of her grandfathers and brothers did to her and her sisters and cousins. Made me want to look them up. Her father and grandfathers were long dead. Darrell and his demented brethren would be unable to get it up for the rest of their troubling lives.

I hit Cara with a double dose of GET OVER IT® picked up the check, told her it was nice meeting her and that I had a hunch we'd meet again.

Never leave home without it.

◊◊

Chapter 40
down to business

"When you're strange
No one remembers your name
When you're strange."

People Are Strange
~ Jim Morrison, Robbie Krieger,
John Densmore, Ray Manzarek

With only three shopping days remaining until Christmas, Andrews the Giant rang Universal Import-Export's doorbell at exactly 7:32 in the morning. Why is it that I keep running into these freakishly tall guys? Andrews was a smidge under seven feet tall. A victim of male pattern baldness, a good-natured, but stand-offish, chain smoker. His SB said he was non-threatening. A trusted courier for THE ERRAND BOYS for decades.

"I have a delivery for a Mr. Julius Briscoe. Is he available?"

"I'm down here."

"Humor is reason gone mad."

"Whatever it is, I'm against it!"

Sign. Counter-sign. Just like in the movies.

Andrews handed me a manila envelope. I slipped him a C-note and a carton of Luckies, escorted him to the elevator, returned to our offices, locked the doors, and opened the envelope. The target was Gilbert 'Gilly' Yocham, the Sunshine State's leading swimming pool manufacturer since '52, Ramona Ransom soon to be his ex-wife. Gilbert was trying to screw her out of millions. Money she had earned as an investor, a business partner, and as the face of *Pools by Ramona,* the dominant player in the bespoke backyard swimming pool racket. Her generous smile and world-famous cleavage graced billboards, bus-stop benches, and television screens from Panama City to Key West.

The phone rang. It was Brenda Burger. She wanted to know if I was planning to go to that New Year's Eve show. I told her that I was. Brenda asked me if I wouldn't mind escorting her houseguest to the show. Not exactly like a date, more like a favor as Brenda would be catering to Tommy Gunn's every backstage whim and wouldn't be able to protect her guest from horny teenage boys.

"You'll like her, Julius. Ilsa Lundy is transferring to Waverley for next semester. She can't live in the dorm until January, so she's staying with me, her senior ambassador. Ilsa's from Los Angeles. I haven't met her yet; we just talked on the phone one time, but she seems kinda shy and doesn't know a soul way out here."

I advised Brenda that I was still of the notion that asking someone on a New Year's Eve date was a committed relationship-level proposition. So Brenda and I arranged to 'run in' to each other this afternoon at MONGO MINGS CHINESE WEST so Ilsa and I would meet by accident and maybe, if we hit it off, and found enough things in common to make it seem like my invitation to the show was a spur-of-the-moment idea, not the result of felony matchmaking. We chatted a few more minutes, mostly about Tommy Gunn's obsession with his infant sons. We said our goodbyes, and I went back to work.

I dug into Gilbert Yocham's dossier. Ramona had offered to pay a quarter of a million up front and another quarter of a million after the autopsy and the reading of Gilly's will. Which Lenny had rejected. They settled on three hundred thousand to the assassin and fifty thousand to the broker. Cash. All of it up front. Non-refundable.

I had never been to Miami and was using the back of my mind to puzzle out the logistics while the front of my mind studied the paperwork. Gilbert Yocham was in his late thirties. Easily twenty years younger than Ramona Ransom. A boy toy gone wrong. Gilly was a little under six feet, had a swimmer's build, sun-bleached hair, piercing blue eyes, and a gold medal-winning smile. Clearly not the monogamous type. He owned a '63 Continental convertible and a vintage Alfa Romeo cabriolet. He wore Ralph Lauren, Miles Gold, and Pierre Cardin. He was an amiable playboy in the prime of his life. Easy to get close enough to kill.

The last page in the dossier was his itinerary. He'd be flying to New York City to meet with several investors about financing his franchising ambitions. I read through the documents again. If Lenny could get me Yocham's flight information, well then, the scoundrel wouldn't leave JFK International alive.

The doorbell rang. I put everything back into the envelope and into a desk drawer. Then I opened the front door. There stood Miles Gold and a couple of suits from the phone company and an engineer clad in branded overalls and a hard hat. 'Intimidated and put out,' complained his SB. They were here to install my scrambler phone and to read me the rules, and burden me with the paperwork. I was told that the main thing to keep in mind is that this device is top secret and no one other than me should ever operate it or even know that it exists. Lenny's scrambler would be installed later in the afternoon.

MONGO MINGS CHINESE WEST does a killer lunch-hour business. MINGS is located across the parking lot from the *Wynnewood Heights Galleria*. Which hosted prominent upscale branded retailers from all over the planet.

Our discount lunch promotion was a smash hit. One MONGO MINGS coupon was good for ten percent off of dine-in, or fifteen percent off take-out orders. MINGS CHINESE WEST'S lobby at lunch hour jams up just like downtown. Galleria patrons waiting to be seated, Galleria employees waiting for their take-away orders, people waiting for other people to arrive for an inadvertent meet and greet. Namely, Brenda Burger and her new gal pal, Ilsa.

Roxanna Chang welcomed me with a great big smile and an SB that said she'd take me to bed. All I'd need do was ask. I couldn't. She's an employee. A valuable one. This time next year, Roxie should be managing MINGS WEST or one of the BIG AL'S I was planning to open next spring. She was too busy to chat and asked if I was joining Mr. Gold and Mrs. Showalter for lunch in private dining suite #8. I told her I was. Roxanna said they hadn't arrived yet, but they should within the hour. They were regulars with reservations.

So, maybe, there is such a thing as a free lunch. If anyone was worthy of a lifetime of free meals on the house, it was Cassandra Showalter. Within months of declaring herself MONGO MINGS CHINESE WEST'S chief publicist, business doubled, then steadily increased each month afterwards.

I stepped outside to wait on Miles, Mrs. Showalter, and maybe even Brenda Burger and her entourage. They were already half an hour late. I faded into a stand of evergreens that shrouded the parking lots and fired up a joint. The last of that Afghani shit. Four hits later, Miles pulled in and parked his Bugatti next to my *FERRARI*. I stepped out of the afternoon shadows and whispered, "Psst. Over here. Miles, Sandra over here."

Here's a little-known statistic for you: one hundred percent of the psychics we've interviewed prefer marijuana over alcohol. Here's another little-known tidbit: Miles Gold, multi-billionaire, philanthropist, educator, pillar of the community, always has the best pot. Miles and Mrs. Showalter sauntered my way, all Fred and Ginger like. Debonair and impossibly cool.

Sandra Showalter abandoned her self-control when she crossed into the hugging zone. She rushed towards me, arms extended, and in her cheeriest, most fawning voice, exclaimed, "Benjamin, my dear beautiful boy, how wonderful it is to see you again. Darling, it's been forever!"

I'm pretty sure I've warned you about her in the past, but in case I hadn't or you have forgotten, Cassandra Showalter, the late Moses Stern's main squeeze and confidante, firmly believes that I am the reincarnation of Benjamin Stern, Mo's son, Lizzie Stern-Gold's birth father. I am constantly reminding Mrs Showalter that if I were Ben Stern reincarnated, I'd certainly know. This usually devolves into a Gordian knot of a conversation I was hoping to avoid.

"Remember Me? I'm Julius. Julius Briscoe. Believe Me Mrs. Showalter. I must tell you that you look very beautiful this afternoon. Miles, you look dashing as always."

We passed the joint around and chatted about the latest episode of *The Fugitive,* current events, the decline of Western civilization, and watched the Normals come and go talking about the true spirit of Christmas, or the wreck of the Santa Express, or the weather or something like that.

◊◊

Chapter 41
liberationists

"Ah, but I've grown older and wiser,
And that's why I'm turning you in."

Love me I'm a Liberal
~ Phil Ochs

We were about to fire up another joint when Brenda Burger, her baby buggy built for two, Tommy Gunn and the *Automatics*, Ilsa Lundy and her tutor/chaperone/bodyguard Lori Vasquez, strolled into view.

Ilsa was wearing a red shoulder-length wig, dark sunglasses, pink high-tops, and an indulgent grin. Kinda like a walking, talking Raggedy Ann. Despite her getup, Ilsa Lundy was a dead ringer for that Francesca Ullman, the headline-grabbing only child of the stars of stage and screen, Nelson and Sarah Ullman. What a coincidence. Ilsa Lundy stood a gawky five feet four inches tall, skinny, eighty-three pounds maybe, blue-eyed, a 100% California girl.

Ilsa wasn't a minute over fourteen, way under the age of consent in every state in the Union. She was still more of a tomboy type than a smokin' hot socialite. What the fuck was Brenda Burger thinking? I sure as fuck am not going to date Ilsa Lundy. She looks like a naive kid. Squiring her to Tommy Gunn's New Year's Eve Rock and Roll show? You can forget about that too.

Francesca Ullman and her captors routinely made the covers of the tabloids we routinely sold out of in each of our stores. Hers was the kind of story I was aware of, but not one I had paid that much attention to. Yellow journalism, lurid gossip. I haven't the time. Which isn't to say that my subconscious was as picky.

It's said that the human brain is capable of storing the memory of every single moment in a person's life. Recalling those memories is an entirely different proposition. It's exactly like waiting on a sneeze that may or may not ever happen. I misremembered Ilsa Lundy to be a spoiled Hollywood brat who went around dressed up as a troublemaker, defacing public property and stealing candy from small children.

Ah-choo. *Gesundheit*.

The actual, true details arrived from the dark recesses of my mind in a blinding flash. A true headslap worthy epiphany. As I now accurately recalled, last year around Easter, thirteen-year-old Francesca Ilsa Lundy Ullman had been kidnapped from The Marlborough School campus by a West Coast group of radical terrorists calling themselves *The Liberationist Society*. Francesca was forced to pose for propaganda photography, brandish a disabled tommy gun during convenience store stick-ups and Savings & Loan robberies. She had to sign gibberishy manifestos that she personally delivered, dressed as a town crier, to the West Coast dailies and select broadcast outlets.

Between their public appearances, *The Liberationist Society* kept Francesca bound, gagged, and blindfolded in a dank, musty root cellar in one of the terrorist's deaf grandmother's houses. They may have been the motliest of motley crews, but *The Liberationists* were not without their standards. Francesca's virginity remained unsullied.

Franny's parents, Sarah Joan Lundy and Nelson Ullman, were America's sweethearts five years running. They were big box office. Paparazzi magnets. In their heyday, the Ullmans starred in, and produced, as many as four romantic comedies a year. Each one of those films grossed millions. The fanzines and tabloids featured cover stories about the Ullmans in every issue. Nelson and Sarah drew crowds wherever they went.

Francesca's gestation and subsequent birth were more closely followed than little Ricky Ricardo's. Her kidnapping more heavily investigated than Charles Lindbergh Jr.'s. The Ullmans posted a reward of $250,000 for the safe return of their beloved daughter. Every able-bodied young man and woman in the state of California loaded up and stalked the mean streets of Los Angeles day and night with nary a sighting of the fetching young junior debutante or any of her demented captors.

Every organization, be it a huge company with hundreds and thousands of employees or something more modest with maybe no more than a dozen on staff, be it a government agency, or some Mom & Pop corner grocery, or maybe even a terrorist cell struggling to succeed in the cutthroat insurrectionism game, all of them have both formal and informal social structures.

The lowest man in the *Liberationist Society's* pecking order was one Kevin Valentine.
Valentine entered into an indentured servitude-like arrangement with the *Liberationists*. KV, his nickname self-assigned, was in deep do-do with several intolerant bookies, a couple of his late girlfriends, and his parole officer, Karim Carpenter, one mean-ass son of a bitch. The *Liberationists* kept Kevin safely hidden, and in exchange,

he did what he was told to do by his betters, which, according to *Liberator Rose,* was everyone else on the planet, including English-speaking domesticated animals.

The *Liberationist Society's* internal politics were as chaotic as the societal changes they intended to impose on the rest of us. Which meant that each member of the organization was expected to be able to perform any of the *Liberationist Society's* routine tasks such as posting posters, disrupting city council meetings, defacing buildings, billboards and taxicabs. There was, however, an exception. The care and feeding of their under age hostage, Francesca Ullman. That duty belonged solely to the leader of the pack, the former Mouseketeer, Arnold Rosenthal.

Arnee Rose (his stage name) suffered from an advanced case of Swanson-Desmond Syndrome, a mental disorder in which the subject cannot tell the difference between a role he plays on film and the ones he may play in real life. In its extreme, sufferers of S-D-S often imagine an entire movie crew filming them from a variety of angles every moment of their unremarkable lives.

Steve South Jr., the character Arnee played on the afternoon television serial, *"Scouts Honor,"* was an Eagle Scout who had earned every merit badge there was to earn. Honest, forthright, noble, confident, and trustworthy, Steve South had gone into the family business right out of high school and presently was a crackerjack apprentice detective at *South and Son Investigations,* discretely located in the Watershed Building in Pasadena, California, US of A.

Arnee Rose was convinced that he was as smart and as clever as Steve South and his staff writers, who were, in actuality, much smarter than most people. What Arnee really was, was perpetually in over his head. If Steve South were an actual person, he would be the antithesis of Arnold Rosenthal, a discontented former child actor turned bicycle messenger and the inept leader of a klutzy anti-American, anti-civilization terrorist organization.

One sunshiny midday last spring, Arnee Rose, in his award-winning role as the bicycle messenger, Steve Swift, was speeding down Figueroa, a rush delivery in his backpack, a generous tip in his immediate future, when, without checking her mirrors, Gail McArthur, who, as it would happen, was also a former Mouseketeer, flung open the driver's side door of her vintage Wagoneer just in time for Arnee to slam into it at approximately 23 miles per hour. He rocketed head-first through the air, arms flailing. His trajectory carried him into the windshield of an approaching sedan driven by an elderly woman who panicked at first and floored the gas, which caused her to rear-end a Brinker Brothers armored truck which was transporting approximately ten million dollars in silver bullion to an undisclosed location. Arnee went airborne once again. This time, he landed flat on his back on the roof of the armored truck, which had gone into self-defense mode the instant Mrs. Negri's Imperial LeBaron slammed into its rear bumper. It was armed before Arnee landed on its now electrified roof. Which saved his life.

Somewhere between the Wagoneer and the armored truck, Arnee's heart had stopped beating. The electrified roof shocked him back from the abyss and into a world of pain. Unimaginable pain. A dozen or so broken bones. A ruptured spleen, third-degree burns, and traumatic amnesia. Wasn't one of the former television star's better days. He would be hospitalized for nearly a year. That was bad news for the delusional insurrectionist, but it was worse news for poor Francesca Ullman, who was bound and gagged in an undisclosed location, a black-out hood covering her head. Who would tend to her basic needs?

Fortunately for Franny, one of the first responders found the 'in case of emergency' card in Arnee's backpack. It listed Kevin Valentine as an emergency contact. Although most would consider it miraculous, KV had the good common sense to tend to the *Liberationist Society's* most valuable asset, Francesca Ullman, the daughter of not one, but two major movie stars. He coveted the reward money as did all of the *Liberationists*. Valentine, however, was the only other terrorist who knew where he and Arnee had her stashed. Time for Kevin to cash in. Or so he hoped.

During a hiatus between romantic comedy shoots, Nelson Ullman, as a favor to his agent, starred in a low-budget western, shot in two frantic weeks in the Mexican desert. '*Kill 'em Dead*' became an instant cult classic, and Nelson's character, Red 'you can't run fast enough' Brown, was to become the antihero that defined the twentieth century.

Francesca and her mother accompanied Nels on the 'Kill 'em Dead' shoot. The chief wrangler on the production was Carlos Vagón. He took a liking to Franny and taught her the ropes. Literally. He was an expert at things most city folk vaguely know exist; knot tying, horse whispering, roping, stalking, branding, dowsing, whistling, yodeling and cursing were among his many arcane talents.

It was there in Guanajuato that Francesca became an apprentice 'ranch hand.' In those two fun-filled weeks, Francesca became adept in the art of knot-tying and, one might think, should have been able to undo her restraints, even blindfolded in a dank and musty root cellar. Unfortunately for her, Arnee was also well schooled in the fine art of knotting. Playing an Eagle Scout on TV had its advantages. He routinely bound Francesca's elbows together. Tied her wrists tightly, and then wrapped her thumbs together with masking tape. Made it impossible for Francesca to slip even the simplest of knots.

Lucky for her, KV Valentine wasn't an Eagle Scout and had never played one on TV. When he retied her to the chair, following a scheduled potty break, it was with a hastily improvised knot that KV believed impossible to unravel. Wrong. Francesca waited for about an hour before she fled the root cellar and KV Valentine's grandmother's house on Vanowen and DeSoto in Brookside. She flagged down a gypsy cab driven by a Rastafarian who went by the name of Porter. As a reward, a grateful Nelson Ullman gave the cabby a one-of-a-kind diamond-studded, solid-gold Omega Sea-Master worth about seventy grand. The rest of the story can be learned by reading between the tabloid headlines.

I caught up with Brenda, Tommy, and their children. They were lagging behind the rest of their entourage, which consisted of Tommy's backup band, *the Automatics,* Francesca Ullman, and Lori Vasquez. Brenda was pushing the buggy built for two up the hill. It had to weigh at least a hundred pounds, what with two chunky infants, Brenda's twenty-gallon purse, two baby bags full of necessities, a bunch of baby toys, and a box of Tommy Gunn souvenir trading cards as cargo.

"Yo Tommy, Man Up, give the little lady a breather, she and I need to have a conversation."

"Julius Briscoe, I know what you're thinking." I had led Brenda aside and answered,

"If you knew what I was thinking, you wouldn't have gotten out of your car. Believe Me Brenda, you don't want to know what I'm thinking."

"Please don't blame me for this, Julius. It's Vice Chancellor Hawkins's fault. He flat out lied to me. I'm a senior ambassador at Waverley. And in case you've forgotten, you are an ambassador also."

I had forgotten. Basically, all Waverley seniors are required to mentor a new Waverley student (a duckling) for the school year. Brenda's freshman duckling was Blythe Bronkowski, who tuned in and dropped out after only six weeks. If I had been assigned an eager, wet-behind-the-ears duckling of my very own, neither Vice Chancellor Hawkins nor Clive Dearborn bothered to inform me.

"You're right, Brenda, I had forgotten. So what did Hawkins tell you?"

"He told me that Ilsa Lundy was a transfer from a school somewhere in California and that she had just turned sixteen and would graduate with the sophomores. I just found out the truth this morning after I talked with you, and that darling girl rang my doorbell. Do you know who she really is?"

"So here's the thing, Lori, Franny's chaperone/ bodyguard has to return to LA, a family matter I suspect, and we need someone to protect her when Fran's out in public. So I thought of you. Julius, I don't know anyone more badass than you. Yeah, sure, you come off all suave and friendly like, but Julius, people don't just like and respect you; they're scared shitless of you.

I don't know why that's true, but it is. No one can keep Franny safer than you can, Julie. And you know I'm right."

I knew Brenda was right, all right? And I didn't like it at all. I've long suspected that I exude a scentless pheromone or something that attracts trouble. Or maybe it attracts Normal females and repels Normal males? Maybe both? Maybe all three?

I didn't feel much like talking. Brenda hadn't lied. We walked towards MINGS. Everyone in her party had stopped to gawk at the Bugatti and the Ferrari. Miles was holding forth. He was regaling everyone with tales of Enzo Ferrari's and Ettore Bugatti's genius for creating fast, luxurious super cars.

"Look there, it's Julius Briscoe. Julius is the only person here today who has driven both of these amazing motor cars. So tell us, Jules, which is the better, my Bugatti or your Ferrari?" Everyone laughed, and then Miles invited all of us to join him and Mrs. Showalter in private dining suite #8. It's our largest private suite; it can accommodate a party of twenty, has a well-stocked wet bar, a lushly appointed conversation pit, three big-screen color televisions, billiard, and card tables.

While lunch was being prepared, Miles and I commandeered the pool table for a game or two of nine-ball. Before Miles had the opportunity to run the table like he usually does, Francesca and Lori sauntered over and asked if they could join us. Gals versus guys. A dollar a ball? Twenty dollars a game? Their SBs cannot lie. They were shameless hustlers. Or so they thought.

During Francesca's convalescence, she had been confined to the Ullman's oceanside estate, which housed every possible attraction designed to distract a disturbed teenager from her troubles and woes. Her absolute favorite quickly became her father's custom made pool table. She and Lori would play several times a day. Francesca quickly mastered the game. She was an impossibly bright young teenager with a good lineage. The talented daughter of talented parents. We accepted their challenge, and won the toss. Miles broke and proceeded to run the table.

"Does he ever miss?" Asked Francesca. She had that same quality Gracie had. Self assuredness bolstered by money, education, breeding, powerful connections and even more money. She was neither timid nor garrulous. Her manners were impeccable. Francesca was preternaturally beautiful. Gracious and earnest. Not a hint of snootiness or entitlement.

"Francesca, he hardly ever misses a shot. Miles grew up named Myron Zoloto in Whitechapel, London. 'A rough and tumble neighborhood if ever there was one' as Miles put it. He learned to play and play very well before he turned ten.

Miles' father, Jacob, owned a casino in a building he also owned, which housed a popular tavern, a bordello on the second floor, apartments on the third, and, rising from the roof, a converted water tower where Jacob and the rest of his family lived. With a pool table on every floor to practice on, Myron was hustling the locals and wayfaring strangers alike before he finished with grammar school."

Francesca seemed to like my answer. She smiled and asked, "How's the food here? Any good?" She had an invincible smile and flirtatious eyes. If only she were a few years older.

"I'm pretty sure you're asking the wrong person for an unbiased opinion."

"Oh, that's right. Brenda did tell me you owned this place. I forgot. Sorry. That's been happening to me a lot. I didn't used to be such a scatterbrain. But getting kidnapped totally messed me up."

I have never *'seen'* an SB quite like Francesca's. All the Normal and Spectral colors with a band of self-doubt and distortion right in the middle, maybe like a sunspot or a deep bruise.
I dosed Francesca with "CHEER UP®." That cloud in the middle of her SB started to melt. Slowly. Then rapidly. Then it was gone. Thorn successfully removed.

Everything the *Liberationists* had siphoned from her psyche was renewed. Her SB brightened. Our eyes met. Her baby blues declared, "Eureka! Hallelujah! Thank you, Julius. Thank you. Thank you. Thank you." If Francesca were a cartoon character, there'd be a crayon drawing of a throbbing heart, pierced by Cupid's arrow, in a thought balloon floating above her head. Francesca studied me. Scrutinized me. Up and down. Back and forth. Inside and out. She gave me one of her invincible smiles, winked, kissed me on the cheek, and said, "Yes."

"Yes?"

"Yes Julius Briscoe, yes I'll marry you."

And that was that. Déja Vu all over again.

I could see the possibility of us getting together someday. True, we hadn't *pair*ed when we first met. It wasn't even love at first sight. But maybe *pair*ing was something just the Golds did. Franny was a cute kid. And smart. Super smart to be more precise. A relationship was plausible, but for the time being, I'll settle for the annoying kid sister I never had. Beyond that? Risky to predict.

"Julius, aren't you a little young to be owning a place like this?

"I'm not sure. I inherited it from a friend of the family's. I did a little favor for him this one time and when he passed, he left MINGS to me." I didn't mention being the reincarnation of Ben Stern, BIG CORNERS, the *undzer shtick*, SLAM, Willie Novichock or *Tabula Rasa*. Radical terrorists? Well there's one thing Francesca and I have in common.

"So, be straight with me, which is the better car? The Ferrari or the Bugatti?"

"I dunno kiddo, it's a toss up. The Ferrari is newer, faster and more agile than the Bugatti. But the Bugatti is cooler looking than the Ferrari and almost as fast. I also have a Jaguar, and it just might be the best of the three."

"You have a Jaguar? So does my dad. He has a dozen of them. He collects. They're all way cool. I like his green XK-E the best."

Well there's another thing we have in common.

◊◊

Chapter 42
christmas eve

"In Jersey, everything's legal as long as you don't get caught."

Tweeter and the Monkey Man
~ Tom Petty, George Harrison,
Bob Dylan, Jeff Lynne, Roy Orbison

"So Julius, what do you think? Will you take the Ransom contract or not?"

I answered his question with one of my own. It was our first scrambled call, and it seemed to be working okay. Lenny sounded a little tinny. I figured I probably sounded a little tinny too.

"Were you able to learn his travel plans? Flight numbers? Hotel reservations?"

"Yes. Cheyanne made a phony call to Yocham's office and finagled the information from a temp who was covering for his secretary, Yolanda, who had just gone into labor a full month earlier than planned. I have that information right here. Let me know when you have pen and paper."

Yocham's plane would land at JFK International Airport the Tuesday before New Year's Eve, at five minutes after two, where, Gilly believed, he'd be greeted by a limo driver provided by one of his potential investors, who, like yours truly, had fallen hard for Ramona Ransom back in the day and was eager to get into ~~bed~~ business with her.

I told Lenny that I'd book a private jet for first thing that Tuesday morning. I'd be traveling as Richard Philbrick and Eli Gold, my spotter, as Stephan Silberberg. We'd land at JFK before nine, have a nice brunch, then stake out the gate where Gilbert Yocham was scheduled to deplane.

"All right, I'll do the job on one condition."

"What condition? You're not going all prima donna on me now, are you, Julius?"

"No, brother. It's nothing like that. Just, if there's a double indemnity clause in Yocham's life insurance policy, our fee doubles. Tell Ramona that fatal accidents often happen in busy places like airports, and if I can arrange one, we'll expect a generous bonus. And that's non-negotiable. Either way, Gilly Yocham is toast."

"Who are you? Julius, you're still in fucking high school and you sound like a character in one of those gangster movies; George Raft, Edward G. Robinson, or Jimmy Cagney. What's with you, kid? How'd you ever get this way?"

"Right after Dad got murdered, Lenny, Mother lost it and tried to get it back by taking Dad's place in BIG CORNERS. Consoling me? Forget about it. Uncle T was weighed down with guilt, but he manned up and helped me cope. You, Lenny? You ran right back to Chicago after Dad's funeral. I had to grow up and grow up fast. When that punk pulled a knife, something in me changed in a heartbeat. Suddenly I had this ability and I instinctively knew how to use it. It's like every Normal I see, Lenny, has this list of their strengths and weaknesses tattooed on their foreheads. Not words, more like animated colors, shapes, and textures, sometimes even lifelike images. They tell me which buttons to push to get a Normal to do what I want. I learn all this about a person in seconds, whether I'm right next to them or in another room. As long as they're close enough, I can read and control them. Walls don't matter."

"What are you saying Julius?"

I told Lenny about my experiences with escaped circus animals, filling station attendants, fetching waitresses, the terrorists at JFK Stadium and the incident at *Wanamaker's*, and that he could now add animal and crowd control and selective permanent amnesia to the list of services Willie Novichock can provide at a cost. Consider the witness and jury tampering possibilities?

My other phone rang. I reminded Lenny to speak with Ramona and get back to me and to have a nice Christmas. Kiss the kids and all that. I answered the normal phone.

"Hey Julius. It's me, Frankie. Whatcha doing?"

"I'm at the office. I thought you were spending the holidays with your folks up in New York City?"

"I am. They arranged for a private rail car for me. Can you believe it? So there'll be no riffraff, no paparazzi, no kidnappers, no encounters with sympathetic strangers. An entire fancied up railroad car all to my lonesome. Sure would be nice to have some company. Imagine the fun we could have?" She was trying to sound sophisticated, experienced, grown up. Actors' kid.

"Kiddo, you know I can't get away right now. I have to work tonight. May I have a rain check?"

"Of course. The very least thing you can do for me, my darling lover boy, is to drive me to the train station, escort me to my private car, then smack me on my cute butt, and give me a soulful kiss farewell, then wave to me from the platform as the train pulls away, a tear in one of your beautiful baby blue eyes. It's something a devoted fiancé should do. Wouldn't you think?"

So it was like that.

Francesca's private rail car was attached to The Manhattan Express, leaving 30th Street Station at two o'clock on the dot. I pulled into Brenda's driveway at quarter past noon and honked the horn and popped the trunk. Best to be early, especially on the last shopping day before Christmas. There'd be traffic. Record-setting traffic.

"You didn't tell me you had a Cadillac too?"

She looked amazing. Francesca was wearing a black wig that ran halfway down her back. She was dressed up for mom and dad in a bright blue designer outfit. She wore one of those floppy hats and that invincible smile. She took my breath away.

"I thought I'd surprise you."

"I had my heart set on a ride in your Ferrari."

"Yeah kiddo, I get that. But I'm supposed to be protecting you, right? And this baby is armored top to bottom. Bullet proof glass all around. Nobody's gonna hurt you while you're in it. Believe Me, Francesca, you're safe as safe can be. Scout's Honor."

"Cool. But you owe me rides in that Ferrari and that Jaguar. If that's okay with you, I mean."

"It's fine with me. Why didn't your parents come down to Philly for Christmas?"

"They're in rehearsals for a movie directed by," she lowered her voice to a whisper and continued, "the great Billy Wilder himself. But don't you tell anyone. Not a soul. Okay?"

"Trust Me, grasshopper, your secret's safe with me."

"Did you just call me 'grasshopper'? Like on that TV show?"

"Do you mean *Kung Fu Troubadours*?"

"Yes I do. Abraham Klein, is his real name. David Kushman is just his stage name. Abe's surfing buddies with my dad. They hang out a lot. Sometimes he's cool. Sometimes he's goofy, or weird, or a little scary. He's handsome, not as handsome as you, not even close, but he's good-looking, nice, and sorta shy." Big whoop-dee-do. Franny Ullman knows a famous actor. Imagine that?

A Red Cap bundled Frankie's suitcases onto a wooden push cart and escorted us to platform 9A where we said our fond farewells minus affectionate butt slaps and soulful kissing. I asked her if she had my phone number. She held up the palm of her left hand. Frankie had written my number, the words, 'lover boy,' and encircled them in a heart. I reminded her that her authentication phrase was, "All you have to do is whistle." Urged her to have a swell time in the Big Apple and all that. And please tell Red Brown that I'm a big fan.

BIG CORNERS #6 is one of our best earners. It's on 47th and Beacon, and serves both the University Park and Squirrel Hill neighborhoods. It features a twelve-seat lunch counter and is non-stop busy night and day. It also does a big Numbers game business and has two drop safes, one each for the legal and illegal operations. Not only that, but BIG CORNERS #6 is surrounded by churches, public parks, and movie theaters. All the major denominations within a two-block radius.

Christmas Eve is #6's Black Friday, no matter which day of the week it falls on. Last-minute gift items, wrapping paper, ribbons, bows, Scotch tape, stocking stuffers, candy canes, gingerbread men, all at reasonable prices. BIG CORNERS, as far as I know, is the only convenience store chain that charges a fair markup. No more than a penny or two higher than supermarket prices. Great-grandfather Samuel figured 'we got you by the balls' pricing was actually bad for business. He figured the best way to attract and keep loyal customers was by treating them fairly and not take advantage.

Usually, Larry Robinette, #6's manager since forever, worked Christmas Eve. His daughter, Marie, was having her first child, and she was due on the 26th. So the Robinettes were off to French Lick, Indiana, for the holidays and to welcome their first grandchild into the world. Julius Briscoe to the rescue.

Like all of our properties with luncheonettes, #6, has to have a minimum of three people behind the lunch and checkout counters. Even though working Christmas and New Year's Eves pays double, it was still difficult to find people willing to work. I begged Margot to help out, and she did.

There's always at least one asshole out there that doesn't have the good common sense to heed sound advice. For example, "don't try to rob a BIG CORNERS store.

They're owned by the mob. If you're lucky, they'll kill you fast. Otherwise, you're in for a slow and agonizing death."

Peter Joseph Cunningham wasn't one to solicit or elicit advice. Good or otherwise. He charged into #6, a red bandana covering his Yosemite Sam-inspired mustache. He was brandishing a chromed revolver and demanding all the money in the cash registers, or else there'd be hell to pay. He was desperate. Down to his last fistful of bullets. So don't you dare fuck with him.

I know I have more notches on my gun belt than most people, but that doesn't mean that I walk around with a massive chip on my shoulder looking for even the tiniest molecule of disrespect to trigger a killing spree like no other. No, I mind my own business. I pay enough attention to the SBs around me only to determine that they pose no threat to me or anyone else. Peter Joseph Cunningham, on the other hand, was a poser.

The store was nearly empty; we had a good twenty minutes before the next Christmas service let out. There was a handful of shoppers: Margot St. James, Hank Levine, and me behind the registers. Killing that clown was, on the one hand, easy as pie. On that practical other hand, not so much. First problem, of course, was Cunningham's age. About nineteen. Although it does happen, a nineteen-year-old having a fatal heart attack or stroke is pretty uncommon. So I did the next best thing. First, I hit the idiot's pause button, then I pulled the shotgun from under the counter, unpaused the schmuck, told him to shut his eyes, and let him have it with both barrels. Rock salt. Tiny cuts on his face and exposed skin. An unanticipated deposit in his tightie whities. Otherwise, he was alive and well.

Peter Joseph Cunningham waddled from the scene of the attempted crime before I could call up the cops.

Twenty minutes later, we were wall-to-wall customers. All of the churches had let out within five minutes of each other. We had all three registers going and could have used two more. Even though they were universally in a hurry to get home, our customers were all polite and friendly. They knew each other socially and chatted pleasantly as they waited their turn in the checkout line. MERRY CHRISTMAS®. Don't leave home without it.

"Julius, could you please hand me down a pack of Chesterfield Kings?" That was Margot at register two. She was too short to reach the cigarette rack suspended from the ceiling. I was about to hand her the Chesterfields when it dawned on me that maybe I ought to check out her customer. Sure enough, it was Johan Manes in the flesh. He was wearing a pea coat and a matching watch cap. He had a tattoo of a Rolex Submariner on his left wrist. I couldn't see his forearms, but he had a package of butterscotch TASTYKAKE KRIMPETS, a bottle of *FRANK'S* Black Cherry Wishniak, a red magic marker, a ball of twine, scissors, a roll of duct tape, a red satin pre-tied bow, and latex gloves in his shopping basket.

Holy fuck. *Aristotle Gutenberg* the serial killer, failed mass murderer, right here in store #6. But what to do? Common sense said to drop the motherfucker right away. He who hesitates and all that. But I needed him to lead me to *Aristotle Rex* and any other *Tabula Rasa* hotshots out there plotting heinous crimes against unsuspecting Normals.

"Excuse me, sir. Don't you work in *Poor Richard's* on the mall? I stopped by there the other afternoon to pick up my personalized *Declaration of Independence*, but you were closed. Any chance I can swing by tonight? It's a Christmas gift for my mom."

"Sorry, kid. You've got me confused with someone else. People are all the time telling me that I look familiar. But I'm not."

He was lying his ass off.

I didn't have too many options. Killing him wasn't one of them. Yet. I paused everyone in the store. Locked the doors, unpaused *Aristotle Gutenberg,* and escorted him to the basement storeroom. I paused him again and locked him in the root cellar. Then I went back upstairs, unlocked the doors, and unpaused everyone else. Business as usual.

◊◊

Chapter 43
the worst christmas ever

"That amazing grace
Sort of passed you by
You wake up every day
And you start to cry."
My Shit's Fucked Up
~ Warren Zevon

Wow, what a night. First, after we closed #6 at a little past midnight, I had to drive Margot to Nadine's house in Devil's Pocket. Just the other day, Darrell O'Hara had tried to prevent a gang-banger wearing war paint and an eagle feather in his beaded headband from robbing the STRAWBERRY MANSION SAVINGS & LOAN, where Darrell was moonlighting as a security guard, and got himself shot dead. Margot wanted to help Nadine and the children cope with their loss. Of course, I was required to make an appearance in the living room, where I soothed the mourners with THERE-THERE®. I left as soon as I could and headed back to #6, where I had *Aristotle Gutenberg* stashed in the root cellar.

Following a heated internal debate, it was decided that I'd question Manes in his apartment above *Poor Richard's*. He'd feel more relaxed in familiar surroundings, and I'd have the opportunity to rummage through his belongings and perhaps stumble upon a clue, maybe even some naughty Polaroids.

I parked at the meter in front of *Poor Richard's*. We entered through the side entrance and took the stairs to the upper floor. Either Pam was away for the holiday or she was dead. Johan Manes' SB was the only one in range.

I don't know shit about antique furniture, but if I did, I'd tell you that the living quarters above *Poor Richard's* housed a million dollars' worth of rare and one-of-a-kind pieces that belonged in museums or in the homes of phony-ass nouveau riche collectors. It's probably a good thing that Elbridge Ross V had the building retrofitted for central air and heating. Otherwise, a philistine like Manes might have converted them to firewood. All of the upholstered pieces were protected by clear plastic custom-fitted covers. I told Manes to sit on one of the Queen Anne chairs in the living room. I sat opposite him, paralyzed his legs, and hit him with a Truth Bomb® and said, "*Aristotle Gutenberg*? How the fuck did you come up with a street name like that? You don't strike me as an inventor or a Christian."

"Who the fuck are you, kid?"

"Well, I'd tell you, but then I'd have to kill you. Which I still might."

"That's cute coming from a punk like you. Sooner or later, I'm going to figure out how to get myself unstuck and kick your ass from here to next Tuesday."

"So is it true that you killed Meredith Carver-Bradford?"

"It's true all right. The bitch had it coming. She totally fucked up the LBJ contract. Embarrassed the rest of us, damaged our credibility. But it wasn't my call, it was *Aristotle Rex's* call, and he wanted her dead. *Aristotle Friedan* was as dedicated to the cause as anyone; she was also dedicated to her one and only hobby: zipless fucking. If you met her standards, and they were variable, well, then she'd take you to bed, and if you weren't careful, give you the clap like she did most of the *Aristotles* on the eastern seaboard. So tell me this kid, do you know why I can't feel my legs?"

"I do, in fact. You cannot feel your legs or move them because I don't want you to."

"You're one of those freaks I've read about in the ENQUIRER."

"You shouldn't believe everything you read. But let's keep going. Did you murder Meredith yourself, or did you have a helper?"

"No, *Aristotle Rex* and *Aristotle Marx* and his sons Milton and Adolph took their turns."

"Who wrote that symbol on her body? What does it mean?"

"It was me. It means 'shame on this age and on its lost principles.' If humans don't mend their ways, they will bring an end to this civilization and launch a millennium of global darkness, savagery, and endless wars. It's my way of warning the great unwashed."

"Mr. Manes, I know I'm 'just a kid', but that doesn't sound like an effective way to deliver such an important message. End of the world, dude, that's some heavy shit. Makes me think you're just another twisted perv loser that likes murdering hot chicks because it gets you off in ways nothing else can. Tell me I'm wrong?"

Manes glared at me, "You're not wrong. You know, I'm beginning to really not like you. Any minute now, I'll bet, I'll be hating your stinking guts."

"Did you know that I'm the guy who prevented *Aristotle Friedan* from shooting the President and her followers from torching the stadium? I'm also the guy that prevented the attack on the Miss America pageant in Atlantic City. And, I'm also the one who ended your siege of Shawnee Elementary. Fourteen of your brainless revolutionists are dead. I'm the one who killed them. How much do you hate me now?"

"I can't wait to beat the living daylights out of you, kid, you fucking little twerp. Why don't you make it a fair fight and release me from this bondage? We'll go at it one on one. May the best man win."

"I'd do that, but I'm thinking I need to keep you alive. Believe Me when I tell you Manes, you're no match for me. And right now, nothing would please me more than to fill you with unimaginable pain and watch you suffer and die, you slimy piece of shit." To make my point, I hit Manes with a micro dose of EXTREME PAIN®. It lasted far less than a second, but to Manes it felt a lifetime. "How many women have you murdered? Did you keep score? Take any trophies? Tell me Manes, have you ever heard of Lingchi?"

"Never heard of it. I saved twenty-six, twenty-eight, thirty-two bitches from their wayward ways, maybe. I kinda lost count when they made me an *Aristotle*. It's not easy mentoring a bunch of snot-nosed know-it-all college pukes. They're all gung-ho and ready to go. Until there's blood. Separates the boys from the men right quick."

"You called it 'the LBJ contract.' Who was the contract with?"

"Can't tell you because I don't know. That was *Aristotle Rex's* deal."

"Who is this *Aristotle Rex?* Where can I find him? What's his name?"

"Nick. Nicholas Shayne. He's in Athens."

"Greece?"

"No, numb nuts, Georgia. He's a professor of Political Science at the university. He's one of the founding fathers of *Tabula Rasa.*"

"Who are the others?"

"Can't tell you. Don't know."

He wasn't lying.

"Tell me this *Gutenberg,* did you kill your grandfather? The cops cleared you, but Pam Peterson doesn't believe them. So how did you pull that off?"

"Easy it was a criss-cross deal. I was attending the opera with the Mayor and Senator Scott and their families while someone else did the deed. After I buried that old coot, I returned the favor. There is, you see, honor among us thieves."

I told him not to move, put on my driving gloves, and searched the place. It was a two-bedroom apartment with the living and dining rooms overlooking Independence Mall, the two bedrooms faced Chestnut Street. The master bedroom had furniture that dated back to before the Revolution, and, I kid you not, a faded, framed needlepoint hanging above the headboard that read:

GEORGE WASHINGTON
SLEPT HERE

The text was embellished with flintlock pistols and muskets with bayonets affixed.

Homes this old often lacked clothes closets. I'm not sure why, but it did create a sizable demand for custom-built freestanding units. There were two in the master bedroom. I searched them both, and the chest of drawers and the bedside tables. Nothing interesting. Nothing incriminating.

The other bedroom? Well, I hit the jackpot. It was set up like a gentleman's study. Wood-paneled walls, walnut, I think, oak flooring, oriental rugs, a drafting table, an elegantly carved writing desk, and a freestanding two-sided cork board. The facing side displayed a pair of promotional posters for *Poor Richard's,* the same ones I saw in Meredith's basement, and pencil sketches of proposed advertising slogans.

I searched the desk drawers and found a Polaroid camera, one of those tiny spy cameras, several boxes of film, a magnifying glass, a fountain pen, fingernail clippers, and a pair of twenty-dollar gold double eagles in a charred and warped Lucite case. In the center drawer, the holy fucking grail. A ledger listing the names, addresses, telephone numbers, psychological and physical profiles, and the family information of every member of *Tabula Rasa* above the rank of *Polemarch.* But no picture book. I finally thought to turn the bulletin board around. The opposite side was covered with photographs of Manes' victims. They documented the stalking, raping, and murdering of maybe thirty young women.

This presented me with a dilemma. Should I kill, disappear or turn him in? I mean, I've killed more people than Manes has. Not by a lot, but enough. I've mostly killed terrorists or murderers. People who had it coming. Not thirty beautiful young women in their prime. Their families deserved some sort of closure. Why not kill him and turn him in? Which is exactly what I did.

"Manes, Listen Up. You're looking worn out old man. Why don't you get into your nightclothes and lie down and get some rest?" He did as I told him. He never woke up. Died peacefully in his sleep. Some villains have all the luck.

I turned off the lights as I triple-checked the apartment for anything I might have missed or any sign that I was ever in the living quarters above *Poor Richard's Souvenir Shoppe*. The side door was self-locking. I checked twice that it was secure, then I walked over to a free-standing phone booth on the corner and called the hotline number. It rang ten times before a sleepy voice answered, "Max Hermann here, who's calling this fucking late?" Shit. I hadn't figured on that. I was expecting that some junior officer would be stuck working Christmas Eve. There was no way he wouldn't recognize my voice. Time to improvise. "Sheriff, it's Julius Briscoe. I found your guy." I told him a version of the truth that had me following the perp from #6 to *Poor Richard's* on the Independence Mall. I sold Sheriff Hermann on the idea that I had trailed Manes on foot and on the #93 bus. So I moved the Cadillac two blocks west and parked it in an underground garage. The *Tabula Rasa* dossier and the double eagles safely locked in the glove compartment.

Sheriff Hermann wanted to take my statement in person and asked me to hang around *Poor Richard's* while he raced from his home in Rose Valley. This time of night it would take him no more than twenty minutes. He made it in fourteen minutes flat thanks to the light holiday traffic, a turbo charged V8 and a loud siren and flashing lights. After I told him a more detailed version of the truth, Sheriff Hermann raced over to the side entrance, rang the bell and pounded on the door. Dead men don't answer no matter how loud you pound. After a good five minutes of knocking and ringing, Sheriff Hermann pulled a set of lock picks from his bomber jacket and sprung the lock in no time. "Don't you need a warrant?"

"Exigent circumstances young Mr. Briscoe. We heard screaming. Remember? You wait right here." He produced a flashlight from thin air and proceeded up the stairs shouting, "Armed Police, sir are you all right?" Sheriff Hermann returned about ten minutes later. His face shone white in the silvery moonlight. "He's dead, Briscoe. Looks like natural causes. Heart attack, stroke, something like that. And he left evidence of his crimes. Young man, you're in for a substantial reward and a commendation from the Mayor and the County Commissioners." Just what I needed. Publicity.

I got back to the Z just after 4:30 a.m. I was bushed. True, I don't need as much sleep as Normals. Four hours a day is all I usually need. Key word here? Usually. I needed to unwind.
I took a long hot shower. It had been a challenging day. As soon as I jumped into bed, the telephone rang.

"Briscoe residence, this is Julius."

"Mr. Briscoe it's Eartha at *You Rang*. I have several messages and there is a caller on the line. Please provide me with your authentication phrase."

"I shot an elephant in my pajamas."

"Thank you. You have messages from Brenda Burger, Eli Gold and there's a vulgar man on the line. He's been calling you every half an hour on the dot. He's very rude and demeaning and he insists on speaking with you. Shall I put him through?"

"All right. I'll call back for my messages."

"Thank you sir. I'll connect you now."

There were clicking sounds and buzzing and whistling then a voice came on the line all condescending and threatening, "Is this lover boy?"

"Have we met? Your voice sure sounds familiar." I thought he sounded just like Boris Badenov, the bumbling Russian spy on the Rocky and Bullwinkle Show.

"Cut the crap. I have your girlfriend Francesca and if you don't come up with a million bucks and fast, I'll fucking kill her."

"Okay, there's no need for bloodshed. First off, you need to put Francesca on the phone. I need to know she's all right and if she is, I'll do my best to get you some money. Nothing else happens until I know she's okay. Okay?"

"Julius, I'm so sorry that he called you. But I wrote your number down on my hand, and honest to Betty, I don't know the unlisted number where my parents are staying, so that asshole called you. He's got a big scar on his face, he's shorter than….." Frankie's deranged kidnapper grabbed the phone from her and practically shouted into the mouthpiece.

"So you know she lives. So now you get me my million dollars before I do something to her that you won't like."

He didn't sound like an experienced kidnapper to me. Amateur. I fucking hate amateurs.

"Listen up pal. A million dollars is a lot of money and it is a national holiday, perhaps you've heard of this one? It's called Christmas? You do know that all of the banks are closed and won't open up again until Monday morning. But I can lay my hands on maybe a hundred grand right now. My family owns cash businesses and there's at least that much laying around in the counting room."

"Counting room? Who has counting rooms?"

"People you don't want to mess with. So how about this. Do you have a car?"

"Yes. I have car."

"So I'm in Philadelphia and you're in the New York City area, right?"

"Possibly."

"So why don't you choose somewhere for us to meet up. Midway between, maybe. It'll get you your money sooner. As long as Francesca is all right, of course."

"I'll call again."

I dressed and took the elevators down to P-10, and into Universal Import-Exports' legendary counting room. I called the service and had Eartha read my messages. Five from Brenda that asked what I had done with Francesca? She seems to have disappeared into Grand Central Station. Eli thanked me for the electric guitar. I bought him a Gibson for Hanukkah, the very same model Chuck Berry plays. The last message from Brenda included an unlisted telephone number for an apartment in The Dakota where Nelson and Sarah Ullman were staying. I asked Eartha to connect me with Ullman.

"This is Nels Ullman speaking."

"Mr. Ullman, I'm Julius Briscoe. I'm a student at Waverley and friends with Brenda Burger and a new friend of your daughter's. I drove Francesca to the train station this afternoon and put her on a private car connected to the 2 o'clock Manhattan Express, and watched the train pull out of the station. I had a very busy day and didn't get home until late. At 5 this morning I got a call from some guy with a thick Russian accent telling me he's kidnapped Francesca and he wants a million bucks or else. I made him put her on the phone and she sounded okay. Calm, cool, and collected. I guess there's no substitute for experience."

"So I told the kidnapper that I can probably come up with a hundred thousand or so and that we should meet up somewhere between Philly and New York. I'm waiting for a call back. He didn't sound too bright. Didn't seem to be aware that coming up with a million bucks cash on a holiday isn't all that easy."

"Julius, thank you for involving yourself. The next time the kidnapper calls, please give him this number. You obviously care for Franny, but putting yourself at risk is out of the question."

"Believe me, sir, there is no risk. I'll keep you posted, sir. You can count on me."

Not ten minutes later, Eartha called to tell me that the rude, vulgar man was calling again.

"So, lover boy, how much money did you come up with?"

"Two hundred eighty-five thousand and change. I can throw in another ten grand in coins if you want. I wouldn't recommend it. A fugitive from justice probably doesn't need to be weighed down. So where should we meet?"

"No coins, good thinking lover boy. In Cranbury, New Jersey, is a lake called Brainerd. On the east end of lake is park, with swings, sliding boards, and picnic benches. Be there in two hours or girl is fish food."

"I'll be there, pal. Just a reminder, you get money when I get girl. Understand?"

"Da."

"If you've harmed her in any way, well, you can't run fast enough. Just so we're clear."

"We're clear. Two hours. Clock is ticking."

I fucking hate kidnappers. I fucking hate New Jersey. The sun hadn't come up yet, and it was already the worst Christmas ever.

◊◊

Chapter 44
greetings from Cranbury New Fucking Jersey

"Wailing down the freeway
Testing out the cruising power
The state trooper trailing
Clocked at 90 miles an hour.
It wasn't me Sheriff…"

It Wasn't Me
~ Chuck Berry

Cranbury, New Jersey, is an old mill town that's seen better times and is just getting by in these. Once an important contributor to the war efforts, Cranbury is just a quiet village filled with quaint old homes and store fronts. It's almost halfway between Philly and New York City. Early morning turnpike traffic was fairly heavy.

I was driving the *FERRARI.* Common sense dictated I should have chosen the armored Caddy. But I opted for faster getaways and better gas mileage. Zero to one hundred in under ten seconds, remember? And I'd promised Frankie a ride in it.

No doubt I was feeling guilty. I should have gone with her, made sure the person that met her at Grand Central Station could be trusted. Asshole kidnappers are incapable of fooling me. And I'd be able to catch the next train back to Philly just in time to go to work at #6.

There was also no doubt that I cared for Frankie. She reminded me of Gracie in many ways. The way she carried herself, graceful, open, empathetic. And yes, I was attracted to her. And yes, she was off-limits for a couple more years.

My relationship with Gracie started out all innocent and chaste. With Francesca it would be like following that same sacred path. Intimate before intimacy, that's the ticket.

I arrived at Brainerd Park with half an hour to spare. The air was chilly, and there was a stiff breeze coming off the lake. Despite the weather, there were a good number of families bundled up and playing on the playground equipment or in the park, tossing footballs around, shagging fly balls, and generally enjoying the best Christmas ever. No sign of Francesca or her captors.

I was lounging on the redwood picnic bench closest to the parking lot entrance. It was filled mostly with rusting entry-level vehicles. Fords, Chevys, Plymouths. The FERRARI a diamond in the rough.

She was in her late teens, early twenties, and introduced herself as Corky Ferguson. She was wearing well-worn and torn Rutgers sweats top and bottom. She had rosy cheeks, brown eyes, a raspy voice, and her reddish hair was cut short.

"You're not from around here, are you?"

"That's amazing! Are you psychic or something?"

"I have my moments. Are you up for some football? We could really use another warm body. Yours looks pretty warm to me."

So it was like that.

"You know, I'd really like to, but I haven't slept since Thursday and I'm meeting someone here. I worry he might not see me if I'm over there on the field. But thank you for the invitation."

She gave me a frown and said, "Well, should you change your mind, we're right over there. Nice meeting you." Guess what her SB told me?

Ten minutes later, a yellow and white worn-out Volkswagen microbus pulled into the parking lot and backed into a space opposite the exit. The driver stepped out of the vehicle. From my vantage point, he looked to be about five foot six, five foot seven, maybe fifty years old, and get this, he was wearing a belted black trench coat with the collar turned up, a black fedora tilted over his left eye, and a semi-automatic Makarov in his right hand. The side door slid open, and another kidnapper configured exactly like the driver stepped out and helped Francesca from the van. She was wearing the same clothing she was wearing yesterday afternoon. She caught sight of me, rose up on her tippy-toes, and called out, "Julius, darling, I'm here."

I walked over to the *FERRARI*, unlocked the boot, and retrieved the briefcase. I set the briefcase down on the roof, and gestured for them to join me. Ten more yards, and they'd be in range.

◊◊

Epilogue

> "Instant Karma's gonna get you
> Gonna knock you right on the head
> You better get yourself together
> Pretty soon you're gonna be dead."

Instant Karma
~ John Lennon

The eyewitnesses all agreed that a yellow and white Volkswagen microbus raced out of the Brainerd Park parking lot at a high rate of speed, nearly running down a young couple who were engaged in a hug of all hugs. The Volkswagen didn't turn left or right onto Brainerd Circle. No, it thundered straight ahead, toppling several memorial benches before it lurched into the lake. There were no survivors.

•

Julius Briscoe pulled his *FERRARI SUPERFAST* into a Texaco filling station at Newport and Cranbury Boulevard. He told the attendant to fill it up with high test and asked if there was a public phone handy. Francesca called the number for her parents. It was answered by an actress even more famous than her world famous parents.

"This is a private, unpublished number. Who's calling please?"

"Your ladyship, it's me, Francesca Ullman."

"Frankie darling is it really you?"

"Who else calls you 'your ladyship?'"

"Only Bogie and that no-good brat Francesca Ullman ever called me *your ladyship*." Lauren covered the mouthpiece, shouted, 'Nels, Sarah, Frankie's on the phone!' She uncovered the mouthpiece and gushed, "Darling girl, are you all right? If they harmed you in any way, I swear, Frankie, I know people. You know what I mean?"

"Aunt Betty, I know people too. My one true love, Julius Briscoe came to my rescue, I just can't wait for you to meet him, he's so beautiful. He brought the ransom money, but they took one look at Julius, got back in their microbus and drove it straight into the lake. Can you believe it? Can I talk to mom and dad?"

•

The recently widowed women, Mary Alice Hopkins and Nadine Brodsky O'Hara, had never in their lives had to sign for a package. They couldn't imagine who had sent it or what it contained. The packages, delivered by a stuffy banker or lawyer type, were about the size of a shoebox, wrapped in heavy, brown, waterproof paper and bound tightly with a length of twine. There were no stamps or return addresses, just theirs, which they would soon be unable to afford. Things can change in the time it takes a battered widow to unwrap a box full of money. Is this a great country or what?

•

On the Tuesday before New Year's Eve, Eastern Airlines flight 1104 arrived on time at JFK International Airport, where it was greeted by a wildcat strike of jetway workers, which required the passengers to deplane the old-fashioned way, down a set of roll-away stairs during a driving rainstorm. Gilbert 'Gilly' Yocham, his line of sight compromised by an uncooperative, wind-blown umbrella, was struck and killed by a baggage trolley driven by a newly promoted transfer agent, who lost control of the vehicle on the rain-soaked tarmac, causing it to slam into Julius Briscoe's target, which triggered a double indemnity clause, which made Ramona Ransom one merry widow indeed.

•

Once her adrenaline levels returned to normal, Frankie asked, "I don't understand, Julius, why did Boris and Tasha run away without taking the money?"

They were headed north on the Jersey Turnpike. New York City was twenty minutes away.

"I don't know what it is about you, Frankie. You're really pretty, super-smart, a little bit silly, and too young to fool around with. Jail bait."

Frankie looked at Julius and began to laugh theatrically, condescendingly. Julius figured it was out of relief. "Julius, my darling, I'm not too young legally. Last year, right after I escaped from the *Liberationists*, we received almost a dozen offers to do television shows and movies featuring all of us Ullmans. If you're underaged in Hollywood and you want to be an actor or a model, well you get yourself emancipated."

"Emancipated? Abraham Lincoln style?"

"More like expensive lawyer style. Not exactly the same. Emancipated in my case means that, under the law, I'm an adult and can work long hours on movie shoots, sign contracts, take a lover, anything I want, really. No more child labor laws to get in the way of my career. Basically, it means that I'm not jail bait. But don't get any crazy ideas about that young Mr. Briscoe. I'm saving it for my one true love. Oh, wait. That's you."

Julius hit the brakes and pulled off the road and parked beneath a graffiti laden overpass. He said "So let me ask you this, Frankie, how are you with secrets? Big ones? Major ones? Can you keep them? Or would you just have to tell someone?"

"I can keep a secret if I have to." She wasn't lying. Nonetheless, Julius hit her with FORGET ABOUT It® and told her everything.

It was like that.

~ fin ~

www.ingramcontent.com/pod-product-compliance
Lightning Source LLC
Chambersburg PA
CBHW070205310726
48976CB00001B/220